CUNNING DEVIL

LOST FALLS, BOOK ONE

ISBN: 1540549712
ISBN-13: 978-1540549716

1

The monster was hiding in the basement, of course.

It was always the basement, or the wine cellar, or the floor space, or the attic.

Easy enough to see why, I suppose. The more benign creatures just wanted to settle down somewhere dark and damp, where they were safe from prying eyes. And as for the nastier monsters, well, what better place than a basement to lie in wait for your victims?

I stood at the top of the stairs and flicked the light switch. Nothing happened.

Of course.

I shot my sister a glare. She was hovering behind me, trying to peer over my shoulder into the gloom. When she caught my look, she shrugged.

"Bulb blew a couple of days ago," she said. "I was going to replace it sometime."

With a grunt, I turned back to the basement. The light from the hallway spilled down the stairs, revealing the shadowed outline of a washing machine. Spider webs shimmered in the corner. Beyond that, the darkness was too thick to penetrate.

It was down there, though. I could smell it. A Stranger. It smelled of sour milk and moldy carpet, of acidic sweat and damp earth.

"You know this isn't my job, right, Alice?" I said. "I'm not

Animal Control."

"Would you prefer I call them?" she asked, her voice thick with false sweetness.

She knew the answer. I had enough of a reputation as it was. The last thing I needed was some hapless Unaware officer getting his face bitten off in my own sister's house. It was hard to cover that kind of thing up.

Alice wasn't really a part of my world, but she was one of the few who had some idea what really lurked in the shadows of this town.

Sure, the legends surrounding Lost Falls had been circulating for years. The town even encouraged them—the rumors brought in the reality TV crews and the paranormal investigators and the tourists who were too stupid to leave well enough alone.

But those of us who knew the truth wanted those legends to stay legends.

Alice hadn't got a good look at whatever had hissed at her from the shadows, but she sure as hell knew it wasn't just a big rat. My sister wasn't prone to flights of fancy. She hadn't known who to call, so she'd called me.

Lucky me.

A banging sound came from somewhere behind me. Guess I must've been on edge, because I nearly jumped out of my skin before I realized it was someone rapping on the door.

"Alice?" a voice called. "Ozzy?"

"Back here," I shouted over my shoulder. Alice was smirking at me. She'd seen me jump. I let her have her fun.

The house creaked as footsteps approached. A man appeared at the end of the hall, his thick gray beard parting in a smile when he saw us. He was a thin old bastard, not an ounce of fat on him. He had that kind of old man vitality that keeps some folks smoking and drinking to the age of 102 while all their friends have long since turned to worm food. His name was Early.

"Heard you've got an unwelcome visitor," Early said to Alice.

She nodded, then gave him a hug and a kiss on the cheek. He wasn't a short man, but Alice still had an inch or two on him. She had the Turner family bones, just like me. Maybe there was some ogre DNA somewhere in the line.

"What took you so long?" I asked when he'd disentangled himself from Alice.

"Trying to find your things, that's what. You ever think about tidying up your cabin? Maybe pushing a vacuum cleaner around?"

"The mess keeps the witches away," I said.

He handed me a leather bag and my truncheon. The truncheon had an iron core and a scuffed and dented silver coating on the hitting end. Symbols and words of power had been engraved along its length.

I'd been out when Alice called, so I'd had Early drop by my place to pick up my equipment. Until we knew what we were dealing with, I didn't want to waste any time.

"Where are the boys?" Early said to Alice.

She gestured. "Upstairs. Valerie's at work."

Valerie—Alice's wife—was an ER doc at the local hospital. They usually traded off for care of their twin boys—Valerie worked early shifts at the hospital, while in the evenings Alice worked at Lost Falls' best and only radio station as a late-night announcer.

"Know what we're dealing with?" Early asked.

I shook my head. "Not yet. Light bulb's blown."

"So use a flashlight."

"It's not 1953, granddad. No one uses flashlights anymore. We've got cell phones."

Truth be told, I'd been a little hesitant about shining lights around until Early arrived with my things. Switching on a light was one thing, but certain Strangers get a little agitated when you point beams of light in their direction. I didn't want this thing attacking me while I was unprepared.

I put down my bag for now, gripping my truncheon tightly in my right hand while I took out my phone with my left. Early joined me, muttering something to Alice as he gently pushed her back into the hallway. Creeping down a few steps, I switched on my phone's light.

Claws scratched on concrete. I snapped the beam toward the sound.

A shadow no more than two feet high darted out of sight behind some old storage boxes, hissing as it moved.

"You see that?" I asked.

"I saw it," Early said.

"The hell is it? A kobold maybe? Some kind of imp?"

"You ever see an imp move like that?"

"You have any better ideas?"

He didn't. "How did it get here?" he muttered, scratching his beard.

"Look. That window there." I pointed the light to the far end of the basement, where a couple of ground floor windows were blocked out by the overgrown garden outside. "It's broken."

"No, I mean, how did it get *here*? We're a ways away from the forest. It's strange."

I knew what he meant. This was a nice little house in a nice little suburb. Alice and Valerie weren't rich, but Valerie's salary meant they didn't have to struggle. There were all sorts of places in Lost Falls where weird things happened and Strangers skulked around, but this neighborhood wasn't one of them.

Still, that was a question for another time. First order of business was getting the damn thing out of here, before my nephews ran afoul of it. I loved those kids.

"Let's get this done." I glanced at Alice. "Might pay to take the boys and wait outside."

"Ozzy—"

"Just in case." Something skittered on the other side of the basement. I snapped my light around, but I couldn't see anything. I exhaled. "This'll be quicker without you breathing down our necks anyway," I said to Alice. "This is a complex, occult operation. We need to concentrate."

She knew me too well to buy what I was selling her, but after a moment's hesitation she nodded.

"All right, fine. Just be safe, both of you."

"I'll look after him," Early said. "Don't you worry."

The contents of my bag rattled as I hefted it. "Close the basement door behind us," I said to Alice. "And lock the front door once you're outside."

"Don't do anything stupid, Ozzy," she said.

"You know me."

She closed the basement door, cutting off the light from the hallway—and our only means of escape. The creature's smell suddenly seemed a lot thicker. It clung to my skin.

The only light now came from my phone. As Alice's footsteps hurried away, I crouched down on the stairs and opened my bag.

"Make sure it doesn't creep up on us," I said. I was whispering now, as if that would make a difference.

"So what's this complex, occult operation you've got planned out?" Early asked.

"You see that dog cage over there?" I aimed the light at it.

"Uh-huh."

"We grab the creature and shove it in there."

"Pure genius," he said.

"No point over-thinking it."

I rummaged through my bag. It looked like Early had found everything. I'd had him gather all the talismans and fetishes and potions I could think of, but without knowing what the thing was we were limited. A sun flare that would stun a vampireling could send a kobold into a rage. And a fetish designed to weaken a kobold wouldn't do a damn thing against a fiend.

So I went for the catch-alls. A handful of old iron nails to lay at the bottom of the stairs to guard our escape. A circle of rope woven from human hair and knotted with animal bone fetishes and silver talismans. And of course, my old trusty standby, the truncheon. I looped the weapon's strap around my wrist so I wouldn't drop it.

"All right," I said. "I think you should go first."

Even in the dim light, I could see Early raising one bushy gray eyebrow. "That so?"

"It is."

"Seems to me this is your family we're protecting here, not mine."

"Guess I'll have to tell Alice not to invite you around for casserole next weekend."

"No need to be scared, Ozzy. You saw how small that thing is."

Something hissed in the darkness. A claw scratched against a pipe.

"Scared?" I said. "No, no, no. I'm just looking at this logically. If this thing really is dangerous, it makes sense that you should be the one to—God forbid—have your throat torn out. Seeing as you're an old man and all. Whereas I've got my whole life ahead of me."

"Ozzy?" he said.

"Yeah."

"Get on with it."

Grumbling, I thrust the phone into his hands. "Fine. But you're holding the cage."

I pulled on a pair of leather gloves I kept in my bag. Never know when you're going to need gloves. I was wearing a thin jacket as well, and I could only hope that would be enough to protect me. I'd gotten a glimpse at the creature's curved claws before it retreated into the darkness.

We slowly descended the stairs. They creaked with every step. Somewhere in the darkness I could hear the creature hissing.

"Don't shine the light directly at it," I said when he started to turn the beam toward the sound. "We'll piss it off."

"I think it's already pissed off."

I was inclined to agree.

I scattered the iron nails at the base of the stairs. They weren't just any old nails. I'd scavenged them from the site of an old mansion on the edge of town that'd been torn down a few years ago. The place hadn't been inhabited for more than a decade, owing to some rumors that it was haunted. It wasn't, though after it'd been abandoned a few of Lost Falls' non-human townsfolk had started holding midnight poker games there.

But that was beside the point. More than a century of history had soaked into the mansion's walls: arguments, lovemaking, the sound of children running in the hallways and the smells of countless family dinners.

That kind of history has a power to it. A power the nails retained. Not every kind of Stranger would be delayed or distracted by the nails, but some would. Worth a try, anyway, if we needed to beat a hasty retreat.

My shoes scraped against the concrete as I stepped over the line of nails. I held my loop of fetishes and talismans loosely by my side as I moved to the center of the basement.

The shadows danced as Early followed me down, keeping the light trained on me. He moved to the dog cage, which was tucked beside the washing machine. The half-full laundry hamper was still lying where Alice had abandoned it, a little boy's T-shirt hanging from the lip. There was a ping pong table folded up and set against the wall, just below the windows. Shards of broken glass glittered in the phone's light, like starlight reflected off a lake.

The rest of the basement was largely being used as storage space. Boxes of old clothes, a moth-eaten couch, a small filing cabinet. An awful lot of places for something to hide.

The hinges of the dog cage door squealed behind me. Without taking my eyes from the darkness, I whispered over my shoulder. "Will it do?"

"We'll soon find out."

I grunted. Tightening my grip on my truncheon, I slowly edged toward the shadows.

Maybe you're thinking I was being overcautious. Cowardly, even. The thing was only a couple of feet high at most. How dangerous could it be, right?

You're thinking that because you've forgotten. All of us have. There are billions of us humans now, all across the world. We gather in huge cities of concrete and steel, belching exhaust fumes into the sky and filling our nights with so much light that even the stars can't compete. We've forgotten fear.

Our ancestors knew better. They knew that safety was an illusion. They knew that on the other side of the door, away from the fire and the hearth, true horrors lurked.

They knew the darkness didn't belong to them.

"Hey, Early," I said. "I'm counting on you to save my ass if this goes bad."

"To hell with that," he said. "I'm running."

He wouldn't run. Early hadn't run from a thing in his life. God knows I'd done enough dumb shit to give him reason to. He was steady.

For a senior citizen, I mean.

A scraping sound, like nails dragging across cardboard. It came from the stack of boxes off to the right. I paused, listened for a moment, then carefully eased forward. I clutched my talisman rope, ready to throw it.

I darted forward, rope raised as I came around the pile of boxes. My lips pulled back in a snarl.

There was nothing there. Where the hell had—
"Right side!" Early roared. "Look out!"

2

I spun as the creature leapt screeching from a darkened ceiling corner. It slammed into me with the weight of a small child. I could taste the stink of it in the back of my throat.

Claws swiped wildly as I crashed into a stack of boxes. Cuts burned across my shoulders. In the bouncing cell phone light I saw bloodshot eyes and long teeth glistening with saliva. The creature went for my throat.

I slammed the butt of my truncheon into the creature's head. There was no silver on that part of the club, no fancy charms or arcane symbols.

Just wood and iron delivered with all the fear-strength I could muster.

The creature fell to the ground, squealing. That kind of blow would've stunned a normal man, if not cracked his skull. But the creature showed no sign of being anything more than annoyed. It skittered about in a circle on all fours, claws clattering on the concrete. Furious eyes glared up at me, slitted nostrils flared. The thing's muscles tensed to pounce again.

I threw the talisman rope that I'd somehow kept hold of. A wild throw. I got lucky. As the creature leapt at me, the loop of rope tangled around its neck.

The creature went rigid, like it'd taken 10,000 volts straight through the skull. One or more of the fetishes on the rope was doing its job. The thing collapsed back to the ground at my feet, sluggishly pawing at the loop around its neck.

"Early!" I shouted, but he was already beside me with the cage.

The creature was gasping as if it was having trouble breathing. I knew how it felt. Little bastard had tried to kick in my rib cage when it jumped at me.

Before it could recover, I grabbed it and shoved it at the cage. The thing managed to gouge another hole in my jacket and scratch up my arm before I got it inside.

In one quick movement, I pulled the talisman rope from around its neck. Instantly, it came back to life. I slammed the cage door in its face.

Early bolted it shut, snatching his hand back as one claw reached through the cage door, trying to snag him. The creature squealed with rage. The whole cage shook.

I slumped to the ground, panting. The cold concrete beneath me was heavenly.

"You all right, boy?" Early asked.

I checked. "Just fine, old man. Just dandy."

"Wasn't so hard after all, was it?"

I decided to let him laugh it up for the moment. Just until I got my breath back.

Early and I lugged the screeching, rattling dog cage back upstairs.

"You're bleeding on the carpet," Early said as we shuffled toward the kitchen.

"Shit." It was a good thing my sister was still outside with the boys. I once spilled a glass of cask wine on the carpet, and I heard about it for weeks.

We dropped the cage on the dining table and I slumped down in a chair while Early fetched my bag of tricks. Out the window I could see the boys screaming around the backyard at a hundred miles an hour, while Alice watched with a look of exhaustion on her face. She caught my eye and I gave her a thumbs-up, then gestured for her to keep the boys outside a little while longer.

I peeled off my gloves and jacket to check myself over. The creature had got me pretty good. My upper chest and left arm were cut up all to hell. Luckily, none of the cuts were too deep. It wasn't until I grabbed a stainless steel frying pan and examined my reflection in the metal that I realized my face had got a taste of it as well. One cut went nearly all the way from my ear to my nose, and it was still dripping blood into my beard. Maybe it'd leave a nice scar, at least.

"Next time it's your turn to wrangle the monster," I said when Early returned. "Hell, this stings."

He sat down next to me and dug through my bag until he found my first aid kit. It contained all the usual things: bandages, gauze, over-the-counter painkillers, plus a few tinctures and unguents of Early's creation. He was the expert on those sorts of things. My eyes always glazed over when he tried to teach me.

"This bleeding's not slowing," I said. "Should be slowing by now, shouldn't it?"

He nodded, peering at the handwritten label on one of his tinctures. "Looks like our friend here is pretty good at exsanguinating its victims."

I didn't much like the sound of that. "You can stop that, though, right?"

"Easy enough." He let a few drops of some green, sludgy mixture drip onto a piece of clean gauze. "This'll burn a little."

It didn't. It burned like the fires of hell. I gritted my teeth as he applied the concoction to the cut on my cheek. The sludge stank like rotting plant matter.

Early's herbal remedies didn't do much for your usual, everyday injuries, but they were essential for dealing with some of the more unnatural causes of illness and injury, the ones modern medicine weren't so good at treating.

Almost immediately the cut on my cheek began to clot. While he applied more of his damn hot oil to my other cuts, I scrubbed flakes of drying blood out of my beard. I'd never get it all.

The creature had finally stopped rattling the cage. It was staring at me through the bars on the door, claws scratching at the base.

I'd thought that maybe once we'd caught it and brought it into the light, we'd be able to figure out what it was. But looking at it now, I felt just as clueless as I had before.

It was vaguely humanoid, with a head too big for its body. Its flesh was an angry red, like it'd spent too long sitting in the hot tub. Darker spots were scattered across the thing's shoulders and upper arms, and the skin looked thicker there, almost leathery.

The creature's arms were unusually long and slender, and each of its fingers ended in those long, hooked claws that'd done such a good job turning me to sushi. But they weren't nearly as scary as the yellowed teeth that filled its snarling mouth like crooked mountain peaks. As the creature glared at me with animal fury, a long, purple tongue rolled out of its mouth, moving like a snake about to strike.

I leaned closer to the cage, careful to stay out of reach of those claws.

"What the hell are you?" I muttered. It didn't answer. Neither did Early. He looked as stumped as me.

It was male, I could tell that much. It wore no clothing, so its stunted genitalia were on display. Beyond that, though, it was a mystery.

Not a vampireling. It'd be screeching with pain if it was, trying to curl itself away from the light. Not a kobold or an imp either. Not anything I'd ever seen before. I scratched my beard as I thought.

"Well, I'm out of ideas," I said to Early. "You?"

He was just finishing up with the last of my cuts. He shook his head and set about applying butterfly stitches to the deepest wounds.

"It's a strange one, that's for sure."

"Think we should put it out of its misery?" I suggested.

"What if it's sentient?"

"It's not sentient. Look at it."

"Still."

I frowned. Maybe he was right. I didn't much fancy trying to murder the poor little bastard anyway. Now that it was in the cage, looking at me with such fury, I had to admit I felt a little sorry for it.

"Well, if we're not going to kill it," I said, "maybe we should give it a name."

"What were you thinking?"

I peered through the bars of the cage. "How about Lawrence?"

"Lawrence?"

"I think it looks like a Lawrence. Don't you?"

Early shrugged. "Well, you could take Lawrence here to Alcaraz," Early said. "If anyone in this town knows what this thing is, it'll be her."

"Not a bad idea." I scratched my beard and smiled. "Not a bad idea indeed."

"I suppose it's the prospect of seeing your lady friend that's got you grinning like an idiot."

I cleared my throat. "I have no idea what you're talking about."

Alcaraz was something of a legend in Lost Falls. She was human—at least I thought so—but given how long she'd been clinging on to life, you had to wonder. She made Early look like a spring chicken by comparison.

The woman had an estate on the outskirts of town, not so far from that abandoned mansion I'd found my iron nails. She kept what I had to imagine was one of the largest collection of live non-sentient Strangers in the world.

Alcaraz had dedicated her life to studying the Strangers. She would know what our creature was, I was sure of it.

Despite what Early said, my excitement about visiting Alcaraz had absolutely nothing to do with the fact that a very nice young woman named Lilian hung around the estate, helping with the creatures and aiding the elderly woman with her studies. Nor did it have anything to do with any sort of ongoing flirtation between Lilian and myself, no matter what Early liked to insinuate.

I did hope she was there, though. Just for the conversation, you know.

"Ozzy?" Early said.

"Mmm?" I was thinking of the last conversation Lilian and I had had. That had been a damn nice conversation.

"Your phone."

"What? Oh." My phone was vibrating so violently it was threatening to throw itself off the table. I snatched it up. I didn't recognize the number.

I pressed the phone to my ear. "Hello?"

"Is this Osric Turner?" It was a man's voice, thin and reedy. I pictured a scrawny little man, with glasses and a receding hairline. Maybe an old sauce stain on the collar of his shirt.

"It is."

"I got your number from an acquaintance. I...I've lost something."

Lawrence snarled and hissed. I jumped up from my seat, moving away from the table so the sound didn't carry down the line.

"What was that?" the man asked.

"Stood on the cat's tail," I said, smiling politely down the phone and adopting the most professional tone I could muster. This was work. A real job, maybe. I couldn't afford to let it get away, not after the dry spell I'd been having lately. "Sorry about that."

"I was told you're good at finding things. Is that true?"

"Depends on the thing," I said. "But yes. Nine times out of ten, someone loses something—or someone—I can find it. I'm sorry, I didn't catch your name."

"Mills," he said. "Brandon Mills."

"And what have you lost, Mr. Mills?"

"It's…something very precious to my mother and me. I—" He stopped, as if struggling to get the words out. Was that a sob? Was he crying?

He was certainly desperate, that much was obvious. That's not unusual among the people who come to me for help. But this was something else.

A kind of guilty excitement flooded me. The guy was having a bad time of it, but a desperate client usually meant a trickier job, and a trickier job usually meant a bigger payout. My bank account was looking a little thin these days. It's hard for a guy in my line of work to drum up business, so I have to take it when it comes. I can't exactly put an ad in the local paper.

"Mr. Mills?" I said. "Are you all right?"

He grunted and cleared his throat. "Yes. Yes. Sorry. Listen, Mr. Turner—"

"Osric's fine."

"Osric. Can you come today? Please? I know it's a Saturday, and I know you're probably busy. I…I can't believe I'm even asking a…a man like you. I just don't know what else to do."

I spoke quickly, before he could break down again. Or worse, talk himself out of it. "Of course. I'll shuffle some things around. Where do you live?"

He gave me the address. I could be there in fifteen minutes. Lost Falls wasn't a big place.

I checked my watch. "Give me an hour."

"Thank you. Thank you."

He hung up.

I was smiling when I returned my phone to my pocket. I had a good feeling about this one. After spending the better part of a week twiddling my thumbs and paging through the local paper to see if I could scrounge up some poor client who'd been the unwitting target of a minor curse, I finally had something tangible. It was shaping up to be a busy day.

Early had gone outside by the time I was done with the call. I could see him through the window, talking with Alice. While the twins were still busy herding a ball around the yard, I took the dog cage out to my van. The creature hissed and shook the cage, but luckily the street was quiet. If there were any neighbors peering out from behind their curtains, I hoped they just thought I was taking an angry dog to the vet.

I had to shove some things around in the back of my van to make room for the cage. The van doubles as my mobile home whenever I have a job that takes me out of town for more than a day or two. When I'm tracking something down, I can't really stop and look for a motel. It weakens the trail, confuses my charms. Better to pull over to the side of some quiet road and close my eyes for a couple of hours.

I threw a blanket over the cage, like you do to your pet budgie when you want it to sleep. Never know, might quiet the thing down. Or at least keep anyone looking in from seeing exactly what kind of strange beasts prowl around the darkness while they sleep safe and sound in their beds.

With that done, I went back inside and picked up the nails I'd left lying at the bottom of the basement stairs. The smell of the Stranger was already starting to fade. I found some air freshener and sprayed it around me for good measure.

It occurred to me then that the creature might not have been alone. And here I'd gone and left my truncheon upstairs. But I had a look around, poked my nose into all the corners, and decided it seemed safe enough. The creature had taken a shit on the floor though. I'd let my dear sister clean that up.

I prepared a couple of simple charms to ward off nasties and left them tucked into cracks in the walls. Then I went upstairs and gave the all-clear. I thought I might've got a hug for that, but apparently Alice reserves all those for Early.

"That looks like it hurts," she said when I approached, gesturing to my cheek.

"Not as bad as these." I showed her the rest of my war wounds, and she let out a low whistle.

"You weren't kidding, were you?" she said. "Thanks, guys."

"What are you thanking him for?" I said, nodding at Early. "He didn't do anything."

"What...uh..." She glanced at the twins and lowered her voice. "What was it?"

"You know we can't tell you," I said darkly. I figured feigning mysteriousness was better than admitting ignorance. Early didn't challenge me.

"Best get that window repaired," Early said to her. "And the light bulb replaced. I don't figure you'll have any more problems, but it pays to be safe."

"I will," she promised. Knowing my sister, she'd probably have iron bars installed on the windows and forbid the twins from going into the basement until they were 25.

Early hugged Alice goodbye, made faces at the twins, and slapped me on my cut-up shoulder. I managed to keep from swearing in front of the kids.

"Good luck with the job," he said.

I guess he'd overhead my phone conversation. I nodded my thanks.

"And tell me what Alcaraz says about that thing," he said over his shoulder as he was leaving. "Might want to ask her to make sure it's not...uh...diseased or anything."

"Diseased?" I took another look at my cuts. "Hell."

I couldn't tell if he was joking or not, and he was gone before

I could ask.

He was just screwing with me. Probably.

I spent a few minutes throwing the twins around the yard. Alice looked on anxiously while the boys squealed with delight.

"I swear to God, Ozzy, if you drop him..." she began while I swung one of them around by his ankles. The rest of the threat was drowned out by the boy's laughter.

When the boys' boundless energy outstripped mine, I set them back to chasing each other around the yard while Alice and I retreated to the patio.

"I should get going," I said.

"This job of yours?"

I nodded. "I've got a good feeling about this one."

"Sit down for a second," she said.

I hesitated, checking my watch. I didn't really have time, but there was something in Alice's tone that told me I wasn't getting out of this. She always did get her way.

The patio chair creaked ominously as I sat down. Alice sat opposite, her eyes on the boys.

"How are you doing, Ozzy?" she asked.

I knew that tone. "Oh, jeez, Alice." I made to stand, but before I could extricate myself from the chair and its too-small seat, Alice was already waving me to stay where I was.

"It's just a question," she said. "You know it's his birthday on Wednesday."

"Really? Slipped my mind." I laid the sarcasm on thick enough for her to drown in it.

She didn't bite. "I was going to go down to the grave about midday. You should come, Ozzy."

"We'll see," I said.

"Ozzy."

"I said we'll see."

She gave me that knowing older sister look.

I threw up my hands. "All right, fine. I'll be there."

"That's what you said last year. I want you to promise."

"What are we, thirteen?"

"You need to come, Ozzy. It'll be good for you."

"So would a colonic, but you don't seem desperate to sign me up for one of those."

She just raised an eyebrow. She was infuriating when she was like this. Becoming a mother had only made it worse.

After a few moments of silence, I dragged my fingers through my hair and leaned forward as far as I dared in the groaning chair.

"Listen," I said. "I'm doing better. I'm not like I was. You can stop worrying about me."

Her mouth formed a line, but she didn't say anything. She just nodded, still looking at me with that same old look.

"All right," I said. "Wednesday, then." I pulled myself out of the chair. I nearly had to snap one of the arms off to manage it. "You really have to get some bigger chairs. Look, I think I bent the leg."

I hollered my goodbyes to the boys—if they heard, they paid no notice—and I kissed Alice on the cheek.

"Ozzy," she said as I turned to go.

"Yeah?"

"When are you going to tell me what really happened to him?"

I shook my head and said nothing.

"He was my brother too," she said.

I sighed. "Just…know that he was avenged."

3

Let me be honest for a second. Not everything I'm going to tell you in this story is strictly true. Names have been changed. I've had to obscure some details, or alter them completely. Trust me when I say there are reasons for that.

But I'm not here to give you the facts. I'm here to tell you the Truth, with a capital T.

So here it is. We are not alone.

There are others who share this world with us. We call them Strangers. That's probably not the best term to use, and trust me, it comes with a lot of baggage. Plenty of people—not all of them human—object to that label. But it's the name that's stuck, and until someone comes up with a better one, it's the one I'm going to use.

It's likely that some of them have always been with us. There are plenty of legends stretching back to antiquity of strange creatures that—if you squint—resemble certain Strangers that still exist to this day. But most of them are more recent transplants to our world. They've been here a few centuries, a millennium maybe. It depends who you believe.

The stories shift, but I'll tell it to you as I understand it.

There was a war. Not here. Somewhere out there. Another place. Another world.

The devastation was on a scale that I doubt any of us can really comprehend. Genocidal. Apocalyptic. Countless creatures, both sentient and non-sentient, were destroyed. Pushed to the brink of extinction.

The survivors were visited by…beings. Beings not of their world, and not of ours either. Beings who had the power to offer them a deal.

The Strangers were offered an escape from the war they were losing. An escape from their doomed world. Passage to another world.

Our world.

I don't know what the Strangers paid for that passage, but knowing who they were trading with, I can only assume the cost must have been astronomical. But they paid it.

And they came to join us.

Not just the sentient Strangers, either. It was them who'd made the deal, but plenty more creatures poured through the passage as well, like rats fleeing a sinking ship.

Strangers were scattered across the Earth, alone in a strange land. Refugees. And they soon realized they had no choice but to hide. There were few of them, after all, and a hell of a lot of us. And for all of humanity's good points, we get awfully vicious when we encounter something we don't understand.

Not that we didn't have reason to fear the Strangers, of course. Almost all Strangers can be dangerous when the mood strikes them, and for some, that's all they know.

Ever since then, the Strangers have been with us. Hiding in the dark corners of the world. A lucky few are able to pass as human and live amongst us, but most of them lurk on the edges of our civilization.

Only trouble is we keep expanding, pushing back the darkness. Every year there's more of us, and fewer of them.

But there are still a few places left in the world where they can hide. Places like this. Places like Lost Falls.

Lost Falls is…well, it doesn't matter exactly where it is. It's a little too small to be called a city. We're nestled in a thickly wooded valley in the middle of nowhere. Used to be a mining town—still is, I suppose. I don't know how many thousands of miles of tunnels and old mine shafts crisscross these hills. Between the forests and the mines and the river and the mountains, there's a place for nearly every kind of Stranger here. For better or worse.

It's a good place to hide. I should know. The Strangers aren't the only people around here who need to stay hidden.

Lawrence scratched and howled in the back of my van as I drove. He was shaking the dog cage so violently I was getting a little concerned he would manage to break out. My brilliant plan to soothe the creature by throwing a blanket over the cage only seemed to have infuriated him more.

The smart thing to do would've been to take him directly to Alcaraz, but the old researcher's estate was a ways away, on the outskirts of the town. I was already running a few minutes late to get to Mr. Mills place, thanks to my dear sister delaying me with her misguided concerns. I couldn't afford to lose the job. The guy already sounded uncertain about hiring me, and I didn't want to give him a chance to change his mind.

So I headed straight for his house. Delilah, the plastic hula girl fixed to my dashboard, danced as I drove.

My route took me on a leisurely drive along Main Street. Gnarled trees lined the center of the road, some of the long branches looming low enough to scrape their leaves on the top of my van as I passed. Scattered among the cafes and shops I passed were tourist traps that sold maps to local haunted houses and T-shirts with cartoon pictures of ogres. Lost Falls' hidden community tolerated that kind of stuff, figuring that it was easier to cultivate misinformation than try to cover up the truth entirely.

The streets were busy, at least as busy as they get around here. I passed a bus that had pulled over to disgorge tourists at an information center dressed up to look like a witch's hut. The locals, out with their families, either tended to eye the tourists with disgust or ignore them completely.

Every now and then, I spotted people wearing heavy amulets or silver bracelets that were too old and tarnished to be purely for decoration. I even recognized a few amulets I'd sold myself, or some that had to be Early's workmanship. It made it easy to identify those who knew—or suspected—that not all of the town legends were complete horse shit. Even during the day, in the middle of town, some folks felt a little safer with some silver or a protection amulet close at hand.

Whatever helped them get through the day. I just hoped none of them ran into any prowling Strangers after nightfall.

The crowds thinned out as I headed back towards suburbia. The only sound I had for comfort was the growling of the creature in the back of the van. I don't listen to the radio much these days. Talk shows bore me and music…music isn't for me anymore.

Mr. Mills' address was in an older part of town. One of the oldest parts of town, in fact. The narrow roads were so potholed I was at risk of breaking my van's suspension if I wasn't careful. The houses here were all wood and brick and flaking paint, packed in tight behind fences and stone walls as old as the town itself. It was a favored location on all the haunted house tours. Most of these places looked the part, at least.

I found Mr Mills' house at the end of a cul-de-sac. It was no better than its neighbors. Weeds had overtaken the front garden entirely, and were laying siege to the house. They'd sent vines to creep up the western wall, and I had no doubt sappers were undermining the foundations as I watched. All in all, quite an impressive shit hole.

"You've got to be kidding me," I muttered.

I grabbed my bag and got out. Before I went to the house, I opened the back door of my van. The dog cage growled at me from beneath the blanket.

With a glance up at the house to make sure no one was looking out the windows at me, I lit one of the small candles I kept in my van for situations like this. While I waited for the wax to melt, I fished a scrap of calfskin parchment from my bag and scrawled a simple written charm on it in black ink. With a bit of luck, the sleep charm might keep the creature docile, at least until I got back. Without a better idea of exactly what the creature was, it was the best I could do.

I folded the parchment, sealing it with a few drops of candle wax. I blew out the candle and left the sealed charm sitting on top of the dog cage.

It was worth a try.

I locked up and turned my attention back to the house. It creaked like it might fall over at any moment.

I pushed open the squealing gate and fought my way through the jungle. A plywood board had been laid over the steps leading up to the veranda, forming a makeshift ramp that'd been screwed in place. It was the only renovation the place had seen this century.

My hopes for this job had fallen somewhat when I first saw the house. They dropped right out the bottom of my boots when I rang the bell and the door creaked open.

I've seen reanimated bodies that looked more alive than this guy. He had the look of a fit, strong man gone to seed in his middle age, so worn down by life he'd given up on the whole enterprise.

His ears were too big for his head, but despite that I got the feeling he probably would've been a bit of a heartbreaker in his youth. Now he didn't even bother to clean the food stains from his jeans. He wore the T-shirt of a band that hadn't been touring in twenty years, which was likely when he'd bought it. He'd shaved two or three days ago—and cut himself pretty badly, by the look of it—but he'd missed a whole big patch under his left ear. The errant beard hairs stood like a tuft of grass in the tundra.

He was an all-round sorry-looking son of a bitch.

I'd been hoping for someone a little desperate, someone willing to pay good money for a job well done. This guy, on the other hand, had nothing left to live for. I doubted he had enough cash to put dinner on the table, let alone pay me what I was worth.

Judging by the look on his face, I guessed I wasn't quite what he expected either. Early didn't have that problem when he visited clients. He had the Gandalf look going on, with the wrinkles and the hair coming out his ears.

Me, not so much. Between the beard and my size, I've been told I look like I belong in a biker gang. I supposed I didn't much resemble the wise old man that Mr. Mills was probably expecting. But I gave him my best smile anyway, trying not to let my disappointment show on my face.

"Mr. Mills?" I said, holding out my hand. "I'm Osric Turner."

After a moment's hesitation, he put his hand in mine. His palm was hard and calloused, but his grip was weak.

He looked at me. "You're the...uh...?"

He wasn't the first person to have trouble deciding what my job title should be. A few centuries back, there were plenty of names to describe folks like me. Pellar. White witch. Cunning man.

There aren't many of us left now. In fact, Early and I are the only cunning folk I know of within two hundred miles of Lost Falls. Once, though, there were more. We were needed.

We were the ones you came to when your crops failed or your prized cooking pan went missing. We were there to track down your son after he wandered into the woods alone. We broke curses and protected against witchcraft. We provided magical assistance for the common folk, all at a reasonable price. And though we weren't always trusted, we were always in demand.

Unfortunately, modern cunning folk—such as yours truly—have to take jobs where we find them.

"Yes," I said, as the man struggled to verbalize. "That's me."

"I thought you'd be...uh..."

This guy had a lot of trouble finishing sentences. I just nodded, smiling politely.

"I get that a lot." I gestured. "May I?"

"Oh, yes, yes. Come in."

The rotten floorboards flexed underfoot as I stepped through the doorway. My initial impression of the house only grew stronger as I followed Mills down the narrow hallway. A wet dog smell hung in the air. Wallpaper was curling off the walls in strips, revealing damp and mold beneath. The spiders had taken up permanent residence around the light fixtures. It would take a battering ram and a SWAT team to get them out.

I glanced through an open bedroom door as I passed, and saw a stack of moving boxes, half of them opened, labeled things like: *Clothes - Brandon* and *Kitchen - Glass - Fragile*. What furniture there was had been scattered half-heartedly about, awaiting the chance to be properly arranged. I got the feeling they'd been waiting a while already.

"New in town?" I asked, trying not to breathe in too much. There was a good chance the air was laced with spores of some deadly flesh-eating mold.

"Hmm? Oh, yes," he said over his shoulder. "Sort of. We needed a change of scenery."

Some scene. How bad was his last place, if this was an improvement?

He threw open a door and we stepped into the living room. It was named for good reason: I think it was the only room that was actually being lived in. The couch was a fold-out, draped with blankets and pillows. There was a small dining table by the wide bay windows, which seemed to be the only place light could penetrate the house.

A woman was sitting in an electric wheelchair beside the table, bathing in the sunshine. She was in worse shape than the house. Both legs had been amputated above the knee. She had her arms, at least, but the fingers were gnarled with arthritis. One eye was completely white, and the other was half-clouded. Her flesh seemed to hang off her bones.

"This is my mother," Mills said to me.

By the look of her, I would've believed she was his grand-mother, but who was I to argue?

Mills laid a hand on the old woman's shoulder and hollered in her ear. "Mr. Turner is here."

She was slow to react, and when she did, her movements were glacial. She turned her head away from the sunlight and her one good eye sought me out.

"Good," was all she said.

"Nice to meet you, Mrs. Mills," I said.

"What?"

"She's very deaf," Brandon Mills said to me. He yelled in his mother's ear again. "He says it's nice to meet you."

Her face twitched into a frown, then with the barest wave to indicate that she understood, she turned back to the window.

"Sorry," the man said to me as he guided me away. "Her mood isn't great at the best of times."

"And these aren't the best of times," I said.

"No. No." He sighed, dragging his hand across his face. "Can I get you anything? Water? Coffee?"

I shook my head. "How about you tell me what it is you've lost?" I suggested.

He sighed again, nodding. "You're right." For a moment, he looked almost as old as his mother. Then he silently gestured, beckoning me to follow.

He led me back into the hallway and into another room. As soon as he threw open the door, I got a lungful of mothballs and dust.

For some reason, this room had carpet, though the rest of the floors in the house were all hardwood. Moth-eaten curtains were drawn across the windows. It was a small room, barely an office, and the spiders were really dug in here.

There was only a single piece of furniture in the room, and it had pride of place, right in the center.

A baby's crib.

It looked brand new, and it was remarkably free of spider webs. A mobile hung over the crib, turning slowly in some hidden breeze.

I grew cold all of a sudden. The sight of the crib brought long-buried memories fighting to the surface.

Images of a crib, not so different from this one, beside a window that'd been thrown wide open. Curtains blowing in the cold of the night. The off-tune scream of a baby. Or what was supposed to be a baby.

"Mr. Turner?"

Mills' voice reached through the memories, dragging me out of the sinkhole. I plastered a smile to my face.

"Sorry," I said. "Got a little light-headed for a second."

"Do you need—?"

"No, no. I'm fine. This crib…"

"Used to be my son's."

The "used to" in that sentence left no doubts as to its meaning.

"I'm so sorry," I said.

"Do you have children, Mr. Turner?"

I shook my head. "But I used to have a younger brother. Theodore. Teddy." How long had it been since I'd said his name? "There were sixteen years between us, so I took care of him a lot. He…uh…he died when he was a baby."

I didn't know why I was telling Mills this. Must've been Alice's talk, getting inside my head. Or maybe it was just the sight of this crib. Hell, this damn crib. I could barely bring myself to look at it.

"My son was eighteen months old." Mills' voice was quiet, but it seemed loud in the confines of this small, still room. "When he died, it destroyed us. My wife and I. The relationship couldn't survive."

I caught a glimpse of a silver chain disappearing beneath the collar of his shirt. I wondered if he kept his wedding ring on that chain. The way he spoke about his wife, I could tell he still loved her, despite the tragedy.

The picture was starting to come into focus. My guess: when they split, Mills' wife got the house. He'd moved here with his mother, using whatever he had left to rent or buy this old dump. Say what you like about Lost Falls, but at least the property prices were affordable enough.

"I feel stupid," Mills said. "I don't…I'm not sure I believe in what you do. No offense."

"None taken."

"I just don't know what else to do. I don't have much money. I—"

"Mr. Mills," I said. "Tell me what I can do for you."

For a moment, I could see the cracks in the facade he was barely keeping together. His lip trembled; he covered it with his hand. He stared at the crib for a moment.

"My boy is gone." He wrapped his hands around the crib's railing. "All I have left of him is this crib. And one other thing. A silver rattle. It's been in our family for more than a hundred years. My mother, she played with it when she was a baby. So did I. So did my son. Now, now it's…"

"Missing," I said.

He closed his eyes and nodded.

"Describe it," I said.

"It's about eight inches long. Ivory handle, with a silver head. There are two rows of bells, four in each row. It's a beautiful old thing. Until yesterday, it sat right here." He gestured to the center of the crib mattress, then turned to me. His eyes were suddenly hard and desperate. For a moment, I caught a glimpse of a different man, a stronger man. Someone used to shouldering the burdens of the world and doing what needed to be done. "Please. I can't explain to you how important that rattle is to me. Me and my mother. I need it back. It's all I have. All I have," he whispered, his voice breaking off at the end. And just like that, the fire in his eyes was extinguished.

All my dreams of a nice big payday had long since gone down the toilet. The man said he didn't have much money, and I believed him. Hell, if that rattle really was an antique, it was probably more valuable than anything else in the house.

But I took another look at that crib, picturing the baby that used to sleep there. In my mind's eye I saw that other crib again, I heard that cry that wasn't Teddy's. And a different part of my brain took over.

"I'll find it," I promised.

Stupidest damn promise I've ever made.

4

There hadn't been a break-in. No one had jimmied the windows to steal the rattle. Brandon Mills said the two police officers who'd come the day before had already determined that, and my own investigation confirmed it.

According to Mills, the cops had taken his statement and promised they'd keep an eye out, but they hadn't seemed convinced that anything criminal had happened. I doubted they even believed the rattle really existed. Even if it did, they probably thought his mother had lost it somewhere (the poor demented old dear).

But the cops were wrong. Silver, like iron, is damn good at soaking up emotional energy.

Silver that old, kept in the same family for so long and used by several generations of little Mills babies, would be brimming with that kind of energy. I figured that maybe, just maybe, it was powerful enough to leave a residue of its existence behind.

I guessed right. The charged powdered silver I scattered over the crib mattress coalesced into a faint shape in the center of the mattress, like iron filings exposed to a magnetic field.

The rattle had been here, all right. But where had it gone?

Here's a little secret of the cunning man's trade: inanimate objects are a pain in the ass to track. Even in situations like this, where the object holds enough memory and history to leave behind some trace of itself, trying to follow that trail is near impossible.

That's not to say I didn't give it a shot.

I'd already sent Mills out of the room before I started doing anything too mysterious. The fewer people who knew how I worked, the safer I'd be. Ordinary people who see magic being performed tend to get a little...anxious. It upsets their world view. Brings out all those terrified, dangerous, torch-and-pitchfork feelings in them.

When I'd poured most of the powdered silver back into its vial—that stuff isn't cheap—I took the last pinch and dropped it into a concoction of my own making. It contained—among other things—a couple of drops of my own blood, the seeds from the first apple to fall from the tree in my backyard that season, and a dash of pureed sheep's liver.

Magic ain't always pretty, folks.

I dipped a cheap silver-plated pendant into the concoction. The silver was new, blank, with no history to mess with my investigations. After letting it sit for a moment, I drew out the pendant and held it by its string, watching it carefully.

I was getting something, but it was faint. The pendant, now primed with the memory of the rattle, was pulling ever so slightly towards the room's south wall.

I went to the wall, one eye on the pendant. It was hard to tell, but I was pretty sure the rattle had found its way over here recently. It wasn't here anymore—if the rattle was still in the house, I would've got a much more pronounced response. But when it'd been taken from the cradle, it had gone this way.

And it had been taken. That's another nugget of cunning folk wisdom, passed down from generation to generation. Get out your pencils. Here it is: inanimate objects don't get up and walk away on their own.

Obvious as it is, it's an important thing to remember. Because while the object itself might be hard to track, people and creatures are a different story. They leave a trail. Scents, hairs, sweat, skin cells. Thoughts, emotions, memories.

So if I could find some hint as to who or what had taken the rattle, I'd be halfway done with this job.

I paced up and down the south wall, all the while keeping an eye on the pendant. The rattle hadn't gone out the window or the door. It'd gone through the wall.

Pocketing the pendant, I ran my hand along the peeling wallpaper. In the bottom corner, the wallpaper was lifting away from the wall completely. I took hold of the corner and pulled it back.

There was a wide crack in the wall, where it had rotted through. It stretched from the floor to about waist-height, maybe six inches across at its widest point.

I already had my suspicions, but that crack cemented them. I pulled out my phone, turned on the light, and crouched to shine it into the crack.

There wasn't much to see in the wall space. It hadn't been insulated, and I could follow the trail of rot from some leak in the ceiling.

But the smell, that was more than the smell of rot. Something had been living in these walls a long time.

"A kikimora? Or a domovoi?" I muttered to myself, but then my light caught on a few strands of long black hair stuck to a nail. That was unusual.

I pulled off my jacket, set down my phone to cast the light as best I could, and stretched my arm into the wall space. It was a tight squeeze. Early's girly little arms would've fit in here no problem.

With gritted teeth and straining muscles, I finally snagged the hairs with the tips of my fingers. I drew them out and looked at them in the light.

The hairs were thick and kinked, with a wet shine to them. I touched them, then rubbed my fingers together. The hairs had a waxy feel.

"Hobgoblin." I smiled to myself.

Hobgoblins were suckers for shiny things, especially silver. I'd bet my left foot that was our thief.

I peered into the wall space as far as my light could penetrate. The stud closest to me was rotten through, but I couldn't see what was beyond.

I stood up and dusted myself off. Moving slowly around the edge of the room, I knocked on the wall, trying to determine exactly where the passageway led. It took me out of the empty nursery and back along the hallway.

Mr. Mills stuck his head out of the living room, apparently drawn by the sound of my knocking. "Do you...uh...need anything?"

I held up my hand, silencing him. "Your kitchen's through here?"

Without waiting for the answer, I went through the door at the end of the hall. It was the kitchen, all right. It had been renovated more recently than the rest of the house, so it was only forty or fifty years old.

Mr. Mills started following me in, but I shooed him away, shutting the door in his face.

"Just need to check something," I said through the door. I heard a grunt, then the man's footsteps shuffled away.

Early always says my manner leaves a little to be desired when I start getting excited about a job. I can't help it. Despite the sometimes sporadic paydays and the occasional bursts of danger, I really do love what I do. The thrill of discovery. Of exploring a world most people no longer believe in.

The stove was electric, the kind with manual dials and a bell that rings when the timer's done. I took it in both hands and hauled it away from the wall.

There was another crack in the wall here, another strip of wallpaper peeling away. I pulled it back, widening the crack, exposing the space inside.

What do you know? A perfect little kikimora hole.
I grinned. "Bingo."

5

A kikimora is a peaceful, benign kind of Stranger. Some live in the woods, but most prefer to make their homes inside human houses. They live off whatever scraps they can scavenge, and in exchange they keep rodents and other pests away.

They usually make their homes behind the stove, because that guarantees them food and warmth. But they also move about the house by making passages in the walls and floor, like the one I'd found in the nursery.

There was no kikimora here, though, and I doubted there'd been one for years. My guess was that the house had fallen so far into disrepair she'd cleared out in search of better accommodation.

And then some hobgoblin had come to take her place. Hobgoblins were like that: opportunistic. They were generally harmless as well, but hobgoblins had a mischievous streak. The hole behind the stove was littered with trinkets the creature had stolen: a single pearl earring, a couple of mismatched socks, and a torn hospital wristband.

No sign of the rattle, though, and no sign of the hobgoblin either. Strange, that it would leave without taking the rest of its haul with it. But then again, maybe it'd been so transfixed by the silver rattle that all these other bits and pieces paled in comparison. Hobgoblins aren't blessed with an overabundance of intelligence.

I would've rather been chasing a kikimora than a hobgoblin. Despite their stupidity, hobgoblins are sneaky little bastards, and overly chatty to boot.

Still, I figured it could be worse. I could be dealing with one of their larger, smarter cousins: a goblin. Hobgoblins are mischievous, foolish, but ultimately no threat to anyone. Goblins, though, goblins are treacherous. As smart as a human, but with a cunning and a complete lack of conscience that make them extremely dangerous.

Vampires hunt because they have to. Chorts and hellhounds and fiends are beasts, acting out of instinct. Trolls and ogres are brutish, but they can be reasoned with.

But goblins are devious. Goblins scheme, goblins plot.

Goblins are too damn much like us.

So I was pretty happy to only be dealing with a hobgoblin, all things considered. I was pretty sure the hobgoblin was no longer here, but it couldn't have gone far. It couldn't drive—it wouldn't have been able to reach the pedals even if it had the necessary brainpower. Which meant the hobgoblin would've toddled off on foot, weighed down by the rattle and anything else it took with it.

I began to stand up, but I paused as I cast one more look inside the kikimora hole. That hospital wristband was awfully small. Almost like it'd belonged to…

I picked it up, looked at the information, and felt my heart sink a little as I saw I was right. The patient's name was Michael Mills. His date of birth was just under two years ago. The wristband belonged to Brandon's son.

By the look of the admission date, he'd had a rocky start in life. He'd been taken back to hospital less than two weeks after he was born, the poor kid. I didn't know what he'd been admitted for, but Brandon Mills had said his son was eighteen months old when he died, so the boy must've survived a while at least after this admission. I wondered if whatever he went in for was the same thing that'd eventually killed him.

I stood up and shoved the oven back into place. Brandon Mills was feeding his mother spoonfuls of instant soup when I returned to the living room.

He looked up expectantly, and I beckoned him over. As he put down the bowl and joined me in the doorway, his gaze lingered over me. I realized he was studying the tattoos on my arms—I'd taken off my jacket when I went rooting around in the wall space. And they were pretty unusual tattoos, I guess. No Harley Davidson logos or half-naked pin-up girls for me. Mostly occult symbols and words of power from a dozen languages—some of them non-human.

They were mainly designed to prevent others from tracking me like I was intending to track the hobgoblin. I figured it was worth it to keep the witch-finders and any other nasties off my back. And if nothing else, I supposed they made me look a little more mysterious.

"I think I can help you," I said.

He had a look on his face, like he wanted to be relieved but couldn't quite shake his skepticism. "You can?"

"You were right. The rattle's been stolen. But I believe I can track it down."

"How?"

I shook my head. "My method's a secret, I'm afraid. Let's just say the thief left some clues."

His skepticism didn't dim, but he was desperate enough to know he had no other choice. He glanced over at his mother, then back at me. "All right. How...um...how much do you charge?"

I told him my usual rate. He paled.

It was worth a shot, at least. Sighing internally, I held up my hand. "Look, I don't normally do this, but I understand how much that rattle means to you." I couldn't believe I was going to do this. Early had poisoned me with all his talk of how a cunning man has to look after his community.

I gave him another figure, a pathetically small one. It would only barely cover my costs. Maybe not even that. I just felt so damn sorry for the guy.

Oh, well. I could always eat at Alice's if money got too tight. She owed me for clearing out her basement, anyway.

Relief swept across his face. For a moment I was afraid he was going to hug me. "Thank you. If you really can do what you say… Thank you."

"You just sit tight," I told Mills. "This could take two hours, or it could be a couple of days. I'll call you when I've got something."

"Thank you," he said again.

I raised my voice, waving to the old woman by the window. "Goodbye, Mrs. Mills!"

Nothing. The woman stared out the window, oblivious to my shouting.

"Don't mind her," Mills said. "She really should be in care, but I just can't afford it at the moment."

"Well, I hope things start looking up for you soon," I said.

I couldn't wait to be out of that house. Mills followed me to the front door, and watched for a couple of seconds as I struggled with the handle. I couldn't get the door open.

"It sticks," he said, taking over. He did some complicated maneuver that involved twisting the handle with both hands while he pressed one foot against the bottom of the door. He gave a grunt of pain as he did it—the guy must've had a bad back or something—and the door finally creaked open.

"I'll call you soon," I promised, and I started down the overgrown garden path toward my van. But Mills kept following me.

"Mr. Turner," he said. "Can I ask you one more favor?"

I pulled open the gate. "What?"

"I want to talk to this thief. I want to know why they did

this to me."

I paused, glancing back. There was something I didn't like in his eyes. Something unsettling.

"I don't think that's a good idea."

"Why not?" he said.

Because I don't think you're stable enough to find out that hobgoblins exist, I thought.

"The important thing is getting your boy's rattle back," I said, avoiding the question. "Let's just focus on that."

That reminded me. I took the hospital wristband out of my pocket and handed it to Mills.

"By the way, I found this when I was looking around."

"Oh my God." He took the wristband carefully, like it might disintegrate at any moment. "I thought we lost this in the move. Where did you find it?"

"Just lying around," I said.

Mills nodded, barely listening. Eyes fixed on the wristband, he dragged the pad of his thumb across his son's name.

"He was born with an intestinal blockage. We didn't catch it until a few days after we got him home. He got so sick, so fast. I couldn't believe it. I couldn't believe how scared I was. I've never been that scared of anything in my life."

I nodded. "Was that how he...?"

"Hmm?" He finally seemed to remember I was still standing there. "Oh, no. They fixed the blockage. We took him home. We were happy. For a little while, at least."

I wanted to ask how the boy had died, but it didn't seem right, somehow. I clapped him on the shoulder. "I'm sorry."

He nodded his thanks.

He was still standing there when I started to climb into the driver's seat. Which meant he was there to hear the screeching growl coming from the back of the van.

I cringed. The sleep charm had done its work on Lawrence, but he had woken when I opened the door. I glanced back and saw the blanket had partially slipped off the cage.

Mills frowned. "What was that?"

"It's just…uh…never mind. I'll be in touch."

I slammed the door and brought the van coughing to life. Just before I pulled away, I glanced in the mirror and saw Brandon Mills looking through the back window, frowning at the shaking cage that wouldn't stop growling.

"Quiet down back there," I said as I drove away. "Or we won't stop for ice cream after all."

I headed home. If I was going to track down the hobgoblin that'd stolen Mills' silver rattle, I'd have to act quickly. All I had of the hobgoblin were a couple of hairs, after all.

What would've been really nice was a big jar of the hobgoblin's urine. You'd be surprised how useful urine is in my line of work. It's potent stuff.

Properly treated, a jar of someone's piss does a damn good job warding off minor witchcraft. It's even better for tracking. With a few drops of urine fresh from the source, I could brew up a potion to track down the producer of said urine to within a couple of feet.

It's a glamorous job, being a cunning man.

But without even a single drop of piss to work with, I'd have to make do with the hobgoblin's hairs. They would do the trick, but the trace would be a little harder.

Lawrence complained the whole way home. I was either going to have to gag him or get myself some earmuffs. I'd never intended to have him sitting in that cage for so long, but I couldn't offload him on Alcaraz until I made a start on tracking this hobgoblin.

Maybe he was hungry, and that was why he was so cranky. With luck, there'd be something at home that the thing would eat.

Home for me was a little one-bedroom riverside house—a

cabin, really—just outside town. It was on Early's property, around the back of his slightly more impressive Victorian. I guess it wasn't much, but to me, it was a mansion.

I owed Early for an awful lot in my life, and the house was no exception. The old bastard would probably let me live rent-free if I wanted, but I wasn't going to let him get away with that.

I headed down the bumpy, forested driveway and parked on the grass outside my cabin. It wasn't until I was hauling the dog cage out of the back of the van that I saw I wasn't alone.

Rhodes was looking particularly menacing today. He was holding a tree saw in one hand as he stared at me from the shade of a willow. He was a little guy, but strongly built, with dark weathered skin and a face that really could've done with a second try.

Early had hired the guy a year or so back to tend to his herb garden and act as an all-round dogsbody. That was Early all over: collecting strays and assorted losers like me and giving them something to do and a place to lay their head.

Of course, it'd been the best decision he'd ever made when he took me under his wing and taught me the tricks of the trade. Rhodes, I wasn't so sure about. He lacked my charm and dashing good looks, that was for sure.

While I struggled to keep the growling, shaking dog cage from leaping out of my grip, I raised my hand in a wave.

"How's it going?" I called to Rhodes across the garden.

He just grunted, turned around, and started hacking at the tree again.

No doubt about it: Early had picked a lemon with that boy.

Juggling the dog cage, I finally got my keys out of my pocket and into the front door. I staggered inside, kicked the door closed behind me, and lugged the creature into the kitchen.

"Settle down, goddamn it." I put the cage on the table. "I'll be back in a second."

The cage continued to rattle as I retreated to the bathroom.

It was good just to have some peace and quiet for ten seconds. I splashed some water on my face, then examined the state of the wounds I'd suffered in Alice's basement.

Early's ointment seemed to have done the trick. I wasn't bleeding anymore, and none of the cuts looked infected by any sort of otherworldly rot. I noticed one of the tattoos on my shoulder had been disrupted by a particularly deep claw mark. Pain in my ass. If it scarred over, that meant a trip to the tattoo artist to fix it up.

"All right, you little shit," I said, coming out of the bathroom. "What do you eat?"

Lawrence didn't respond, of course. In fact, he had grown awfully quiet. Had he gone back to sleep?

I went over to the cage, peered inside. The creature had pulled himself into the very back corner of the dog cage, like a wounded animal. He spat and hissed at me.

"What's got you so worked up?" I asked him.

A voice came from behind me. "That would be me, I'm afraid."

6

I jumped so high I nearly slammed my head into one of the ceiling beams. Spinning, I staggered back, reaching for a weapon.

"Oh, did I scare you? I am sorry, Osric."

His face was not the sort of face you want to find suddenly appearing in your home—or anywhere else, really. It was a mishmash of features: a squat, fat nose below two eyes of different shape and color; lips that were too red for the tone of his skin; teeth that looked like they'd been arranged at random.

The rest of him was no better. I called him a "him", because he spoke with a male voice, but his body neither confirmed nor denied that assumption. He had the wide hips of a woman, but the broad chest and thick neck of a lumberjack. Even though he was sitting, I could see his arms were too long—they would've hung nearly to his knees if he'd been standing.

He was sitting on the stool in front of my piano. As I stood there gawping, he took off his top hat. The guy was wearing a real, honest-to-god top hat. On a Saturday afternoon, no less.

When I decided I was no longer having a heart attack, I pointed at the front door.

"Get out."

"Osric—"

"No. Get out."

"My dear boy," he said with a lopsided smile. "Surely you

have time for an old friend."

I realized I was distractedly rubbing at the small patch of scar tissue on the right side of my head, where the hair no longer grew. Tightening my hand into a fist, I forced my arm back to my side.

"What the hell do you want, Dealer?" I demanded.

"Perhaps I'm just here for a nice chat with my favorite customer," he said.

"I doubt that. How the hell do you always get in, anyway? This place is supposed to be warded."

Still smiling, the Dealer swiveled on his seat, set his hat down beside him, and gently laid his long fingers on the keys of my piano.

"I always wondered why you kept this," he said, ignoring my question. He tapped a piano key. The sound was like fingernails scraping on metal. "You threw away everything else." He tapped another key; this one was like the moan of an injured tiger. "But the piano you kept. I never understood why."

"Don't you dare—"

But his fingers were already moving. They danced across the keys, swift and elegant. His whole body got into it. His eyes were closed, but his head was swaying. His shoulders rose and fell and his foot feathered the pedals. He smiled, lost in the music.

I clapped my hands over my ears, grinding my teeth against the cacophony of discordant sounds bouncing around the inside of my skull. It was agony.

"Stop!" I roared.

The racket continued.

I stomped over and kicked the stool out from under him. The Dealer toppled backward and the sound cut off with one last tortured squeal.

I caught him by the lapels of his jacket and slammed him against the piano.

"Stop," I snarled in his face.

He wasn't scared of me. That only infuriated me more.

"It's a little out of tune." The Dealer smiled lazily, reached out a single finger, and pressed a key. "That was Rachmaninoff's second piano sonata, if you were wondering. I'm still getting the hang of the third movement."

I wanted to break his misshapen face. For a moment, I entertained the thought of slamming the piano's fallboard shut on his fingers a couple of times.

But it wouldn't do me any good. Taking a deep breath, I released the Dealer.

He smoothed out his lapels, regarded me for a moment, then pulled down his lower eyelid and pointed at his right eye. "I got this eye from a nine-year-old girl. Did I ever tell you that? She had a brain tumor, and I offered to excise it for her in exchange for her eye. Poor girl was so scared." He touched his throat. "This voice is from the nineteenth century. It belonged to one of the French soldiers of Napoleon's Grand Armée, during his failed invasion of Russia. I bought it from the soldier in exchange for a warm greatcoat, a week's worth of rations, and a talisman that would ward off the Cossacks' bullets." He smiled, as if remembering the moment fondly. "Do you know what the soldier's last words were, before I took his voice?"

"Don't wear it out on pointless stories?"

"He called me a demon." He shook his head. "You humans are so superstitious." He laid his hand on my shoulder, like we were old pals. "But of everything I've bought, over all these centuries, I think your music is my favorite purchase."

He stretched his hands out in front of him, admiring them. I reconsidered my decision not to break those fingers.

"Such an amazing talent," he said. "I got lucky with you, Osric. I always thought—where are you going?"

I walked away from him, opened the fridge, and took out a beer. I pressed the cold bottle to my throbbing head. It didn't help.

"Got another one of those?" the Dealer asked.

I slammed the fridge closed.

"Never mind," he said. "I'm not very thirsty after all."

The dog cage on the table hissed and shook. Whatever that creature was, it didn't much care for the Dealer. That much we could agree on.

I cracked open the beer and downed half of it in a single gulp.

"What do you want, Dealer?"

"It's not what I want. It's what I can do for you, my friend."

I brushed past him and unlocked a door leading off the cabin's main living area. A sharp acidic smell hit me as I opened the door. "I'm too busy for your shit today. Come mock me another time."

"No need to be like that." He followed me into the back room. "I have information to trade. Information that will interest you greatly."

"Pass."

I pulled the light cord and the bulb overhead flickered uncertainly to life. This was my workshop, my laboratory. Wooden workshop tables were set around the walls of the small room, littered with vials and pouches and Bunsen burners. The shelves above were even more crammed with ingredients, everything from table salt to chicken feathers to the pickled tongue of a kelpie.

I gathered an armful of vials and bottles, then pulled up a stool and got to work. I had a shelf full of grimoires and archaic books of the occult filled with *thees* and *thous*, but I didn't need a recipe for this particular spell. It was one of my bread-and-butter jobs, and I could recite the preparations in my sleep.

"Don't be so hasty," the Dealer said. I could feel him peering over my shoulder as I worked. "I wouldn't offer you this information if I didn't think it was useful."

I turned to face him. "Because you're always so fair in your dealings, right?"

His smile faded, replaced with a serious frown. "I am. Always. My brethren haven't always been so discerning, but I always ensure that my customers get a fair deal. I give them what they want most. What they need most. I never trick anyone. I never force anyone into any deal they don't want."

His breath had a rotten stink to it. So did the rest of him. I didn't know for sure, but my theory was that the flesh and organs and body parts he bought from other beings had a limited shelf life. The Dealer had visited me half a dozen times in the last seven years, and every time there was something different about him: a new hand, or nose, or set of lips. As if he was replacing the dying parts of himself.

"You prey on the vulnerable," I said. "You said so yourself. The little girl with the brain tumor. That French soldier."

"Survival isn't free, Osric. You of all people should know that."

I forced myself to turn back to my work. Getting pulled into an argument with him was a waste of my time. I had a job to do. A job that I was barely going to break even on, granted, but a job nonetheless.

I struck a match and lit the Bunsen burner. While the Dealer hovered over my shoulder, I brought a few ingredients together and set them boiling.

The Dealer had fallen silent for now, but I could feel him watching me as I worked. I couldn't be bothered trying to toss him out.

Even though he was the one who'd granted me my ability to work a cunning man's magic, he was no expert in it. He'd traded it from someone in some other place, some other world, and sold it on to me in turn. In exchange for the part of me he wanted most.

My music.

That music had always been inside me. As long as I could remember, I'd heard it in the back of my head.

There was only a hole there now.

I was six when I decided I wanted to be a concert pianist. Most kids wanted to be fire fighters or astronauts. Not me.

But no one took me seriously. I was a big kid even then, a tough kid from the wrong side of town with a father who'd split and a mother who worked minimum wage eighty hours a week to keep us afloat. Pianists were classy, and I was anything but.

When I was eight, a teacher of mine asked me what I wanted to do when I grew up. I told her, expecting her to laugh like all the others. But she didn't. She didn't pat me on the head and go off to help the gifted kids. She had me wait behind after school, sat me down behind a tinny little keyboard, and started to teach me.

I worked hard. Damn hard. I flunked most of my subjects over my teenage years, but I kept on playing. I won some competitions, and eventually I scraped together enough cash to buy myself a real piano. The piano I still own.

I played, and I played, and I played. It was the only thing I was good at. But I was really fucking good at it.

And then I won a scholarship for a prestigious music school. It was what I'd hoped for since I was a kid. There was nothing that could've made me give that up.

Or so I'd thought. Turns out, you make a man desperate and angry enough, there's not much he won't sacrifice. The Dealer knew that all too well.

Still, the Dealer was right about one thing: I'd made my decision willingly. Would I do it again, knowing what I know now?

That, I hadn't quite figured out.

I banished the thoughts, turning my attention back to the concoction I was brewing up. The Dealer had draped himself over the bench next to me, watching as I removed the brew from the burner.

"You're wasted on this kind of work, Osric," he said. "You know that."

"The client I'm helping might disagree."

"Perhaps. Perhaps."

Finally, I took the small zip-lock bag from my pocket. Inside were the hobgoblin hairs I'd found at Mills' house. With a pair of tweezers, I carefully extracted the hairs and dropped them into the flask. The concoction bubbled and hissed, and a stink like sulfur wafted off. I corked it quickly, before I stunk the whole damn place out.

I downed the last of my beer, tossed the bottle into the trash on the other side of the room, and pushed back my chair.

"Well, thanks for stopping by," I said to the Dealer. "Now, if you don't mind getting the fuck out of my house…"

"You haven't given my offer any thought yet."

I stood. "Oh, I've given it as much thought as it deserves."

"I'm trying to help you, Osric. You're in danger."

"Uh-huh," I grunted, unconvinced. I scanned the shelves, looking for my eyedropper. Where the hell had I left it this time? Oh, there. The Dealer was leaning on it. I nudged him aside and pocketed both the dropper and the newly brewed potion.

The Dealer followed me out of my workshop. "You should take this seriously, my friend. There are forces moving against you, even as we speak."

I sighed. He was never going to leave me alone at this rate. "Fine. I'll bite. What kinds of forces?"

He gave me a sly smile—it was particularly creepy with these new lips of his—and waggled a finger. "That's as much as I can tell you for now. Consider it a free sample. For the rest of it, you'll have to pay."

"Here we go. How much this time, huh?"

He pursed his lips and looked to the ceiling, like he was doing sums in his head. Like he actually had to think about it.

"Let's say…a kidney. Left or right, I don't mind."

I snorted.

"You don't need both kidneys," he said. "And you'll need them a lot less if you're dead. Please, Osric. I implore you."

"Your imploring has been noted. Now get out."

He stared at me for a moment, then sighed and lifted his hands in defeat. "If you refuse to see reason, what can I do?"

He picked up his ridiculous top hat, set it atop his head, and strolled toward the door. The dog cage hissed and whined as he passed.

"I hope you don't come to regret your decision," he said as he opened the door. "I truly hope that."

"Bye-bye, now."

"And I hope your friend Early doesn't come to regret your foolishness either," he said over his shoulder. And then he shut the door behind him.

My guts tightened. "Wait," I shouted after him. "What did you say about Early?"

I rushed to the door, threw it open. He had vanished.

"Dealer!" I roared. "What did you mean about Early?"

A startled trio of sparrows took flight. I glared after them.

Across the yard, by the main house, that bastard Rhodes was crouched by Early's chicken coop, staring at me like I was a madman. I supposed, from over there, it was a fair assessment.

I waved, stepped back inside, and closed the door. The Dealer was just screwing with me. It was what he did.

A kidney. Hell. Slimy bastard.

Shaking my head, I went back to the table and checked I had everything I needed. The potion I'd concocted would need a little time to reduce, which gave me time to drop by Alcaraz's.

I scraped together the contents of my refrigerator into a sandwich, poked a chunk of it through the bars of the dog cage, and stuffed the rest down my throat. Inside the cage, Lawrence hesitantly approached the hunk of bread and meat.

The presence of the Dealer seemed to have cowed the thing somewhat. He sniffed the sandwich chunk, gave it a testing lick, then snatched it up in its claws and shoved the whole thing into his mouth. He even sucked up the crumbs afterward.

"See," I said. "I'm not so bad."

The creature gave me a look like he still wanted to rip my face off.

I grabbed the cage and started for the door. But as I passed the piano, I paused.

My fingers stretched out on their own, brushed along the well-worn keys. Just as I did almost every day. Hoping that some part of it would come back to me. Hoping that there was some fragment the Dealer had missed, when he'd cut into my brain and taken out the music.

Just a simple little tune would do. Beginner grade stuff. Every now and then I pulled out all my old books, tried to start learning it all from scratch.

But every time I tried, my mind would go fuzzy. The keys seemed to shift and dance in front of me. The music on the page was nothing but gibberish, no matter how hard I studied it.

Nothing but a waste of time.

I slammed the fallboard down over the keys and put the past where it belonged. I had work to do.

7

Alcaraz's estate was really something. She'd probably bought it for a pocketful of buttons and a shiny brass kettle back in 1903, and now it had to be one of the most expensive properties in Lost Falls.

Or at least it would be if she ever sold it. I'd heard rumors that some rich dude had been sniffing around the last twenty years, trying to get the old woman to sell up so he could develop it into a golf course and luxury hotel. Alcaraz hadn't sold, and she hadn't had the good decency to die either. I wondered if she was staying alive just to spite him.

The estate was set atop a ridge overlooking the valley in which Lost Falls and the river were nestled. High stone walls surrounded the perimeter, the manor house peeking over the top. It was a lonely, winding road to get out there, and the house loomed above me the whole way, as if watching my approach.

The gate was closed when I arrived, but she hadn't changed the code since the last time I'd come. Alcaraz was always a little lax about security, especially considering the kinds of things that were on her property. Then again, maybe they were why she didn't have to worry. Even the more ignorant townsfolk had heard rumors of strange roars and growling echoing down the valley on moonless nights. The only people who came up here when they weren't invited were the occasional tourists, and even they tended not to stick around too long once their skin started prickling.

I drove up to the house. The driveway was lined with overhanging trees, and the grounds beyond were lush with overgrown gardens and artificial lakes slick with algae.

Before I went in, I took out the potion I'd brewed and rested the flask on the dashboard to mature. Moonlight would've been best, but sunlight would do the job as well.

I lugged the squirming dog cage up to the grand double doors that formed the manor's entrance. It was four stories tall, and each of those stories was lined with windows. But most of the windows were blacked out or shrouded with curtains, giving the place a still, silent feeling, like the owners had packed up and left a long time ago.

I pressed the buzzer, and heard a bell ringing in some distant corner of the house. Lawrence rattled the door of the dog cage.

"Knock it off," I said. The creature paid me no attention.

After a few seconds, I hit the doorbell again. Nothing. It wasn't unusual for Alcaraz to get wrapped up in some experiment she was doing, or to be so busy studying the mating behavior of bloodfiends that the whole rest of the world passed her by. I think that was half the reason she kept Lilian around.

I tried the door. It opened.

"Hello?" I called out as I stepped inside. "Doctor? Lilian?"

My voice echoed in the cavernous entrance hall. It was a disconcerting sound.

All across the entrance hall, grotesque creatures had been stuffed and mounted to the walls. Some kind of man-sized Stranger that vaguely resembled a giant bat had pride of place. It stood hunched at the bottom of the stairs, glaring at me with glass eyes as I came inside. A small brass plaque was affixed to the base, no doubt detailing the taxonomic information Alcaraz had gathered on the beast. I decided I'd rather not get close enough to investigate.

The lights were on, but when I called out again, I still got no response.

A growl drifted down from somewhere overhead, and I could hear snuffling in another part of the house.

The sounds were unsettling, but they weren't unusual. Most of the manor's bedrooms and sitting rooms had been repurposed into holding cells for the innumerable Strangers that Alcaraz studied.

Still, I was starting to get a little creeped out. Where was everyone? For a moment my thoughts flashed back to the Dealer's warning. I couldn't believe I was letting the bastard get inside my head.

To prove to myself I wasn't scared, I let the door swing closed behind me. It shut with a thud.

"Doctor Alcaraz!" I called again. "You upstairs?"

If she was home and not answering, she had to be pretty deep in something. Dealing with one of her creatures, probably. I started for the main stairs, resigning myself to the idea I'd have to spend the next half hour searching every room of this damn house.

But then I heard someone respond to my call. I couldn't make out the words, but it was someone speaking, not some Stranger growling. The sound seemed to come from the landing at the top of the stairs.

"Lilian?" I said. "Is that you?"

The figure of a woman appeared on the landing and began to stagger down the stairs toward me. I froze with my hand half-raised to wave.

It wasn't Lilian. Not Alcaraz either. The woman was slim, redheaded, beautiful, and young—all of about nineteen.

Oh, and she was naked. Not a stitch on her.

She stumbled quickly down the stairs, clutching at the banister with both hands. Big blue eyes fixed on me. Her fear was as naked as the rest of her.

"Please," she said. "Help me."

"Hell," I breathed.

I dropped the dog cage, earning a squawk of annoyance from the creature inside. I ran for the stairs. The woman didn't seem to be injured, but by the way she was moving, something wasn't right.

As I made my way toward her, I scanned the landing above. Where was Alcaraz? What was going on? Who was this woman?

"What happened?" I said. "What's going on?"

"Help," she said. "Please me."

My steps faltered. "What?"

She continued to stagger down the stairs, staring at me with those big wet eyes. "Help please. Help me. Me. Please."

I stopped. Licked my lips. My throat was awfully dry all of a sudden.

"Help," she said again, just the same way she'd said it before. She had no accent, but the way she was speaking…

"Shit," I whispered.

"Please." She reached for me with one hand. "Please."

I began to back away. The rising panic in the back of my brain wanted me to turn and run for it.

That would've been a very bad idea.

The woman's steps were becoming sure-footed now. She was coming on faster. That same look of fear remained in place, like it'd been painted there.

I glanced back. Too far to the door.

A sunflare. That would buy me enough time. I had one in my bag…

…which was sitting in the front passenger seat of my van. Might as well have been in China.

So my hand went to the one thing I had on me. My truncheon, hanging from the loop in my belt. I'd put it there before leaving my place.

Maybe the Dealer's warning had sunk in more than I

thought.

"Help," the woman said. She'd released the banister, and now both arms stretched toward me. Her red hair shimmered around her bare shoulders, as if it had a life of its own. "Help. Help. Help."

Without taking my eyes off her, I grasped the pommel of my truncheon and twisted. It was screwed on tight, so tight I thought it'd frozen shut. But I put some elbow grease into it, and it started to come loose.

The woman was coming quicker. Her fingers seemed to grow longer before my eyes. Her face shifted, became sharper. Those baby blues grew narrow.

I stumbled back as fast as I could. My fingers desperately unscrewed the pommel. The caged creature I'd left on the floor screeched in fear.

"Please," the woman said one last time.

And then she was flying at me.

8

She wasn't beautiful anymore.

The woman's hair twisted and coiled like a pit of snakes. She came at me snarling with teeth like steak knives. Her claws swung. She was a blur.

The truncheon's pommel came loose in my hand, exposing a sharpened wooden point. I thrust the truncheon forward as she leapt.

The sharpened point sunk into pale flesh. There was no blood. But let me tell you, she had a pair of lungs on her.

Her howl of pain was like a knife being dragged down my spine. Didn't help that her mouth was about three inches from my ear.

Her momentum carried her forward. She slammed into me, weighing a hell of a lot more than her slim form would suggest. A bony elbow drove into my solar plexus and all the wind went out of me.

We went down together. She was on top, which was really fucking bad news. I twisted aside as jaws snapped at my neck. A claw swiped across my chest, making the wounds I'd taken in my sister's basement look like paper cuts.

The point of my wooden stake was still jammed into her stomach. It was the only reason I was still alive.

Because this woman was no woman at all. She was a vampire. A breed of lesser vampire, to be more specific. And what the hell she was doing wandering about free in Alcaraz's house, I had no goddamn idea.

I had more pressing things to think about.

Contrary to popular belief, stakes don't kill vampires very effectively. Decapitation is the trick if you want to kill a vampire. Burn the body if you want to be sure.

But a stake to the heart will paralyze a vamp, at least for a while. Trouble was, I hadn't got her in the heart. I'd hit about eight inches south of there. Given the speed of her, I was lucky I got her at all.

She was hurt, but she wasn't paralyzed. And she was extremely pissed off.

I wrenched one arm free and grabbed her by the throat. With my other arm, I drove the stake in deeper.

That was enough to convince her to give up on bleeding me for the moment. She got her feet under her and leapt upward, pulling herself free of the stake.

She sailed into the air, spun, and dug the hooked claws of her feet into the wall. She hung there upside down, back arched as she snarled down at me. One claw swiped at the light fixture hanging beside her, and the light flickered out.

Now was my chance. With one hand clutching my wounded chest and the other desperately grasping my truncheon, I pulled myself to my feet and staggered for the door.

There was a thud and a crack of splintering floorboards behind me. I glanced back. The vampire had landed in a crouch on the floor. She was fully transformed now, a predator in its purest form. The hole in her stomach was already closing over.

I kept running. My legs were getting tangled. The adrenaline was keeping the pain at bay, but my shirt was soaked with blood. I risked another glance back and saw the vampire standing tall, her nostrils flaring at the scent of my blood. In the darkness, her pupils glistened like pools of black ink. For a second the only sound was the rattle of her breath and the squeal of my shoes on the floor.

Then the dog cage in the center of the entrance hall screeched and jiggled in place.

The vampire's head snapped toward Lawrence.

Lesser vampires aren't sentient, but even in the grip of bloodlust they have a certain amount of animal intelligence. She could see I was nearly to the door, and I had a weapon that could cause her pain. If she came for me and I got outside into the sunlight, there'd be even more pain for her.

The caged creature, on the other hand, offered no resistance.

She snarled at me once more, snapped her jaws, and turned to the dog cage, hunger in her eyes.

It was the perfect distraction. I was home free.

So I—being the bone-headed idiot I am—stopped.

I could tell you it was because I still needed to unravel the mystery of what this little creature really was, and how he'd got into my sister's basement.

I could tell you that I needed to know if the creature had brothers and sisters that might come looking for him, and maybe find my nephews instead.

But I'd be lying. I wasn't thinking about any of that. Hell, I don't know what I was thinking. Maybe, sometime in the last couple of hours, I'd started to like the poor little bastard. He had probably only been looking for a dark, quiet place to hide, after all, and here I'd come, a big blundering human, to capture him and stick him in a cage. Maybe my conscience just couldn't quite bear the thought of that vampire tearing the door off the cage and sinking her fangs into the throat of that child-sized little creature.

Reasons didn't matter. What mattered was what I did.

I stopped running. I turned back to face the vampire.

It stalked toward the cage, hunched over, head thrust forward, claws clicking on the hardwood. The cage rattled and shook, the creature inside squealing frantically.

I glanced around the entrance hall. Below a board of pinned and labeled insects, there was a polished troll humerus set atop a wooden vase stand. I tossed the troll bone aside, grabbed the stand by its leg, and stomped on it. The leg splintered near the top, and with one more good kick the top of the stand sheared off.

Leaving me with what was essentially a three-foot long wooden stake.

I slid my truncheon back into my belt and looked up, gripping the table leg in both hands. My vandalism had attracted the vampire's attention again. She was crouching above the dog cage, but her black eyes stared at me, watching to see what I'd do.

She bared her teeth. It was a sight to set knees quivering.

I swallowed and adjusted my grip on the stake. When had it got so slippery?

"Come on, then," I said. I pressed my hand to the scratches on my chest and held out my bloody palm. "This is what you want, isn't it? Why have stinking Stranger blood when you can have human?"

Slowly, the vampire sank to all fours and slunk toward me like a jaguar. She began to circle me, her eyes never leaving mine. I turned in place, threatening her with the point of the stake.

Then she struck. She was a pale blur, zigging and zagging toward me. The black shine of her eyes filled my vision.

I stabbed with the stake, felt it hit flesh. But it was a glancing blow. Screeching, the vampire darted away again. She stopped a few feet away, watching for an opening. Her eyes grew wider. She licked her lips, staring at the drops of blood staining the floor.

Out of the corner of my eye, I glimpsed movement at the top of the stairs. A woman's figure appeared, half-hidden in shadow.

For a moment, I feared the worst: the vampire wasn't alone. I could barely handle one; with two vampires I'd be drained dry in twenty seconds.

I should've run while I had the chance.

But then the woman moved into the light, and I saw I was wrong. She was no vampire.

She was wearing clothes, for one thing—a set of work overalls stained with God-knows-what. And she was armed. She lowered her rifle, braced it against the landing's railing, and aimed down the sight.

"Lilian!" I shouted.

That was as far as I got before the vampire was coming at me again.

I heard a single *pop*, like a violent puff of air. The vampire darted to the side and something whizzed past, striking the floor behind me. Up on the landing, Lilian raised her rifle to reload.

The vampire swiped at me, but it was a feint. As I thrust with the stake to keep her at bay, she skittered past me, leapt off the wall, and came flying at me from another angle.

No time to think, no time to defend myself. I threw myself to the ground as the vampire sliced through the air above me. She landed, twisted, and struck at me. I was already rolling away, scrambling to get to my feet again.

There was another *pop*, another sound of something striking the ground. Lilian swore and started reloading again.

Before I was fully up the vampire threw herself into another attack. She didn't seem to give a shit about Lilian. I didn't even know if she'd realized the woman was up there. Her focus was entirely on me. The bloodlust had taken over.

I barely managed to bring the table leg up as the vampire struck me. The wooden point drove into her flank and she screeched in agony. But this time she didn't pull away. She used her momentum, twisting past me. And she twisted the slippery stake right out of my hands.

With a howl, she tore the stake from her side and hurled it across the entrance hall. I suddenly felt very vulnerable. Staggering back, I pulled my truncheon from my belt once more, holding the short point out like a dagger.

"Keep her still!" Lilian's voice echoed down from the landing. "Keep her still, goddamn it!"

Of course. Keep her still. What a great fucking plan. Why hadn't I thought of that? Keep her still. Hell.

I looked around once more. My gaze fell on the blacked-out windows near the door.

The vampire charged with a snarl. My first instinct was to defend myself, my second instinct was to run. I did neither. I was fading, and I couldn't keep up the fight much longer. So I turned to Plan C.

I darted to the side, grabbed the mounted troll humerus from where it'd fallen, and hurled it at one of the blacked-out windows.

Glass shattered. As the vampire pulled back an arm to swipe at me, a thin beam of sunlight pierced the entrance hall.

The vampire staggered back with a shriek, dazed and shielding her eyes. I knew she would only be stunned for a second or two. There just wasn't enough sunlight to cause her any real pain.

So I charged forward, raised the pointed end of my truncheon, and plunged it into the vampire's chest.

She fell to the floor screaming. Before she could squirm away, I raised my foot and stomped down on the truncheon hard, driving the stake further into her heart.

Her muscles tightened and she went suddenly rigid. Her eyes bugged out and she gasped for breath. The bestial visage faded, human features rippling back into view.

The *pop* of Lilian's rifle sounded one more time. A wood-tipped dart struck the vampire in the neck. The vampire's eyes opened wide in shock.

For what seemed like forever, the creature strained against the stake in her chest. Slowly, her movements began to fade. And then finally her eyes slid closed, and her body went limp.

I swayed on my feet. The burning pain of the wounds in my chest came roaring to life.

"Forget it," I said to no one in particular. "I'm going back to bed. I give up on today."

Up on the landing, Lilian rested her rifle against her shoulder. "Hey, Ozzy. Nice of you to stop by."

9

My shirt was a write-off. Doctor Alcaraz offered to find me a new one, and before I could protest she'd produced one from some long-forgotten wardrobe. By the look of it, it'd last been worn in the early days of the Cold War. It was far too tight, but after several minutes of badgering I finally accepted it.

Early wasn't around to play nurse this time, so I patched myself up. Lilian was nice enough to fetch my kit from the van, and I spent the next fifteen minutes bandaging my chest and trying to hide the fact that my hands wouldn't stop shaking.

Twice in one day I'd been scratched up. I bet the Dealer was laughing it up right now.

"All right," I said as I gingerly pulled on the borrowed shirt, trying not to burst the seams. "Now will someone please explain to me why you had a baiter vamp running loose?"

We were on the second floor, in what had once been a guest bedroom. It was a little less inviting now, what with the blacked-out windows and the reinforced floor-to-ceiling cage dominating one wall.

The vampire was in the cage, snoring peacefully on the thin mattress in the corner. The sleeping draught that Lilian had shot into the creature was potent stuff, beyond anything I—or maybe even Early—could cook up. It had also returned the vampire to her human form, which had the unpleasant side effect of making it look like we'd kidnapped a naked young woman and trapped her in our dungeon.

But the cuts on my chest were a painful reminder of what she truly was. Baiters were a kind of lesser vampire that used camouflage to attract their prey. This one was designed specifically to look like a helpless victim. But she wasn't sentient. She couldn't even truly speak. The words she'd spoken were about as meaningful as a parrot mimicking the sound of a washing machine.

Doctor Alcaraz was puttering about the room, scratching notes in a notebook by the dim orange light of the single remaining bulb in the light fitting overhead. So it fell to Lilian to give me the story. She sat with the dart rifle across her knees. While she talked, she fiddled idly with the bolt.

"We had a break in last night," she said.

"What?" I found that a little hard to believe. Anyone who knew what was kept here would know to stay far away. Except me, apparently, but I've never been accused of being particularly smart.

"It happens from time to time," she said, shrugging. "Judging from the shattered window on the top floor, it wasn't a human intruder. Some sort of flying creature. Sometimes predator Strangers smell the prey creatures here. Think they can get themselves a nice meal of imp and sprite."

She said it so nonchalantly. As if the kinds of Strangers who'd come hunting here were nothing to worry about. We were talking seriously nasty creatures here: hellhounds, fiends, lesser vampires.

I glanced back at the sleeping baiter vampire. "Her, you mean?"

Alcaraz made a *hmmph* kind of noise and muttered something to herself. Apparently I'd said something stupid.

Lilian seemed to get the joke as well, but she contented herself with smirking at my expense. I didn't mind. When she smirked, her nose kind of wrinkled up, which did strange and unspeakable things to me.

"Do you see any wings on her, Ozzy? Besides, it usually takes more than one itty-bitty little baiter vamp to muscle through our wards."

"She didn't look so itty-bitty from where I was standing."

"She's just one of our guests here," Lilian said. "Whatever got in here damaged a number of our cages when it was trying to get at its prey. A few creatures got out. The roggenwolf is still unaccounted for, but by the blood in its cage, I'm guessing it was the unfortunate victim of our intruder." She jerked her head toward the vampire. "She was the last one running around. I've been hunting her through the house most of the day."

"Then I guess I did you a favor, showing up when I did."

"Yeah. You made a great chew toy. Really distracted her nicely."

"Didn't you see my stake-work? That was pretty nice, I thought."

Lilian made a non-committal noise, then put her hands behind her head and stretched out in her chair. She was a razor blade of a woman, tall and skinny and sharp all over.

She blew a stray hair out of her face, took a granola bar out of her pocket, and opened it.

"Hungry?" she asked.

"Starving."

She broke the bar in half and tossed me the larger piece. I watched as she took a bite of her half.

"Interesting," I said.

"What is?"

"What you're eating."

She frowned and gave me a funny look.

"Never mind." I shrugged, smiling to myself. In my head, I crossed out two items on a list: vampire and ghoul.

You see, Lilian wasn't human. That much I knew for sure. She had to make frequent visits to the town hag, presumably to refresh her glamour—the spell that kept her looking human.

Only trouble was I didn't know what kind of non-human she was. And she wouldn't tell me.

So it had become a kind of game between us. We even had a bet running. If I couldn't guess what she was before the last day of winter, I had to shave my beard off. But if I did guess correctly, she was going to take me out for a five-course dinner at the Black Cat, the fanciest restaurant in town.

I really wanted to win that bet. I liked my beard.

I'd never seen her eating before, but now that I'd watched her bite into that granola bar, I could rule out the possibility that she was either a greater vampire or a ghoul. Which was something of a relief, to be honest. Going on a date with a vampire seemed like an incredibly stupid idea.

Something else had been tickling the back of my brain as well. When the baiter vamp had been attacking me, she'd paid no attention to Lilian up there on the landing. Maybe it was just the bloodlust, but I almost got the feeling that the creature couldn't sense Lilian at all.

Very interesting.

"All right." Doctor Alcaraz slammed her notebook shut and turned back to us. "The baiter's wounds are healing nicely. I wish I could be as positive about the incredibly rare mountain troll humerus you casually threw out the window."

She shot me a glare. As if I were to blame for trying to keep my blood inside my body.

Alcaraz turned to Lilian. "I'm impressed by the success of the hag's new sleeping draught."

"Told you it would work," Lilian said.

"Hang on," I interrupted. "You mean to tell me you weren't sure that dart would put the vampire to sleep?"

"*I* was pretty sure," Lilian said.

"Pretty sure," I repeated flatly. "And what was the backup plan if it didn't work?"

She shrugged. "You could've handled her, couldn't you?" She eyed me with a smile, waiting to see if I'd admit just how close I'd come to losing that fight. I was trapped.

I just scowled and kept my mouth shut.

"Never mind," Alcaraz said. "It all worked out. Most of the damage is repairable, and the only irreplaceable loss was the roggenwolf. A rare beast, these days, but nothing to be done about that. Now, I suppose this creature here is what prompted your visit."

The dog cage was sitting on a table next to me, surprisingly quiet. Lawrence's encounter with the vampire seemed to have left him a little traumatized.

I knew exactly how he felt.

Alcaraz pushed her coke-bottle glasses up on her squat little nose and peered through the cage door with a frown on her face. She was a big, round woman, permanently hunched over with no neck to speak of. Between that and her glasses, which made her eyes seem twice their normal size, she always reminded me of an elderly owl.

While she studied the creature, I gave her the story about my sister's basement. I left off how badly I got cut up by the little bastard. It was kind of embarrassing.

Lawrence snarled and swiped a claw at Alcaraz through the cage door, but the old woman didn't flinch.

"Hmm," Alcaraz said when I was done talking.

I waited patiently for her to elaborate. After a couple of minutes, no further explanation was forthcoming. I cleared my throat.

"Well?"

"Well what?" Alcaraz said, not even looking at me.

"What is he?"

Alcaraz ignored the question.

Lilian leaned in close to me, confiding in a loud whisper, "She has no idea."

"I have no idea *yet*," Alcaraz corrected. "And the sooner I'm allowed to get on with my work, the sooner I can have an answer for you. Is that acceptable, Mr. Turner?"

The way she asked didn't really leave much room for disagreement. "Very acceptable. Thank you." I stood. "I'll leave him in your capable hands."

I didn't think she even heard me. She'd already become distracted again, scribbling something in a new notebook. "Girl, I'll need some more of that scrying potion. Fetch some for me, will you?"

"You used the last of that a week ago," Lilian said. "Remember?"

"Then go get some more from the hag," the old woman said. "Give her two cockatrice eggs, this time, and no more. I won't have her fleecing us again. And while you're at it, we need a new fixative suitable for bloodless organisms. And—are you writing this all down?"

I decided it was my cue to leave. I met Lilian's eyes, grinned, and waggled my fingers goodbye. She grimaced and turned back to face the old doctor's browbeating.

Strangely, I was a little sad to be leaving Lawrence behind. I looked over my shoulder when I got to the door and saw him watching me through the bars of the cage.

The little bastard was kind of cute, in an ugly sort of way.

Against my better judgment, I interrupted Alcaraz as she continued to issue instructions and reprimands to Lilian. "Doctor. You're not going to…stuff him or anything, are you?"

She fixed me with her bug-eyed glare. "No, Mr. Turner. I normally wait until they're dead before I do that. But in your case, I might make an exception."

I was pretty sure she was joking, but I got the hell out of there in a hurry, just in case.

As soon as I got back to my van, I stripped off the ancient shirt Alcaraz had given me and pulled on one of the spare

T-shirts I kept in the van. I popped a couple of painkillers to ward off the burning of my chest wounds, and followed them up with a swig of one of Early's special tinctures. It wouldn't do much for the pain, but it would keep the shakes at bay. Nearly getting killed by a vampire does terrible things to your mental fortitude.

My tracking potion had finally matured. The color had gone a deep, murky crimson. Just what the doctor ordered. I plucked the bottle off the dashboard and uncorked it.

"All right, Delilah," I said to the plastic hula girl on my dashboard. "Vacation's over. Time for you to earn your keep."

I used my eyedropper to extract some of the potion from the bottle. Carefully, I applied a single drop to both of her upturned hands.

For a moment, she just quivered in place. Then, slowly, she began to tilt to one side, like she was being pulled on by an invisible string.

Delilah had picked up the hobgoblin's trail.

I smiled. "Gotcha."

10

My muscles ached and the claw marks on my chest still burned like someone had rubbed chili sauce into the wounds, but it felt damn good to be on a job again.

It had been a weird afternoon, that was for sure, and I knew I'd be having nightmares about that damn baiter vamp for a few weeks to come. But for now I could put all that aside and get back to basics.

This was proper cunning man's work. Nothing flashy. Nothing dangerous. I wasn't cut out for that kind of stuff, not anymore. I left all that behind years ago, when I ran back to Lost Falls with my brother avenged and my mind in tatters.

It had been Early who'd picked up the pieces, put me back together. He showed me I could be someone else. Someone who helped people. Someone I could be proud of.

It wasn't glamorous, and there wasn't much money in it. But there was nothing quite like breaking a bad curse or reuniting a man with something precious that'd been taken from him. It just felt…*good*.

After all the excitement at Alcaraz's place, it was getting late by the time I was on the trail of the thieving hobgoblin. I'd picked up some drive-thru on the way, and now I was polishing off the last of the cold fries in the bottom of the bag.

The last glimmers of sunlight disappeared behind the thick forest of the valley. Clouds were moving in fast. It'd rain tonight. That made things a little trickier. Rain could disturb the hobgoblin's trail as surely as it wiped away footprints. I couldn't afford any more delays.

Delilah the hula girl danced on my dashboard as I drove, pointing the way. By the way she moved, I guessed the hobgoblin was a few miles outside town. Assuming the creature hadn't ditched the rattle somewhere along the way, I could be finished with the job and be back home soon after midnight. Maybe I'd even have a chance to get Early to check on my wounds before I collapsed for the night.

The thought of bed soon had me yawning. The fight with the vampire had really taken it out of me, and my bones were growing heavy now that the adrenaline had stopped pumping. I sucked up the last of my Coke, hoping the caffeinated sugar water would keep me awake.

Delilah pointed me south, across the Rosetta River. The main township of Lost Falls hugged the north bank of the river. Further downstream were the Falls themselves, but my route took me in the other direction. As I crossed the bridge, my headlights washed across a chipped and bird-shit-stained statue of a cartoon river troll. It was what passed for a town mascot around these parts.

Out of habit, I rolled down the window and tossed a coin into the river below. It was highly unlikely that there was a real troll down there, but I'd had a bad enough day already. I didn't want to take any more risks.

As I left the lights of the town behind, the dark of the forest seemed to press in close. The only light around was a flashing red bulb atop a radio tower ahead. Up there on that hill was the town's radio station.

I checked the time. My sister would be working at the station right now. I rarely listened to the radio nowadays—seeing as music meant nothing to me anymore—but tonight, to ward off the dark, I switched on the radio and twiddled the dial until

Alice's voice crackled to life.

"-come back to Falls Radio, where we're taking your calls until three a.m., the witching hour. I hope you're all safe and sound this evening. Before the break we heard from a gentleman driving out near the mountain, who reported seeing the shadow of a large beast dart across the road in front of him. Just a stray dog, or something more? I'll let you decide. Ah, looks like we have our second caller of the evening. You're live with Alice, what do you have for us tonight?"

Alice loved playing up the town's legends, and even I had to admit she was pretty good at it. When she was working she adopted a soft voice that made the hairs on the back of your neck stick up, even if you knew that most of what she was saying was complete bullshit.

"Hello?" the caller said. "Am I on the air?"

"You're live right now, ma'am," Alice said. "Tell us why you're calling."

"It's about that creature by the mountain, the one that other man called about. I saw it too."

"Another sighting. This story is heating up. What's your name, ma'am?"

"Carol."

"What did you see, Carol?"

"Well, my husband and I were driving back into town. We were visiting my mother, you see, because she's sick. Smoked all her life, and now she's got the emphysema. So we'd been out of town for a few days, visiting her, but my husband had to get back for work, so—"

"Tell us about the beast," Alice interrupted.

"Oh, yes, well, we were driving into town—we were coming from the east, you see—and as we came around the corner I saw this shadow on the side of the road. So I yelled at my husband to stop the car, because I thought it might be a person. Like maybe they're hurt or something."

"And then what happened?"

"We pulled over, and I jumped out and ran back toward the shape. I could see it was moving a little. So I called out, I said, 'Are you all right?' And then, and then it kind of lifted its head."

"It wasn't a person?" Alice said.

"No. No it wasn't. It was like…like a big, black dog. But not just big, like, really big. As big as my husband. Bigger. And my husband's not a small man. This…this thing, it looked like there was blood on its nose. It was dark, but I'm pretty sure there was blood on it. Its fur was matted, you see. And…and…"

"What, Carol?"

"It had no eyes."

"No eyes? Are you sure? You said it was dark."

"I'm sure." The woman's voice quivered. "There were just holes. Holes where its eyes should have been."

I grinned to myself as I listened, shaking my head. The beast was almost certainly some poor injured dog. Hit by a car, probably.

"What did you do then, Carol?"

"I froze," the caller said. "For a moment, I just froze up. And then the creature growled. I've never heard a sound like that in my life. So I turned and I jumped back into the car and I screamed for my husband to drive."

"Did your husband see the beast?"

"No. It all happened so fast. He hadn't even got out of the car. But I saw it. I saw it with my own eyes."

"Thank you so much for your call, Carol. There you have it, listeners. A second sighting of this strange beast lurking on the edge of town. If anyone else out there has seen it, please call us now. And if you're driving out near the mountain tonight, friends, then be careful. When we come back from the break, we'll be talking to Francesca Kaufmann about her new book, *Heartflesh: The Vampire Conspiracy*. If you're concerned, like I am, that our government has been infiltrated by blood-drinking creatures of the night, you won't want to miss this. Don't go anywhere. We'll be right back."

I was impressed. My sister could be pretty earnest when she put some effort into it.

I half-listened to the rest of the program as I drove deeper into the forest. Unlike the eastern road, which was apparently lousy with blind werewolves, my route was nearly empty. Logging trucks used to pack this road, but the timber industry had moved out of here in the last decade. Bad for the town, but at least it meant I had the road to myself.

The hobgoblin had apparently chosen to stick to low ground, which was fine by me. Delilah's dancing grew more insistent with every passing minute.

I was getting close.

A roadside cafe emerged out of the darkness ahead of me. All the lights were off, no cars parked outside. As I drove past, Delilah's hula dance spun back to point behind me.

I stopped in the road and examined the cafe in the side mirror.

"Found you," I muttered.

11

I did a U-turn, switched my headlights off, and pulled quietly into the cafe's parking lot. No point spooking the hobgoblin. With luck, it'd be asleep right now.

It wasn't that I was afraid of getting hurt—hobgoblins were generally harmless, if a huge pain in the ass. I just didn't want the thing making a run for it. If it got scared and bolted into the forest, I'd have a hell of a time trying to follow.

And unlike the hobgoblin, not everything in the forest was harmless.

Before I got out, I took a moment to look over the cafe. It had seen better days. The sign read *G ld Dig ers Cafe*, having long since lost the *o* and one of the *g*s. They seemed to be going for an old-timey mining theme, with a wooden facade and a faded cartoon prospector looking sourly down at me.

The front doors were chained closed. The hobgoblin had probably found a back way in. The little bastards were good at that.

"Found yourself somewhere pretty nice to spend the night," I said. "Not willing to sleep in the wild, huh? Must've gone soft."

No point taking my whole kit in with me. I prepared a simple written charm, then pocketed a chain of coins and small silver bells—they were good for distracting and entrancing hobgoblins. If that failed, I also had a fetish made of twine and chicken bones. I didn't want to use it unless I had to—the fetish was designed to overwhelm the hobgoblin's mind with fear, freezing the creature in place. Not exactly pleasant.

Last of all I pocketed a set of lock picks and hung my truncheon on my belt. I felt stupid, bringing the weapon, but after the day I'd had, I wasn't taking any chances.

Taking a deep breath, I climbed out of the van and quietly shut the door. A quick glance showed me that there were no cameras watching the parking lot. That made things easier.

Even without streetlights, the waxing moon gave enough light for me to see by. I only hoped I was done before those rainclouds came in and smothered the light.

As I made my way around the side of the cafe, I reached into my pocket and found the silver pendant I'd used to absorb the echoes of the rattle's history. I let it hang down. It swung ever so slightly. No doubt about it, I was in the right place.

There was a high wooden fence around the back of the cafe, with another chain keeping the gate locked. The gaps in the bottom of the fence were far too small for me to fit through, but a hobgoblin would've had no problem.

Glancing along the fence, I decided the easiest place to scale it would be where it met the side of the cafe. There was a drainpipe bolted to the wall there. I tested it, and decided I could trust it to hold my weight for at least a couple of seconds.

I pocketed the pendant, grabbed hold of the drainpipe, and hauled myself up. My wounded chest didn't thank me for it. Grunting and panting and trying not to swear out loud, I got my hand to the top of the fence and scrambled over. With one last groan, I threw myself unceremoniously down on the other side.

"Son of a bitch," I muttered as I picked myself up, prodding gingerly at my wounds. Felt like one of the cuts had broken open. Just what I needed.

I looked around. The cafe was even less impressive from back here. Smelled a hell of a lot worse, too, though I put that down to the overflowing dumpster sitting nearby.

I guess I couldn't really complain. I was trespassing, after all.

My silver pendant pointed me to the rear service door on the other side of the dumpster. A touch of the handle told me it was locked, but at least this door didn't have a big thick chain on it. I crouched down in front of the door, took out my lock picks, and got to work.

I was a little rusty, but after a couple of minutes the lock gave way under my tender ministrations. The legacy of a misspent youth.

The handle turned. Silently, I eased the door open. It was pretty damn dark inside. I peered into the gloom for a few seconds, letting my eyes adjust. And then I stepped inside.

If a patrol cop showed up now, I'd have a hell of a time explaining myself. I'd gone from petty trespassing to full-blown breaking and entering. In my defense, I was here to remove another trespasser from the premises. You could even say I was a hero.

All right, maybe that was pushing it.

The service door had brought me into the kitchen. I could just make out the shape of the central bench top and the appliances set along two sides of the narrow room. A long, empty window looked out at the counter area and the cafe itself beyond.

I felt along the wall beside me until I found a set of light switches, but I didn't flip them yet. I held my breath and opened my ears. I couldn't hear anything moving, not even a rat.

Where are you hiding? I silently asked the hobgoblin.

The kitchen was the most likely place. Slipping off my shoes, I padded quietly to the center of the kitchen. The floor was disturbingly sticky.

I took the chain of silver bells and coins out of my pocket, letting them jingle as I laid the chain in a rough circle on the floor. In the center of the circle I put down the sealed written charm I'd prepared earlier. The charm was designed to make the chain irresistible to feeble-minded creatures like hobgoblins.

I retreated back to the service door and rested my fingers on the light switches, ready to flip them. I waited.

For a minute, maybe two, nothing moved. I stayed where I was, as still as the rest of the cafe.

And then I heard something shuffling in the darkness.

"What is it?" a voice whispered, on the edge of hearing. "Where's the jingle-jangle? Ah!"

A shape moved in the corner of the kitchen, in the space between the oven and the wall. So small I barely noticed it. But as I watched, the shadowy figure slid out of the darkness, moving cautiously toward the chain of bells.

The creature would be lucky to be a foot tall. It walked hunched over, its long nose leading the way. It was impossible to make out details in the dark of the kitchen, but I could see long, stringy hair dangling from its head, nearly touching the ground. As its head snapped back and forth, searching for danger, large yellow eyes flashed, reflecting what little light there was.

"Mmm," the creature muttered. "Look at the jingle-jangle. Pretty jingle-jangle."

My charm was doing its job. Not that it was particularly difficult to trick a hobgoblin. Frankly, they were so damn stupid it almost wasn't worth wasting the ink.

The creature was dragging something along behind it. A small sack about the size of a sock. Something inside was rattling.

I smiled in the dark. *The rattle.*

With one last glance around, the hobgoblin let go of the sack and reached out a long arm as thin as a chicken's leg. It took hold of the chain and lifted it. As the bells rang, the hobgoblin giggled with delight.

"Look at it jingle! Look at it shine! Look at it—"

Something in the creature's demeanor changed as it fell silent. It whipped its head around, suddenly nervous.

Guess the charm had worn off. Maybe this creature wasn't quite as weak-minded as the other hobgoblins I'd dealt with in the past.

Still, it had seen the trap far too late.

I flipped all the switches at once. The kitchen was flooded with light. Screeching and shielding its eyes, the hobgoblin staggered back, dropping the chain of bells and grasping blindly for its sack.

But I was already halfway across the room. As the creature turned to run, I grabbed it by the scruff of the neck and lifted it into the air.

The hobgoblin screeched in fear. It scrambled and twisted, trying to shake itself out of my grip. Poor bastard never stood a chance.

"No!" it screamed. "Leggo! Leggo!"

"Oh, pipe down," I said. "I'm not going to hurt you."

If it understood what I was saying, it gave no sign. I sighed and held it aloft, getting a better look at it.

It was a female, I think. Kind of hard to tell. It was wearing some scrap of fabric that had been turned into a poncho. There was a big letter "E" on the front and part of an "M", but the rest of the word was back with whatever was left of the T-shirt.

She looked about the same as all of her kind: wrinkled, gray-skinned, and ugly as hell. The creature's ears, eyes, and nose were all too large for her tiny proportions. The rest of her was rail-thin—I could make out the shape of tiny bones beneath her skin. In between screams and the nonsense she was babbling, her yellowed teeth chattered like a roomful of typewriters.

As she tried to wriggle free, I tugged the sack out of the hobgoblin's grasp and upended it on the floor.

"No!" she screamed. "Give it!"

I ignored her. Among the coins and crumbs of bread and

cheese that fell out of the sack, there was my prize. The baby's rattle.

Just picking it up, I could sense the history and memory that the silver held. The bells jingled softly as I shook it.

"Give it!" the hobgoblin screeched.

"It's not yours," I said. "It's going back to the person it belongs to."

"No! No, no, no!" She kicked wildly, her big eyes seeming to grow even bigger. "Can't! The blood! The blood!"

"What?" I could barely understand her. "What blood?"

"Blood and boiling and death and silver. Can't have! Give it!" She pulled herself up and bit the flesh of my thumb.

"Ow." I shook her and she dropped down, dangling from my fingers once more. "Quit it. What are you talking about?"

"Blood! The blood!"

I rolled my eyes and pocketed the rattle. That'd teach me for trying to talk to the damn creature.

You know, I was starting to revise my opinion on hobgoblins. Maybe they were as bad as goblins after all.

I reached down to pick up my coin and bell chain, but just as I was pocketing them my phone started buzzing. While the hobgoblin continued to struggle in my grasp, I fished my phone out of my pocket and pressed it to my ear.

"Yeah?"

"Hey, Ozzy. It's Lilian."

"Lilian. Hey." I straightened a little, like maybe she could sense my poor posture through the phone. I had the sudden urge to check myself in a mirror, make sure my hair looked okay. "Let me guess, this is a booty call."

"You wish." She wasn't half-wrong. But her voice said she wasn't in the mood for joking around. "You find people, right? That's a thing that you can do?"

"There's a lot of things I can—ow!" The hobgoblin had used the distraction to sink her teeth into me again. "You bite me one more time I drop you into the garbage disposal."

"Who, me?" Lilian asked.

"No, I'm talking to… You know what, never mind. Long story. What do you need?"

"You know how Alcaraz sent me to trade with the hag?"

"Yeah, I seem to remember the good doctor talking your ear off about that."

"Well, the hag's not here," she said. "I dropped by about an hour ago, knocked on the door, no response. Didn't want to go home empty-handed, so I hung around for a while. Something didn't feel right, so I started snooping. Found the back door unlocked, so I went in."

"Hell, you must have a death wish," I said, but Lilian ignored me.

"I'm still here now. No sign of the hag. But I think someone's been searching the place."

"Yeah? Why do you say that?"

"Just a feeling. Her place is always a mess, but there's usually a pattern to it. Now things seem out of place."

"That's not a lot of evidence to send out the search party."

"I know, I know. It just…it feels wrong. I think you should come have a look."

I'll be honest, that sounded like the worst idea I'd heard in a long time, and I was old enough to remember the *Super Mario Bros.* movie. Getting involved in a hag's business was a good way to spend the rest of your life as a toad.

Hags and witches have forever been confused with each other, but they're not the same thing. Witches are human. They made a deal to obtain their powers, just like I did.

Hags are decidedly inhuman. They can pass as human— they are the undisputed champions of glamour magic, after all. But they are Strangers. They are powerful. And they are not to be trifled with.

Going into the hag's house uninvited and poking around

the place sounded…well, like I said, I kind of like not being a toad.

I was trying to think it over, but it was hard to concentrate with a squirming hobgoblin in my hand. She'd started getting even more agitated, squealing and babbling so loud I had to hold her at arm's length to keep her from drowning me out while I was talking to Lilian.

"The light!" the creature was screaming—or at least that's what I thought she was saying. It was hard to tell. "Leggo! Give the silver and leggo! Gotta run! Gotta fly! The blood!"

"What's that noise?" Lilian asked. "Are you watching *Alvin and the Chipmunks*?"

"I never wanted to murder the chipmunks this much."

I started carrying the hobgoblin toward the exit. I didn't want to put her down until I was about to leave—I had a sneaking suspicion she'd take the opportunity to try to steal the rattle again, and I didn't like my chances of catching her twice.

"Listen," I said to Lilian, "I've had a hell of a day. I need to sleep for a very long time. And if you can't find the hag, I'm willing to bet it's because she doesn't want to be found."

"Maybe." She sounded unsure. "What if someone did something to her?"

"I doubt it. The hag's more powerful than you know."

"You're probably right. I just…I don't know what to do."

I knew what she meant. It wasn't like she could go down to the police station, file a missing person's report. Not for the hag. We couldn't risk stirring up trouble in Lost Falls.

"Look, go home and get some sleep," I said. "That's what I'm planning to do. If the hag still hasn't shown up by morning, I'll come take a look. Sound good?"

She sighed. "I guess so."

"All right. I have to go deal with something. I'll call you tomorrow."

"Thanks, Ozzy."

The fact that she hung up without insulting me once told me that the whole thing was still troubling her. I paused, staring at my phone, and considered calling her back and telling her I'd changed my mind.

She knew the hag better than me, after all. Maybe trusting her instincts wasn't such a bad idea.

"Oh, no!" The hobgoblin's screams reached a new, even more painful pitch. "No, no! He here! Hafta run! Run!"

"Goddamn it. Just be quiet for a second," I said. "I'm trying to think."

"Not the curse! Not the curse! The blood!"

I stopped by the back exit and shot the creature a look. "Curse? What curse? What are you—?"

A shoe scraped against concrete outside. Before I could move, a figure filled the doorway, blocking my exit.

The light from the kitchen fell on the face of my client, Brandon Mills. Somehow, he was looking even shabbier than he had this afternoon. He let a pair of bolt cutters clatter to the ground beside him.

And then he raised a pistol and pointed it at my chest.

12

"Stay where you are, Mr. Turner," Brandon Mills said. "Do exactly what I say."

There was desperation in his eyes, desperation mixed with the pain of a deep-seated sadness. But the hand that held the pistol was steady, experienced.

A cold dread spread through my gut, freezing me solid. All I could do was stand there, gaping like an idiot. It took me a moment to realize the hobgoblin was still in my grip, weeping and wailing.

"Drop the phone," he said.

I did what he said. I know when to pick my battles.

"Listen," I said. My voice came out a rasp. I tried again. "Brandon—"

"You have it?" he asked.

"What?"

"The rattle. You have it?"

"In my pocket," I said.

He held out a hand. "Slowly."

He didn't have to tell me twice. Doing my best not to agitate him, I pulled out the rattle with my thumb and forefinger and handed it to him. He glanced at it quickly and shoved it in his pocket.

"All right, Brandon," I said, swallowing thickly. "You've got the rattle. Now how about you put down the gun, huh?"

The pistol remained pointed at me. It was worth a try.

I'd been running on automatic since I saw the gun, but now my brain was slowly rebooting, and it had some questions about this whole damn situation. How had Mills found me here? And what the hell had I done to make him think he needed to bring a gun to get the rattle back?

"Now that thing," Mills said, twitching the gun toward the hobgoblin.

"What about it? It's just—"

"Hand it over."

I hesitated. My mind flashed back to earlier that afternoon, to the look Mills had had in his eyes when he said he wanted to confront the thief. I saw the same look in his eyes now, burning twice as bright.

The hobgoblin was annoying, but it was sentient. I didn't want to see what Mills would do to the poor creature.

"Brandon, just calm down, okay? I can explain."

His face twisted. "Give me the hobgoblin!" he snarled.

"I... You know what she is?" I rearranged the pieces in my head, trying to make the puzzle fit together. It wasn't working. "All right, all right, just wait a second. I don't know how much you know about hobgoblins, but they're not exactly little Einsteins, okay? She's no master criminal. She saw a shiny thing, she took it. But you've got it back now. No harm, no foul."

Mills took a step forward, and for a moment I saw a hint of the man he used to be. A hard, tough man. No stranger to violence. Not the broken, shambling mess of a man I'd met this morning, but a man to be afraid of.

Cop? Soldier? Gangster? I didn't know.

"I won't ask again, Mr. Turner," he said, leveling the pistol at my head.

The hobgoblin had given up trying to squirm free. She hung limply from my hand, crying silently. Every now and then she muttered something, but the only words I could make out were:

"My insides."

I considered my options. I considered them carefully.

My truncheon was hanging from my belt. One good hit with that and Mills would go down. But one good hit would be awful hard to come by.

Mills was maintaining a few feet of space between us, just close enough that if we both stretched out our arms we could touch fingertips. Not far, really. If he hesitated, maybe I could close in before he got a shot off.

I didn't think he would hesitate.

Maybe you're thinking: "Ozzy, you dumbass, just do some magic. Blow him away."

Trouble is, magic doesn't work that way, at least not the kind I do. I can't shoot fireballs from my hand. This isn't *Dungeons & Dragons*. I needed time. I needed to prepare potions and charms and fetishes.

And besides, I was a cunning man. I used magic to help people. I was no witch.

That gun was as deadly to me as it would be to you. And I don't care how brave you are, there are few things more terrifying than staring down into the dark of a gun barrel, knowing there's a bullet inside waiting to aerate the back of your head.

I handed over the hobgoblin.

She didn't fight. She had no fight left to give. Mills grabbed her roughly in his free hand, crushing her arms to her side. She gave a grunt, like she couldn't quite get enough air.

Mills eyed her as I handed her over. A look of profound relief spread across his face, like he'd just been acquitted of murder.

With his gaze fixed on her, I let my other hand slide into my pocket.

"All right." He took a breath and waved the gun at me. "Let's go."

"Where?"

"Outside. Move."

He backed out the door, giving me room to follow. I watched for my chance to make a break for it, but it never came.

"Turn off the lights," he said. "Close the door."

I did what he said, and the door locked behind me with a click. The first cloudy fingers had begun to snuff out the moonlight, but I could still make him out as he gestured for me to move.

I complied, walking ahead of him, past the overflowing dumpster and out through the gate he'd unlocked with the bolt cutters. I started to head toward the parking lot, but he stopped me.

"This way," he said, and he gestured to the forest.

My chest grew colder. "Why?"

"Just walk."

I took another look at the gun. Then I did what he said.

My shoes crunched on the dirt as we walked a couple dozen yards away from the cafe, away from the street lights. Mills was always behind me, too far away for me to jump him, too close for me to make a break for it.

When I was just about to reach the tree line, my foot caught an exposed root. I stumbled and went down, just managing to get my hands out in front of me. I panted, breathing in the earthy smell of moss and dirt and fallen leaves.

"Get up," Mills said.

I pushed myself up onto my knees, but I didn't stand. I mean, what was the point?

"Tell me," I said, looking back at him. "Was it all a lie? Just a sob story? The crib. The dead son."

I don't know what compelled me to speak. Fatalistic apathy, maybe. Maybe I just wanted to see if I could incite him to anger, distract him enough that he'd drop the hobgoblin. No need for her to die too.

His eyes met mine, and in the last glimmers of moonlight I

saw the fire in them. "Don't you fucking talk about my son. You hear me?" He came a step closer, close enough I could smell his sweat. "You hear me?!"

Maybe it wasn't a lie after all. Swallowing, I raised a hand in placation. "All right. All right. I'm sorry. I did all this to help you, remember? I'm trying to help. I'm trying to understand."

"Just shut up."

"What is this really about? Just tell me that, Brandon."

He took a shaky breath and glanced back at the hobgoblin in his hand. "I don't have a choice," he whispered. I don't think he was talking to me.

I answered him anyway. "We always have a choice. Always."

He nodded slowly, a sad smile flickering across his face. "You're right. And I've made mine."

He looked at me. And I saw what his decision would be.

His finger moved to the trigger.

I lifted my hand, opened my fist, and let the fear fetish I'd pulled from my pocket dangle from my finger. The chicken bones twisted and spun in the web of twine.

It didn't affect Mills. It wasn't designed to.

The hobgoblin screeched. It was a scream of purest fear. The fetish's power overwhelmed the creature's mind, driving out logic, rationality.

The screech was a sound to make ears bleed. I was ready for it. Mills wasn't.

He grunted in sudden pain, jamming his eyes shut for a moment. I'd hoped he'd toss the hobgoblin aside. He didn't. Instead, his hand tightened around her. Her scream cut off as the air was pushed from her lungs.

My other hand gripped my truncheon and pulled it free. I only had a second. No time to line up a real hit. As I pushed myself up, I threw my weight forward and thrust the pommel into Mills gut.

It was a good hit, all things considered. I delivered it with all the force I could manage.

It wasn't enough.

Mills doubled over, all right. But I was right about him—he wasn't as soft as he looked. He flowed away from the blow with surprising speed, already recovering from the shock of the hobgoblin's scream. The strike hurt him, but he didn't let that pain stop him.

Nice try, I thought to myself as I watched the gun come back up. *But not nice enough.*

He shot me in the stomach.

The truncheon slipped from my fingers, landing with a thud in the dirt. I gaped at Mills, at the smoking gun in his hand. I staggered forward, reached out, grabbed him by the hair.

He grunted and elbowed me in the chest, shaking me loose. My ears were still ringing with the sound of the gunshot when I hit the ground. That hurt worse than the bullet itself, at first.

Then I coughed, and that got things moving again. It suddenly felt like someone was stirring up my insides with a hot poker.

I tried to get up, and found I couldn't. My thoughts were coming in bursts—fear and confusion suddenly giving way to pure understanding. I couldn't see where my truncheon had gone. I put a hand to my abdomen and it came away streaked with something dark and wet.

I squinted up through blurry eyes, saw Mills standing over me. He had the nerve to look sad about the whole thing. I lay back down on the ground—damn, the earth was cold—and laughed.

"You asshole," I rasped. "I even gave you a discount."

"I'm sorry," he said as he lifted the gun again.

This time, he shot me in the chest.

13

The human body is a strange thing. Punch a guy just right, you can kill him, without even meaning to. Hell, you know what the leading cause of unintentional death in the home is? Falling over. Thousands of people die every year slipping in the shower or falling down the stairs. A life can be snuffed out so easily.

And then there's the other side of the coin. Soldiers in battle who get shot three times and don't even notice until the firefight is over. People who are still alive after their parachutes fail to open.

Strange how we can be so fragile, yet so resilient.

Don't get me wrong. I'd taken a bullet to the gut and another to the lung. I was dying. I just wasn't quite dead yet.

The world flashed past in tiny slices.

Being dragged through the soil and rotting leaves, into the dark of the forest.

Struggling to breathe. Drowning, drowning in my own blood.

The heavy panting of the man who killed me, the sour-sweet smell of his breath as he leaned down to riffle through my pockets.

The hobgoblin's wailing, her cries, her screams, screaming, screaming…

A baby's scream echoes through the house, cutting through my sleep for the third time that night. Endless fucking wailing, the kind of sound that makes you want to go in there and throttle the kid until he shuts up. Just shut up, SHUT UP!

He's screaming because he's sick, screaming because he hurts and the doctors don't know why, screaming and screaming and nothing soothes him.

I don't care. If I had my way, he'd never have come along in the first place. Alice and I were already teenagers when Teddy was born. We were already a family. We don't need a goddamn baby in the house. Shitting and screaming and why won't he shut the fuck up already?

That does it, if he doesn't pipe down right now, I'm going to go in there and I'll...I'll...

Rain pattered around me. It dripped from the leaves overhead, running in tiny waterfalls onto my hands, my neck, soaking through my clothes. Some of it dripped into my mouth.

I couldn't move away, but I didn't want to anyway. I tried to swallow. I was thirsty, so thirsty...

I've been left alone with Teddy. Again. Mom can't take the screaming, she has to go out, has to drive around for hours and hours and come back stinking of cigarettes and cheap liquor. Alice moved out of town a month ago, off to journalism school. So here I am, alone with a goddamn baby.

All I want to do is sit at the piano, practice this piece I need to practice, but Teddy's wailing again, wailing loud enough to shake the walls, and somehow it gets worse every time I hear it.

I want to leave, just head out the door and never come back. But I can't do that, because I'm the only one here, I'm supposed to look after a fucking kid that I never signed up for.

So I stomp down the hall and throw open the door to his room, my head pounding. I open my mouth to shout.

And the screaming stops. It just stops, just like that. And for a moment, it's the most beautiful sound in the world, the sound of silence.

But then I realize the silence sounds wrong. It's too still. Too complete. It pounds in my ears louder than his screams ever did.

I don't want to go over to the crib, but I do, I have to, and I see him there, curled up, wooden, wilted, like...

Fallen leaves between my fingers. I grabbed at the ground as I was dragged into the shallow hole, but all I caught were leaves.

The rain was falling heavier now, but I barely felt it. I was still alive, but I didn't know how. I didn't know why. After all I'd done, this was such a stupid way to die.

I heard a scraping sound, then a shovelful of dirt fell on my face. I tried to cough, tried to move my head away, but I couldn't. All I could do was lay there, lay there and be buried alive...

They bury Teddy in the tiniest coffin I've ever seen. I didn't know they made coffins that small. I'm seventeen, and I'm starting to realize there's a lot of things I still don't know.

I wished for this, wished for him to be gone. Now he is. And the worst part of it? I'm thankful for the silence.

I hate myself for that. I hate the other people at the funeral for looking at me like they know my shame. I hate Teddy for being dead, and I hate Alice for crying, and I hate Mom for already being drunk. I've forgotten everything else except hate.

The first chance I get, I break away from the mourners and leave the cemetery and disappear into town. If Mom and Alice look for me, they don't find me.

I want to get drunk and hit someone, but I can't get into a bar and they're all empty anyway, this being Lost Falls, the ass end of nowhere. So I find an alley and I punch a dumpster and I throw bottles against the wall until I realize what a stupid fucking kid I must look like. And I can't be a kid, not anymore. So I go to the park and I sit down on a bench and I stare at nothing for a while.

Until someone sits next to me. Not just sharing the bench—he sits as close to me as he possibly can, his hip pressed against mine. And before I can say anything, before I can tell him to piss off, he leans in close and says something that stops me cold.

"Your brother wasn't in that coffin."

I turn to stare at him. He's the strangest man I've ever seen. Misshapen, asymmetrical, like none of his body parts are supposed to go together. He looks at me with a pair of mismatching eyes, studying me like I'm some vaguely interesting museum exhibit.

"There was something in that coffin," he says, "but it wasn't your brother. How does that make you feel, Osric?"

Everything goes red and the next thing I know I have my fists bunched in his coat and I'm pulling him close enough to smell the faint stink of rot that comes off him.

"Who the fuck are you?" I say.

"A friend, Osric. A friend who knows the truth about your brother." He bears his teeth in a smile that makes my skin prickle. "And I have a deal for you."

The dirt turned to mud around me. I blinked, staring up at the sky through the clumps of soil that covered my face. It was a shallow grave.

I couldn't hear the hobgoblin anymore. A car started somewhere nearby, then the sound of the engine faded into the distance. All that remained was the rain, and the forest, and the mud.

I waited for my death.

I gasp awake in a motel bathtub filled with ice.

Disoriented, shaking violently, I pull myself out of the tub and collapse on the tile floor. I'm naked and my flesh is blue with cold. There's an ache in the side of my skull, and a feeling of emptiness that goes far deeper.

I grab the washbasin and haul myself to my feet. My legs nearly go out from under me again on the slippery floor. I snatch a towel off the rail and wrap it around me, still shivering.

I catch a glimpse of myself in the mirror. My eyes are sunken, my flesh drawn and tight. It looks like I've doubled in age overnight. There's a shaved patch on the right side of my head. Gingerly, I touch the red-stained bandage affixed there. Memories start to come back to me.

I can hear the TV playing in the other room. Wrapping the towel around my waist, I ease open the door with my foot.

I'm alone. The motel room is beige, from the carpet to the light fixtures. The curtains are pulled, leaving the TV the only source of light.

My clothes are folded on the bed. And next to the pile is a book.

I can tell the book is old before I even touch it. It has a cover of red leather, with silver embossing on the spine. As I open it, the thick parchment crackles and gives off a smell of dust and time. The text inside is all written in a tight, cramped hand.

It's a black book. An evil book.

A word springs out at me from the pages. A word that the strange, misshapen man said to me, as he explained what'd happened to Teddy. As he laid out the deal he had for me.

Changeling. My brother had been taken, replaced with something else. Something not human. Something not even truly alive.

That was what had screamed endlessly. That was what had wilted and died. That was what had been buried. But Teddy, the real Teddy was still out there somewhere, if the Dealer could be believed. In the hands of foul creatures. Monsters. Goblins. Like out of a goddamn fairy tale.

A sudden horrific screaming pours from the TV, and I slap my hands over my ears. A commercial for laundry liquid is playing.

But instead of the usual jingle, all I can hear is screeching.

That's not right. How does the song go again? I can't remember.

Slowly, understanding dawns on me. I recall what the Dealer bought from me in our trade. My hand goes again to the side of my head, to the hole in my skull where he took out the music.

I switch off the TV, put the grief out of my mind. My music is gone. But there's something else in its place. A new power, a new knowledge. I can feel it inside me, pressing against the inside of my skull, whispering for me to use it.

I get dressed and pick up the old book. It seems to whisper to me as well. It tells me my brother is still alive. It tells me it knows how to find him.

I sit down and start reading.

That last memory seemed to hang in my mind for a very long time. It came with a feeling worse than the pain in my gut.

Shame. For what I'd done trying to get Teddy back. For the knowledge that in the end, I'd failed.

I tried, Teddy. But it wasn't enough.

I faded again. And somehow, when I drifted back into consciousness, I was still alive.

The world seemed sharper now. One last gasp before I died for good. My mind gave itself a kick start, running through my options. Trying desperately to find a way out of all this.

I couldn't die here in this hole. I couldn't die drowning in mud and my own blood. Not without saying a real goodbye to Alice, and throwing the twins around the yard one more time. Not without thanking Early for all he'd done for me, for saving me from myself.

And not without wrapping my fingers around Brandon Mills' throat.

Footsteps. The sound of shoes squelching through mud. It came to me through the earth. I tried to open my mouth, tried to call out. Nothing. I could barely breathe through the thin layer of dirt.

The footsteps were coming closer. They were strange footsteps, heavy and dragging. Not the footsteps of Brandon Mills.

The footsteps stopped. But they were close. I tried again to speak, but the hoarse whisper I managed was drowned out by the sound of the rain.

My hand. Maybe that would work. My right hand was laid across my stomach, just beneath the thin layer of dirt. If I could reach up, push my fingers to the surface, I might catch the person's attention.

Summoning the little energy I had left, I focused on the index finger of my right hand. *Move. Come on. Just a twitch.*

Nothing. And then the tiniest movement.

Heart surging with hope, I tried again. And again my finger moved, the mud shifting around it. With all of my effort, I pushed for the surface.

Cold air and rain touched the skin of my fingertip. I wanted to cry. With my finger sticking out of the mud, I wiggled it back and forth, the only movement I could manage.

There was a grunt and I felt the person shift next to me. Dirt and mud were swept from my face. And as I blinked and squinted, I found myself looking up into the same misshapen face I'd seen in the memories flashing through my dying mind.

The Dealer smiled down at me in the darkness. "A kidney doesn't seem too high a price now, does it, Osric?"

14

I groaned.

Raindrops struck my face like falling needles as the Dealer cleared away the dirt over my torso. He knelt beside me, his fine suit now soaked through and splattered with mud. He didn't seem to care much.

He cast an eye over my wounds and tutted. "This is very bad, Osric. Five, maybe ten more minutes and even I won't be able to help you."

I tried to speak, but no sound came out. I moved my lips anyway.

What do you want?

The Dealer seemed to understand. He grinned and gave me a friendly pat on the shoulder. "That's the right question, my friend. I knew you'd come to your senses eventually." His smile faded as he looked me over. "It's a pity you had to suffer so greatly to learn your lesson. But then, that's you all over, isn't it, Osric?

I gave him a death glare. It's easy to do when you're so close to death yourself.

"All right," he said, "I suppose you want me to save your life, don't you? It'll cost you, though."

Kidney, I mouthed.

The Dealer chuckled. "Come now, Osric. Let's be reasonable. When I offered to buy your kidney, I was selling information.

Information that might have prevented you from ending up in this position. The situation is different now. I'm going to have to work hard to save your life. That's worth more than a simple kidney, don't you think?"

Go to hell.

"I'm going to pretend you didn't say that." He stroked his chin, then snapped his fingers. "How about this? I'll do the work on credit. I'll save your life, my friend, and give you a little time to do what you need to do. And then in—oh, let's say five days—I'll return. And I'll take your body."

I tried to laugh. Bad idea.

I'm using it, I mouthed.

"Not for much longer," he said. "In fact, you're not really losing anything at all. I give you another five days of life, in exchange for use of your body once that period expires. Seems fair to me." He pulled back his sleeve and checked a gaudy women's watch. "Let's call it midnight. So when the clock strikes midnight and Friday begins, you surrender your body to me. If you take the deal, of course." He glanced around at the forest, then smiled down at me. "Though I don't see anyone else lining up to outbid me."

A sudden spasm gripped at my stomach, bringing with it a wave of new agony. My vision was narrowing. I was finding it harder to focus on the Dealer.

"You're running out of time, Osric," he said. "Take the deal."

He was right. I was fading fast. I could no longer feel my legs, and my arms were going the same way. There was a buzzing in my head, like my skull was filled with bees.

Transfer clause, I mouthed.

"Hmm? What do you mean?"

I could barely move my mouth now, but I tried. *Exchange... equal value.*

"Interesting proposition." The Dealer smiled as he thought it over. "If you can find something else of equal value, you want to trade that instead of yourself."

I blinked in the affirmative.

"You know if you want to trade another person, they have to be a willing participant."

Fine.

He tapped the side of his cheek with a long finger as he considered the proposal. I could barely see. Everything was so cold.

Finally, he slapped his knee and then reached out, gripping my limp hand. "You drive a hard bargain, my friend, but you've got yourself a deal."

He released my hand and pulled open his coat. Before my vision went black, I thought I saw him pulling surgical clamps and a scalpel from pockets sewn into the inner lining of his coat.

"Hold still," he said. "This might sting a little."

15

I dreamed that a baiter vamp was tearing open my stomach, feasting on the blood of my abdominal aorta. As I screamed, she looked up at me, blood dripping down her chin and onto her soft naked flesh. She put a finger to my lips, silencing me, and returned to her meal.

I dreamed of Alice dressed all in black, crying at a funeral. Twin coffins sat at the front of the church, both child-sized. But when I stepped up to the open caskets and looked inside, instead of her boys I saw only dolls, crudely whittled from logs. Crosses were painted where their eyes should've been.

I dreamed of a black beast with no eyes, whining by the side of the road. Lilian crouched by its side, rubbing its flank. "Get help!" she shouted at me.

I dreamed of Lawrence, the strange little creature I'd found in Alice's basement. His back was turned to me. He rocked back and forth, crying.

I dreamed of the hobgoblin, pinned to a wooden board with nails through her hands and feet. Arcane symbols were painted across her flesh, and all the while she screamed, "The blood! The silver! The death! The curse!"

I dreamed of Brandon Mills' mother, crippled and deaf, sitting in the dusty light streaming through the living room window. She looked at me through the one eye that could still see, and she just shook her head, like she was disgusted with me.

And I dreamed of Brandon Mills himself, the man, the myth, the murderer. The bastard who'd killed me.

I won't tell you what I dreamed of doing to him.

I woke slowly, over hours. It wasn't like waking up in that motel room bathtub, after the Dealer took my music. That had been a gasping, instant kind of wakeup. I was younger back then, after all. And I hadn't just been shot.

No, this time, I had to drag myself out of the black. This time, it hurt like hell.

There was something banging on the wall behind me. It was followed up with grunting and the fake moans of a woman who didn't quite have the whole "fake orgasm" thing nailed down.

Good to see the Dealer's taste in motels hadn't changed much in the last few years.

I pried my eyes open and squinted up at the ceiling. The sunlight trickling through the cracks in the curtain was nearly blinding.

It was a motel room, all right, right down to the stock artwork of a sailing ship on the wall opposite me. The bedside clock read 11:18 in big glowing numbers that hurt to look at. The mattress was so lumpy I wasn't sure it could legally be called a mattress anymore.

Still, it beat the ice bath.

My mouth tasted like a gas station bathroom. I ached from my toenails to my eyebrows.

But I was alive. Blessedly, intoxicatingly alive. I sucked in the damp, moldy motel room air, tasted the sweat and filth and stale sex that'd soaked into the walls. I'd never smelled anything so good in my life.

With a groan and a string of curses that I won't repeat here, I levered myself up on the bed. The room spun a few times, then got bored and settled down. On the bedside table next to me was a big bottle of water and a packet of over-the-counter painkillers. I cracked open the water and washed down a pair of tablets before guzzling the entire bottle.

When I finally came up for air, I gathered my courage and looked down at myself to see what the damage was.

I was naked. Bastard hadn't even left me my boxers. I expected to still be covered in mud and dried blood, but my skin was so clean I looked like I'd been run through an industrial-strength dishwasher. I touched my beard. It was clean as well, and—I sniffed—the Dealer had oiled it.

Not creepy at all.

As for my bullet wounds? Oh, they were still there, all right. I could feel the flesh burning with every movement. But the wounds had been cleaned and sutured and sealed with clear bandages. I could still feel the ache in my chest where the bullet had struck, but I didn't seem to be having trouble sucking in air. And though my gut still hurt, it felt more like I'd taken a couple of good wallops to the stomach, rather than a bullet.

I found a needle mark in the fold of my left elbow, where I guess the Dealer had dumped some fresh blood into me. I didn't want to think about where he'd found that blood.

I was in damn good shape, all things considered. Hell, the Dealer had even sutured up the vampire's claw marks on my chest.

My delight at being alive was dampened when I realized why the Dealer had taken such good care of me. In five days, he hoped to inherit this body of mine. No wonder he wanted it fixed up so nicely.

Five days to live. The words bounced around the inside of my skull, but I couldn't seem to assign meaning to them. None of it felt real. Some part of me still hoped that the whole night—the hobgoblin, the shooting, everything—had all been a bad dream. Maybe I'd eaten something bad and hallucinated it all.

But as I pulled myself unsteadily to my feet and staggered across the room, that last fading hope was finally snuffed out entirely. On the shelf beside the TV, some clothes were piled, still with their tags on. Beside them were my things: keys, phone, truncheon. No sign of my wallet—Mills must've swiped it. On top of the folded clothes was a note, signed at the bottom with the Dealer's strange symbol.

No question about it. The Dealer had sewn me up better than any human surgeon could've, then left me here to recover. In five days, he'd return to demand his payment. And unless I found something better to offer him, he'd leave with my body.

I could try to run, try to escape my debt. Somehow, I didn't think it would work.

Besides, I had more important things to do with the time I had left.

I checked my phone. The Dealer must've found it inside the diner's kitchen, where I'd dropped it. There was a fresh new crack on the screen. I tried to turn it on, but it was dead. Hopefully just the battery.

I put the phone back down on the shelf and noticed something else sitting there. A small black box, the plastic casing broken along the seams. Some of the wiring inside had been pulled out. There was a magnetic strip along one side of the casing.

I turned it back and forth in my hands for a few seconds before I figured it out. It was a GPS tracking device.

A hacking laugh escaped my throat. Hell, I was stupid. These tattoos of mine were supposed to ward off tracking by mystical means, to keep the witches and witch-finders from the door. Mills hadn't bothered with any of that. He'd just slapped a GPS tracker on my van, and let me lead him right to the hobgoblin.

I had a look at the clothes that'd been left for me. They were pretty up-market threads: a button-down business shirt, slacks with a crease down the front, designer underwear. Not my usual T-shirt and jeans. I checked the price tags and nearly keeled over again. If the Dealer could afford clothes like these, why did he even want my body?

My own clothes were nowhere to be seen, and I had a vague recollection of the Dealer having to cut off my bloody T-shirt. So I ripped the tags off my new clothes and started pulling them on, feeling guilty for soiling them. I had to admit, they fit well.

As I dressed, I read the note the Dealer had left for me. It was written in looping cursive, the kind you just don't see these days. I wonder if he bought his handwriting off someone from the nineteenth century as well.

Osric,

I hope you are feeling well, my friend. It took all my considerable skills to drag you back from the brink, and once or twice I almost lost you completely. I am extremely glad that it did not come to that. Yours is a fine body, and I will be honored to call it my own.

You have likely already found the tracking device your client attached to your vehicle. Rest assured that it has been disabled. In future, I would suggest you be a little more careful about these things. Although I suppose that is unlikely to be a concern of yours for much longer.

Speaking of your vehicle, you should find it parked outside. Your client was in too much of a hurry to properly dispose of it.

I hope your new clothes are to your liking. A little different from your normal attire, I know, but I think they will suit you. The jacket is hanging in the wardrobe. You should find a couple of things in the breast pocket which may prove useful to you.

I lowered the letter and opened the wardrobe. Sure enough, there was a suit jacket hanging there. I slipped it on, feeling overdressed, and took out the contents of the breast pocket.

The first thing I found was a small wad of cash, enough to keep me going for a few days. But it was the other thing that caught my attention. A small, sealed plastic bag, with a clump of gray hair inside. There was blood on the roots, as if it'd been ripped out by force.

A memory came back to me, of the instant Mills first shot me. A memory of me staggering toward him, grabbing at his hair. I must've ripped a chunk of hair out.

Dark thoughts swirled in my head, and I tucked the bag of hair back into my pocket. I couldn't go down that road. Not again.

I continued reading the Dealer's letter.

Don't worry about the motel room. I paid in advance. Take as long as you need. But I am sure a man in your position has plenty of things to be getting on with.

Oh, that reminds me. In the interests of protecting my new investment, I have decided to loan you some small trinkets of mine. Your little club is cute, but I feel like you need to be more appropriately armed for your current business. Have a look in the box I left in the bottom of the wardrobe.

I glanced down at the wardrobe. There was a small unmarked box sitting there. It made a rolling, rattling sound when I picked it up and set it on the desk. I flipped the lid open.

He'd given me a gun. It was a simple, snub-nosed revolver. When I picked it up, it sat heavy in my hand. It wasn't loaded, but a collection of bullets were rattling around the bottom of the box. Most of the ammo looked pretty standard, but when I looked closer I saw there were also a half-dozen silver-plated bullets. I pocketed the ammo, then picked up the other item inside the box.

It was some kind of bottle. Smaller than a tennis ball. Almost spherical, except for a flat base. Gold and silver loops ringed it from top to bottom. It had a strange metal cap etched with impossibly fine patterns. Its blue surface was slightly translucent. I peered closer, holding it up to the light.

Something moved inside.

Swallowing, I put it carefully back down and returned to the Dealer's letter.

The gun is self-explanatory. I normally do not care for such things, so in truth I am glad to part with it. The spirit bottle, though, is much more interesting. I acquired it many years ago, from a mystic woman who had been shunned by her people and wanted me to help her get revenge. I have always wondered exactly what kind of entity dwells within the bottle. The mystic claimed it was a nefarious spirit, highly dangerous, but she could not tell me more than that.

I would advise you not to use the bottle unless you have no other options. There is no telling how the entity will react to freedom. It is entirely possible that it will devour you whole. I understand that this fact limits its usefulness as a protective measure. I have decided, however, that it is a risk I am willing to take. If you decide to open it and things end badly for you, then at least I will have sated my curiosity. And when you live as long as I do, such small satisfactions become the greatest pleasures of all.

Nevertheless, try to take good care of that body. I did a fine job piecing you back together, if I do say so myself. Try not to get shot again.

I'll see you very soon.

Sincerely,

Your friend.

After that, the Dealer had written the symbol he used instead of a name. I wondered if he got the idea from the artist formerly known as Prince.

"Hell," I muttered to myself, eying the spirit bottle. I was pretty sure the Dealer was playing a joke on me. I just wished I understood his sense of humor.

I went back and forth on it a few times, but in the end I

gingerly picked up the spirit bottle and tucked it into my pocket. As long as I didn't open it, I was pretty sure everything would be okay. And if things got bad enough that I needed a Hail Mary play, then the contents of the bottle would be the least of my worries.

There was a small postscript at the bottom of the letter.

P.S., Eat up. I expect you are starving after your ordeal. You like Chinese, do you not?

I looked around, wondering if I'd missed a box of Chinese somewhere. I couldn't see anything, not even in the minibar fridge. Now that he mentioned it, it felt like I hadn't eaten in days.

There was a knock at the door. I froze, mind whirling. Who knew I was here? Had the Dealer been followed? Had Mills come back to finish the job?

Another knock. I could see a shadow in the crack beneath the door. It looked impatient. Silently, I picked up my truncheon and moved to the door.

"Who is it?" I said, standing to the side of the door in case someone started shooting.

"Delivery."

I twitched the curtain, peeking out the window. A young Asian dude in a red uniform was standing there, two big bags in his hands. He was chewing a toothpick and looking bored.

"Goddamn it, Dealer," I muttered.

I opened the door, and the smell of the Chinese food hit me instantly. It took all my strength not to descend on it immediately like a vampire in the grip of the Hunger.

"Eric Tuner?" the delivery guy said.

"Close enough." My mouth was watering as he handed me the bags. "How much?"

"Already paid for. Have a good day."

He turned to leave and I started to close the door, but a thought came to me.

"Hey!" I called after him. "What day is it?"

"Huh? It's Wednesday."

Shit. It'd been Saturday night when I followed the hobgoblin to that roadside cafe. Saturday when I'd been shot. And Sunday midnight when I'd made the deal.

I didn't have five days left. I had 36 hours. I'd lost three and a half days recovering from my near death experience and subsequent surgery.

Well, I could afford to lose a few more minutes while I devoured this food. I set it all up on the bedside table and cracked open a box of sweet and sour pork. I stuffed it in my mouth as fast as I could work the chopsticks.

But something was distracting me from the MSG-laden deliciousness. Wednesday. The word was sticking in my head. Wednesday.

Wednesday.

I stopped chewing suddenly, my eyes going to the bedside clock again.

"Shit!" I said with a mouthful of pork. Then I grabbed my keys and the bags of Chinese and ran for the door.

16

I don't like cemeteries.

I mean, I know no one really *likes* cemeteries. But I went out of my way to avoid them wherever possible.

For one thing, more than a few Strangers are drawn to the dead. You remember those iron nails I had, the ones soaked in the memories of the house? Well, think how many memories there are in the bones of a dead person.

And that's not even mentioning the Strangers who have darker motives to hang around dead bodies. Ghouls, for example. They eat dead flesh. Dead human flesh. And while most of them don't hunt humans unless they're absolutely starving, watching one chewing on a dead man's thigh is enough to put you off your dinner.

In truth, though, those aren't the only reasons I hate cemeteries. They're just too quiet, too empty. They encourage you to think about loved ones who've passed away, and about your own fleeting existence. And as of a couple of days ago, my existence was fleeting at breakneck speed.

But I came anyway. I was late, but I came. I'd made a promise.

Alice's back was to me. She was kneeling in front of Teddy's gravestone, a fresh bouquet of flowers laid on the grass beside her. For some reason I expected her to be all in black, like she had been the day of Teddy's funeral, but instead she was wearing a long-sleeved floral dress that actually succeeded in making her look vaguely lady-like for once.

"Sorry I'm late," I said when I came up behind her. "You wouldn't believe the traffic."

She jumped at the sound of my voice, spinning around and leaping to her feet.

"Ozzy." She tackled me with a hug that I swear knocked something loose inside me.

I grunted in pain, but before I could complain, she released me and punched me in the shoulder. Not a lady-like punch either, no matter what the dress would have you believe.

I staggered back a few steps, clutching at my shoulder. I was pretty proud of myself for not falling over.

"Son of a—" I said through gritted teeth. "Goddamn it, Alice. What the hell?"

"Where the hell have you been?" she demanded, advancing on me. "I've been calling you since Sunday. I went around to your house, and Early hadn't seen you either. I… What are you wearing?" She packed her snarl away and brought out a concerned frown to replace it. "You look like death. Are you hurt?"

"I am now." I rubbed my shoulder. "Hell."

"Ozzy," she said flatly.

I paused. My first instinct was to give her a story. But Alice would see right through the lie. I sighed.

"I'm here," I said. "That's what matters. I'm here for Teddy. I just want to stand here awhile."

She studied me, her mouth forming a tight line. Finally, she nodded, turning back to Teddy's gravestone. I put my arm around her and we stood there as a cold wind whipped around us.

It was a simple gravestone. Just his name and the dates of his birth and death. Not the true date of his death, of course. Just the official one. But that was okay. It was just a date.

"He was taken," I said.

Alice tensed against me, but she said nothing.

I licked my lips and closed my eyes, trying to make the words come. "You remember that night he first started screaming? The real screaming, I mean. When we went in there and found the windows wide open and he was screaming like he'd never screamed before. You remember that?"

"I remember," she said.

"That wasn't him. He'd been taken. Replaced with something else."

"Replaced? What...what are you talking about?"

"It wasn't him," I said again. "The thing that was lying there screaming, it wasn't him, Alice. It wasn't even alive."

She shook her head, face twisted in pain. "I don't—"

"It was a puppet. A doll, designed to look like Teddy. You understand?"

"No. No, I don't understand." She wiped a hand across her face, silent for a moment. "Who? Who took him?"

"Something that wasn't human."

"What—" She swallowed. "What did they want with him?"

I shook my head. I still didn't know for sure. "Mischief, maybe. Power. There's power in the bones of the young and innocent."

"Oh, Jesus."

She pulled free of me, turned away to cover her face. I let her go. There was a lump in the back of my throat, and I couldn't swallow it down. I didn't want to talk about this. I'd spent years trying not to.

But I had to. She had to know. Someone had to know, after I was gone.

After a few minutes, she straightened her back and turned to me again. "Those years you were away. You were looking for him."

I nodded. "Someone...someone told me the truth. Told me

what I'm telling you now. Gave me a chance to find him."

"And did you?"

My cheeks were wet. I nodded again. I didn't trust myself to speak.

Alice touched my arm. "And?"

"I was too late."

She already knew that. She had to. I didn't look at her face as I said it.

She slipped her arms around me once more, hugging me. It was all I could do not to fall to my knees and bawl like a baby.

"This isn't where he's buried," she said after a while, her face pressed against me.

"No."

"Where is he?"

"By the bottom of the falls. I thought he'd like that."

"He would." She broke the embrace. "You should've told me this before."

"I know. I just couldn't."

"So why now?" she asked.

I hesitated. I'd just finished laying a whole lot of truth on her, but there were still some things I couldn't bring myself to talk about. Like my impending death. And the black rage that was bubbling away deep in my stomach.

I hadn't felt rage like this since I saw what'd been done to Teddy. It was a part of me I wasn't proud of. But it was there nonetheless.

The monster inside me wanted to be let off the leash.

"Ozzy," Alice said, looking at me like she could sense what I was thinking. "What's going on? Where have you been?"

"Job got more complicated than I expected," I said. "I have to finish sorting it out."

Her face hardened. "Don't do that."

"Do what?"

"You're shutting down again. Like you always do."

I smiled. "And you're nagging me again. Like you always do."

"Ozzy—"

I grabbed her by the shoulders, kissed her forehead. "Don't tell anyone you've seen me, okay? Not even Early. I need to keep things quiet a little while longer."

"Wait—"

"Love you," I said.

And then I turned and strode away.

Promise kept. Now I had one more matter to attend to.

It was a while until Alice's swearing finally faded into the distance behind me. She sure can shout, my sister.

I didn't take the main driveway to my place. I didn't want to risk getting caught by Early if he was around. So I turned down a narrow forest road about a quarter-mile from home, parked my van, and walked along the river until I came to the back of the property.

I'd found my kit in my van, just like the Dealer promised, but that was all cunning man's stuff. For what I was planning, I needed a couple more things. Things that Early had once made me swear up and down that I'd destroyed.

I scanned the property carefully as I jumped the fence, but I couldn't see anyone moving in the windows. Rhodes' pickup was in the driveway, but Early's car was nowhere to be seen. He was probably out on a job. Maybe my luck had turned.

There were notes pinned to my front door from both Alice and Early. And one—interestingly enough—from Lilian. Hadn't expected her to come all the way down here looking for me.

Then again, I had promised to go have a look at the hag's place with her on Sunday morning, see if I could learn anything. That must've been what prompted her visit here.

I hoped she wasn't too mad at me. Chances were the hag had reappeared by now anyway.

I supposed I might not end up seeing her before my body was no longer my own. We'd never get to see who won our little bet. Surprising, how much that thought ached.

I forced the feeling aside. It was a distraction, a distraction I couldn't afford. There was a clock in my mind, slowly ticking down.

The monster wouldn't wait much longer.

Someone had been into my cabin while I was gone. I knew it as soon as I walked through the door. Had to be Early. He was the only one allowed through the warded doorway. He probably wanted to make sure I hadn't had a heart attack on the toilet or something.

There was another note on the table from Early, telling me that Alice was threatening to make a police report about my disappearance. I hoped Early had talked her out of it. He knew how badly that would work out for everyone.

I found an old crowbar with my tools under the laundry room basin. I took it with me into my workshop, where dusty glass vials reflected the light of the orange bulb overhead. I stripped off my fancy new suit jacket and tossed it out of the room.

"Sorry about the floor, Early," I said.

Then I plunged the sharp end of the crowbar into the space between two floorboards.

It took five minutes to open up a large enough hole in the floor. When you're still recovering from a couple of gunshot wounds, five minutes of work really takes it out of you. Panting slightly, I wrenched off the last splintered floorboard and reached into the space beneath.

The coat was shabbier than I remembered. It was bundled up, but I could already see how frayed the hem was. I pulled it into the light. The leather was dark brown. As I unwrapped it, I could hear parchment crackling. There were dozens of protective charms stitched into the lining. I hoped they were still functional.

I pulled on the coat, feeling the weight of it settle about my shoulders once more. Glass vials clinked together in the many pockets. The sound made a shiver run down my spine.

There was another bundled package in the hole in the floor, right where I'd left it. I swallowed as I took it out and laid it on the undamaged floor beside me.

I could still back out. I could still put all this stuff away, bury it back where it belonged. I could go have a beer with Early, tell him what a crazy few days I'd had. I could go around to Alice's place, hug her wife and get my ass kicked on the Playstation by the twins. I could go to a movie with a couple of friends. Hell, I could even see if I could score an actual date with Lilian, and to hell with our bet.

I could've done a lot of things. But I didn't.

I untied the string on the bundle and let it fall open. It contained two items. A wax doll and a book. I tucked the wax doll into my pocket, next to the revolver the Dealer had given me.

The book was the same ancient tome I'd found after I crawled out of that ice bath. A black, evil book.

I wouldn't need it. I already knew everything I needed to.

I laid the splintered floorboards back in place, leaving the evil tome there in the hole I'd opened up in the floor.

I just wished I couldn't hear it laughing at me as I switched off the light and left the cabin.

There was still no sign of Early when I reemerged into the sunshine. I wasn't stupid enough to think Alice would actually keep my presence secret. He'd be coming back soon, and I didn't want to be around here to face him.

I crept around to the front of his house, pulled a scrap of paper out of my pocket, and penned him a note.

Early,

I'm sure Alice has blabbed by now, but anyway, I'm back, so you can stop worrying about me.

The job went bad, and I have to set it right. I'll tell you about it when I can.

Do me a favor. Check in with Alcaraz, make sure she hasn't turned our little friend into some new ornament for her entrance hall. She said she wouldn't, but I don't trust that woman. Did you know she keeps a live baiter vamp in her house? Who the hell does that?

Anyway, got to go do some things. Stay out of trouble, old man.

Ozzy

I paused, looked back at the driveway, and then brought the pen to the paper once more.

P.S., Tell Rhodes I'm sorry for stealing his car.

17

I didn't take Rhodes' pickup truck purely to be an asshole. Brandon Mills would recognize my van if he saw it. The pickup was less conspicuous.

And I desperately wanted to get the drop on the bastard.

I crunched through the gears of the worn-out pickup all the way across town. Rhodes did a pretty good job tending to Early's gardens, but he apparently had a lot less interest in keeping his vehicle in shape. I was worried the whole thing would rattle itself to pieces at any moment.

Brandon Mills' house was at the end of a cul-de-sac, which meant I couldn't drive by the place while I was scouting it out. Instead, I parked up on the side of the road a few doors down and slid down low in my seat.

The weeds seemed to have gained another foot in height since I'd last laid eyes on the house. Mills' station wagon was missing from the driveway. He was out. Murdering some other poor sap, maybe.

I settled down in my seat, eyes on the house, and waited. I didn't have to wait long.

Half an hour later I heard a car approaching from behind, and a glance in the mirror showed me it was Mills' station wagon. I slid down further in my seat as it passed, but Mills didn't look in my direction.

He pulled into his driveway and got out of the car. Shooting me didn't seem to have improved his mood any. With the look of a prisoner at a hard labor camp, he got some grocery bags out of the car and lugged them toward the house.

Strange, I never thought about murderers visiting the supermarket. Guess they still have to eat.

When his back was to me, I slipped out of the pickup and pushed the door quietly closed. With a glance at the empty street, I hurried toward Mills' house.

Mills was busy fumbling with his keys while both his hands were full with bags from an upscale grocer. He got the door open as I reached his driveway. He still hadn't noticed me.

I withdrew the wax doll from my pocket. A bloodied clump of Mills' hair was stuffed in its mouth, and it had been washed in a potion of stagnant water and bog grasses. A vague sense of disgust washed over me as I gripped it in my hand, like I was holding something dead and rotten. My heart hammered in anticipation just the same.

As I came up the driveway behind him, Mills finally seemed to hear me. He turned and his eyes met mine. I bared my teeth at him. With a look of silent shock, he dropped the shopping bags and reached to the small of his back.

Our ancestors used to be terrified of witchcraft, with good reason. It could wrack a man with agony, or wither his flesh, or destroy his livelihood. It could strike at any time, unseen, unknowable. People were so terrified they started accusing anyone and everyone of being a witch. Thousands of innocents were drowned or burned or hanged in the frenzy of fear.

You want to know the difference between that kind of witchcraft and the kind of magic I can do?

There isn't one.

I squeezed the wax doll in my grip, crushing it tight. Mills went suddenly rigid, arms pinned to his side. The air was pushed from his lungs. His eyes bulged above his open, gasping mouth.

"How does that feel, Brandon?" I said as I stepped over

a puddle of spilled milk. "How does it feel being unable to breathe? How does it feel to know you're dying?"

His eyes rolled with panic. I shouldn't have been enjoying this. But I was. Oh, I was.

I grabbed his rigid body by the front of his shirt and shoved him inside. He hit the floor like a sack of shit. I kicked the door closed behind me and crouched beside him, grinning.

"You see, I chose to become a cunning man," I hissed in his ear as I relieved him of the pistol tucked into the back of his pants. "Someone showed me I could use my power to help people, instead of hurting them. And I was glad to leave that part of my life behind."

Mills stared at me, desperately trying to take a breath. I squeezed the doll harder, and his face grew even redder.

"But I didn't forget, Brandon. I still remember how to hurt people. I had a lot of practice, after all. And you made a big fucking mistake crossing me."

I eased my grip on the doll, and Mills sucked in a wheezy breath. Grabbing him by his collar, I dragged him down the hall.

"Where's your mother?" I said.

"B...bed," he wheezed. "She's ill."

I grunted. It was probably a mercy for her. She wouldn't have to watch her son die.

I dragged Mills into the light of the living room and dropped him in the middle of the floor. My rage was burning through my muscles, giving me strength. The monster inside me was straining at its chain, demanding to be let loose entirely. Demanding I open Mills' throat, hack him to pieces, bury him in a shallow grave and salt the earth above him.

Once, I might've done that. But there was an Early-shaped angel on my shoulder, trying to rein the monster in. Telling me this wasn't right. Telling me this would solve nothing.

Truth was, I didn't want to solve anything. There was

nothing to solve. I was a dead man already.

But I stayed my hand, at least for the moment. With Mills gasping on the floor, I stood up and began to pace.

"You have no idea how badly I want to end you," I said. "You killed me, you bastard. You fucking killed me!"

He strained for the tiny amount of breath I allowed him. "I...I'm sorry."

I barked a laugh. "You're sorry? You're sorry?!"

"Sorry," he rasped.

I shook my head, paced across the room, slammed my hand down on the table. I sucked air through gritted teeth.

"What did you do with the hobgoblin?" I said.

"I..."

"What?" I turned back. "What was it about? Huh?" I waited, got nothing. "Tell me!"

He shook his head, or at least I could see him trying to. He could move his limbs maybe an inch each way at the moment. I was tempted to crush that out of him again. Or maybe just toss a vial of witch's fire onto him, watch him try to writhe. Yeah, that sounded satisfying.

"Can't..." he said.

"Can't what? Can't tell me? You will."

"No. I'm sorr—"

I crushed the wax doll tight again, tighter than I had before. Panic flooded his eyes once more as he went rigid.

"Stop saying you're sorry," I snapped. "We're past sorry, Brandon. Tell me why you did it."

I eased my grip, giving him enough air to speak. He remained silent.

"Tell me, Brandon," I said. "Tell me!"

With a snarl, I took the doll's right leg between my thumb and forefinger and began to bend it up. Brandon groaned with pain as his knee was slowly twisted the wrong way.

"Why did you do it?" I demanded.

"They took my son!" he screamed.

His words went through me like a knife. I released the doll's leg. Mills let out a sigh of relief.

I dropped to his side, grabbing him by the collar. "What did you say?"

"My son. Michael. They took him. They have him. They made me do it. I'm sorry. I'm so sorry." Tears began to well up in his eyes.

"Shut up," I said, but it came out a whisper. I couldn't hold onto my rage; it was slipping through my fingers, pouring away like sand. And in its place there was only shame. "What are you talking about? Who has your son?"

"I don't know."

"Don't lie to me."

"I don't know!" he said, and he really was crying now. "I didn't have a choice!"

I realized I was still gripping the wax doll, keeping him paralyzed. I released it and he instantly put his face in his hands, curling up into a ball.

"Hey!" Grabbing him by the shoulders, I hauled him to his feet and shoved him into a tattered armchair. I leaned over him. "Hey! What the hell is going on? Where is your boy?"

"They took him," he whispered again.

I pulled his hands from his face. "Tell me how it started, Brandon."

He licked his lips, looking up at me through wet eyes. "It was at night. They took him at night. Took him right out of his crib."

"When?"

"A month ago. And they…they replaced him. They replaced him with something else. But it wasn't him. It wasn't Michael."

Just like Teddy. Another changeling. Could it be true?

I searched Mills' eyes and found no hint of a lie. My hands started shaking. I stuffed them in my pockets.

"How did you know?" I said.

"Someone...something came back, after I buried what I thought was my son. It came back in the night, and told me it had Michael. I tried to grab hold of it, demand answers. But it was dark, and it slipped away."

"And you didn't see this thing?"

He shook his head. "It seemed almost human. But its smell... its smell was all wrong. And its voice was like sandpaper. My wife didn't believe me. That's why I had to leave." He paused, looking down at the floor. "And then, one night, the thing came back. It said it would return Michael if I gave it what it wanted."

"What did it want?"

He swallowed. "A hobgoblin. The thing that took Michael, it told me how to trap a hobgoblin. I did what it said. But then the hobgoblin got away, and I had to find it, so I came to you, and...and..."

"All right, all right." I exhaled, dragging my hand across my face.

"That thing said no one could know. It said there could be no witnesses."

"All right, I said!"

Blood pounded in my head. I wanted to crush Mills for what he'd done to me. I wanted to squeeze the wax doll until the last of his life was choked out of him.

But I couldn't. I couldn't. I believed him.

He'd done all this to try to save his boy. How could I fault him for that, after all I'd done to try to save Teddy?

"What did you do to the hobgoblin?" I said.

Mills was still sobbing. When he didn't answer me, I shook him and repeated the question.

"The thing told me to leave the hobgoblin tied up in a bag at the foot of my bed that night. I was so tired, I couldn't stay awake. When I woke up, the bag was gone."

"And your boy?"

He sniffed and shook his head. "I don't know. The thing said it would be back. But...but I still haven't heard anything."

Of course you haven't, I wanted to shout in his face. What kind of idiot was he? Changeling children didn't come home.

Chances were the boy had been stripped for parts within a day of being taken, like a stolen car. Maybe he was still alive, being raised as the slave of some nefarious Stranger. But no matter what orders Brandon Mills carried out, the boy wasn't coming back. Not unless someone went and brought him home.

I squashed that thought before it could spread. The boy wasn't my problem, and I had enough of my own to deal with without taking on more. Besides, he was almost certainly dead. The sooner Mills came to terms with that, the better.

But when I opened my mouth to say the words, I couldn't bring myself to. He was pathetic enough already. I didn't want to see what he'd become when that one last hope was taken away from him.

Maybe it was stupid to pity the bastard. He'd killed me, after all. But when I looked at him sitting there, sniffing and sobbing, my anger found a new focus.

Mills had been used. He was a pawn, like me. But somewhere out there was a player, and I wanted nothing more than to make him choke on his own chess board.

"All right, Brandon," I said. "Listen here. Is there anything else you haven't told me? Because if I find out you're keeping something from me..."

"That's all I know. I swear." He met my eyes, and I nodded slowly.

"Good. From now on, you're going to sit in this house, tend to your mother, and stay the hell out of my way. I'm going to get to the bottom of this. If anyone or anything contacts you, you give me a call right away. And if you can't get in touch with me, you talk to my friend Early." I gave him Early's phone number. "You understand?"

He nodded. "Okay."

I gave him one last glare to make sure he got the message, then I headed for the hall. Just as I was about to leave the living room, he called out to me.

"What about my son?"

I paused, sighed. Couldn't leave it alone, could he?

"Your boy, he's..." I looked into his puppy dog eyes and sighed again. "Tell me about him. Tell me about your boy."

"Tell...?"

"Describe him to me."

Mills licked his lips. "He's...he's nearly two. Tall for his age. Dark haired. His eyes were blue when he was born, but they turned green." His lips trembled. "He has the biggest smile I've ever seen. And he smiles at everything. Everyone. I've never met a happier child. I don't know how that happened. How did I make such a perfect son?"

I screwed up my eyes, tried to form a picture of Michael Mills in my head.

But all I could see was Teddy.

"Do you think he's still alive?" Mills whispered.

No, said the voice in my head.

But what if he was? What if he was?

Teddy was dead. But maybe this boy wasn't.

Damn it. I grunted. "Look, I'll do what I can."

A smile broke across his face. "Thank you," he said, sniffling. "Thank you."

"I'm not doing it for you," I said.

I got the hell out of there before he could start crying again.

As I made my way back down the hall, I heard the creak of bedsprings from behind a half-open door. I paused. After a moment's indecision, my curiosity got the better of me and I eased the door open a couple more inches with my foot.

The room had a musty, retirement home kind of smell. The curtains were pulled, but they were thin and tattered, letting shafts of light in through the gaps and tears.

Brandon's mother was asleep in bed, covered in dusty blankets. Her wheelchair sat in the corner of the room, like a watchful guard dog.

She breathed with a rattling hiss. One arm dangled out from under the covers, bathed in a strip of light coming through the crack in the curtains. A band of gold glittered in the sunshine. She was wearing a wedding ring that had been etched with a pattern like naked tree branches.

I wondered what had happened to her husband. Was he dead too?

That led to other questions. Had Brandon told her what had really happened to his son? And if he had, did she believe him?

I felt a sudden wave of pity for the woman. She was already crippled and deaf. She'd lost her grandson, and now she'd been brought here, to this damp wreck of a house to slowly fade away.

Just as I was about to back away, the old woman's eyelids fluttered open. She turned her head, and in the dim light her one good eye met mine.

Something in her stare made my blood run cold. I stood frozen for a moment as she silently stared at me. Then I pulled the door closed and backed away quickly, cringing at every creaking floorboard.

It was a relief to throw open the front door and emerge into the thick tangle of the house's front garden. Everything in that place creeped me the hell out.

I enjoyed the cold afternoon sunlight as I strode away from the house. Funny, how sharp the wind seemed now, how bright the light was. I was slowly coming to terms with my fate, and my senses were greedily sucking in every sensation they could, before it was too late.

Part of me wanted to just stay like that forever, staring up into the sky. Part of me wanted to let it all go, just accept that my time was up.

But when I reached the street and saw what was waiting for me, I knew any chance of being content with my lot had gone straight out the window. Because standing there next to the stolen car, watching me approach, was Early.

And he looked fucking furious.

18

It takes a lot to make Early mad.

Sure, he can be a bit of a grumpy old bastard at times. He doesn't suffer fools, and if he doesn't get his morning bowl of bran flakes, you can bet you'll be hearing about it.

But deep down he's the wise and gentle brand of cunning man. He takes in the world's problems, gives them a look over, and starts fixing them without complaint.

Must be all the herbal tea he drinks.

That was how I knew Early truly did care about me. Because as soon as we were both shut in the relative privacy of Rhodes' pickup, he really ripped into me.

It was an impressive thing to watch. There was waving of arms and frothing at the mouth and everything. At one point he even used the phrase "worried sick." Like I was a five-year-old who'd gotten lost at the mall.

I just sat there behind the wheel with my head hanging, mumbling apologies every so often and hoping he'd hurry up. I couldn't waste all day getting yelled at.

I probably would've got away with a short scolding if I hadn't stolen Rhodes' car. So I guess it was my own fault, really.

Sometime during the tirade I started wondering how Early had managed to track me down here. He gave me the answer soon enough, without me having to ask. Get this: GPS again. It was the bane of my life. For some reason Rhodes had actually gone to the effort to fit this damn rust bucket with an anti-theft GPS tracking device. I sometimes wondered if Rhodes was even from this planet.

It was about five minutes into Early's rant that he finally recognized the coat I was wearing. His eyes widened as he stared at the tattered leather. The anger left his face, and in its place was a disappointment so sharp it cut.

"Why are you wearing that?" he said quietly.

Taking a deep breath, I began to tell him what'd happened. Now that he'd got all that shouting out of his system, he listened in silence while I laid everything out.

I didn't hold back like I had with Alice. Telling her everything would've endangered everyone. Centuries of unspoken law dictated that I kept the full truth hidden from her.

But Early was a cunning man, just like me. So I told him everything: Mills, the job, the betrayal.

And once I started telling the story, it all came tumbling out of me. I could hear the rage in my voice as I told him about the shooting; it tasted like bile in the back of my throat. I swallowed it down.

When I told him about the deal I'd made with the Dealer, Early closed his eyes and let out a sigh like a deflating balloon. He knew as well as I did that a deal like that was final.

Finally, it was all out there. My words seemed to hang in the pickup's cab, heavy and smothering. I was breathing heavily, suddenly exhausted. I felt like I could sleep for days. If only I had that long.

For a few seconds, Early just sat there, staring out the windshield, hands balled into fists in his lap. Then he turned to me and gripped my shoulder.

"My boy," he said, his voice thick with sorrow.

"I'm not dead yet," I said.

He nodded, but we both knew it would take a miracle to save me. The transfer clause I'd added to the deal was a long shot. There were only a couple of people in the whole world who might willingly sacrifice themselves up to the Dealer in my place, and I wouldn't let them.

Early, for instance, would undoubtedly leap at the opportunity to take this bullet for me. He loved that kind of thing. Even if I agreed to it—which I wouldn't—I doubted the Dealer would consider his creaky old bones to be worth the same as mine.

We lapsed back into silence for a few minutes. We were still in the cul-de-sac near Mills' house, and now that I'd spilled my tale I could feel my time ticking away again. Early's car was parked behind my stolen pickup. I'd gathered from his earlier tirade that my sister had blabbed to him as soon as I'd left the cemetery. Tattletale.

As I watched, Early seemed to come to terms with everything I'd told him. His face hardened and his voice became matter-of-fact.

"This business with the hobgoblin worries me. Did this Mills character say anything about why his tormentor wants the creature?"

"No," I said, relieved to put aside the issue of my mortality for now. "But I'm going to go out on a limb and guess that whatever it is, the hobgoblin isn't happy about it."

He nodded grimly. "I have a bad feeling about this. Hobgoblins don't make enemies easily, and they're not much use for anything. Not alive, at least. But I've heard of a few very old and very powerful curses that require the flesh of a hobgoblin."

I'd heard of them too, and as he said it, something came back to me. "Before I got shot, the hobgoblin was screaming something about a curse. Blood and silver and a curse."

Early grunted. "I don't like this. I don't like this at all."

"Talk to the hag," I suggested. "She might be able to shed some light on this."

"I would," he said. "But she's nowhere to be found."

I looked at him. "Still?"

"You've heard?"

"Lilian called me just before I got shot, said the hag was missing. Asked me to help find her. I figured she would've shown up by now."

"Well, she hasn't," he said with a sigh. "In fact, I just came from her place. Her disappearance is starting to worry people. She's never been gone this long before. I was asked to have another look. I don't have your skill with tracking, but..." He shook his head. "Nothing. No sign of her. Some of her wards have been broken, but the place is such a mess I can't even tell if anything else is missing."

He didn't say it, but I could tell he was thinking the same thing I was. Was the hag's disappearance somehow linked to the hobgoblin and whoever had been manipulating Brandon Mills?

The timing made for an interesting coincidence. Stranger things had happened in Lost Falls. Still, it didn't smell right.

"I'm going to have to call a conclave," Early said, his voice heavy.

"What? No. Come on."

"I don't have a choice. This keeps getting worse, Ozzy. First the hag goes missing, and now we're dealing with change-lings as well. If someone harmed the hag, they're extremely powerful. And if they're working a curse, they could be a threat to everyone. This needs to be discussed properly."

"No, we need to *do* something. Not gather up the local freaks and spend the next three days arguing over what font the minutes should be typed up in."

He frowned and opened his mouth, but I cut in before he could speak.

"Look, the hag's disappearance is concerning, I'll give you that. But it's a dead end. I want to find Mills' tormentor. And we both know the first place we should go looking for him."

"We don't know anything," he said.

"Oh, come on!" I threw my hands up in the air and accidentally punched the roof of the pickup. "Don't give me that false diplomacy bullshit. Not now. I don't have time for it, Early. Literally."

His face tightened as if he was in pain, but the grimace vanished so quickly I wondered if I'd been imagining it. He turned to me, fixing me with his hard gray eyes.

"This is bigger than you, and you know it. I know you're angry. I know you want to rip and tear. Believe me, I know. But this is what cunning folk do, boy. Cunning folk have a responsibility to their community. Cunning folk have to be wise. They have to think, they have to talk it out." He cast an eye over my coat once more, and I was suddenly ashamed of it, of the vials of black liquid stuffed into the pockets and the weight of the revolver pressing against my side. "Are you a cunning man, Ozzy? Or are you something else?"

I licked my lips. Damn the old bastard.

"Well?" he said.

"Fine. All right. We'll do it your way."

He nodded sharply. "Good. I'll call the conclave tonight. It's short notice, but we don't have a choice. You're going to need to tell your story to them."

"What? I—" I sighed. "Hell. Yeah, okay. I'll tell them what they need to know. But I swear to God, the first one of them to interrupt me is getting cursed with genital warts."

Early's bushy gray beard parted in a smile. "Fair enough. I'll meet you back at home." He climbed out of the pickup, but before he closed the door he paused and looked back inside. "This boy. The Mills baby. You think he's still alive?"

"I don't know," I said quietly. "Maybe it's better if he isn't."

Early frowned and nodded his understanding.

There were worse fates than death, after all.

19

Rhodes was standing in the driveway waiting for me when I got back to Early's. Something told me he was a teensy bit annoyed about me stealing his pickup.

I parked beside him, got out, and held out the keys to him.

"Listen," I said. "I'm really sorry about taking your truck. It was an emergency, and—"

He snatched the keys out of my hand, shot me one last glare, then turned and stalked back around the side of the house. For a guy who was more than a head shorter than me, he sure could stomp about.

I gave him a few seconds' head-start, then went into the house. Early wasn't back yet—he was still out making calls and rounding up the usual suspects—so I rooted around in his fridge and helped myself to a beer and half a roast beef sandwich.

It was agony waiting for nightfall, when the conclave would form. I had just over 30 hours to live, and here I was, sitting around and waiting for the town freak show to arrive.

After I'd eaten, I went to my cabin, pulled a selection of my grimoires and occult texts off the shelves, and carried them back to Early's place. I sat down at the table and started leafing through the books, trying to find some mention of a spell or curse that used hobgoblin flesh as an ingredient. But dark magic like that was beyond anything I specialized in. I found nothing.

I slammed my last grimoire closed, disheartened. To take my mind off things, I checked my wounds. The stitches were all holding. In fact, aside from a dull ache at each of the wound sites, I was feeling surprisingly good. The fatigue was another story, but I chased down my beer with a couple of cups of coffee, and that perked me right up.

Early made it home soon after. He came straight in and started scurrying about the place, clearing away dirty dishes and sweeping the floor like a bachelor expecting to bring his date home that night.

"Why don't you just have the conclave meet somewhere else?" I said as he hurried past. "Ollie's Diner, maybe. You know, neutral ground."

"Public meetings are dangerous. Too many of us show up at Ollie's at once and we start drawing eyes." He thrust a pile of old newspapers into my hands. "Go put these in the back room."

I grumbled and moaned and did as I was told.

Alcaraz and Lilian were the first of the conclave to arrive. Lilian was there more as Alcaraz's assistant than as a participant in her own right, but that was splitting hairs.

They were stuck standing at the front door until Early let them in. The walls of the old Victorian were warded to the eyebrows, crammed full of protective charms, witch bottles, worn-out leather boots, and talismans of iron and silver. They kept witchcraft at bay, and also made it damn near impossible for guests to enter without being invited in.

When Early finally gave them the okay, Alcaraz shuffled straight into the sitting room that Early had set up for the occasion and sat herself down on the best chair. Lilian came in behind the older woman, curious eyes studying the old house. She saw me and gave me the once over.

"Where the hell have you been?" she asked.

"Long story. You'll hear it later." I paused. "Sorry I couldn't follow up the business with the hag."

She shrugged, but by the way her eyes clouded over, I could tell she was even more worried than she had been when she'd called. I didn't think she was concerned for the hag's wellbeing. Lilian needed something from the hag, and she needed it bad.

While Alcaraz snapped open a book she'd been carrying, Lilian came over and joined me at the back of the sitting room.

"Nice coat," she said.

"Thanks."

"Did you get it out of the dumpster behind a thrift store?"

"All right, all right."

"Seriously, you look like a homeless pirate."

"A pirate can't be homeless. His home is the sea." I mimed moving a chess piece. "Check and mate."

The rest of the conclave drifted in over the next hour, as the sun slowly set. It was a pretty pitiful turnout. There was a minor charm dealer who made his living telling fortunes down by the dock, and a token member of the ghoul community—if you can call that fractured mob a community. She sat in the corner, all skin and bones, gnawing on her fingernails as her eyes darted about the room.

"How long do you think it's been since she fed?" Lilian whispered to me. "Poor thing looks starved."

"Offer up your arm if you're so concerned," I said.

"Ghouls only eat dead flesh."

"Well, cut it off then," I said. "It'll die soon enough."

Lilian frowned. "She's not exactly a great representative to send, is she?"

"No one likes to attend a conclave at the best of times, and Early called this one on short notice. He's lucky anyone at all showed up." I paused. "Probably better this way. You know what the rivalries in this town are like. Maybe we'll save ourselves some bloodshed."

A few more freaks filled in the other chairs. The last person to show up was a guy I'd never seen before. In fact, he looked so out of place among the rest of us weirdos that I wondered if he'd gotten lost and was looking for directions. He had a kind of effeminate beauty to him, all narrow features and carefully sculpted blond hair. He was dressed in pastels, and to top it all off he was wearing a beige scarf.

Lilian made a kind of purring sound when she saw him. I didn't much like the way she was eying him. I didn't much like it at all.

As Early led the newcomer in, I caught the old man's eye and shot him a questioning look. Early scratched his nose, then touched his throat as he lowered his hand.

I looked back at the beautiful man and swore to myself as I caught Early's meaning. "You've got to be kidding me."

"What?" Lilian said.

I gave a bitter laugh, shaking my head. "That's classy. Real classy. The vampires sent a swain."

The man noticed me glaring at him. He shot me a smile so bright I saw stars. He strolled over, turned his smile on Lilian for a moment, then addressed me.

"You must be Osric Turner," he said, holding out a hand. I didn't take it.

"Uh-huh."

He let his hand fall. The smile never left his face, but his eyes were glazed and distant. "My name is Isaac. I'm afraid my mistress, Miss Lockhart, couldn't make it to this conclave. She sent me as her representative in this time of crisis."

"Uh-huh."

He paused, and somehow his smile got even brighter. "I'll go take my seat." He nodded once more at Lilian, then drifted away.

"A swain," I muttered when he was out of earshot. "Guess we know how seriously Sonja Lockhart and the rest of her brood are taking this."

Sonja Lockhart was the undisputed heavyweight champion of greater vampires in Lost Falls. If lesser vampires like the baiter vamp I'd fought at Alcaraz's house were the baboons and chimpanzees of the vampire family, greater vampires were the humans. They'd overcome their more bestial urges. They could speak, think, scheme, paint pictures, appreciate Mozart.

Greater vampires knew better than to hunt humans. That would be crass, not to mention risky. But Lockhart, like the rest of the small brood of vampires that held sway in Lost Falls, still had to feed. Which was where people like our pretty new guest came in.

He was a swain. A human bloodslave. Beneath that beige scarf of his, I knew I'd find the puncture wounds where he'd allowed his mistress to feed. It was arousing, supposedly. Addicting. The swain became devoted to the vampire who fed on him. A real marriage made in heaven.

It was a hell of a snub from Lockhart, sending a swain instead of one of her brood, or coming herself. Even Early wasn't looking happy about it. Considering the fact that Early had some unpleasant history with the vampires, I couldn't blame him.

Finally, as the swain took his seat, Early moved to the front of the room, stroking his beard nervously. He never was any good with public speaking, even if only a handful of individuals had come to the conclave.

"I'll skip the formalities, since there are so few of us here," Early said, and his eyes lingered on Isaac the swain as he said it. "There have been some troubling events in the last few days, and I'm concerned about the consequences for our community. By now I'm sure you're all aware of the disappearance of the hag."

A few scattered nods answered him.

"I've visited her home myself," he said, "and she's left no

trace that I can detect. Even her familiar is missing."

I'd never seen the hag's familiar myself, but I'd heard it was some kind of great bird-like creature. Well, not a creature, exactly. More like a magical construct. It was supposed to protect the hag, follow her orders, do her bidding. Wherever the hag was, the familiar wouldn't be far away. Unless, of course, she'd died or become grievously injured. Without the hag's magic, the familiar would soon wither and die.

Early continued. "I'm sure I don't have to tell anyone in this room how great the implications are. The hag has protected this town since its founding. Not out of the kindness of her heart, I'll grant you. But whatever her motives, her presence has helped keep the rest of us safe from witch-finders and other creatures who would hunt us."

My eyebrows raised. That was news to me. I always knew the hag was powerful, but beyond that I'd done my best to steer clear of her.

I kept my mouth shut about my ignorance, though. In the eyes of everyone else in this room, I was still a newcomer to this world, this community. I could do without being the butt of everyone's jokes.

"And of course, the hag also provides higher magical assistance to those in our community who require it," Early continued. "Including glamours for those who wish to pass as human. We are greatly weakened by her loss."

"Not all of us," Isaac said. The swain was sitting casually, his arm draped across the back of the chair. He had the kind of smile I wanted to staple to the floor.

Early's bushy eyebrows hung low over his eyes as he regarded the swain. "Your mistress is powerful, but there are things even she cannot do. With the hag gone, the vampires are exposed. As are we all.

"But that isn't the only reason I've called this coven," Early continued, addressing the whole room again. "I believe we have a rogue element in town. Someone carrying out practices that have long been forbidden. Ozzy?" He gestured to me.

The eyes of the room turned to me. Suddenly I wasn't terribly excited about public speaking either. Lilian nudged me, muttering something that was probably either supposed to be encouraging or mocking. I wasn't listening close enough to tell.

I moved to the front of the room. Swallowing, I started to give them the Cliff's Notes version of the story. I told them about Mills, and the job, and the betrayal, but I left out the part where I got shot. I didn't feel much like telling a roomful of weirdos about my impending demise.

My throat was dry when I got to the end. I fell into awkward silence, and the eyes of the room blinked at me.

"That's it?" said the dockside charm-seller. He didn't seem to be alone in the sentiment. Isaac gave me a pitying grin.

"Yeah, that's it," I said. "What more do you want? The hobgoblin said—"

"It's a hobgoblin," the charm-seller sneered. "Who cares what it said? It has a brain the size of a Tic Tac."

"You think someone snatched a man's child and used it as leverage just so he could get himself a pet hobgoblin? Someone wants that hobgoblin for something, and I'll tell you this: it won't be something good."

"You have to admit," Lilian said, "it's a little thin, Ozzy."

I stared at her. *Et tu, Brute?* She gave an apologetic shrug.

"You don't believe me," I said.

"Of course I do," she said. "I'm just worried you're jumping to conclusions. I mean, he's not wrong." She nodded at the charm-seller. "It's just a hobgoblin."

"Forget the damn hobgoblin," I said. "At the very least, we've got a changeling child out there somewhere. Maybe dead, maybe alive. That's supposed to be strictly forbidden. Do none of you care about that?"

"You don't know there's a child," the charm-seller said.

"Have you ever seen it?"

"I saw the goddamn crib, is that good enough for you?"

"Ozzy," Lilian said, making soothing gestures. "Look, we're not saying something strange didn't happen to you. I just think we have more important things to focus on. The hag is the real concern."

There was a thud of a book slamming shut. Alcaraz, who barely seemed to have been paying attention during my story, laid the book she'd been reading in her lap.

"All right, girl," she said to Lilian. "You've said your piece, and embarrassed yourself enough. As have you," she said to the charm-seller, whose face soured. "The boy is right. We would be fools to ignore this business with the hobgoblin."

I'll admit, I was surprised that I was getting support from Alcaraz's corner, but I took a great deal of pleasure in it nonetheless.

"Wipe that smug smile off your face," she snapped at me. "This is serious."

Way to burst my bubble.

"Since when are you so concerned about the welfare of hobgoblins?" the charm-seller said to Alcaraz. "You probably have a few caged in your basement."

"Oh, keep silent," Alcaraz said. "I honestly wonder how anyone confuses you for a wise man. Are you all so short-sighted? We have a missing hag, a changeling child, and a kidnapped hobgoblin. At least Early and the boy seem to realize the danger here. Hobgoblins are not smart creatures, no, but their flesh holds a great deal of latent magical residue. Far more than goblins. More than lesheys as well, perhaps even more than vampires. Creatures like this have long served as ingredients in the darkest of curses. Only a fool would ignore the signs."

The charm-seller sneered. "Fool? I wouldn't throw that word out too often, Doctor. You're the one who can't keep her creatures from breaking out, so I hear."

I snapped bolt-upright, the realization striking me like 50,000 volts straight to the nipples. "Holy shit."

"What?" Early said. The rest of the room had paused their argument to stare at me.

The mention of the break-in at Alcaraz's house had sparked something in the back of my mind. Why hadn't I made the connection before?

"Was anyone else listening to Falls radio on Saturday evening? *Nights with Alice.* Anyone?"

Isaac the bloodslave turned his grin on me. "You mean that mundy woman who tells ghost stories?" Mundy—mundane— was what some in our community called humans who were unaware of what lurked among them. It wasn't a nice term.

I narrowed my eyes at him. "I wouldn't take that tone with me, bleeder, or Lockhart will have to find herself a new foodbag."

He drew himself up, his grin gone in an instant. "You threaten a swain of the most powerful vampire in—"

"Enough!" Early said, getting between us. "Now isn't the time." He looked at me. "Ozzy, what is it?"

I tore my eyes away from Isaac. "Saturday night. People were calling in to the station, talking about a big black beast out near the dam. A beast with no eyes." I looked at Alcaraz. "Did you ever find your missing roggenwolf?"

"No," she said slowly. "But roggenwolves have eyes."

"The witness made it sound like the beast had been injured. Eyes gouged out, maybe."

She was quiet a few seconds, and the lines on her face seemed to deepen. She looked down at the book in her lap, tapping the cover with one nervous finger. "It is said that their eyes hold the eyelight of all those they've hunted. If it's true, they hold a great deal of power. But it would be a cruel thing to do to the beast."

Lilian seemed to have gone a little green. The other members of the conclave were looking confused, but I turned to Early and saw he was as troubled as I was.

"What if someone broke into Alcaraz's specifically to get their hands on the roggenwolf?" I said. "They could have smashed open a bunch of other cages to cover their tracks, then fled with the roggenwolf."

Early chewed his lip and glanced at Alcaraz. "It would've been difficult. But not impossible."

"Eye of roggenwolf," I said. "Flesh of hobgoblin. Do you think…?"

"A curse," he said, nodding. "A dangerous curse."

He swallowed, then addressed the room. "That settles it. We can't ignore the signs. We must assume someone is planning to work some very dark magic, and until we know otherwise, we must consider them a threat."

"I don't get what the big deal is," the charm-seller said. "You two are cunning folk, aren't you? You break curses for a living."

"Personal curses," I said. "Curses that affect one person, or a family. Curses that bring disease and misfortune. Stuff like that we can deal with. This…this is bigger. Much bigger."

"Let's assume for a moment that you're right," Isaac said, though his tone suggested he wasn't convinced. "Someone really is working some big spooky curse. What does that mean for us?"

Early frowned. "Best case scenario? Even if our rogue conjurer isn't able to work the curse correctly, they're drawing attention to themselves. Which will draw attention to us."

"We can deal with the mundies," Isaac said flippantly. "My mistress has swains within the local police force."

"It's not law enforcement I'm worried about," Early said. "With the hag missing, Lost Falls is vulnerable. If the witch-finders detect this curse, who is going to keep them away?"

A hush fell over the room. Everyone here had something to fear from the witch-finders. They were no kinder to Strangers than they were to witches and sorcerers.

"So what's the worst case scenario?" the charm-seller said after a moment of silence.

Early's eyes clouded. He stroked his beard, thinking. "I recall an old story from the time of the witch hunts. A small, isolated community had fallen on hard times. Crops were failing, and no reason could be found. Livestock began to die in the night, the meat rotten by morning. The townspeople watched their children grow thin. Whispers of witchcraft began to spread, and panic gripped the town.

"Suspicion fell on a young woman, a farmer's daughter, who had a reputation for being free with her affections. As the town grew hungrier and hungrier, they turned on her. Accused her of being a witch. A posse formed one night and surrounded the house, threatening to burn the place down. In the end, it was the girl's own father who handed her over to the crowd to be hanged.

"The crops recovered, and the livestock stopped dying. The townsfolk congratulated themselves, thinking they'd killed the witch and ended their troubles. But the girl wasn't the witch. It was her lover, the blacksmith's apprentice. And when the town killed that girl, the boy found a new target for his fury.

"At first there were disappearances. A wandering wise woman vanished between one appointment and the next. A young maiden, the same age as the woman who'd been executed, was taken from her bed. Strange howls came from the woods at night, and the dismembered corpses of unnatural beasts began to appear around the town.

"The blacksmith's apprentice was preparing a curse. A black curse, powered by pain and flesh. A curse that would give him the vengeance he craved." Early paused. "It was a tax collector who found the bodies a few days later. They were lined up in rows in the town square. Hundreds of them. The whole town. Men, women, children. Just lying in the mud, eyes closed as if they were sleeping. Except for one person: the father of that young woman who'd been hanged. He'd been nailed to a tree by his wrists, his chest cracked open and his heart carved out. There were crows about, and dogs, but none of the animals would go near the bodies. They could smell the stink of witchcraft on them." Early looked around. "That's the kind of curse I think we're dealing with here."

He let silence fill the room. Lilian let out a low whistle. No one else made a sound.

"If Osric and I are right," Early said, staring out at the room, "if someone really is trying to work a curse of that magnitude, then the events of the last few days could affect everyone in this room. This community, this whole town could be at risk. Until we have answers, we have to be cautious."

"Wait a minute," the charm-seller said. "Let's not get stupid. No witch within five hundred miles could work magic like that."

"The hag could," Lilian said quietly.

That shut everyone up. The ghoul in the corner had run out of fingernails to chew on and had moved onto her toes. Even Isaac wasn't looking so sure of himself.

If the hag had turned on us, we were in big trouble.

Early turned to the charm-seller. "You have friends among the witches, don't you?"

"Friends?" The charm-seller looked like he was about to spit on the floor, but he caught Early's eye and stopped himself. "I wouldn't call them that."

"We need to find out what they know. Can you do that?"

The charm-seller hesitated, frowned, then nodded. "Fine. I'll see what I can do. But I want it noted I still think this whole thing is bullshit."

"Treating with the witches, cunning man?" Isaac said. "It's not like you to deal with the devil."

"We all have to, sometime or other," Early said quietly. He clicked his fingers at the ghoul in the corner. She jumped, pulling her toes away from her mouth. "We also need feet on the ground, gathering information from the community. Can you round up your brothers and sisters, get the word out about what's going on?"

The ghoul scratched her head nervously. "Ah, um, yeah, yeah, okay. I'll try."

"Good." Early nodded. "See if anyone has any information about the hag's whereabouts. And listen out for anything else that seems strange."

"Yeah." The ghoul was nodding enthusiastically now. "Yeah. I can do that."

"I'll search my notes," Alcaraz said. "I can pass along everything I know about the use of hobgoblins and roggenwolves in spells."

"Good." Early stroked his beard. "We need to find out what this curse is. It might give us a clue about who is responsible."

Isaac stood. "If it is the will of the conclave, I believe my mistress may be able to assist. Miss Lockhart has the most extensive library of the arcane in this town. She doesn't possess the hag's knowledge, but the answer to your question is almost certainly somewhere within her archives."

Early's face remained neutral, but I knew him well enough to see he was uncomfortable seeking the aid of the vampires. But I guess we didn't have much choice. "All right. I'd like Ozzy to be the one searching the archives."

"What?" I said. "No way. I've got other things to do."

"Your apprentice's presence won't be necessary," Isaac said. "We can find the information ourselves."

"Ozzy," Early said. "We all need to—"

"No." I stepped in close, lowering my voice so the rest of the conclave wouldn't hear. "I'm sorry, Early, but no. I came here, I talked to your conclave. I did things your way. But I already have something I need to do. The Mills kid could still be alive. I need to find whoever took the boy. Whoever used me. And we both know where I'm going to find them."

The old man held my gaze, frowning as he studied my face. I set my jaw. I wasn't backing down. Not this time.

Without answering me, he turned to Isaac. "I'll be in touch with your mistress soon. Start your search." He looked around the room. "Are we all clear on what we're doing? Yes? Then let's get to it. We can't afford to waste any time."

Murmuring quietly, the ragtag conclave began to disperse. The ghoul was the first to dart off, with Isaac swanning along behind. Lilian shot me a questioning look on the way past, but I ignored her, and she was shooed on by Alcaraz before she could ask any questions.

I heard the front door creak shut, and then a couple of vehicles starting outside. Silence returned to the house.

And then Early and I were alone.

20

"I know you're angry," Early said to me.

"I'm way past angry."

"But I think you're making a mistake. You pulled yourself out of this hole once before. I don't want you falling back in."

I turned away, stared into the empty fireplace. "You've got to do things your way. The cunning man's way. I get that. And I think you're right, we're going to need help to get to the bottom of this. But I'm not going to go sit in a vampire's library and page through dusty old books. I can't, Early. Not when I know what I need to do."

"And exactly what is it you think you need to do?" he said.

"You already know the answer."

"Tell me anyway."

I spun back to face him. "Who do you think stole the Mills boy, Early? Huh?"

"Ozzy—"

"It was a goblin, Early. It has to be."

He frowned. "Or maybe that's what you want it to be."

I couldn't believe what I was hearing. "Drop the wise man act, for one goddamn minute. We're looking for a creature capable of replacing a baby with a convincing replica. We're looking for a creature conniving enough to use the boy to blackmail his father. It's a goblin, Early. It has to be. I'm going back to the Mines."

I turned to leave, but Early didn't let go of an argument that easily. "Goblins can't work curses like the kind we're talking about."

"Then maybe we're wrong about that. Or maybe someone else is involved as well. I don't know, and I don't much care. You're this community's wise man. You have to protect them. I understand that. And I know you want to protect me. But it's too late for that. I'm not like you, Early."

He paused, his eyes hard above the gray of his beard. "So you've made your decision then? About whether or not you want to be a cunning man."

"Looks like it."

"Is this really all it takes? One changeling child brings back memories of your brother, and all of a sudden you're donning your witch's cloak and turning a man into a puppet?"

My hands tightened into fists. "He killed me!" I shouted. "He killed me, Early, do you understand that? He shot me dead. I did everything you said. I gave it all up. I became a good person. I did it for you, and for Alice, and the twins. I did it because I missed the start of those boys' lives, and I wanted to be around for the rest of them. I wanted them to be proud of me. I wanted *you* to be proud of me."

I stomped about the room, the vials in my coat rattling with every step.

"And for what?" I said. "I was good, I wanted to help, and I got killed for it. I lost Teddy a long time ago. And now I'm going to lose everything else. Can you at least try to understand that? Can you try to understand why I have to do this? I have one day left, that's all, and I'm going to spend it well. I'm going to find that boy, it he's still alive. And then I'm going to get my revenge." I dug my nails into my palms. "I'm going back to the Mines. I'm going to find out which bastard goblin is responsible for all this. I'm going to drag him out of his hole. And I'm going to make him answer for what he—"

I stopped, my jaw slamming shut with a click. Lilian was leaning against the sitting room doorway, arms folded across her chest as she studied me. I couldn't read the expression on her face.

"I thought you'd gone," I said to her after a few seconds. It was the only thing I could come up with.

"I heard shouting."

Hell. How much had she heard? I didn't want anyone's pity. But the look she was giving me wasn't pity. I couldn't work out what it was.

"You're going to the Mines?" she asked.

I glanced at Early, then nodded. "Yeah."

"I'll come with you."

"What?" I said.

"What?" Early echoed.

"I want to help find the hag," she said. "I...I need to. If we don't find her, I'll have to leave Lost Falls."

I frowned. "What? Why?"

"I just will, okay? Things will be very bad for me if we don't find her. I trust your instincts. If the hag is connected to all this, maybe we'll find some clue in the Mines. Besides, you'll need someone watching your back."

I scratched my head. I hadn't been planning on this. Last time I'd gone to the Mines, I'd done it alone. It hadn't even occurred to me that anyone might want to help.

But maybe she was right. Maybe I did need someone watching my back. Maybe I needed someone along to keep me level.

"It'll be dangerous," I said.

"No shit."

I shot Early another look. His face was a mask again. I shrugged. "I'll be glad for the company."

"Good," she said with a nod. And that was settled.

Or so I thought.

"This is all pointless," Early said. "You won't be able to get into the Mines."

"I did before," I said.

"The goblins have tightened their wards since the unrest. They've become even more afraid of outsiders."

He gave me a hard look at that, which wasn't entirely unwarranted, I suppose. When I'd gone to the Mines before, all I'd wanted was to get Teddy back. But my actions had stirred up the whole damn wasps' nest.

"How do you know?" I said.

"I talk to people."

"Well, I'll find a way in. Every ward-net has holes."

"Maybe." He sighed and glanced at the door behind him, as if coming to a decision. "Are you sure you have to do this, Ozzy?"

"I am."

He nodded grimly. "Will you do one thing for me?"

"What?"

"Remember what I've tried to teach you."

Something sat heavy in my chest. I nodded slowly. "Of course."

His face was still troubled, but he seemed resigned to my decision now. He glanced at the door again, then held up a hand. "Wait here a second."

Without explanation, he left the room, closing the door behind him. I stared after him in confusion for a moment, before shooting Lilian a look.

"What was that about?" she asked.

"I have no idea." I cleared my throat. "So...uh...how long were you standing there?"

"Quite a while," she said. "Surprised it took you so long to see me."

"I was distracted," I said.

"So I gathered." She pushed off the doorway with her hip,

crossed the room, and pressed her fingers to my throat.

"Uh...what are you doing?" I tried to lean away, but she grabbed me and held me still.

"You still have a pulse," she said.

"Yeah."

"Then you're not dead yet."

I shook my head. "You don't understand. At midnight tomorrow—"

She put her hands on either side of my skull and pressed tight. Her eyes burned. "You'll know when you're dead, Ozzy. Until then, you're alive. And you better act like it. Understand?"

"Not really." I'd obviously touched a nerve, but I had no idea how.

She set her jaw, her hands tightening on my skull. For a fleeting moment I was afraid she was going to try to snap my neck.

Something cold washed over me, like I'd been dunked in ice water. Black dread filled my chest.

Terror beyond reason. It obliterated my vision, shut out thought. I opened my mouth to scream.

And then it was gone. I staggered back, collapsing into the armchair Alcaraz had vacated. I gasped for breath, felt the delicious warmth of life spread through my bones once again. I nearly wept.

"What...what was that?" I croaked, rubbing my skull. I looked up at Lilian. "What *are* you?"

She waggled her finger at me. "We still have a bet, don't we?" She leaned over me, gripping the arms of the chair. "Life feels a hell of a lot better, doesn't it? Don't let it go lightly. Fight for it. Fight for it with everything you have."

"All right, all right," I said. "Jesus."

"You don't need another demonstration?" She reached for my temple again, and I flinched away.

"I get the picture."

"Good."

She held out her hand to me. I hesitated, then took it gingerly. Nothing happened this time. All I could feel was her soft, warm flesh in my palm.

She hauled me to my feet and held me until I stopped swaying. I looked into her eyes.

"You scare the hell out of me, you know that?" I said.

She just grinned.

I took a few breaths, letting the warmth creep back into my toes. I felt reinvigorated. I felt alive.

She was right. I wasn't dead yet. I still had the transfer clause. My one slim chance of escaping my debt. And if I couldn't use it, well, I was going to fight for every breath just the same.

I opened my mouth to ask her what she'd done to me, but just then I heard a raised voice from down the hall.

"You hear that?" I asked Lilian.

She nodded. "Sounds like an argument."

I hadn't been able to make out the words, but it had been Rhodes' voice I'd heard. Curious, I crept to the sitting room door and eased it open.

The voices had gone quiet again, but I could still hear them arguing in hushed tones. They were somewhere down the hall, near the back door. Another voice—Early's—said something I didn't catch, but I could just make out Rhodes' response.

"This is a bad idea."

Again Early's words were too quiet for me to make out. I started to creep down the hallway, trying to get closer.

"You shouldn't be eavesdropping," Lilian whispered.

I glanced back at her. "Chicken?"

She scowled and followed silently behind me.

"It's too dangerous," Rhodes said. "I can't go back. If they catch me—"

"I know. I know." Early was using his patient, understanding voice. Rhodes seemed to find it as infuriating as I did. He grunted in frustration.

"The hag is missing. You know what that means. Once I change, I can't reverse it. You're asking me to give all this up."

"For a while. We don't know the hag is gone for good."

"And if she is?"

"We'll figure out an alternative," Early said.

I moved silently closer, avoiding the creaky floorboards. I sidled up to the open back door. I could see Rhodes on the back porch, facing the river. Early stood behind him, palms upturned in supplication.

"He won't be able to do it without you," Early said.

Rhodes hung his head. "I want to help. You know that. But I don't trust him. I can't. Not after what he did."

"He's changed."

"Has he?"

Early sighed and leaned against the railing next to Rhodes. "This is a big sacrifice. I can't make you do it. But you know you can't hide here forever. You can't hide who you are. Sooner or later, you have to face that. You have to face what you left behind."

"You're insufferable," Rhodes said.

"So I've been told."

Muttering something to himself, Rhodes dug a small vial out of his pocket. The thin milky liquid inside shone in the moonlight. Didn't look like any concoction I knew of, and the vial itself was nothing like the ones Early and I used. This one looked old, the glass uneven, as if it'd been hand-blown.

I watched as Rhodes pulled the cork out with his teeth and spat it over the side of the porch. He held the vial to his lips, hesitating.

"I only had a few days left anyway," he said, like he was trying to convince himself of something.

Then, shoulders stiffening, he threw back the vial, drinking its contents.

Behind me, Lilian made a noise. "Was that...?"

I glanced at her. She was peering out the window as well, frowning.

"What?" I said.

Her eyes widened. "Oh, shit," she whispered.

A sound like bones cracking came from the porch. I followed Lilian's stare.

Rhodes was hunched over, hands clenched on the porch railing. His face was turned away from me, but I could see his tensed muscles. He groaned as another series of pops and cracks rang out.

I didn't know what the hell I was looking at. Was he hurt? Early put a hand on his shoulder to comfort him, but Rhodes lashed out, growling and shoving him back.

"Hey!" I shouted. Lilian grabbed at my arm and tried to pull me back into the hallway, but I was already through the door, catching Early before he could fall. "What the hell are you doing?"

Rhodes snarled. He glanced at me and then covered his face, turning away.

But not before I saw the bones of his skull shifting beneath his skin.

"Ozzy!" Early looked shocked to see me. He brushed away my hand. "I'll explain in a minute. Please, just wait inside."

I ignored him. Rhodes staggered to the far end of the porch, and I followed. His clothes seemed to grow looser on him as I watched. There was another loud *crack* and he grunted, grabbing at the corner post. His fingers had grown longer, thinner, and his skin had taken on a worn texture, like tree bark.

"Rhodes," I said. "Look at me."

"Fuck off!" he snapped. His voice had become harsh and guttural.

"Look at me!"

Hands grabbed at my shoulders. "Let's go back inside,"

Lilian said. She tried to pull me back, but she couldn't move me.

"Rhodes!" I yelled.

There was one last *pop*, and finally the transformation was complete. Panting, Rhodes slumped to the floor, his back to me. The sharp points of his vertebrae poked against the fabric of his now-loose shirt.

"Look at me, Rhodes," I said.

Slowly, Rhodes turned toward me. Except he wasn't Rhodes anymore.

He stared at me with eyes that had grown large and sunken. They shone yellow in the moonlight. The rest of his face was narrow and pointed, cheekbones unnaturally high. His ears rose to points and a long crooked nose drooped from the center of his face. He peeled back his lips, revealing pointed yellow teeth.

My hands curled into fists.

"Goblin," I growled.

21

I advanced on the goblin, fists clenched at my side. He hissed and dropped into a crouch, lean muscles coiling beneath his green-gray skin.

"Stop!" Early roared.

The force of his voice stopped me in my tracks, but I didn't turn my back on the goblin that'd once been Rhodes. It took all my willpower not to throw myself at the creature.

I knew this goblin personally.

Early stepped between us and stuck a finger in my face. "Ozzy, don't."

I licked my lips, staring at the goblin over Early's shoulder. "You knew? You knew this whole time?"

"Yes," Early said.

My blood pounded in my temples. "He's been living a hundred yards away from me for more than a year, and you knew? You let him?"

"Yes."

I let out a roar of frustration at the calm in his voice. Behind Early, the goblin eyed me warily. The bastard was as ready for a fight as I was.

A trickle of deglamouring potion still trailed from the corner of the creature's mouth. Glamours—potions that allowed someone to change their form—were way above Early's pay grade. The hag must have been supplying the creature with the potion to disguise his true nature. And more than likely, Early had been paying through the nose for it, since I doubted the goblin had the funds to spare.

"Rhodes," I said, seeing the name in new light. "Cute. Real cute."

Lilian came up behind me. She took my arm again, and this time she really dug her fingernails in. "Ozzy, what the hell are you doing? So he's a goblin. So what?"

I laughed bitterly. "He's not just a goblin. Are you?" I said to him. "Are you?!"

He hissed again, backing away. I ran into Early's open palm and realized I'd taken another step forward.

"This little bastard's name isn't Rhodes," I said. "It's Rodetk. He spent two years trying to kill me. All to defend the goblins who took my brother!"

I shouted the last few words, unable to control myself any longer. I tried to shove past Early, but the old man was surprisingly stubborn, and with Lilian clinging to my arm I couldn't get my balance.

"I told you this was a bad idea!" the goblin said, jumping nimbly up onto the porch railing.

"Osric!" Early said. "Be calm."

"Calm? I'm calm, Early. I'm very calm. You can watch while I calmly throttle this little fuck."

"You're not going to hurt him. You're not that person anymore."

I scowled, but I stayed where I was. Damn him.

"Explain, Early," I said. "Explain quickly."

"He's not going to harm you. He left the Mines."

"Why?"

"That's his story to tell, not mine," Early said. "I found him, gave him amnesty. I helped him arrange the glamour. I helped him get back on his feet. Just like I did for you, Ozzy."

I glared at Rodetk. How could Early talk like this? Like

I was somehow comparable with this creature. I went to the Mines to try to get Teddy back. I didn't start this.

The goblin's thin black hair hung down below his ears, but it didn't cover the scar tissue across his cheek. A scar that I'd given him. I resisted the urge to rub my left forearm, where he'd once sunk his teeth into me.

"He wants to help," Early said.

"Good for him."

"He can get you into the Mines."

"What?" I glanced at Early, then turned my glare back to the goblin. "No. No way. I can find my own damn way in. He's not coming with me."

"Fool," Rodetk spat. "They'll catch you in five minutes."

"I'll take my chances." I looked at Early. "He'll sell me out the instant he gets the chance. Or maybe he'll just kill me himself."

"If I wanted you dead, I would've done it long ago," the goblin said, and he gave me a vicious grin. "I know where the gardening tools are kept."

"That's enough!" Early said. "Both of you. You're on the same side now, whether you like it or not." He looked at me. "You want to get into the Mines?"

"Yes, but—"

"You want your revenge?"

"I—"

"You want to find the Mills boy, if he's still alive?"

"Of course I do," I said through gritted teeth.

"Then you need to take whatever help you can get." Early turned to Rodetk. "You're still willing to help?"

The goblin let out a low hiss, then nodded. "Yes. But not for him."

"That's good enough." Early gave me a look. "Ozzy?"

I ran my tongue along the points of my teeth. This was madness. Bad enough trusting a goblin, but *this* goblin?

"You know he hunted me, right?" I said to Early. "Did he tell you that?"

"I told him everything," the goblin snapped. "I told him I did my duty."

"And what the hell does a goblin know about duty?"

Rodetk bared his teeth and snarled.

"Ozzy," Early said. "I trust him."

I met the old man's eyes. They were hard, steady.

"He's not who he used to be," Early said. "Neither are you."

I hesitated.

"Come on, Ozzy," Lilian said. "Don't be a jackass. We need him."

I sighed. "All right, fine. But if he stabs me in the back, I want you all to remember I told you this was a bad idea."

"If I stab you," Rodetk said, "it won't be in the back." He jumped down from the porch railing. "We'll be taking the boat upriver. We leave at dawn."

He pushed past me, heading back inside. I stared at his back until he disappeared from sight.

Early laid a hand on my shoulder. "This is as hard for him as it is for you. Go easy on him. He really is trying to help."

I just grunted.

"Alcaraz is waiting in the car," Lilian said. "I better take her home before she tears my head off. She is not going to be happy when I tell her what I'm doing tomorrow." She paused. "See you at dawn, then?"

I nodded. "Pack light."

She said goodbye, shared a look with Early, and went off to drive Alcaraz home. I turned away from Early and slowly unclenched my fists.

"You should get some sleep while you can," Early said. "I'll head to Miss Lockhart's library in the morning and see if I can shed any light on the nature of this curse. We have two possible ingredients at least: eye of roggenwolf and flesh of hobgoblin."

He paused. "And changeling as well, maybe."

"And silver," I said. "The hobgoblin mentioned silver."

"With any luck, we'll have an answer by the time you get back from the Mines."

"Uh-huh."

I started down the porch steps, heading back to my cabin. My shoes crunched softly on the grass. Exhaustion pulled at my bones, but somehow I doubted I'd be getting much sleep tonight.

"Ozzy," Early called. I paused and looked back. "Rodetk is a lot like you, you know."

"Yeah," I said. "That's what I'm afraid of."

22

I eased open the door of the boathouse to find I wasn't the first one to arrive. Rodetk was lit by an electric lantern that hung from a nail on the wall. He paused at the sound of the creaking door, a red plastic fuel tank in his hands.

He was covered from head to toe: gloves on his hands, a hoodie covering his long ears and stringy hair, a bandanna across his face, and a pair of dark glasses over his eyes. But he couldn't do much to hide his long thin limbs and the slight inhuman hunch to his back.

I closed the boathouse door behind me, shutting out the pre-dawn light. For a moment, the two of us just stared at each other as the river lapped at the boathouse's foundations.

Rodetk was the first to turn away. He clambered into the dinghy and fitted the fuel tank to the outboard motor. I carried my backpack over and laid it next to the boat ramp.

"They still use you to scare goblin children," Rodetk said as he prepared the dinghy. "Work hard, do what you're told, or the *Natiz-Tuk* will get you." He raised his head, but I couldn't see his eyes behind his dark glasses. "The witch in the shadows. If you're bad, he'll come for you. He'll boil your blood, carve out your spleen, and grind your bones to dust for his spells."

"Sounds like I need a new publicist," I said.

He grunted. Climbing out of the boat again, he fetched a small pack he'd left lying in the shadows below the electric lantern. By the look of it, he was taking even less than me. Guess he didn't plan on being there long.

I had a change of clothes and a little food in my backpack—most of the food you can find in the Mines is intended for goblins, and I'd had my fill of that four years ago.

Everything else of importance I had on me. I was still wearing my coat loaded with vials and charms and fetishes. If this went bad, I wanted as much protection as possible.

My truncheon of silver and iron and wood hung from my belt, and in my right coat pocket was the revolver the Dealer had given me. I'd brought the Dealer's spirit bottle with me as well, though I figured if I needed to open that, we were already way past screwed.

"So what's this plan of yours for getting into the Mines?" I said.

"There's an old mine shaft on the west side of the mountain," Rodetk said. "It caved in about eighty years ago, so it was never properly warded. It was cleared out by smugglers. That's how I got out of the Mines. It's how we'll get back in."

"Since when was it so hard to get into the Mines?"

"Since the sorcerer came." He threw his pack into the dinghy with unnecessary force. "Khataz's paranoia is worse than ever now. He doesn't want anyone going in or out of the mountain without his knowledge."

Khataz was the ruler of the Mines, the Lord of the Deep. But I didn't know about any sorcerer. There were always a few goblins who dabbled in dark magic—including the leader of the mob who'd stolen Teddy away. The way Rodetk had said it, though, this was something different.

"What sorcerer? What are you talking about?"

"The sorcerer you brought down on us."

"Me?"

Rodetk pointed a long gloved finger at me. "You. It was your black magic that killed the boss of the Snatchers. He choked to death in front of his people. We couldn't keep that secret. The witch in the shadows was no longer just a rumor."

"So?"

He lifted his balaclava and spat. "So Khataz got scared. Decided to put his trust in a foreign sorcerer. After that the Guard was disbanded. Things just got worse from there. That's why I had to leave. You're the reason I had to leave my home."

I shrugged. "You never needed to get involved."

"You were hunting goblins," he snapped. "Like a monster in the dark. I was Lieutenant of the Guard. It was my duty to stop you."

I scowled. "You were protecting the goblins who took my brother."

"I was protecting my home! I knew nothing about any changelings. I knew nothing about any of it!"

The boathouse door creaked open. Rodetk and I spun at the sound, cutting our argument short.

Lilian slipped inside, carrying a small duffel bag and wearing the same clothes she'd been in last night. She gave each of us a hard stare.

"I could hear the two of you from outside," she said. "Maybe you shouldn't be yelling about changelings for all to hear."

Rodetk turned away from me. "You're late," he said to Lilian.

"Alcaraz had me out all night," she said. "I've been busy setting traps in the forest, trying to recover our missing roggenwolf."

She looked remarkably well-rested for being awake all night. Unnaturally so. I filed that little tidbit of information away. Chances were I wouldn't live to find out what she was, but old habits are hard to break.

"Find any sign of it?" I asked.

She shook her head. "Poor beast is almost certainly dead by now."

"Your pity is misplaced," Rodetk said while he unlocked the

chain holding the dinghy in place. "Roggenwolves are dangerous beasts. Hunters of the weak. Whatever pain it suffered, it has inflicted worse."

"Even so," Lilian said.

I thought about the kind of person who'd be capable of separating a roggenwolf from its eyes. Someone clever, cold-blooded.

I knew a few goblins who fit the bill.

"Are you two just going to stand there?" Rodetk said. "Or are you going to help me get this boat in the water? We've got a long way to go yet."

The dinghy and the boathouse belonged to a friend of Early's who had a house about a mile upriver. The guy knew we were taking the boat, but not why. We got out on the water before he could wander by and ask any awkward questions.

I was a little concerned by how low the dinghy rode. There was water in the bottom of the boat, sloshing about our feet. Every few minutes I did a quick check to make sure it wasn't getting any deeper.

"Afraid of getting a little wet?" Rodetk scoffed, his hand on the motor.

"I just know what lurks in this river," I said.

Lilian nodded her agreement. "Vodyanoys."

"And rusalki," I said.

"A kelpie hunts near here as well."

"More than one."

Rodetk stared at us for a moment from behind his dark glasses, trying to tell if we were joking. He shuffled away from the side of the boat and cast a wary eye at the water flowing past.

The whine of the outboard motor accompanied us as we powered upriver. The water was murky and thick with algae. An early-morning fog hung over the river, at times nearly completely obscuring the shore. This was why Rodetk wanted to leave at dawn, I guessed. With the fog hiding us, neither human nor goblin would notice us.

This far upriver we had the river almost to ourselves. Only once did we pass another boat: an old man in a wooden rowboat drifting slowly downriver. He was dressed in a blue coat, with a broad-brimmed hat hanging low over his eyes. His lips split in a wide smile as we passed.

I felt a prickle on the back of my neck. Something told me he wasn't entirely human. All three of us grew silent and kept our eyes on him until he disappeared back into the fog.

You can never be too careful.

After another fifteen minutes, Rodetk steered us toward a small tributary whose entrance was overgrown with the dangling fingers of a willow tree. We all ducked as we passed through, but a few dew-covered leaves still slid along the back of my neck.

With the forest pressing in closer now, the air seemed thicker, the fog clinging tighter. The sun had broken the horizon, but it couldn't penetrate the canopy here.

Birds fluttered and sang but fell silent as we passed. Now that we were well away from town, Rodetk finally removed his dark glasses and pulled down his bandanna.

"Not far now," he said. "We'll bring the boat ashore and travel the rest of the way on foot."

I nodded, looking up at the mountain before us. The thick forest reached right to the summit, an endless wall of green and brown. There was nothing to indicate that the mountain's interior was crisscrossed with mine shafts. The gold had dried up in these hills nearly a century back, and the forest had retaken the dirt roads and railroads and mining settlements that'd littered the land.

"You're sure you can get us inside?" I said to Rodetk.

"I haven't been back in a year," he said. "I'm not sure of anything. I can take us to the only hole in the wards that I know of. That's all I can promise."

It would have to do. There were answers somewhere inside the mountain. I was sure of it.

"All right," I said. "Once we're inside, we'll have to act fast. Unfamiliar human faces will get noticed. We get the lay of the land, ask around, find out what we need to know. We're looking for any information about kidnapped hobgoblins or changeling children."

"And if we find out that the changeling boy is alive?" Lilian said quietly. "If we find out he's there?"

I paused. "We improvise."

Rodetk grunted. "The man with the plan," he muttered.

We traveled in silence another few minutes, then Lilian spoke again.

"Oh, I almost forgot," she said. "Alcaraz has been making progress on identifying the creature you found."

So much had happened in the last few days, it took me a moment to work out what she was talking about.

"You mean Lawrence?"

"What?" she said.

"That's what I called him."

She raised an eyebrow.

I cleared my throat. "So what is he?"

"Alcaraz still isn't entirely sure. It's been hard to figure out without the hag's scrying potions. But she found a couple of references to similar creatures in an old reference book. And apparently there's an interesting scar on the creature's abdomen that she says is almost certainly made by—"

"Quiet," Rodetk hissed as we rounded a bend in the river. "Silence from now on. Khataz and his sorcerer have patrols in the area."

He cut the engine and we drifted toward the riverbank. As soon as we felt the dinghy's bottom scrape the mud, Rodetk leapt overboard and started dragging the boat further ashore.

With some reluctance, I lowered myself into the shallow water as well and trooped through the mud to help him get the boat out of the water. This was just how I wanted to be spending my last day on Earth: in the company of a goblin who'd once tried to kill me, and with wet socks to boot.

We dragged the boat a few yards onto the bank, hiding it in the shelter of a gnarled, drooping tree. While Lilian grabbed our stuff, Rodetk and I found a few fallen branches and covered the dinghy as best we could.

Pressing his finger to his lips, the goblin gestured for us to follow. The fog was burning off rapidly as the sun rose higher. For a couple of minutes we trudged along, following the riverbank upstream. Part of me began to wonder if Rodetk even knew where he was going.

Another thought stuck in my head. This could all be some goblin trick. Lure us out here. Maybe lead us right into an ambush. Maybe we'd never even make it inside the Mines.

I studied Rodetk's hunched back as he crept through the forest ahead of us. His motives were hard to fathom. Goblins were crafty, and they had long memories. And Rodetk was more cunning than most.

He'd only been a lieutenant in the Lord's Guard when he'd hunted me through the twisting caverns of the Mines, but it had soon become clear he was the brains of the operation. The only time I'd nearly been caught by the Guard was when I'd fallen into a trap Rodetk had laid.

Was this another trap?

Early trusts him, I thought. But Early was only a man. He could make mistakes.

Rodetk threw up a hand. We all stopped. We stood rock solid for a few seconds, the only sounds the rustling of trees and the beat of my heart. I watched the goblin as he scanned the terrain, and I let my hand drop to touch the revolver in my coat pocket.

If he betrayed us, he wouldn't live to enjoy it.

Finally, he turned and jerked his head at us. Lilian and I exchanged a glance and crept forward to where he was standing.

We were on the outskirts of what had once been a small village. Dilapidated wooden buildings that were little more than shacks were clustered around what had once been a single main road. The remains of an abandoned horse-drawn cart sat in the middle of the road, overgrown with grass and moss. One of the buildings had a sign hanging loose over the entrance, but the sun had long since bleached it clean. I caught a glimpse of the river through a gap in the trees. There'd once been a jetty here, but all that was left were a few rotten posts sticking out of the water.

This was an old mining village. The hills were dotted with small abandoned settlements like this. A few of them were now home to opportunistic others: imps and fiends and even the odd troll.

This place looked uninhabited though, and probably with good reason: most Strangers wouldn't settle this close to the Mines, for fear of being hunted by any goblins that ventured aboveground.

Rodetk crooked a finger at us. We huddled together, our heads nearly butting.

"This road leads to the mine shaft entrance," he breathed, pointing. Calling it a road seemed a little generous to me. Ten yards out from the village, the forest swallowed the trail completely.

"We can follow it up," the goblin said, "but we'll stay off the road itself. We don't want to run into any smugglers."

"Or Khataz's men," I said, and Rodetk nodded.

"Lead on," Lilian said.

The goblin circled back into the forest, the two of us a few steps behind. Lilian and I had to fight through the underbrush, getting snagged on every branch and thorn bush, but Rodetk moved as swiftly and easily as if he were taking a stroll down Main Street. I blamed my size. If I were a skinny runt like him, I wouldn't have a problem either.

It didn't get any easier to see the road once we were back in the forest, but the goblin seemed to know where he was going. Soon the land began to rise and we found ourselves trudging uphill, which only added to the misery of wet shoes and a forest that seemed intent on swallowing us whole.

We were silent as we walked—or as silent as we could be, panting and fighting through the forest as we were. If there was anyone else on the mountain, I didn't hear or see them.

Every now and then Rodetk would gesture for us to stop while he looked around warily. I took the opportunity to catch my breath and have a drink. Maybe it was unkind of me, but I would have been a lot happier if Lilian was struggling a little more. I mean, she hadn't slept all night. Where did she get her energy?

As we climbed higher, the forest started to thin out a little. I guess it had grown tired scaling the mountain as well. With our path clearer now, Rodetk picked up the pace.

Until finally the goblin came to a stop once more. At first I thought it was just another momentary pause, but then Rodetk hissed and pointed at the hillside in front of us.

It took me a moment to make out the mine shaft's entrance. It was well camouflaged with thick overgrowth. Instead of wooden beams, the entrance was formed by the exposed root structure of a tree further up the steep hillside.

Lilian crouched beside me and scanned the forest. "No sentries."

"Khataz doesn't know this hole exists," Rodetk whispered. "He trusts his sorcerer's wards to control comings and goings in the Mines." He glanced around once more, then gestured for us to follow. "Come."

"Wait," I said, reaching into one of my inner coat pockets.

It'd been a long time since I'd worn the coat, but it was like a second skin to me. I could still remember where everything was kept. I pulled out a small stick talisman shaped like a person and tied with kikimora hair. A glass marble hung in the center of the stick man's chest.

Rodetk drew back a little, eying the talisman warily. "What is that?"

"It reacts to wards. Witch bottles, charms, curse traps, anything that restricts passage. I want to be sure."

I glanced around once more, then crept out of the cover of the underbrush, holding the talisman out. As I moved toward the mine shaft, I moved the talisman in a wide semi-circle in front of me. The marble in the center remained still.

I edged right up to the mine shaft entrance and peered inside. It sloped down a few feet, but beyond that was pitch blackness. A faint smell wafted out, stale air and something else, something living. It brought me back, back four years, back to the dark of the tunnels and the thrill of the hunt and the fear and rage and desperation that had once powered me.

I wished it didn't feel so enticing.

I cast a glance over my shoulder and saw Rodetk and Lilian a few steps back, watching me. Holding my breath, I moved the talisman slowly through the entrance, ready to pull back at any moment. The marble didn't move. I reached in further. Nothing.

I exhaled. Rodetk was right after all. Tucking the talisman back into my pocket, I looked back at the others.

"It's clear," I whispered. Lilian looked relieved, but Rodetk just nodded. He joined me by the entrance.

"Stay close," he said as he entered. "You never know—"

A flame sparked to life inside the mine shaft, pushing back the dark. The orange light of a match flickered across a trio of weathered goblin faces. They grinned in unison, baring sharp teeth.

"Guests," the biggest of the three said. He raised a rifle and pointed it at Rodetk. "How lovely."

23

I thought about running.

The big goblin must've read my mind. He swung his rifle around and stuck it in my face. "Where d'ya think you're going, huh?"

I kept my mouth shut. Behind me, Lilian swore softly.

"Well, don't just stand there," the leader of the goblins said. "Come on in. Let's take a look at ya."

He backed off a few steps, his two cronies hunched and grinning beside him. Rodetk shot me a glance, then the three of us followed the flickering match light into the dark of the tunnel.

The ground was soft beneath my feet. Dirt and leaves and moss made the mine shaft entrance seem organic, some natural indentation in the land, but as we shuffled down the shaft I caught sight of rotting wooden beams supporting the ceiling. Rusted old lanterns sat about, dormant. The shaft was just wide enough for Rodetk and I to stand side-by-side, with Lilian behind us.

I studied the three goblins as best I could in the flickering light. They all wore a mix of human clothes and items either made from scratch or recycled from other garments. The leader, in particular, was looking pretty fancy. Once it had been through a spin cycle, the shirt he was wearing wouldn't be out of place at any office building in town.

All three had bare feet. I knew from experience that wouldn't be a disadvantage for them. Goblins were quick-footed little bastards.

I had no way of knowing if the rifle was actually loaded. It was a bolt-action, so if we rushed him he'd probably only be able to kill one of us.

I figured maybe there were better ways out of this predicament.

A few yards back, an alcove widened off the side of the mine shaft. A curtain made of a bed sheet was strung across the opening, and when one of the goblins swept it aside, I caught a glimpse of a little living area scattered with crates and boxes and lit with a series of candles. The goblins' match had almost burnt down to nothing, so he shook it out and gestured for us to follow into the candlelight.

"Listen—" I said, but the big goblin hissed at me to be silent. Wielding the rifle one-handed, he grabbed a candle holder and held the light up to Rodetk's face. He frowned.

"Don't I know you?" he said.

"Maybe," Rodetk said. "I used to work in the Lower Pits."

"Pit boy, huh? What ya doin' here, then? This place isn't for the likes of you." He jerked the rifle at me and Lilian. "And why you bringing humans here?"

"They're my trading partners."

"Yeah?" The big goblin eyed me up. "What're ya trading, then?"

"What's it look like?"

Rodetk reached over and jammed his hand in my pocket. All three goblins snarled and took a step back. But Rodetk just pulled out one of my vials, a concoction of heart's bane. He held it up to the light.

"This here's a sleeping draught," Rodetk said. "Powerful stuff. Couple of drops would put a river troll to sleep for a week. And this"—he put the heart's bane back and reached into one of my inner pockets, pulling out a silver flask—"well, you take a sip of this and you'll be able to go for days, if you know what I mean." He jerked his head toward the crotch of the smallest goblin. "Bet you could use some, huh?"

The other crony snickered at his friend, but the leader growled at them and they fell silent again. He narrowed his eyes, studying me.

"You sorcerers?" he said.

I went along with Rodetk's story. "Just a humble potion maker." I jerked my head at Lilian. "She handles the business end of things. I work my art."

"We got enough problems with sorcerers here already," the big goblin said.

"We're not here to cause trouble," Rodetk said. "All we want to do is help out the little guy. Make a little money on the side. And we want to do it quietly."

One of the cronies whispered something in the ear of the big goblin, but he just hissed and waved him back. For a few seconds he looked from Rodetk to me to Lilian and back.

I was doing my best to keep my face neutral, but inside my heart was hammering. He wasn't buying it. Swallowing, I slowly moved my hand toward the pocket that held my revolver.

"This ain't a bloody highway. We don't let just anyone haul their shit through here," the goblin said. "How'd you find our tunnel?"

"Big Nang told me about it," Rodetk said.

"Big Nang's dead."

"Wasn't always. Just like this wasn't always your tunnel."

"Well, it is now. And anyone wants to smuggle potions through our tunnel has to pay the tariff."

Rodetk scowled. "What's the point in smuggling if you still get taxed?"

"Because unlike Khataz, we won't just take all your shit for ourselves and throw you in the dungeons."

"For Christ's sake," Lilian said. "Let's just pay him and get going. We have an appointment to keep."

"Lady's got some sense," the big goblin said. He lowered his rifle. "We only take human cash."

"How's this?" A small wad of cash appeared in Lilian's hand. I didn't see where she pulled it from.

The eyes of the cronies widened. Even the leader hesitated, rubbing the point of his chin.

"Yeah, all right. That'll do, I guess."

Before she could change her mind, he reached out and snatched the money away. He glanced at it for a moment, then made it disappear as deftly as Lilian had made it appear.

"Tun," the goblin said to the smallest of the trio. He waved his hand. "Show them the way down. Make sure they don't get spotted by the Lord's people." He smiled at us, showing his pointed teeth. "Your meeting goes well, maybe we can do business again."

The little goblin snapped to attention, near beaming with pride. I hadn't noticed it at first, mainly because I'd been somewhat distracted by the rifle pointed at me, but the small goblin wasn't much more than a boy. He crooked his finger at us.

"This way, this way. Watch your step. Gets tricky down here."

He grabbed a rusted miner's lantern off a nail driven into a support beam, lit it with one of the candles, and bounded off into the dark. We hurried after him, leaving the other two goblins behind to count their cash and pat themselves on the back.

I let out a breath I hadn't realized I'd been holding. As we followed the glow of the lantern, I shot Rodetk a look.

"You didn't say anything about mobsters trying to hold us up," I hissed.

"They're not mobsters," he whispered. "And I didn't know

they'd taken hold here."

"That was quick thinking," Lilian said to him. "You did good."

"Thanks."

I grunted. We were damn lucky, that was all. I snatched the silver flask out of Rodetk's hand and waved it at him. "You shouldn't go touching things you don't understand. What if one of them had wanted a swig of magic Viagra?"

"Why, what is it really?" he asked.

I tucked it back into my pocket. "Witch's fire."

"Oh."

"Yeah. Oh."

Up ahead, Tun had paused with the lantern, waiting for us. "Careful," he said as we approached. "Two ways down, but I only recommend the one."

He held out the lantern, and I caught his meaning. We were at the top of a steep, narrow staircase carved out of the mountain itself. There was a wall of stone to the left. And on the right, nothing but a sheer drop down.

I didn't know how far down it went—the lantern's light didn't reach the bottom. I decided I wasn't in a hurry to find out.

Without waiting for a response, Tun started down the stone stairs. Swallowing, I followed.

"So you said you make potions, right?" Tun said over his shoulder.

"Uh-huh. Among other things." I kept my eyes on my feet and my hand on the left wall. The stone steps were smooth and a little damp, which wasn't making me any more confident.

"You...uh...you have anything to keep monsters away?"

"Depends. What kind of monster?"

"The Blind Beast."

"What?"

"You haven't heard?" he said. "You're lucky it didn't attack you on your way up. It's been haunting this here slope of the mountain for days now. One of the smugglers I know, she saw it herself two nights ago. Out there, on the mountain. A big black beast, like a shadow, she said, only it was the scariest shadow she'd ever seen. Teeth as long as your arm, but no eyes. That's what they say. She was near shitting herself when she came running in, screaming and wailing."

A black beast with no eyes. I didn't dare glance back at Lilian, but somehow I felt her stiffen behind me. *The roggenwolf.* It was still out there somewhere.

"Khataz put a bounty on the beast's head after it savaged one of his sentries," Tun continued. "They're sending out hunting parties. But I have to go out on the mountain tonight, and if they don't catch it…I could really use something to scare it away. If you've got anything like that."

He glanced back at me with wide pleading eyes. Sighing, I dug through my pockets until I found a round glass vial.

"If you see the beast," I said, handing him the vial, "throw this at its feet. And then run like hell."

He grinned with excitement. "How does it work?" He reached for the cork.

"Don't," I said, grabbing his hand before he could uncork the vial. "The fumes won't kill you, but you open that here and you'll be out cold in seconds. Along with the rest of us."

He glanced at me again, then gingerly tucked the vial into the folds of his shirt.

We were far enough down the staircase now that I couldn't see where it started, and I still had no idea where the bottom was. This couldn't be part of the original mine complex, but that wasn't surprising. The goblins had spent a century expanding the Mines far beyond the original shafts. I doubted any one person—human, goblin, or Stranger—knew all the paths that ran through the mountain.

"Who's this sorcerer your boss was talking about?" I asked

after a few more minutes descending into the darkness. "A human?"

Tun shook his head. "A goblin sorcerer. I've never seen him, but everyone knows he's more Lord than Khataz is now. Everyone hates him, but there's nothing we can do."

"Your boss called him a foreigner," I said.

"Yeah. I don't know where he's from, but it's nowhere around here. Got some foreign name. We just call him Likho. He's brought nothing but bad luck since he arrived." He looked at me, then shrugged, smiling sheepishly. "That's what everyone says, anyway."

Despite the minor terror of descending a staircase in the dark, excitement bubbled in my gut. It had to be the same sorcerer Rodetk had mentioned. The one Khataz had brought in to defend the mountain against witches like me.

If this sorcerer really did have Khataz in his thrall, he was skilled. Powerful. Powerful enough to work a curse like the one we were investigating?

I knew it'd been the right call to come to the Mines. Now all we had to do was find this sorcerer, figure out what he was doing, and put a stop to it.

I thought about turning around right then, going back to town, and gathering the troops. But I immediately scrapped the idea. I didn't have time for that. And anyway, we'd been lucky enough to get into the Mines once without drawing attention to ourselves. Getting in again, especially with more of us in tow, would be a lot more difficult.

And besides, who could I call on to help? Early, certainly, but if it came to a serious fight there wasn't a whole lot he could offer. Alcaraz would be less use than a wet rag. The vampires would almost certainly refuse to fight unless they were threatened directly, and the ghouls wouldn't be any different.

No, it was better we did this now and did it quiet, without a fight. We would find proof that this Likho was the one working this curse, the one pulling Mills' strings.

And then, when the time came, we'd strike. I'd teach this sorcerer what became of people who crossed me.

I'd done it before. I could do it again.

Early's voice was in my head, urging me not to go back down that road. And maybe I wouldn't have to. Maybe.

The end of the staircase came so suddenly I didn't even notice it. Suddenly, we were on flat ground again, and Tun was leading us into another tunnel cleverly hidden behind a door disguised to look like part of the wall. This tunnel was wider than before, and after a few more minutes it began to merge with other tunnels that split off in all directions.

Signs of life began to appear out of the dark: distant echoes of tools and machinery, the smell of something cooking. Lights and muffled laughter came from some of the side passages, but Tun lead us down one tunnel after another, avoiding all other goblins.

He looked back at us and put a long finger to his lips, and we nodded our understanding. I didn't know if we were avoiding spies or Khataz's people or if we were just navigating some other mob's territory, but I didn't ask.

And then, finally, we passed through a curtain and stepped onto a ledge overlooking a cavern bigger than any stadium I'd ever seen.

Lilian stopped beside me, drawing in a sharp breath at the sight of it.

I didn't know what was the most breathtaking aspect of the city beneath the mountain. Maybe it was the way it seemed to climb the walls of the cavern, buildings stacked on top of buildings, whole town blocks precariously jutting out on foundations carved from the mountain.

Maybe it was the thousands of lights that sparkled in every corner of the cavern. Some came from flames, but many more were electric: naked orange bulbs and flickering fluorescent strips and multicolored Christmas lights strung along walls and windowsills.

Or maybe it was the movement of it all: goblins hurrying here and there, climbing staircases and hurrying along stone bridges, like a hive of insects going about their business.

"There's so many," Lilian said in a low voice.

I nodded. I'd felt the same way the first time I'd laid eyes on the Mines. In truth, the population beneath the mountain was only a fraction of Lost Falls', but to see them all here, crammed into this space, living out their existence in the bowels of the mountain just a few miles outside of town, it was humbling, to say the least.

"I have to get back," Tun said. "Boss'll need me."

Rodetk nodded. "We'll find our way from here. Go safe."

"You too." The little goblin bobbed his head once more, patted the pocket where he'd stowed the vial I'd given him, then darted back the way we'd come.

Lilian was still staring slack-jawed at the city. If she wasn't careful, she was going to plunge over the edge of the outcropping and end up getting a closer look at the city than she wanted.

When Tun had disappeared back into the dark, Rodetk turned to me, exhaling. "I got you inside. Now what?"

I scratched my beard, thinking. "We need a source of information. Someone who knows what's going on here. Someone who can tell us about this sorcerer."

Rodetk cocked his head to the side, then nodded to himself. "I think I know just the goblin."

24

We threaded through alleys and passageways, sticking to the dark corners of the Mines. It wasn't hard. The maze of tunnels that ran through the mountain reached every corner of the city, as long as you knew how to navigate them.

These tunnels had been my home four years ago while I searched for the people who'd stolen Teddy. The lights here were few and far between, providing ample darkness to hide those who didn't want to be found.

That included us. Lilian and I weren't the only human faces in the city—there were even a few human families who'd lived down here for more than a generation, their ancestors snatched from the surface in decades past. But we were clearly surface-dwellers, which meant we'd be noticed if we stuck to the main walkways. Hawkers would try to part us from our cash, while Khataz's people would undoubtedly want to get a little more intimate with us.

Small squads of Khataz's soldiers patrolled the markets and the living areas. They didn't have uniforms, not quite, but they wore jackets and hats splashed with white paint, which made them plenty recognizable. Most were armed—rifles, shotguns, clubs, knives. Wherever they marched, other goblins would disappear, hurrying away with their heads down before they could draw attention to themselves.

It was a cold atmosphere. Nothing like I'd experienced the

last time I was here. Maybe the everyday goblin on the street had been scared of me back then, worried about the witch in the shadows, but that was nothing like the quiet fear that filled the air now. No one was brave enough to step out of line or even loiter in place. Whatever Khataz and his sorcerer had done, they'd scared the people good.

We weren't the only ones using the back passages to avoid the soldiers. Other goblins moved in the shadows, speaking in whispers and growing silent until we passed. Smugglers, thieves, assorted scum. They'd always lived in these parts of the Mines, but there seemed more of them now. More than once we were walking down a supposedly empty passage, only for me to glance back and see golden eyes watching us from the darkness.

I had ways of averting unwanted eyes from myself, but I couldn't hide all three of us. Our best defense was speed. We had to get what we needed before word of our presence spread.

While Rodetk led the way, Lilian hurried alongside me, holding her bag tight against her to keep it from rattling. She walked with her eyes open wide, one hand touching the roughly carved rock wall of the tunnel.

"How can you see anything down here?" she whispered.

Honestly, I couldn't really. But in my years here I'd gotten used to relying on sound and touch more than my eyesight. You got a kind of sixth sense for these passageways after a while.

I took a small vial from my pocket. "Put a couple of drops of this in your eyes. It'll make it easier."

She grimaced, pushing the vial back at me. "No thanks."

"It won't hurt. Stinks a bit, but it'll help you see."

"No potions," she said firmly.

I scratched my head. "Well, I guess I can make a charm that'll help you instead. I've got some things in my bag. Just tell me what you are, and I'll whip up something that'll work for you."

Her eyes flashed in the dark and she shook her head. "You're not getting out of our bet that easily."

Rats. With a shrug, I tucked the vial back into my pocket.

"You're holding up pretty well for a man who thinks he's been shot dead," she said to me.

"Thanks."

"You're still angry about it?"

"You could say that," I said.

"Early thinks you should let it all go. Make peace."

"I wish it was that easy."

A small smile flickered across her face. I think she thought it was too dark for me to notice. "The anger is good. It's powerful. It's righteous. Use it while you can."

I glanced at her. "Didn't expect to hear that from you."

She ignored me. "But it can't take you all the way. When it's time, do what Early says. Let it all go. Because if you don't..."

She seemed like she was going to say more, but instead she closed her mouth and let the words hang in the air. I studied the shadow of her face in the dark, trying to make some sense of her. I've studied grimoires written in medieval German that were easier to read than she was.

"Why'd you come here with me?" I said. "Really. I know you want to find the hag, but there are other ways you could have helped. You could've stuck around helping the ghouls. You could've gone with Early to Lockhart's library. But you came here. Why?"

She hesitated, then glanced at me. "You've been a good friend to me since I came to Lost Falls. The community isn't always welcoming to outsiders. I guess you know that."

I nodded. "They're a bit of an ornery bunch, I'll give you that."

"Well, I figured us outsiders have to stick together," she said. "And besides, you deserve to find out the truth about what happened to you." She looked straight ahead, and whispered to herself in a voice I don't think I was supposed to hear. "We all do."

Rodetk pulled up his hood to hide his face as he squinted out the tunnel opening. "There are eyes everywhere here," he said. "If I'm recognized, Khataz's people will be on us before we can blink."

"What do we do?" Lilian asked.

The goblin looked us over, his lip curling. "Act like you belong."

He slipped out of the tunnel and joined the bustle of the walkway. Lilian and I followed.

We were on one of the middle levels of the city, in what I guess you'd call a residential neighborhood. Buildings rose up on either side of us, cobbled together from wood and stone and leather and fabric of all colors. It was halfway between a medieval city street and a refugee camp. Power cables ran along the walkway and formed tangled networks overhead. Lights hung down like beads of dew from a spider web.

We had to hurry to keep up with Rodetk as he weaved among the other goblins on the narrow stone walkway. Goblins huddled in small knots of twos and threes, muttering quietly to each other as they moved. Most of the snatches of conversation I heard were in English, apart from the occasional scattering of goblin words. There was no unified goblin language, and the goblins who'd settled under the mountain here nearly a century ago had come from countless backgrounds—leading to an awful lot of ethnic tension—so English had become a kind of *lingua franca* for them.

From the open windows of the buildings around us came the smell of woodsmoke and cooking fires, meat roasting and strange subterranean vegetables stewing. I knew from experience that most of what came out of the grub farms was damn near inedible, but after our trek up the mountain and down into its bowels I was getting hungry enough that it didn't smell so bad.

Rodetk turned down an alley, leading us deeper into the press of buildings. Finally, after two more bridges, he waved us to a stop and we pressed ourselves into the shadow of an overhanging balcony.

"There," he hissed, pointing across the walkway to a doorway at the top of a long and crooked wooden staircase. "That's it."

"How can you be sure she still lives here?" I said.

"That's her mark above the door."

When I squinted, I could just make out the symbol painted above the doorway in faded red-brown. Blood, most likely. Part of an old superstition some goblins still clung to. It was supposed to ward off wandering spirits who might come seeking shelter and flesh to eat.

Hell, maybe it worked. I was smart enough to know there were an awful lot of things about the world I didn't understand.

"No lights inside," Rodetk said. "She's probably not in."

"Let's find somewhere to wait." I looked around and spotted a dark alley behind us, where we'd have a decent view of the doorway. "There."

We settled in, slumping down with our backs against the wooden walls on either side of the alley. Lilian and I shared a drink of water and a chocolate bar. She offered the water bottle to Rodetk, but the goblin waved it away.

A pair of Khataz's soldiers trooped past outside, swaggering like they owned the place. With a shout, one of them snagged the collar of an elderly goblin trying to hurry past with a sack slung over his shoulder.

"Where d'ya think you're going?" the soldier snapped, ripping the sack from the goblin's hands.

He tossed the sack to his comrade while he shoved the elderly goblin up against the wall. As the second soldier upended the sack on the ground, the first kicked the elderly goblin's legs apart and began to search him. The other goblins on the street quickly disappeared, eyes carefully turned away.

"Stop your bloody squirming," the soldier barked. "Big sack for an old worm. What are you trying to sneak into midtown?"

The other soldier held up a couple of gnarled grey vegetables that looked a little like turnips. "Healroot."

"That's a restricted item," the first soldier said in the old goblin's ear. "You should know better, worm."

"No, you don't understand," the goblins begged. "My sons, they—"

"Tell it to the Justice. Come on, move."

They dragged the old goblin away. His cries echoed down the street, but no one came to help him.

The three of us hunched down in the dark of the alley, staying still and silent until the soldiers were gone.

"I didn't know it had got this bad," Rodetk muttered, almost to himself. He stared at the backs of the soldiers through narrowed eyes, his long fingers scratching at his calf. "I should've come back sooner."

"Why did you leave?" Lilian asked.

Rodetk glanced at me, his eyes meeting mine. For a moment, it felt like we were back in the bad old days, on opposite sides, doing our best to kill one another.

"I had to flee," he said, "for my own safety."

"What do you mean?" she said. "I thought Early said you were in the Lord's Guard."

"I was," he said. "Until Likho came. The sorcerer…he knew those of us loyal to the city—loyal to Khataz—would be a threat to him. We'd try to keep him from casting his spells over Khataz. So he had half the Guard poisoned in a single evening. It was only luck that I avoided the same fate."

I remained silent while Rodetk spoke, trying to suppress the guilt churning in my stomach. Was this all my fault? Rodetk had said that Khataz had brought in the sorcerer because of me. Khataz had never been the most stable ruler, but if I hadn't come in and stirred things up, would it have got this bad?

I didn't like goblins. I had my reasons for that. But that didn't mean I wanted all this.

All I'd wanted was to get Teddy back.

Rodetk was looking at me again, frowning as if he could read my thoughts. He glanced away.

"Likho murdered my men," he said. "Now I see he's laid claim to my home as well. If I get the chance, I'm going to put a knife in his throat."

"No," I said. "Not until we know more about this curse."

The goblin spat. "The curse is your business, Turner. I told Early I'd help you. I owe him that much. But if we see Likho, I won't let him slip away." He lowered his voice. "Not again."

I dragged my hand across my face. He was going to get us all killed.

But before I could argue, Lilian pointed to the doorway across the street. "Look. There's a light on."

"She's inside," Rodetk said, jumping to his feet. "She must've come in a back way. Come on."

Before I'd even pulled myself up, Rodetk slipped out of the alley. Lilian shot me a look and we set off after him.

The walkway was quieter now, even though the soldiers had moved on. I didn't know what time it was; down here beneath the mountain, time seemed to have little meaning. We made our way to the building across the way, where Rodetk was waiting at the bottom of the wooden staircase.

"Whatever happens," he whispered, "we can't let her out of our sight. We can't afford to have her raising the alarm."

I nodded.

"Wait," Lilian said, looking from Rodetk to me. "What exactly are we talking about here? You're not planning to hurt her, are you?"

"It won't come to that," Rodetk said. He crooked his finger

at us and started creeping up the staircase. She frowned, but after a moment she nodded. We followed Rodetk up the stairs.

When we reached the top, Rodetk gave us a look. I nodded. We tugged aside the leather curtain that hung over the doorway and strode inside.

A small, hunched goblin woman looked up from her desk, her eyes widening behind gold-rimmed spectacles. She squealed and threw back her stool, still clutching a pen in her hand. The papers on her desk fluttered at our entrance.

"Don't be alarmed, storykeeper," Rodetk said. "We just want to ask you some questions."

25

"You…you can't be here," the storykeeper said to Rodetk. She backed away until she bumped into another teetering pile of papers stacked against the wall. A small fire burned in the brick fireplace behind her. "Khataz says you're a traitor."

"From what I've heard," Rodetk said, "Khataz doesn't even speak with his own tongue anymore. He has his sorcerer do it for him."

The storykeeper's eyes grew even wider as I stepped out of the shadow of the doorway behind Rodetk. "Who are these humans? Why have you brought them here? Khataz has forbidden all surface-dwellers except—"

"Never mind them," he said. "Now sit back down, before you have an aneurysm."

When she didn't move, Rodetk rounded her desk, picked up her fallen stool, and planted it back on its legs. Trembling, the storykeeper sat.

She was dressed simply but neatly in the hand-stitched blue robes of her profession. Storykeepers were the guardians of goblin history. When the goblins had fled to Earth along with the rest of the Strangers, most of their knowledge had been lost. It was up to the storykeepers to ensure that didn't happen again. Some acted more like investigative reporters than historians. They could gain access to almost anyone in the Mines, from the lowliest mobster to the Lord himself.

Which, of course, was why we were here.

"I'm calling in your debt," Rodetk said to her.

She hesitated. "I…I don't know what you're talking about."

"You don't?" Rodetk leaned over her. "You don't remember your father's disgrace? A disgrace I made disappear?" He sneered. "You know, I always thought that was hypocritical of you. A storykeeper is supposed to be pure. Supposed to bring the truth to the people. When it came to your family's secrets, though, you were more than happy to hide them. You were more than happy to beg." Rodetk shrugged. "But I suppose, if you've changed your mind, I can find another storykeeper who would love to hear what your father did."

"No!" she yelped. "No, please."

"Then you'll answer our questions?"

"Yes. Anything."

"Good." Rodetk turned to me.

"Tell us about Khataz's sorcerer," I said. "Tell us about Likho."

She swallowed. "What about him?"

"Are the rumors true?" Rodetk asked. "Does he have Khataz in thrall?"

"Likho is just here to advise the Lord," she said woodenly. "He is a servant of the city."

Rodetk slammed his open palm down on the desk, and a few sheets of paper fluttered to the floor. "I didn't ask you to recite his propaganda."

The storykeeper curled into a ball. "I know little of sorcery. But…but the Lord's mood has soured in the last year. He seems…tired. Tired and nervous. Most of his proclamations come through Likho now. He has become increasingly concerned for the safety of the city."

"Is that why his soldiers are stomping about everywhere?"

She gave a jerky nod. "He enforces strict curfews. Monitors all trade into and out of the mountain. Goblins are encouraged to report on their neighbors if they suspect subversion."

"And the council lets him?"

"The council no longer has the power to overrule him."

Rodetk scowled and opened his mouth again, but I cut in before he could speak. We were wasting time. We weren't here to talk politics.

"What have you heard about a curse?" I said.

"Curse?" The storykeeper looked at me. "What kind of curse?"

"A bad one."

"I told you. I know little of sorcery."

"What about changelings?" I said.

The goblin woman shrunk further into herself. *Changeling* was a dangerous word down here. "Please, I don't—"

"Answer the question, storykeeper," Rodetk snapped.

"Rumors!" Her eyes darted between us over the rims of her spectacles. "That's all I've heard. Some speak of hearing the cries of human children inside the Tower. But it's just a rumor! The practice is outlawed. Even Khataz wouldn't—"

Something on my face made her stop talking with a squeak. Lilian touched my back, murmured in my ear.

"Take it easy," she said. "Use the anger. Don't let it use you."

She was right. I couldn't be the boy I'd once been. I exhaled through gritted teeth, getting myself under control.

"So you don't know anything about the abduction of a human boy. A baby, name of Mills?"

She shook her head. "But...but if there are changelings, Likho has to be responsible. He's been rounding up every goblin proficient in the dark arts, having them executed or sent to the dungeons. All sorcery is forbidden now, except that performed by Likho himself."

Lilian stepped forward, and the storykeeper seemed to notice her for the first time.

"You know the hag who lives in Lost Falls?" Lilian asked.

The storykeeper hesitated, then nodded. "I have heard of her."

"She's missing. What do you know about that?"

"Nothing. What does that have to do with us?"

I studied her face and found no sign that she was lying.

"Never mind," I said. "This Likho, where is he now?"

The storykeeper thought for a moment. "He rarely goes far from the Lord."

"The Tower?" I asked.

She nodded.

"He must have chambers inside," I said. "A lab where he works."

She nodded again.

I planted my hands on the desk and leaned over her. "You're going to take us there."

"I… No. No, I can't."

"You carry the keys to the city," Rodetk said. "You can go places we can't, storykeeper."

"But not there!" she squealed. "Not there!"

She started to rise, but Rodetk put a hand on her shoulder and pushed her back down onto her stool. He leaned down and began to whisper in her ear.

I strained to hear what he was saying, but I couldn't make it out. The storykeeper grew still as she listened. Her eyes flickered to me. Her fear faded slightly, replaced by a look that was thoughtful, almost calculating.

I exchanged a glance with Lilian. Whatever Rodetk was saying, it seemed to be working.

He moved away from her ear, hand still on her shoulder, and gave her a meaningful look. She swallowed.

"The sorcerer has rooms in the Tower," she said, her voice shaking. "But that's not where he works his magic. There is a secret chamber near the Tower's base, unknown to all but a few. That's where he goes, when he's not at the Lord's side. It should be empty now." She took a deep breath. "I will take you there."

"How did you manage that?" I asked Rodetk in a low voice as we followed the storykeeper along a small private tunnel.

"I talked to her in a way only a goblin would understand," he said after a moment. Then he hurried forward to make sure the storykeeper didn't get too far ahead.

"Cryptic bastard," I muttered to Lilian. She just gave me a condescending pat on the shoulder.

Through openings in the passage we caught glimpses of the Tower looming over us. Unlike most of the buildings in the Mines, it wasn't just a ramshackle hovel made of timber and stone and leather. It had been carved out of the mountain itself, all stone columns and grand archways. This was where the council gathered—or at least where they used to—and where the Lord addressed the people of the city.

But the passage we were using was completely deserted. The only sign of life was the sound of rodents scurrying about in the shadows.

"No guards around," Lilian said. "Are we sure this is the right place?"

"Likho puts little trust in guards," the storykeeper said distractedly. She was balancing an open book in one hand as she walked, using a flashlight to illuminate the pages. "One of my predecessors recorded the location of the chamber. It's supposed to be right here." She looked up, shining the flashlight up and down the passageway. "I don't understand. There should be a door."

"We haven't seen a door for a quarter of an hour," Rodetk said. "We haven't seen anything. You must've taken a wrong turn."

"I followed the directions perfectly," she said.

"Then the directions are wrong."

"Maybe not," I muttered, glancing along the wall. I crouched down, pulled a piece of parchment from my bag, and began to scribble a charm. "Lilian, grab a candle out of my bag and light it, will you?"

She gave me a weird look, but she did what I asked. It took me a couple of tries to get the charm right; it wasn't the kind of magic I was used to dealing with. This was more subtle than witchcraft.

I folded the parchment and snatched the candle out of Lilian's hand. Rodetk frowned as I dripped wax on the parchment to seal it. The storykeeper just covered her eyes and turned away, moaning to herself about forbidden sorcery.

"What is it?" Lilian asked.

"Charm of True Sight," I said, holding up the paper. "*Bon appetit.*"

I shoved the charm in my mouth and swallowed it.

"Jesus, what the hell, Ozzy?" Lilian said.

The parchment scratched at the back of my throat, making me gag. Screwing my eyes up tight, I massaged my throat, helping the charm make its way down.

A burning, prickling sensation began in the back of my skull and moved to the space behind my eyes.

Finally—and thankfully—the charm dropped all the way down into my stomach. I took a deep breath and opened my eyes.

The passageway looked pretty much the same as before. The light from the storykeeper's flashlight flicked across the walls that'd been hewn from the rock by goblin hands.

Except this time, a few feet behind the storykeeper, there was a door I hadn't noticed before.

It wasn't invisible, or anything like that. It was just hard to focus on. Like when you can't find your keys, even though they're sitting right there in front of you.

Even now, with the charm, my eyes tried to slide past the door. I couldn't look at it straight on. As I approached it, I kept it in my peripheral vision. It was a heavy wooden door reinforced with iron. The handle was trimmed with silver.

A clever little piece of work. It looked dull and ordinary, just like it was designed to do. The wards that kept it hidden had been worked into the door itself.

"Where are your keys, storykeeper?" I asked.

She looked at the wall beside me, confused—her eyes slid past the door, unable to focus on it. But she dug through her robes and took out her iron ring of keys.

"This is the one," she said, selecting one of the keys on the ring. It was iron, plain and unadorned just like the rest. "But I don't—"

I took the key from her and slid it into the lock. The well-oiled lock turned smoothly. I opened the door.

The others sucked in air as the door's illusory wards were broken. It was a satisfying sound.

"Guess he's useful for something after all," Lilian said. Rodetk nodded.

"Shut up," I said. "Just let me have this."

I turned back to the doorway. It opened onto a tightly coiling staircase.

Just what I needed. More stairs.

With the charm still working its magic on me, I studied the doorway for any other wards or traps, but I couldn't see anything. The sorcerer thought he could rely on his little hiding trick.

"This is it," the storykeeper said. "I did what you asked. I have to get back before someone—"

Rodetk grabbed her by her robes as she turned to leave. The goblin woman let out a low wail.

"Uh-uh. You're staying with us, storykeeper." Rodetk pushed her forward. "Move."

26

I unhooked my truncheon from my belt and pulled my ward-detecting talisman from my pocket. Taking a deep breath, I started down the stairs. Lilian stuck close behind me, silent as the dead, while Rodetk and the storykeeper took up the rear.

The stairway was narrow, only a little wider than my shoulders. Like the walls, the stairs themselves had been carved out of the mountain. They were short and steep, made for nimble goblin feet, not my great big trotters. The stairwell coiled down into the mountain, lit by electric lanterns burning in recesses cut into the outer wall.

Soft sounds echoed up from below: bubbling and hissing and dripping. But I heard no voices, no footsteps. With luck, the storyteller was right and the sorcerer was off holding court right now, giving us free rein of his lab.

I kept one eye on the ward-detecting talisman as I descended, but the marble didn't move. It occurred to me that Likho might be able to weave some kind of goblin ward that my talisman couldn't detect. I knew little of his magic, after all.

Screw it. Too late to stop now. Besides, if anything was going to give us away it would be the storyteller's sniveling. I swallowed down my nervousness and continued on.

Suddenly, I was at the bottom of the stairs. I paused, grip tightening on my truncheon, and stepped through the low archway into the sorcerer's lair.

The wide, circular room was crammed to the gills with stuff. Just...*stuff.*

There, a ramshackle wooden bookcase stretching to the ceiling and creaking ominously, stocked full of books much like the grimoires I kept in my workshop. And over there in the fireplace, what looked like a large wok re-purposed as a cauldron, sitting over the last embers of the fire.

The sad remains of a cat lay on a table in front of me, its belly opened up with a surgeon's precision. Overhead, hanging low enough to brush the top of my head as I moved, were hundreds of animal bones, feathers, talismans, and dried herbs.

"Oh, God," Lilian whispered as she emerged behind me, covering her mouth and nose. "What's that smell?"

There was more than one smell. Strongest of all was the stink of death and decay, maybe coming from the poor dissected cat, or maybe there was some rotting meat still left on the animal bones hanging from the ceiling. But there were other smells as well, and almost all of them stuck to the roof of my mouth and made me want to heave. The sweet, pungent stink of strange herbs I didn't recognize. A black, smoky smell. Something sharp, like formaldehyde. But there was one subtle, coppery smell that stuck out to me most.

"Fresh blood," I whispered.

I couldn't tell where it was coming from. A couple more lanterns were scattered about the place, but darkness and towering piles of junk still swallowed up large chunks of the room.

The storykeeper made a groaning sound as she and Rodetk reached the bottom of the stairs. I turned and hissed at Rodetk.

"Keep her quiet!"

"You want to babysit her?" he snapped back. He turned to the storykeeper. "Why are you moaning, anyway? You're in Likho's lab. There must be centuries' worth of occult knowledge here. This should be paradise for you, storykeeper."

She didn't quit her moaning entirely, but she did get a little quieter as she looked around the room with fresh eyes. It would have to do.

I returned my attention to the chamber. Was the Mills boy here? Even if he wasn't, we still needed to find some evidence of the sorcerer's involvement in the curse. And we needed to find it fast, before he returned and found us here. But where did we start?

I glanced back to see everyone looking at me, waiting for instructions. Like I was the goddamn leader of our little gang of Scooby Doo mystery solvers. Hell.

"Spread out, I guess," I said. "But don't touch anything. If you find anything, tell me."

"What exactly are we looking for?" Lilian asked.

"I have no idea."

She raised an eyebrow. "Great. Thanks, fearless leader."

We each picked a path through the clutter and began to explore the room. Rodetk kept a firm hand on the storykeeper, while I went to investigate the contents of the wok in the fireplace. There was barely enough room to move. Once I caught sight of something skittering across the stone floor, scurrying beneath piles of crap. It was either a small rat or a large cockroach.

Whatever had been in the wok was now unidentifiable, but it was definitely animal-based. I gave it a whiff, choked down the urge to vomit, and moved on.

There had to be something here. Some hint of what the sorcerer's plans were. If we could figure out what Likho was trying to do, we could figure out how to stop him. I had a few good ideas on that front, and most of them involved putting a bullet in the goblin sorcerer's head. But we couldn't act until we were sure.

See, Early. I can be patient. I can be extremely patient.

On a recessed shelf in the wall, I caught sight of a violin that looked as old as the Mines. One of the strings was broken and the veneer was scuffed, but it was a beautiful piece of work. Piano had always been my forte, but I'd dabbled with the violin as well.

As I studied the instrument, the old ache in my brain started up again, and I touched the scar on the side of my head. How could I miss music, when I couldn't even remember what it sounded like? It made no sense. But I found myself reaching out for the violin just the same, as if maybe this time, when I plucked the string, it would all come flooding back to me.

"Ozzy!" Lilian's urgent whisper carried across the room. "You have to see this."

I paused and let my hand drop to my side, turning away from the violin with a sigh. I didn't have enough of a future left to keep living in the past.

I weaved through the maze of junk, following the sound of Lilian's voice. I found her standing near the back wall of the room. She'd pulled back a heavy leather curtain to reveal an alcove set into the wall. As I approached, the smell of blood grew stronger.

"What—" I stopped and stared. "Holy shit."

Lilian nodded. "Yeah."

Six iron cages were secured to the wall, each of them maybe a cubic yard in size. A whole lot of newspapers had been stolen from somewhere, torn up, and used to line the bottom of the cages.

And in each of the cages—bar one—sat a creature. They were humanoid, sallow-skinned, each the size of a toddler. They had big heads and long, slender arms that each ended in three hooked claws. They looked out at us through half-lidded eyes, breathing rapidly as they slumped against the bars of their cages.

"Holy fucking shit," I said. "Are you seeing this?"

"I'm not blind," Lilian said.

"They're the same," I breathed. "The same type of creature

as the one I caught in my sister's basement. They're just like Lawrence." I rubbed my head, trying to make things fit together. "What the hell are they all doing here?"

She shook her head. "I was hoping you could tell me."

Rodetk and the storykeeper hurried over to us. "What is it?" Rodetk hissed. "You two need to keep quiet! If the sorcerer finds us here—"

"Shut up for a second." I looked at the single empty cage, then glanced at Lilian. "Do you think...?"

Lilian pushed me aside and went to the empty cage. The creatures followed her with their eyes as she got near, and a couple lazily bared their teeth, but they all seemed too exhausted to care. Lilian pulled open the empty cage door, the squeal of the hinge echoing through the room. She picked up a handful of shredded newspapers and sniffed them.

"Ew," I said. "You know they've been shitting in that, right?"

"Obviously," she said, tossing the newspaper back and brushing her hand on her pants. "I'd say it's about a week old. Maybe less."

"So the creature I captured, the creature I brought to Alcaraz...it could've escaped from here?" I shook my head. "And then it...what? Sneaked out of the Mines, climbed down a mountain, crossed the river, and ended up in my sister's basement? Seriously, what the *hell* is going on here?"

If anyone else had any answers, they weren't sharing them. The storykeeper bent down to examine something on the ground beside the cages, while Lilian and I stood around scratching our heads. Rodetk looked at us like he was waiting for us to fill him in, but I was a little preoccupied.

The more I thought about it, the less sense it made. We'd come here seeking a changeling child and evidence of a curse, and instead we'd found this.

It couldn't be a coincidence. But what did these creatures have to do with anything? One little weird Stranger was bad enough. Now we had six of them, and even Alcaraz didn't know what they were.

"Do they have any scars?" Lilian asked suddenly as she peered into the dark of one of the cages. "Damn it, we need more light."

"What do scars have to do with anything?" I said.

"Before I left this morning, Alcaraz mentioned something about the creature you brought to her. It had a scar on its flank. She said it looked almost like a surgical scar. Maybe they all have the same scar. Maybe Likho's been doing something to them."

Rodetk peered over my shoulder, using his superior night sight to see what we couldn't. "I can't see any scars," the goblin said. "But why are they being bled?"

"What?" I said.

"Look." He pointed at the arm of the closest creature.

I snatched the flashlight out of the storykeeper's hand and shone it at the creature, so those of us without goblin eyes could see what the hell he was talking about.

A thin plastic tube had been inserted into the crook of the creature's elbow. It was filled with the deep red of the creature's blood.

The tube trailed out the rear corner of the creature's cage. As I followed it along, I saw more tubes coming out of the other cages. They met up, held together with cable ties and string. And together they trailed toward the patch of floor the story-keeper was examining.

Except as I shone the flashlight down, I saw it wasn't just a patch of floor. Something like a wooden trap door was set into the floor. It was oval-shaped, hinged on either side like a pair of narrow double-doors. The tubes draining blood from the creatures disappeared through a small opening at the top of the doors. And when I listened carefully, holding my breath, I could hear a gentle *drip, drip, drip* coming from within.

Distant memories called to me. Old stories of Early's I'd half-listened to. I was so busy trying to remember them that I didn't even notice the storykeeper moving until she wrapped her fingers around one of the trap door handles and began to pull it open, eyes wide with curiosity.

Lilian was the fastest of us to react.

"No!" she shouted, pushing past me and shoving the storykeeper away.

But it was too late. The trap door flew open.

In a single instant, I saw what was inside. Below the doors there was a recession, like a bathtub set into the floor. It was filled almost to the brink in thick, red blood.

The blood pool glistened in the light from my flashlight. Before the trap door had fallen fully open, a shape began to break the pool's surface. A goblin face, but sharper somehow. His eyes were closed, like he was sleeping.

Lilian had overbalanced herself when she shoved the storykeeper aside. She stumbled in front of the pool and stared at the face rising out of the blood, her eyes widening in horror. I opened my mouth to shout a warning.

The goblin's eyes snapped open.

Then, suddenly, it was moving.

The goblin leapt up from the pool, showering us with droplets of blood. Red-stained steel glistened and spun.

And before I could move, the goblin plunged the tip of his spear into Lilian's chest.

27

My throat slammed shut, turning my shout into a strangled cry. Three inches of sharpened steel stuck out of Lilian's back. She stared down at the spear that'd been driven into her, her mouth hanging open.

The goblin tugged on his spear, and Lilian gasped as the spearhead was dragged back through her. With a snarl, the goblin kicked her. His iron-shod boot slammed into Lilian's stomach, throwing her back into a bookcase. Tomes and scrolls collapsed onto her in a cloud of dust.

It had all taken less than a second.

The goblin was lean and stringy, a foot taller than Rodetk. He wore no shirt, and blood dripped from the sharp points of his exposed ribs. Aside from a pair of leather trousers, the only items of clothing he wore were iron boots and a rimless hat that clung to his head so tightly it might've been part of him. It was stained unnaturally red with the caged creatures' blood.

Redcap. The word bubbled up from the recesses of my mind. A vicious breed of goblin, faster and stronger and more bloodthirsty than even the worst goblinkind could muster. I'd thought they were a myth.

I was wrong.

My eyes flickered down to taken in Lilian's fallen body, buried in books and dust. My heart lurched once, twice. Hot blood pounded in my ears.

I leapt at the redcap, truncheon swinging.

He spun back toward me, but before he could bring the spear's point around I was on him. With a snarl, he lifted the spear in both hands, trying to block my overhand blow.

I slammed the truncheon down on the shaft of the spear. The wood splintered, and the spear snapped in half.

My weight carried me forward. I crashed into the redcap, shoving him back and pinning the spear tip against the wall. The storykeeper squealed and scurried away as we scuffled. I slammed my forehead into the goblin's long nose, and I felt something crack.

But the redcap was fast. Damn, he was fast. Hissing, he drove a knee into my gut. As I doubled over, he whipped the blunt half of the spear across my face.

I staggered back, spitting blood. He leapt and kicked me square in the chest. I hit the ground hard.

"Intruders!" the redcap screeched as he came at me, the steel-tipped half of his spear point-down in his left hand. "Intruders in the sorcerer's—"

A book flew out of nowhere and cracked against the redcap's head. He grunted, spat, then snapped his head around to search for the source of the attack. I turned my head as well, one eye closed to correct the double vision.

Rodetk stood crouched and hissing. In his hand he clutched a long, curved dagger he must've found among the artifacts that cluttered the shelves.

The redcap snarled and charged at Rodetk. The monster's iron boots barely seemed to touch the ground. Rodetk's eyes widened, lifting his knife. And then the redcap was on him.

I rolled to my side, groaning, trying to lift myself up. My lungs burned. The chamber was spinning around me. The redcap's movements were a blur as he struck and stabbed and kicked, driving Rodetk back.

I had to do something. I reached for my truncheon, but I'd

dropped it somewhere, and I couldn't see it in the dark. Didn't matter. The truncheon was too slow. I needed something else.

My hands went to my pockets as I staggered to my feet. Witch's fire? No. The chamber was filled with books and chemicals. I'd burn the place to ash, and us as well.

My hand brushed the spirit bottle that the Dealer had given me. But that idea was even worse than the witch's fire. I'd have no idea what I was unleashing.

The gun. I touched the revolver in my pocket. It'd be loud. Too loud. It'd bring guards running. I couldn't.

Rodetk cried out. Blood poured from a cut on his forearm. As he dropped his blade, the redcap hooked his leg around Rodetk's and brought him toppling to the floor.

"Shit!" I muttered, digging my hand into my pocket. The redcap raised the half-spear, preparing to shove the steel point into Rodetk's throat. Rodetk raised his hands in one last desperate defense, eyes wide with fear.

I pulled out the revolver and squeezed the trigger.

The crack of the gunshot echoed in the confined space. The silver round punched through the redcap's temple, leaving the flesh blackened and smoking. He swayed for a moment, crouched above Rodetk, half a spear still clutched in his hand.

Rodetk shuffled back as the half-spear fell from the redcap's hand and clattered against the stone floor. With a look of surprise in his eyes, the redcap slumped face-down.

Panting, I lowered the smoking gun. My ears were ringing. Rodetk stared at me, still stunned. He nodded.

"Thank you."

I turned away with a grunt and nudged the redcap with my shoe. As I watched, the red of the goblin's hat faded. Its bloody stain pooled on the floor, mixing with the blood coming from the hole in his head.

It had to take some nasty magic to turn an ordinary goblin into something like this. I looked at the five caged creatures, their blood still being drained to fill the pool the redcap had been bathing in.

Nasty magic indeed.

Lilian. I spun around and found her lying at the base of the bookcase where she'd fallen. My chest tightened, and for a moment I couldn't breathe. I rushed to her.

"We have to go," Rodetk grunted as he picked himself up. "They will have heard that shot."

I began to shove aside the books that had half-buried Lilian's body. "In a minute."

"We don't have a minute."

"Shut up!" I snapped at him. "Get those creatures out of their cages. Take those damn tubes out of their arms."

"But—"

"Just do it!"

I turned back and pulled the last scroll from over Lilian's face. She was as gray as the stone floor beneath her. Her eyes were closed. I felt for her wound, but I couldn't find it.

"Lilian," I said, grabbing her by the chin and shaking her roughly. "Lilian, goddamn it."

She was limp. I had to stop the bleeding. But I couldn't see where she'd been stabbed. Where the hell was the wound?

I felt for a pulse. Couldn't find that either.

She couldn't be dead. She couldn't be.

"Lilian!" I thumped my fist against her sternum. Her body shook limply under the force of my blow. Her head lolled to the side. "Lilian!"

I brought my fist down once more. Lilian's eyes snapped open.

With a screech, she arched her back and sucked in air. Her muscles tensed, her hands curling into claws.

"Lilian!" I grabbed her by the shoulders. She was alive. She was alive!

But something was wrong. Her gasp didn't stop. She just

kept sucking in air, kept making that horrifying sound. Her mouth was open wider than I thought possible.

She turned her eyes on me. She had no pupils. Something dark and smoky moved through the whites. Her mouth pulled down in a furious sneer. One hand snapped forward, trying to grab me by the throat.

But as I jerked back, she went limp again. Her arm fell to the floor. Her eyes fluttered closed.

"Lilian?" I said.

She opened her eyes again. There was no screaming this time. No weird smoky eyes. With a grunt of pain, she gripped her stomach.

"Oh, Christ," she said. "I…I'm all right." She looked around. "What happened to the redcap?"

"Forget that," I said. "You've been stabbed. Let me look at it."

I tried to push her arm aside, but she stiffened. "I'm fine. It only grazed me."

"Grazed you? It went right through you!"

She raised herself up on one elbow, looking down at her stomach. I could see a tear in the fabric, but there were only a few spots of blood. "It's dark in here," she said. "Your eyes are playing tricks on you." She winced and rubbed her head, where she'd slammed against the bookcase. Her color was already coming back. "Damn it. Help me up."

She was lying. I knew what I saw. That spear had gone through her.

I couldn't believe she was alive and talking, let alone able to stand. But when I took her hand, her skin was warm, and when I pulled her to her feet, she didn't fall.

She started to turn away, but I kept hold of her hand.

"How?" I said.

"Turner!" Rodetk called. "We have to go!"

He had all the cages open, and he'd removed the tubes from

all five of the strange little creatures. But they still sat in their cages, staring blankly. They'd lost so much blood they could barely move. I didn't want to have to carry them out of here, but I couldn't just leave them. Whatever they were, they deserved better than this.

I found my truncheon on the floor and hooked it to my belt. Putting aside the mystery of Lilian's miraculous survival, I went to the cages and grabbed one of the creatures. It clung to me lazily, threatening to chew on my ear.

"What are you doing?" Rodetk snapped. "Didn't you hear me? We have to go!"

"We're bringing them with us," I said, trying to grab another creature out of its cage as it swiped at my hand. "Lilian, take the gun out of my pocket. Rodetk, you grab those two, and…" I paused, looking around. "Where's the storykeeper?"

My answer came a moment later when I heard heavy boot steps on the spiral staircase. "They're down there!" the story-keeper's voice echoed down the stairs. "They made me take them. They made me!"

I swore. "Lilian, my gun! There must be another way out of—"

Goblins began pouring out of the stairwell, snarling as they moved to surround us. They clambered across tables and leapt from walls, traversing the junk-filled chamber as easily as if it were empty. Spear tips gleamed and guns were cocked.

Before we could move, they'd spread about us with unnatural speed. There were eight of them, and they were redcaps, every last one of them.

"Surrender!" hissed the one I took to be their leader. He held a rifle that looked like it'd last been used to hunt dodos. He aimed it at me, which I didn't think was very fair. Lilian was the one who could take a spear through the chest and live to tell about it.

I looked around for escape. There was none.

There was a shuffling sound, then another figure emerged from the stairwell. The goblin was tall, though not as tall as the redcaps that'd fanned out around us. He wore a hooded black robe, and the only weapon he carried was a staff of gnarled wood. A black strip of fabric was wrapped around his head, covering his left eye. Around his neck he wore a necklace tied with animal bones.

I knew a sorcerer when I saw one.

"Likho," I whispered.

The goblin sorcerer shuffled into the chamber and stared at us with his single eye. He was dragging the storykeeper behind him. She seemed to be trying to get as far away from him as possible without actually tearing herself out of his grasp. She raised a shaking finger and pointed at us.

"There," she rasped. "That's them."

A smile twisted his lips. "Take them."

28

The redcaps took my truncheon and my revolver.

It wasn't all bad. I got a little pleasure out of the hiss of pain one of them gave when he touched the silver head of the truncheon. Most goblins weren't bothered by silver, but then these weren't ordinary goblins.

I was the only one they bothered to bind. A redcap tied my hands behind my back so tight it made my fingers tingle.

"What's the matter?" I said as he pulled the last knot extra tight. "Scared of the big bad witch?"

He just sneered.

The smell of blood hung about the redcaps. As they herded us into better light, I noticed their skin had a faint tinge of red to it. A side effect of their blood baths, I guessed. None of them gave any sign that they regretted being altered by Likho's sorcery. They were true fanatics.

Likho gestured to one of the redcaps. "Return the little ones to their cages." He had a smoker's rasp. When he spoke, his lips only moved the barest amount, like he was afraid talking too much would give him wrinkles.

The redcap nodded and started rounding up the strange little creatures we'd freed, carrying them back to their cages. They made angry little whining sounds that stung a lot more than they should've.

"Good idea," I said to Likho. "You already lost one, I see."

The sorcerer fixed me with his eye, his chin moving side to side. Something about him made it hard to meet his gaze. I did it anyway.

"You're a witch," he said. "Your kind is forbidden here."

I said nothing.

"I'll see you burned for what you've done," he said with a twisted smile. He cast his eye over Rodetk. "I knew I would see you again one day, Lieutenant. But I didn't expect it to be under these circumstances."

Rodetk bared his teeth and hissed.

"Nothing to say?" Likho asked.

"Not to you, sorcerer."

With a twirl of his robes, Likho spun around. "Fine. You can explain yourself to the Lord."

I had the point of a spear in my back the whole way up the stairs. The redcap just kept it there, prodding me with every step.

"Will you knock that off?" I said. "Or are you going to make me shove that thing down your throat?"

The redcap glared at me with red-tinted eyes and gave me a few extra pokes for the hell of it.

We reached the top of the stairs and kept on walking. Likho shuffled along ahead of us, one hand on his staff and the other clutching the storykeeper by the robes.

Lilian and Rodetk both looked okay, given the circumstances. There was a nasty cut on Rodetk's forearm that hadn't stopped bleeding, but he wasn't complaining. When I glanced at Lilian, she caught my eye and raised her eyebrows, as if to ask: "How are we getting out of this one, fearless leader?"

I wished I knew the answer.

Everything had gone to hell. I was running out of time. I had less than twelve hours until I had to surrender my body to the Dealer. And yet we still hadn't found the Mills boy—dead or alive—and I didn't even know what curse Likho was working.

I glared at the sorcerer's cloaked form as we were led down a stone corridor. He had to be the one who'd blackmailed Brandon Mills. I'd been killed because of this son of a bitch.

And now I wasn't sure I'd be able to repay the favor.

A pair of redcaps threw open a large set of double doors. Likho strode through, leading us into the hall. He raised his staff and thumped it against the floor.

"Lord," Likho said. "We have captured the intruders."

A round, aged goblin blinked and looked down from his throne.

Khataz didn't look like much of a lord. He was haggard, sickly. As the redcaps herded us into the small but well-lit hall, the Lord of the Deep hunched his shoulders and squinted at us.

"Eh? Who? Let me look at them." He gripped the arms of the throne to push himself shakily to his feet. Beside him were the only other occupants of the room: two more pike-armed redcaps standing guard in the shadows of the columns that flanked the room.

"They're insurgents, Lord," Likho said. "Here to destroy us."

"Insurgents," I muttered. "That's a new one."

The butt of a spear slammed into my back. I dropped to my knees, gasping for breath.

"Insurgents?" Khataz trembled, and clutched at his throat as if he were under attack. His eyes darted about wildly. "Here?"

"Don't fear, Lord." Likho glided smoothly over to Khataz and put a hand on the goblin's shoulder. "You're safe now."

At the sorcerer's touch, Khataz's eyes glazed over. His trembling slowed, and he nodded. "Yes. Yes. I'm safe. Thank you."

Maybe the rumors we'd heard weren't so far off after all. Likho was clearly using some kind of sorcery on Khataz, keeping the Lord of the Deep docile.

I'd never met Khataz before, but he'd always had a reputation for his fiery temper and swift—if reckless—decision-making. This goblin here, though, was a scared puppy, not a ruler.

"Lord!" Rodetk called out. "It's me. It's Rodetk."

Khataz blinked and squinted like he was having trouble seeing. "Rodetk. I know that name."

"I was a lieutenant in the Guard, remember? I'm here to—"

Likho moved a finger and one of the redcaps kicked Rodetk in the back of the head. The goblin slumped face-down on the floor with a grunt.

"Silence!" Likho snapped, his calm facade breaking for a moment. "Traitors don't deserve to speak."

The sorcerer took a few deep breaths, his composure returning. Khataz opened his mouth, but Likho touched his shoulder and the Lord of the Deep went slack-jawed again.

"Your *lieutenant* has betrayed you, Lord," Likho said. "He brought a witch into the mountain. Doubtless the same witch that's been plaguing us. He and his lackeys are here to work dark magics against us."

The sorcerer gestured to Lilian as he spoke. Judging by the look on her face, she didn't like being called my lackey. I thought it had a certain ring to it.

Khataz's eyelids fluttered. "A witch?" he groaned. "No, no, no."

Likho muttered soothing words in his Lord's ear, then snapped his one-eyed gaze back to me.

"Confess, witch," the sorcerer said. "Tell us how you plan to destroy us."

"I'm no witch," I said. "I'm a cunning man."

"You're a witch! Don't think I haven't noticed the shifts in the whispers of the Earth. I have sensed the darkness building. You seek to curse us all."

I blinked. "You're the one working curses, goblin."

"I am the protector of this city!" Anger bubbled through his facade again. He stalked toward me, finger outstretched, animal bones rattling about his neck. "You send your minions against us, you work to destroy us, but it is you who will be destroyed!"

"Minions? Do you see any minions here?" I looked past the sorcerer at Khataz, who swayed drunkenly on his feet. "Lord, listen to me. I'm not here to harm you, or this city. I'm here to track down a missing human child and prevent a curse. Your sorcerer—"

"No more lies!" Likho screeched, and the electric lights wired to the ceiling flickered and dimmed. Even a few of the redcaps shifted uneasily. "Several days ago you sent your familiar to abduct one of the little ones. But that wasn't enough, was it? You had to come and abduct them all. You send blind beasts to haunt the hillside and savage our men. But I will not let you curse us all, witch! Your plans have failed!"

He sprayed saliva as he shouted. I had to lean back to avoid being rained on. This rage and paranoia didn't seem to suit the sorcerer.

Because they're not his emotions, I realized. Khataz's paranoia was seeping through their connection, corrupting the sorcerer. Likho had absorbed some of the Lord's fears into himself.

The sorcerer spun and gestured to a pair of redcaps. "Show them. Bring in the creature. The witch will see his failure."

One of the redcaps hesitated. "Sorcerer, it could be dangerous—"

"Bring it!"

The redcaps stiffened. "Yes, sorcerer." His voice slurred like Khataz's. I got the feeling Likho was using his magic to influence the redcaps' minds as well. He had created them, after all.

The two redcaps disappeared through a side door. As soon as they were gone, Likho glared at me and paced away. His face twisted, like he was trying to get control of himself.

I shot Lilian a look. I saw my own confusion mirrored in

her eyes. This wasn't playing out like I'd thought it would.

A few hours ago, things had made sense. Likho had seemed the obvious suspect. I figured he'd snatched Brandon Mills' baby and was using the boy to manipulate Mills. He was gathering the ingredients for a powerful curse that could wreak havoc upon its target.

And our course of action had been simple as well. All we had to do was prove the sorcerer was responsible, then figure out what his plan was and put a stop to it. Maybe give him a few extra kicks to pay him back for what he'd made Brandon Mills do to me.

But now things were sliding out of focus. Likho was powerful, sure—turning goblins into redcaps was no easy feat, and neither was manipulating the mind of someone like Khataz. But it was clearly straining him. Was he really capable of working a curse as powerful as the one we were imagining?

And what was all this rambling about minions and familiars? I wasn't strong enough to command a familiar. That was high-level magic.

Maybe the sorcerer was just trying to confuse us. Cover his tracks, perhaps. But I couldn't figure out why he'd bother. He had us. We were already as good as dead.

Rodetk was only just picking himself back up off the floor. He planted his hands and pushed himself to his knees. There was blood matted in his stringy black hair.

"Hey," I muttered. "You all right?"

He spat a glob of blood on the floor and gave me a grin. His teeth were stained red. "Didn't think you cared."

"Who says I do?"

"Quiet!" Likho snarled.

Rodetk ignored the sorcerer. "You're not going to talk your way out of this, Turner. I think you know that."

Something about the way he said it gave me pause. I opened my mouth, but Likho swooped in again, his cloak streaming behind him.

"I told you to be quiet! You will answer my questions, witch, and otherwise you will keep silent!"

I smiled up at him, my mouth clamped firmly closed.

From outside the chamber came a deep growl that rumbled through my chest. It was a sound to awaken primal fears. Beside me, Lilian breathed, "Oh, shit."

She'd cottoned on before me, clearly, but I didn't have to wait long to find out for myself. The door swung open. And a new terror entered the room.

The beast was closer to the size of a bear than a wolf. It stalked into the room on all fours, black fur hanging limp and matted from bulging muscles. The creature's lips were peeled back, revealing teeth that looked like long splinters of bone.

But this was no mere beast. There was something intelligent about the noises it made, the way it moved. Something unnatural. I felt like it was staring right through me, despite the fact that its eye sockets were empty. They dripped blood endlessly down the side of its snout.

"Our roggenwolf," Lilian whispered.

I just nodded.

The beast was so menacing I almost didn't notice the iron muzzle that covered its snout, keeping it from fully opening its jaws. A silver-wrought collar was secured around its neck, and a second harness had been fashioned from ropes and leather to go around its body. The two redcaps accompanied the roggenwolf, keeping the beast at a distance with long poles attached to the beast's collar and body harness. The roggenwolf growled and twisted about in frustration, trying to snap at the redcaps through the muzzle.

"God," Lilian said. "What have they done to it?"

She wasn't just talking about the beast's missing eyes. Wounds gaped on the roggenwolf's flank and shoulders, oozing blood. They looked fresher than the gouged-out eyes.

The goblins obviously hadn't had an easy time capturing the roggenwolf.

"You see, witch?" Likho said. "We've captured your monster."

I looked at him. "You're a special kind of stupid, aren't you?"

The sorcerer gestured and the two redcaps urged the beast over to us. It obviously didn't like being pushed around like this, but it went along with it. When it stood less than three feet away, it fixed me with an eyeless stare and growled. Its breath smelled of sulfur.

"Now, witch, you will answer my questions," Likho said. "Or you, your lackey, and this traitor will be fed to the animal one by one."

The roggenwolf strained against its bonds, sniffing the three of us. Rodetk edged back when it snarled at him, but Lilian remained calm and still. As it turned to her, growling, I saw her mouth moving slightly with near-silent whispers. The roggenwolf's growls got a little quieter.

Somehow, I didn't think Lilian was going to be able to save our asses playing roggenwolf whisperer.

"Who are you working with?" the sorcerer asked me. "I can see into your soul. You're not strong enough to work a curse on this scale. Who aids you?"

"I'm not working any curses," I said. "I'm trying to stop one."

"Liar," Likho hissed. "Stop lying!"

"Where's the changeling, sorcerer? Where's Michael Mills? What have you done with him?"

"Quiet!" He thumped his staff on the floor and the roggenwolf snapped its jaws in anger behind its muzzle.

The sound seemed to draw Khataz out of his stupor. He blinked a few times and looked around, his gaze settling on the roggenwolf.

"Sorcerer!" he said. "Why is there a beast in my chamber?"

"No need to fear, Lord," Likho said. "Your soldiers captured it, remember?"

"They did?"

"It has been haunting the mountain for days. Sent by the witch." Likho turned back, considered us for a moment, then pointed a finger at Rodetk. "Let the traitor be the first to die. That should loosen the witch's tongue."

"Wait a second," I said. "What are you—?"

Something struck the back of my head and I nearly hit the ground. When I could see again, I looked up and saw that Rodetk's eyes were wide with fear.

A redcap came forward, warily approaching the growling roggenwolf, and began to undo the muzzle.

My mind spun. The sorcerer seemed as scared of this curse as we were. Was I wrong? Was someone other than Likho really responsible for all that had happened?

But if he wasn't working it, then who was?

Likho stood before Rodetk, sneering. "Any last words before I feed your traitorous tongue to the blind beast?"

"You're the traitor, sorcerer," Rodetk spat, his eyes fixed on the roggenwolf. "You were brought here to protect the city against the witch in the shadows. But all you've done is whisper poison in the Lord's ear and create these...these abominations!" He pointed at the redcaps.

"Be calm," Lilian hissed. "You're angering the roggenwolf. Don't move. Don't make eye contact with it."

But Rodetk wasn't listening. The redcap pulled the muzzle from the beast's snout, nearly losing a finger to the creature's teeth.

The blind roggenwolf snapped its jaws at the air, growling with rage. Rodetk tried to shuffle back, but the redcaps behind him held him in place.

Lilian returned to her whispering, trying to placate the roggenwolf. I watched, helpless, trying to think.

"Sorcerer," I said. "Listen to me. You're right, someone out there is working some dark magic. But it's not me. And if it's not you, we need to figure out who's responsible."

Likho ignored me. His attention was fixed on the roggen-wolf. It seemed like Lilian's whisperings were working. The beast was beginning to calm.

With a snarl, the sorcerer jabbed his staff at one of the creature's open wounds. The beast howled with pain and snapped its jaws closed inches from Rodetk's nose.

"Wait!" Rodetk said. "Wait! Storykeeper! Tell the Lord in the Deep what I said to you. Tell him why I'm here."

At Rodetk's shout, the storykeeper jumped. She'd been so quiet I'd nearly forgotten she was here, which I guess had been her goal. She was clinging to one of the columns in the corner, shaking.

"Tell them!" Rodetk shouted as the roggenwolf strained for him.

She licked her lips and bobbed her head, nearly losing her glasses in the process. "He...he said he was fulfilling the orders the Lord of the Deep gave him. He said he was bringing you the witch in the shadows."

"Just as I promised!" Rodetk pointed at me. "This isn't just any witch. This is the *Natiz-Tuk*. This is the witch in the shadows. And I have brought him to you."

29

I stared at Rodetk, not believing what I was hearing.

Likho raised a hand. The redcaps pulled back the roggen-wolf a couple of feet, and Rodetk sighed with relief.

"I never turned my back on the city," Rodetk said. "I'm no traitor!"

"Speak," the sorcerer snapped. "What do you know?"

Rodetk glanced at me, swallowing. "I've been working for his master for a year. All the while gathering information on the witch. I know his powers, his weaknesses. This was the chance I needed to bring him back to the Mines and uncover his true plans. I led him into your hands."

I gaped. I'd been right all along. It was a trap.

"You little shit," I growled. "I should've let that redcap kill you! I should've killed you myself!"

I lurched for him, but the redcap behind me grabbed me and held me still. My sudden movement set the roggenwolf growling again, but Lilian continued to murmur soothingly to it.

"You're right," Rodetk said to Likho. "The witch and his master are planning something. And not just them. They've been holding secret meetings with the vampires. The ghouls as well, and others. They're gathering their strength."

Likho leaned forward, eager. "For what?"

"To bring the Mines under their sway," Rodetk said.

"What?" I said. "What the hell are you talking about?"

Likho spun and cracked me across the face with his staff. I saw stars.

"If he speaks again, kill him," Likho said to the redcap behind me.

"The witch knew he had to take the redcaps out of the equation," Rodetk continued, speaking quickly now. "That was why he was taking the little ones. He planned to use their blood for his own purposes. And he intends to poison you."

I opened my mouth, fighting through the pain in my skull, but the sharp steel pressed against the back of my neck made me reconsider.

What was Rodetk talking about? Was he just trying to save his own skin however he could?

Rodetk met my eyes. "He carries a flask of poison. I can show you. I can prove it."

Licking his lips, Likho nodded. "Slowly." He gestured to one of the redcaps. "Watch him."

With one eye on the roggenwolf, Rodetk slowly rose. He held his hands out, showing he was unarmed, and edged over to me. The roggenwolf growled as the goblin passed, but Lilian increased the intensity of her whispers, and the beast remained still.

Khataz seemed to be growing more alert again. He shook his head, like he was trying to clear the spider webs from his mind. He started forward to see what was going on. But his redcap guards intercepted him, gently but firmly directing him back to his throne.

"What's happening?" Khataz said to the redcaps. "Isn't that man part of the Guard?"

Likho spoke distractedly over his shoulder. "Just a security matter, Lord. It'll be dealt with soon."

Rodetk crouched down in front of me. He held my gaze as he reached into a pocket sewn into the inner lining of my coat. He turned back slowly, showing Likho the silver flask he'd taken from me.

"It's poison," Rodetk said. "Designed to burn the victim alive from the inside out. I watched his master brew it for him."

I looked at the flask, then at Rodetk, catching on at last. I swallowed.

The goblin was mad. But what choice did we have?

"He's lying," I said. "It's just whiskey."

"Is that so?" Likho said. He nodded at the redcap behind me. "Smell it."

Rodetk unscrewed the cap and held it steady as the redcap leaned in. Even from here I could smell the sharp stink of it. The redcap reared back.

"It's not whiskey," he hissed.

"Like you would know," I said. "You were made in a fucking bathtub."

The redcap bared his teeth, but said nothing.

Likho smiled. "Don't worry, witch. I believe you. In fact, you look like you could use a drink."

He gestured with his fingers, and suddenly the redcap had me in a headlock. I jerked and twisted, but the redcap only gripped me tighter. The stink of his blood-tainted skin was overwhelming.

"Rodetk," the sorcerer said. "You say you're not a traitor? Prove it to your Lord. Give this witch a taste of his own medicine."

Rodetk swallowed, nodded, and turned to me. He raised the flask. "Drink up, witch."

He shoved the flask's opening into my mouth so hard it cracked against my teeth. Foul, bitter liquid filled my mouth.

He withdrew the flask and the redcap holding me clamped his hand over my mouth and nose. I couldn't breathe. I couldn't move. The arm tightened around my throat. Blood pounded in my head.

I could hear the roggenwolf growling and snarling nearby. I held the liquid in my mouth, fighting against the foul taste.

"Swallow it," Likho hissed.

My lungs began to burn. I grunted and twisted in the redcap's grip. The eyes of the room were upon me.

Which meant I was the only one watching as Rodetk snatched a knife from the belt of the unsuspecting redcap and stabbed the creature in the side.

The redcap snarled with pain. His grip on me loosened for a moment.

I tore myself free of his grasp, breathing in deep through my nose. Leaving the knife embedded in the redcap's side, Rodetk grabbed Lilian by the shoulder and pulled her to the floor.

I reared back and spat the liquid in a spray aimed at the redcaps behind me.

It wasn't whiskey. It wasn't poison either.

It was witch's fire.

A gout of bright green flame burst from my mouth. The heat of it hit me like a wave, scorching my skin and singeing my eyebrows.

The two redcaps that were suddenly enveloped in fire came out considerably worse. They were still writhing when their blackened bodies hit the floor.

Rodetk was right. We weren't talking our way out of this.

The chamber was suddenly filled with screams. Likho and his redcaps instinctively sprung away from the green fire. The redcap who'd been holding me staggered back, clutching the knife in his side as the light of the unnatural fire shone in his wide eyes.

The two goblins holding the roggenwolf's control poles momentarily forgot their duty as the gout of flame swept past them. One of them dropped his pole, and the other one leapt back, flinching at the sudden heat.

A split second later, the two of them realized their mistake.

Their faces contorted, and the one who'd dropped his pole scrambled to pick it up.

They were too slow.

The roggenwolf snarled and bounded away. The redcap still holding his control pole was flung across the room by the beast's sudden twisting. The other redcap found himself staring into the dark expanse of the roggenwolf's maw.

Then the creature's jaw closed around his head, and I don't think he saw much after that.

I tried to struggle to my feet, my wrists still tied behind my back. Rodetk reappeared at my side, the silver flask still in his hand.

"Again!" I rasped.

He brought the flask to my cracked, burned lips, poured the rest of the witch's fire into my mouth, and spun me to face the mass of redcaps coming at us from behind.

I sprayed fire like a flamethrower. The redcaps fell back, shouting, leaving behind another couple of charred corpses.

Rodetk dropped down behind me and started gnawing on my bonds with his sharp goblin teeth.

The chamber was in chaos. The storykeeper fled screaming to the far corner of the room. Khataz was being herded to a door at the rear of the chamber by his two redcap guards. Likho staggered back, staring with wide eyes, his lips moving rapidly.

With blood dripping from its maw, the roggenwolf turned away from the redcap it had savaged. It fixed me with its eyeless gaze and growled, its hackles raised.

I swallowed, my throat dry and burning. The beast's lips peeled back and it advanced on me.

Lilian stepped between us, her hand raised toward the roggenwolf. The beast stopped in its tracks and sniffed at her outstretched hand.

"We're not the ones who hurt you," she said authoritatively.

The beast paused, regarding Lilian for a moment. Then,

with a growl, it streaked around us, hurling itself at a trio of redcaps. They toppled like bowling pins. Lilian lowered her hand and exhaled. She was trembling.

As the roggenwolf ripped through the redcaps, something shiny went flying and slid across the floor.

"My gun!" I yelled at Lilian. "Grab it!"

She leapt for the weapon as a rifle cracked nearby. Something whizzed past my head. The redcaps I'd driven back with the witch's fire were regrouping. One of them worked the bolt of his rifle and took aim again.

Lilian snatched up my revolver and snapped off a shot at the redcaps. The goblin with the rifle flinched, his shot flying wide.

Finally, Rodetk chewed through my bonds and the ropes fell from my wrists. Blood rushed back into my fingers.

Another shot flew overhead. I dived to the ground, landing on top of a redcap who'd been torn to pieces by the roggenwolf. It was the same redcap who'd taken my bag and truncheon. I slung my bag over my shoulder, picked up my truncheon, and grabbed Lilian by the elbow.

"Come on!" I yelled.

I pulled her along as she fired. One of the redcaps cried out. I didn't stop to see whether he went down.

We hurried toward the main chamber doors. But before we were halfway there, they burst open, and another half dozen redcaps poured into the room.

With a choked cry, I skidded to a halt and pulled Lilian behind one of the chamber's columns. More gunfire cracked, following us. A bullet slammed into the column two inches from my head, scattering fragments of stone and dust in all directions.

"I'm out," Lilian said, snapping open the revolver's cylinder and letting empty casings fall to the floor.

"Bottom right pocket," I said. "Give them silver."

She stuck her hand in my coat pocket and started feeding

the rest of the silver-tipped cartridges into the revolver. Rodetk ducked behind the next column along from us, holding a spear he'd grabbed from a downed redcap.

"Hey!" I yelled. "Rodetk. You call Early my master one more time, I break your pointy goblin nose. You hear me?"

He shot me a sharkish grin. "Had you going for a second there, didn't I?"

"Boys," Lilian said through gritted teeth as she ducked out of cover and snapped off a couple of shots at the redcaps moving to flank us. "Maybe we do this later."

One of the redcaps caught a silver bullet in the stomach. A wound opened up in his abdomen, the edges black and foul like rotted meat. As he died, smoke poured from his screaming mouth.

The magic that'd been used to grow these redcaps didn't react well to silver. That was a weakness I could use.

I pulled a spherical glass vial from my bag and hurled it. The glass shattered as it hit the floor, spilling a cloud of glittering silver high into the air.

Redcaps screamed as the powdered silver touched their skin. A couple made the mistake of inhaling as they did so. They clutched their throats and clawed at their eyes, their weapons clattering to the floor as the pain overwhelmed them.

It was horrific to watch. But it bought us a few seconds. I glanced around the chamber.

The roggenwolf was still on the rampage. Several new cuts marred its flanks, and the tip of a broken pike was jammed in its rear leg. But that only seemed to make it angrier.

Still more redcaps were rushing into the room, and with them came other goblins, the white-painted soldiers we'd seen marching the streets.

We needed to get the hell out of here.

I grabbed Lilian and pointed to the side of the chamber. "The door we came in through. That's our exit."

She nodded and held up the revolver. "I'm out again."

And I had no more silver bullets. We'd be doing this the hard way.

"All right." I shoved some normal cartridges into Lilian's hand and dug another vial out of my bag. "Get ready to move."

But at that moment the lights overhead flickered again. I noticed something: the sound of a rising voice speaking in a tongue I didn't recognize. Likho was chanting. There was something eerie about it. He was speaking with more than one voice at once.

As the lights dimmed, I had the strange sensation that there were other people in the chamber, other beings, just out of sight. I shivered as I felt their gaze sweep across me.

"Shit." Likho was doing something. And whatever it was, I didn't like it.

Without thinking, I hurled the vial I was holding. It cracked at Likho's feet, and a cloud of silver billowed around him. Sparks flared within the cloud, and the other presences in the room faded from existence. I breathed a sigh of relief.

Likho himself wouldn't be harmed by the silver, but it had been enough to disrupt his sorcery. I heard him coughing as the cloud faded. With a flutter of his cloak, he turned and made for the door the Lord of the Deep had fled through.

"He's getting away!" Rodetk snarled.

"Forget him," Lilian said. "We have to get out of here."

"He killed my men. He made my people into slaves." Rodetk gripped his pike in both hands. "He's not leaving here alive."

Rodetk burst from cover before either of us could shout.

The little bastard had guts, I had to give him that.

A couple of scattered shots followed him, but at that moment the roggenwolf barreled through the main body of goblins, and suddenly they had more important things to worry about.

Likho had a head start. He pulled up the hem of his robe as he ran for the door. Rodetk sprinted after him, snarling.

Rodetk hurled the pike at the fleeing sorcerer. It wasn't exactly an Olympic-medal-winning javelin throw. The heavy pike slapped the ground behind the sorcerer, twisted, and spun.

The shaft of the pike struck Likho in the back of the legs. The sorcerer went down in a tangle of robes. Cursing in some language I didn't understand, he started to pull himself to his feet.

But Rodetk was already on him. The goblin snatched up the pike again and leapt at the fallen sorcerer.

Likho wasn't out of tricks yet, though. He spun to face Rodetk at the last second, dodging the point of the spear. With a hiss, the sorcerer ripped off the rag that concealed his left eye.

Or what should have been his left eye. There wasn't even an empty socket there, like the roggenwolf was sporting. There was just a hole.

A hole that moved and shifted like a drowning man trapped beneath a layer of oil.

The sorcerer spat a word. The blackness burst from his eye socket, buzzing around Rodetk like a cloud of insects.

Rodetk screamed. The sound cut through all the shouting and fighting and gunfire that filled the chamber. Not a scream of pain. A scream of horror. The kind of horror that breaks a man's mind and turns him into a gibbering wreck.

The sorcerer closed his puckered eyelids over the hole, and the blackness began to dissipate. As Rodetk stood there, frozen, Likho reached for the necklace of bones he wore.

"Shoot the sorcerer!" I said to Lilian. "Now!"

But she was too distracted by the regrouping redcaps to act. I could only watch as Likho ripped one of the bones from his necklace. With a sick smile, he snapped it between his fingers.

Rodetk's scream became a strangled cry. He collapsed to the floor, writhing, as dark blotches and boils began to rise across his skin.

"Hell," I breathed.

The goblin's mouth foamed. He twisted his head to the side and let out a roar of pain. There was nothing behind his eyes.

"Get to the door!" I yelled to Lilian. "Cover us."

"Cover...? Wait, where are you—?"

But I was already running. I sprinted across the open chamber with head down and teeth gritted. A bullet struck the floor beside me and ricocheted past, smashing into the Lord's throne and sending splinters of stone flying. I didn't think about it. I just dug my hand into my pocket and rummaged as I ran, pulling out a bag of prepared herbs.

Likho had left his curse to do its work. I caught a glimpse of his robes disappearing out through the far exit as I reached Rodetk's side. Part of me wanted to chase the sorcerer down and beat him until there was nothing in his robes but mincemeat.

But I dropped to Rodetk's side instead, grabbing him by the jaw. Somewhere back across the chamber, the roggenwolf roared with renewed rage. I didn't pay any attention.

Rodetk stared through me. His eyes danced, like he was entranced by something only he could see. The boils were growing fast. His skin was slick was sweat as I held him still.

I wrenched open his jaw and shoved the mixture of herbs into his mouth. His jaw slammed shut again, nearly taking my index finger clean off. The spread of boils slowed, and some of the pain left Rodetk's face. But he wasn't cured. Far from it.

"Ozzy!" Lilian shouted. "I can't hold them!"

I looked back. Lilian had made her way to the door, but the redcaps were closing in fast.

The roggenwolf was in bad shape. It had left half a dozen mauled redcaps in its wake, but it was badly wounded and backing away from the pikes of a gang of regrouped redcaps.

If we wanted to leave this place alive, we had to leave now.

I grabbed Rodetk and hauled him over my shoulder in a fireman's carry. He weighed practically nothing.

A scrap of cloth on the floor beside him caught my eye. I

shoved it in my pocket without thinking. As I ran back toward the cover of the columns, I dug one last vial out of my pocket and hurled it across the room.

It shattered against the floor with the sound of a banshee's scream. I closed my eyes as a sudden burst of blinding light ripped through the chamber. Redcaps cried out, stunned by the sunflare. It was designed to ward off vampires, but goblins— with their eyes attuned for darkness—didn't much like them either.

Lilian was shielding her eyes when I got to her. Squinting, she pointed the gun at me.

"Whoa, easy!" I said. "It's me."

"Jesus, Ozzy. Little warning next time."

"You want to tell me off, or you want to get out of here? Huh? Thought so."

I grabbed her by the elbow and hauled her blinking and swearing toward the door.

We ran.

30

Well, I call it running. "Staggering" might be a better word. "Lurching," maybe.

Lilian was still half-blind, bouncing off walls. And me, I was hauling a writhing goblin on my shoulders. My ribs ached like all get-out, and my burned, cracked throat stung with every breath.

Spitting witch's fire took its toll.

But we were moving. We careened down stairs and burst out into the long, empty corridor where the door to Likho's chamber had been hidden. My charm of True Sight had long since dissolved in my stomach, hiding the door from my eyes once more.

It didn't matter. We couldn't afford to stop, not even to try to free the little ones from their cages again. We had one plan.

Haul ass.

As the corridor flashed past, I heard a panting behind us. My brain told me to just keep on running, that looking back was a good way to trip over my own feet and never get back up again. But I couldn't help myself.

The roggenwolf was following us. It bounded along with a loping, limping run, its tongue hanging out of its mouth.

My heart skipped a beat. But after a moment's terror, I realized the beast wasn't trying to run us down. It was keeping pace with us.

The beast was badly wounded. So badly wounded any natural creature would've been long dead. Long gouges had been ripped from its flanks, exposing ribs. A bullet had torn away most of the roggenwolf's right ear, and two snapped spear tips still stood embedded in its flesh.

But on it ran with us, shaking its eyeless head, following by hearing and scent and whatever otherwordly senses it had.

Roggenwolves were savage creatures, known to hunt down unwary humans for the sport. But I guess the beast figured we were just its best chance of getting out of here.

The corridor branched and we veered left. That was the way back to the main city. At least, I was pretty sure it was. We'd gotten so twisted around following the storykeeper through all these unused tunnels I could barely keep track.

We were suddenly in a passage that looked like part of the old system of mine shafts, with ruggedly cut walls and wooden beams supporting the ceiling. Had we come this way? I couldn't remember.

It couldn't be much further. Once we got to the city, we could lose ourselves among the crowds, or sneak back into the dark corners I was more familiar with. We could retrace our steps from there and return to the surface.

Part of me rebelled at that thought. We weren't done here. The Mills boy could still be down here somewhere. We hadn't found out all we needed to know. Hell, all I had now were more questions.

But Rodetk wouldn't last that long. He needed Early's skills to break the curse that ravaged his body. He was a bastard and a goblin, but he'd saved us back there.

He wasn't going to die if I could help it.

We staggered past an animal-skin painting that'd been hung in a small opening in the shaft. I recognized it from our earlier journey down here. We were on the right track.

"Nearly...there..." I said to Lilian as I fought for breath. She just nodded grimly.

But just as I was beginning to hope that we might actually get out of here alive, I heard the clanking of iron boots behind us.

I risked another glance back. The roggenwolf was loping along a few yards behind us. And further back, gaining rapidly, came the redcaps.

They sprinted along the corridor and clambered along the walls, leaping from beam to beam. They moved faster than I thought possible. There was murder in their eyes.

"Run!" I shouted at Lilian.

She hadn't dared look back. "What is it?"

"Just run!"

I pushed myself harder, legs pounding until they burned. My lungs couldn't draw in enough air. I ran as fast as my straining body could bear.

It wasn't enough. The sound of the redcaps' boot steps were growing louder by the second. We weren't going to make it.

I slapped at my pockets as I ran, trying to determine what I still had available to me. My pickings were slim. No more silver bullets. No more sunflares. No more witch's fire. No more powdered silver bombs. About the only thing left of any use was my truncheon. And once the redcaps swarmed over us, even that wouldn't be any good.

But what choice did we have? We couldn't outrun them. We couldn't hide. We had to stand and fight.

Well, it wasn't like I was planning on living much longer anyway. The Dealer could come take my body once the redcaps were done tearing it to pieces.

I glanced at Lilian. She met my eyes. Nodded. We both knew what had to happen. I adjusted Rodetk on my shoulders, preparing to throw him to the ground. I couldn't hold him and fight at the same time. Maybe, if we were lucky, one of us would live long enough to drag him out of here.

It didn't seem very likely.

But at that moment a hissing shout rose up among the redcaps. I looked back.

The roggenwolf had turned. It blocked the corridor, its hackles raised as it snarled at the approaching redcaps. Their sprint had slowed as they readied their weapons.

One redcap tried to scamper up the wall to get past the roggenwolf. With a roar, the beast reared up on its hind legs and swiped the goblin back to the floor with its massive paw. The roggenwolf took the redcap in its teeth, bashed its head against the wall, and hurled the shattered goblin toward its fellows.

This was our chance. But as I pushed the last of my energy into my burning legs, Lilian looked back and saw what the roggenwolf was doing. She began to slow, her eyes wide.

"What are you doing?" I yelled.

"We can't"—she took a deep breath—"leave it to die."

She stopped, began to turn, but I grabbed her by the elbow and pulled her on. "Rodetk dies if we stop," I panted. "We all die. Run. Run!"

I gave her a shove. Her eyes burned with fury. But she started running again. Every few seconds she cast another look behind her.

I didn't look back. Not anymore. I just ran.

A roar rang out behind me. It shook the corridor and rattled my skull. It was followed by the sound of fighting, of redcaps dying, of steel and gunfire. Then even that faded as we continued our mad run to freedom.

We burst out onto a rocky platform overlooking the Mines' main cavern. The sounds and smells of the underground city hit me like a splash of icy water. I staggered, disoriented for a second, then found my bearings and looked around.

"Follow me," I said.

We slowed our mad dash to a hurried jog. My muscles were just about worn out. One look at the walkways running through the Mines showed the place was crawling with every soldier Likho could muster.

Word had spread. They were looking for us.

Goblins were being shoved off the streets, back into their homes. There were no crowds to hide in. But we were back in territory I knew now. Back in the shadows I used to haunt, the shadows that hid me from Rodetk's guardsmen and the vengeful mobs.

I led Lilian on through the dark, staying clear of the soldiers. We didn't speak. Unless you count Rodetk's feverish moans, of course.

He was in a bad way. More than once I had to pull him off my shoulders and clamp my hand over his mouth while we waited for a patrol to pass.

Finally, we came to the hidden door leading to the long staircase and the forgotten mine shaft. We slipped through and began to climb.

If it had seemed a long way down, it was even longer going up. My muscles trembled with every step, threatening to throw both me and Rodetk off the edge. Lilian lit one of my candles to give us some light to see by.

As we came at last to the top of the stairs, a goblin voice called to us. "It true, what they're saying?"

I squinted up and a light flickered to life. We stared into the faces of Tun and his two smuggler friends. The big goblin still had his gun, but at least he wasn't pointing it at us. We paused.

"Depends," I said. "What are they saying?"

"Some humans and the blind beast tried to gut the sorcerer in his lair." The big goblin's eyes flickered across Rodetk's writhing form. "Helped by a traitorous ex-Guardsman."

"Word travels fast in the Mines," I said.

"What else we supposed to do besides gossip? TV reception is dog shit down here." He cocked his head to the side. "Is it true, then?"

I eyed up the three goblins, trying to decide what they'd do to us. Would they try to turn us in for a reward? As tired as I was, I was past caring.

"More or less," I said.

The big goblin fingered his gun and thought about it. "'Bout time someone gave it a shot, I figure. Come on, then. We'll make sure no one follows you out."

I just nodded my thanks, too exhausted to say anything else.

We emerged into dazzling late afternoon sunshine.

For a while there, I'd wondered if I'd ever see the sky again. You'd think, after all the time I'd spent in the Mines, I'd be used to being underground. I wasn't.

We staggered halfway down the mountainside, then took a break in a copse of trees that sheltered us pretty well. I lowered Rodetk from my shoulders and had a better look at him.

Beneath the boils, his face had gone a pasty green-gray. His yellow eyes were wide and staring, but whatever they were seeing wasn't of this world. The blood vessels in his eyes had gone black.

I prepared a simple concoction of the herbs I had in my bag, chewed them up, and pushed the paste into his mouth.

But I was buying time, and nothing more.

"What did the sorcerer do to him?" Lilian asked as she wiped the sweat from her face.

"I'm not sure exactly. A bewitchment curse of some sort. Early will know."

I hoped.

"Likho," she said. "He's not the one responsible for everything, is he?"

I shook my head. "I don't think so. But he's tied in somehow. He has to be."

He has to be. Or all this was for nothing.

Early was right. I should never have gone back to the Mines. I should never have brought Lilian and Rodetk with me. Rodetk was dying in the worst kind of way, and Lilian, well...

I looked at the hole that'd been sliced in her top by that redcap's spear. I'd seen that spear go right through her. The hole in her top was placed dead center, just above her navel. The spear hadn't skimmed her, like she'd claimed. But the flash of skin I could see through the tear showed no sign of damage.

I opened my mouth to ask her again what the hell had happened. But she'd sensed my gaze. She covered her torn top with her hand and picked up my bag. "We should keep moving."

Her face left no room for argument. I shouldered Rodetk and gave her a nod. "Yes, ma'am."

31

The boat was waiting for us where we'd left it, just outside the abandoned mining settlement. We shoved it back into the water, loaded up Rodetk, and brought the engine coughing to life.

The sun had fallen by the time we started downriver. Out here, away from the lights of the town, the stars reigned from horizon to horizon. We navigated by the light of the full moon.

As we headed back toward town I wracked my brain, trying to make sense of it all.

If Likho wasn't working this grand curse, then who was? And why? Who had snatched Brandon Mills' boy? Who was responsible for the hag's disappearance, and the cruelties that'd been inflicted on the roggenwolf? Was it the hag herself, or was there another player in town?

Damn it, what the hell was going on here?

I wasn't as good a helmsman as Rodetk, but I managed to guide the dinghy back into the boathouse without crashing into anything or running aground. We leapt out, re-energized. Rodetk made a rasping sound with every jagged breath he took. He wouldn't last much longer.

Luckily, Lilian had driven her car to the boathouse this morning. We loaded Rodetk into the back and drove back to Early's place in about ten seconds flat. I didn't even have time to buckle my seatbelt.

I made a mental note to never, ever let Lilian drive me

anywhere again. She was a maniac.

I kicked open Early's front door and charged inside, Rodetk in my arms. "Early! Help, now!"

The old man appeared in the hallway, holding a kitchen knife and an unshucked corn cob. We'd caught him in the middle of making dinner. He took one look at Rodetk and said, "Kitchen table. Quickly."

Lilian and I rushed into the kitchen behind Early. He swept the junk off the table and I laid out Rodetk's writhing form.

"What happened?" Early demanded as he threw open a hidden cabinet in the back of the pantry and began pulling out vials and potions and bundles of herbs.

"Some kind of bewitchment curse. I don't know exactly. I've never seen anything like it."

Early peeled back Rodetk's eyelid, studying his pupil and the color of the flesh on the underside of his eyelid. Rodetk snapped his jaws at Early, but the old man barely seemed to notice.

"Suspension charms," he said. "Now. We need to slow his heart before this thing spreads any further. What happened?"

Lilian lit candles for me and I started scribbling out charms while I told Early everything I could remember. He listened in silence, nodding as he stripped off Rodetk's clothes and examined him. His face was set in a look of determined concentration.

I folded the paper charms and gestured for Lilian to bring me the candles. I sealed them with wax, then laid the first one on Rodetk's bare chest.

At the paper's touch, the goblin's muscles tightened. With a noise like groaning metal, he began to thrash.

"Hold him!" Early shouted.

I threw my weight onto his arms and chest while Early took his legs and Lilian held his head. The goblin was surprisingly strong. He moaned and tried to twist out of my grasp. I held him so tight I was afraid I'd break his arms.

Slowly, the first suspension charm began to take effect, and his movements grew weaker. I took the chance to layer more charms across his shoulders and stomach.

"Good," Early said, wiping his brow with his sleeve. He thrust a mortar and pestle into my hands. "The marsh-herb concoction I showed you. You remember it?"

I nodded.

"Prepare some and start making poultices for the boils. Lilian, hand me that blue vial."

Nodding mutely, Lilian rolled up her sleeves and started acting as Early's assistant. She was a little out of her depth, but she was handling herself well. She'd had plenty of experience helping Alcaraz take care of the Strangers they kept. It wasn't like they could take them to a vet.

"What else did you find?" Early asked as he worked. "Is this goblin sorcerer the one we're looking for?"

I hesitated, then shook my head. "I don't think so. He's doing some dark magic there, but nothing on the scale we're looking at. He knew something about a curse, but he seemed to think we were responsible." I paused, looking down at Rodetk. "You were right. I shouldn't have gone there."

"It was a good lead," he said. "Rodetk thought so."

"Really?"

Early nodded, drawing up a murky grey potion into a needle-less syringe. "That's why he agreed to go with you. He was sure that a goblin was responsible for stealing the Mills boy. He couldn't let that stand."

I glanced down at Rodetk. He was so still now I could barely tell if he was breathing. "We didn't find the boy. Maybe he was there. Maybe not. But we'll never find out. If Likho or some other goblin was snatching children, they'll have gone to ground by now. We made a hell of a commotion."

Early nodded grimly as he squirted his potion into the

corner of Rodetk's mouth. "We always knew it was a slim chance. Changelings are rarely recovered."

That didn't make me feel any better.

"All the noise you made might convince our villain to abandon the curse," Early suggested.

"Or maybe they'll speed things up, now that they know we're onto them."

"You never were much of an optimist, were you, boy?"

"What about Lockhart's library?" I said. "Tell me you found something there that can untangle this mess."

"Nothing conclusive," he said. "I spent all day searching the library, cross-referencing with the notes Alcaraz gave me. Even enlisted some of Lockhart's swains to help. I couldn't find a recipe for the curse itself."

"But? Tell me there's a but, Early."

"But," he said, "I found more references to similar curses. More tales like the one about that farmer's daughter. They all seem to rely on the creation of something called a Blackheart. An extremely powerful fetish, capable of causing death and disease on a mass scale. But it's hags' magic. Can only be wielded by a hag."

"And we've got a missing hag," Lilian said.

Early nodded as he dripped some potion I didn't recognize onto the tip of Rodetk's tongue. "This is a curse of revenge. The Blackheart is grief given form. Not the kind of curse we can break easily. We need to either disrupt the casting ritual, neutralize the emotion that's powering it, or destroy the Blackheart. Or we're in a lot of trouble."

"Exactly what scale of trouble are we talking about here?" Lilian asked.

"Potentially? Genocidal."

She grimaced. "Kind of wish I hadn't asked."

"We have to find the hag," I said. "And fast."

"You think she's behind this?" Lilian said, shaking her head.

"I don't believe it. I saw her just a couple of days before she went missing. She gave no sign she was planning anything like this."

"She's a hag," I said. "If she was planning something, she'd be able to keep it a secret."

"If she was planning something, she'd be able to do it cleanly," Lilian countered. "She wouldn't have worked through intermediaries like Mills. She wouldn't have let any witnesses live."

I chewed the inside of my cheek. She had a point. The hag could be vicious, but she wasn't reckless. She was careful, patient.

But if it wasn't the hag, and it wasn't Likho, then who the hell was responsible? There weren't that many powerful magic users in Lost Falls.

"There's something else," Early said. "All the stories of the Blackheart had one thing in common. It was always created beneath a full moon."

I glanced out the window. At the full moon shining high in the sky.

"Ah, hell. Tonight, then?"

Early nodded. "Tonight."

Well, at least my last night on Earth wouldn't be dull.

Sighing, Early put his hands down on the table. I'd applied the marsh-herb poultices across every boil I could see on Rodetk's body, but the goblin's condition hadn't changed. Early's potions hadn't helped either.

"He's not improving," Early said, looking down at Rodetk. "I can't break the bewitchment."

Rodetk breathed with shallow, rattling breaths. The blackness had spread from the blood vessels in his eyes to the pulsing veins and arteries of his arms and neck. They snaked beneath his skin, twitching like black worms.

Early closed his eyes and put his hands to his head, deep in thought. There were black bags under his eyes. He looked all of his years and then some.

"The bone," he said finally. "The bone the sorcerer snapped when he cast the curse. What was it?"

Hell, he might as well have asked me what color underwear Likho was wearing. It had all happened so fast. And I'd been kind of busy trying not to get shot. I closed my eyes and tried to picture the moment in my mind.

"It was…kind of…hell, I don't know. It was a fucking bone! Six inches long, maybe? Curved, I think." I threw up my hands. "I don't know what else to tell you."

"Curved?" Lilian said. "You're sure it was the curved bone he broke?"

"I…I think so."

She looked at Early. "The sorcerer had a wing bone on his necklace. It was the only one that was curved. Harpy, maybe, or sirin."

I'd never seen either creature myself, but I knew a little about them. They were both winged Strangers, foreign to these parts, who looked something like a cross between a bird and a human woman. Both were vicious in their own ways.

"Sirins are magical," Early said. "They bewitch the minds and bodies of their victims. The sorcerer could've incorporated that power into his curse." He shook his head. "I can't break that kind of bewitchment here. Maybe if I could get my hands on some sirin urine—"

"Alcaraz has a sirin," Lilian interrupted. "A live one."

Hope surged in my chest. Urine saves the day once again.

Early looked at me. "Ozzy."

"I got him." I picked up Rodetk, doing my best not to disturb the suspension charms.

"We need to get him to Alcaraz's as soon as possible," Early said. "I don't know how much longer we've got. It might already be too late."

Early's cell phone started ringing as we headed for the door.

He tossed his car keys to Lilian.

"Put him in the car. I'll be there in a second."

We hurried out to Early's car. A sharp breeze cut through the night. Lilian threw open the back door and I shoved Rodetk inside.

"Hold on, you little bastard," I said in a low voice. "I didn't carry you all the way down that mountain for nothing."

Early came out a few seconds later. He said a couple more words into his phone, then hung up.

"That was Malika," he said. At my blank look, he clarified. "The ghoul who came to the conclave. She's been talking to the ghouls and the rest of the community, trying to pin down the hag's last movements before she disappeared."

"And?"

"She spoke to an ogre who might've been one of the last people to see her. He visited her place to get his glamour renewed. And when he was leaving, he saw someone else arriving. Two someones. It was, and I quote, 'a sad man and a old lady wif wheels.' That was all Malika managed to get out of him. Mean anything to you?"

The words bounced around the inside of my skull a few times before sinking in. And then I laughed. I couldn't help it.

"That son of a bitch," I whispered. "He fooled me. Twice." I shook my head in amazement. "I'm so fucking stupid."

"Ozzy?" Early said.

I wiped the bitter smile from my face. "I think I know who's working our curse."

He glanced at Rodetk in the back of the car, then set his jaw and turned to me. "Go."

I hesitated. "Are you sure? What about—"

"Go!" he said. "Both of you. I can get Rodetk to Alcaraz. If I can't save him, neither can you. You need to shut this curse down before it gets started."

I turned to Lilian, intending to tell her I could deal with

this myself if she wanted to go with Early and Rodetk. But I swallowed my words when I saw the look in her eyes.

"I'm not letting you do this without someone watching your back," she said.

"I know. I was just going to ask which of us is driving."

"Me," she said, leaving no room for discussion.

We were going to die on the road. I knew it.

Without warning, Early reached out his weedy little old man arms and grabbed me by the shoulders.

"Be careful, my boy."

Before I could reply, he released me and reached into the back seat of his car. He pulled something from beneath the seat and held it out. It was a pump-action shotgun.

I stared. "You've been holding out on me, old man."

"Alternating lead and silver slugs," he said. "Just in case."

Lilian grabbed it out of his hands. "Don't worry," she said to Early. "I'll take care of him."

And with that, Early nodded once more, jumped in the car, and gunned the engine. The wheels spun and he left a cloud of dust behind him as he raced off down the driveway. I turned to Lilian, eyed her and the shotgun.

"You know, that suits you. Really brings out your eyes."

"You want to flirt, or you want to stop this curse?"

"I can't do both?" I said.

"Afraid not."

I shrugged. "Then let me introduce you to someone very close to my heart. His name is Brandon Mills, and he's the man who killed me."

32

Brandon Mills had fooled me twice. He wasn't going to get a chance to do it a third time.

Mills' story had sent me off on a wild goose chase into the Mines. A chase that'd left Rodetk clinging to life by his fingernails. A chase that we'd only survived ourselves thanks to a roggenwolf that was now almost certainly dead. A chase that had cost me precious hours, and brought me closer and closer to the time when the Dealer would return to claim my body.

And the worst thing was I had truly, honestly believed Mills. I'd been struck deep by his whole damn sob story, his tale of an abducted son.

Had he known about Teddy? About the guilt I harbored? Had he used it to play me?

I'd been sure it was goblins. It fitted everything I knew about the world. I'd gone to the Mines again, just like I'd done all those years ago. I'd been ready to take my revenge on whatever cave-dwelling monster had done this.

But this time there was no scheming goblin. This time it was plain old garden-variety human evil.

I still didn't know the why, or the what. I didn't really care. I had the who, and that was enough.

We approached the front door of Brandon Mills' creepy old house under cover of night.

I held my wax doll in my hand. The bloody clump of Mills'

hair was still stuffed in the doll's mouth. It had probably lost some potency in the last day and a half, but it would be enough. And if not, I had a truncheon I was eager to introduce to Mills' kneecaps.

Lilian strode along beside me, shotgun in hand. She had a face like the angel of death. I remembered what she said, about using the anger when the time was right. She was channeling her anger now, that much was plain.

I tried the front door. It was unlocked.

Caution overrode my anger for a moment, and I tested the door for any wards I hadn't noticed the first two times I'd been here. It was clean. Didn't surprise me. If it'd been properly warded, the hobgoblin wouldn't have been able to get in in the first place.

I glanced at Lilian, nodded. With her jaw set, she raised the shotgun. I threw open the door.

The hallway was as black and cold as a tomb. I reached in, found the switch, and flipped it. The light grudgingly came to life, catching the swirls of dust generated by the sudden breeze. Nothing else moved.

With one hand on the wax doll and the other gripping my truncheon, I crept inside. The revolver in my pocket slapped against my side with each step. I was out of silver rounds, but lead would do just fine.

Lilian closed the door behind us and we paused, listening. The house made all the usual old house noises: creaks and groans and the whistle of the wind coming in through some crack in the wall. But there was nothing else.

I gestured silently to Lilian. We went room-by-room, Lilian covering me with the shotgun while I threw open doors. The guest bedroom was empty aside from the moving boxes that still hadn't been unpacked. I checked the main bathroom next. It had been scrubbed clean.

I nudged open the door to Mills' mother's bedroom. It still

had her smell. The curtains were pulled, and the sheets had been stripped. There was no sign of either the woman or her wheelchair.

No one in the nursery or the living room. Piles of dirty dishes and empty take-out boxes littered the kitchen, producing a hell of a stink. Flies buzzed around in circles, making little black tornadoes above the sink.

Only the two plates sitting at either end of the dining table looked recently used. By the look of things, Brandon Mills and his mother had had themselves a fine meal not more than a couple of hours ago. But they weren't here anymore.

"Shit," I whispered, lowering my truncheon and looking around the empty living room. "No one's home."

"I don't know about that," Lilian said. "That mold patch looks developed enough to start wearing a suit."

I rubbed my beard in frustration. I had all kinds of pent-up emotion I wanted to work out on Brandon Mills' face. And the bastard didn't even have the decency to be here.

So where the hell was he? Where were they both?

Hell. It was just after nine. Only three hours until midnight. Three hours until the Dealer returned to claim his due. I had to find Mills while I still had time.

"Let's look around," I said. "See if he left some clue about where he went."

"There's nothing here, Ozzy."

"Look anyway."

"We already have," she said. "There's nothing."

I shook my head. I couldn't accept it.

"Can't you do your cunning man thing?" she said. "Track him that way?"

"I could," I said. "If I had time and the right ingredients. I've got neither."

She frowned. "Then maybe we should hide in wait. If Mills comes back, we can ambush him."

"What if he doesn't come back? What if he's out there right now, working the curse?"

She chewed her lip. "Then we're already too late."

Real ray of sunshine, this one. But she was right. Goddamn it, she was right.

"I need to call my sister," I said suddenly.

"What for?"

"You heard what Early said. Whatever this curse is, it's bad fucking news. We don't know what will happen if Mills succeeds. And I don't want my family sticking around to find out. Is there anyone you need to call?"

Lilian hesitated, then shook her head. "No. I'll…I'll switch off the lights. We don't want Mills knowing we're here if he comes back."

I nodded and stepped into the hallway, bringing my phone to my ear. It went straight to voicemail.

"This is Alice. You know what to do."

Shit. She'd switched her phone off, which meant she was probably at work. The beep came, and I hesitated for a second, unsure what to say.

"It's me," I said. "I'll try to call you at the station in a second, but in case I can't get through…" I trailed off and sighed. "Listen, some things might be going down. I can't go into detail. I told you I had a job go bad, right? Well, it's getting worse by the second." I shook my head. "I'm rambling. The point is you need to get out of town. You and Val and the boys. For a few days, at least. Leave tonight. Just put some distance between you and Lost Falls."

I heard a switch flip, and the living room went dark. Lilian moved about quietly, and even though I knew she wouldn't be trying to eavesdrop, she wouldn't be able to help overhearing.

"I'm sorry I can't explain," I said into the phone. "Just know that this isn't me being crazy. Get out of town. Seriously. I love you all." I sighed. "Okay, I'll try to call you at the station."

I hung up just as Lilian switched off the hallway light. Darkness descended, until the only light came from my phone's screen. I scrolled through my contacts, trying to find the number for the radio station's reception. I knew I had it somewhere.

But just then I noticed a sliver of light out of the corner of my eye. I lowered my phone.

"What the hell?" I whispered. "Lilian, come look at this."

She walked back down the dark of the hallway to me. A couple of near-empty moving boxes had been stacked up against the wall where the hallway turned a corner. But there was a crack of light coming through a gap in the wall behind them.

Lilian saw it too. Without a word, I pushed the boxes aside.

I'd be exaggerating if I called it a hidden door. Now that I'd moved the boxes, the handle and door frame were pretty obvious. But it had been designed to fit in smoothly with the wall, right down to the wallpaper. A thin strip of light came through the crack in the door.

Lilian and I moved into position without exchanging a word. She readied her shotgun, and I pulled open the door.

It was a staircase leading down to the basement.

Hell. Why was it always a basement?

There was a light on downstairs, illuminating the stairway. By the looks of it, Brandon Mills had made only one renovation in the entire house, and it was here. A stair lift had been installed in the stairway, giving Mills' mother a way of getting downstairs. The bucket seat was sitting at the end of the track, at the top of the stairs.

A smell floated up from the basement. It wasn't so different from the smell of blood in Likho's chamber, only this time the smell was old, stale, the smell of meat beginning to turn.

I glanced at Lilian, gesturing with my eyes. She nodded. Taking a deep breath, I started down the stairs.

Whatever was down there, I knew it wouldn't be good.

33

There was a horror show waiting for us at the bottom of the stairs.

For a second I just stared at it all, letting it soak in. I couldn't speak.

Lilian reached the bottom of the stairs and gasped. She kept the shotgun raised, even though there was nothing to aim at.

Nothing alive, at least.

The basement was part rec room, part satanic ritual chamber. A couple of battered, cigarette-burned couches were being used as shelves, holding an unordered collection of vials and powders and small boxes of unknown content. A huge trunk, wrought with tarnished silver, was pressed up against the far wall, with a grimoire open on top.

There was even a little bar at the far end of the basement, but unfortunately for me all the booze had been ransacked long ago. In its place was a tray of dirty knives and a lumpy mess covered with a bloodstained cloth. The cloth crawled with flies. There was also a blowtorch and what looked like a thick clay bowl. A simple manual wheelchair was sitting at the bottom of the stairs.

Pride of place was given to a pool table, no doubt abandoned by the house's previous owners when they decided they couldn't be bothered hauling the damn thing back up the stairs. And upon said pool table was the star of the show.

Brandon Mills lay face up on the pool table, buck-naked, staring blankly at the ceiling. Lit candles were planted around the rim of the table, next to the pockets. They were all burnt half down, sitting in puddles of wax. Arcane symbols had been painted in a neat, tidy hand all across Mills' naked flesh—at least the parts that weren't covered in blood.

Mills, the son of a bitch, was dead. Dead before I could make him pay for what he'd done to me.

Just my luck.

"Maybe we should check for a pulse," Lilian suggested.

Her idea of a joke. Brandon Mills' chest was a bloody mess. His ribcage had been cracked open by one of those surgical spreaders. Mills was dead. No doubt about it.

I felt tired all of a sudden, like all the furious energy that'd been keeping me going was sucked out all at once. I wanted to lie down on one of those flea-ridden couches and sleep for a week.

If only I had a week.

"What's that?" Lilian whispered.

"What's what?" I tore my eyes from Mills' corpse to see what she was looking at.

She was looking up, in the same direction Brandon Mills' dead eyes were staring. There was something pinned to the ceiling.

Apparently feeling neither my disgust nor my fatigue, Lilian leapt nimbly up onto the pool table, placing one foot on either side of Mills' head. She reached up and plucked the thing stuck to the ceiling.

She dropped back down beside me. She was holding a Polaroid photograph. It was no professional picture. The focus was off, and the whites were blown all to hell. But it had a special quality to it all the same. It was a picture of a baby, not more than a couple of months old, with a mop of dark hair. A pretty damn cute baby. An easy baby to love.

A woman was holding the baby to her chest. The woman's face fell outside the frame, but from the way she held him, I was almost certain it was the boy's mother.

I took the picture from Lilian and flipped it over. On the back, someone had scrawled: *Michael, 6 weeks.*

Michael. Michael Mills.

"This was what he was looking at when he died," I said. "A picture of his son."

"Nice of his killer to give him that."

I grunted and pocketed the picture.

Lilian bent over Mills' body, examining him. "His heart is gone."

I nodded. I'd already guessed that much.

"Can't see any other wounds. No bruising." She looked at me. "I think his chest was opened when he was still alive."

I nodded again. Mills' face was frozen in a scream of pain. But his eyes were wide open, staring up at the ceiling with all the intensity a corpse could muster.

"Were we wrong?" she said. "Was he just a victim after all?"

"I don't know," I said. "His arms and legs aren't tied. No bruising there either. So either he was held in place by some kind of magic, or…"

"Or what?"

"He went to his death voluntarily."

Lilian's eyes widened and she turned back to the massive, gaping wound in his chest. "How could anyone suffer that willingly?"

I didn't have an answer for her.

I went over to the bar, careful not to step on a spray of Mills' blood that'd soaked into the carpet. Most of the flies in the room were buzzing around the lumpy cloth-covered pile on the bar, rather than Mills' body. His death had been recent. Maybe no more than an hour ago, given the look of him.

But whatever was under the cloth on the bar had been dead

a while longer.

I couldn't bring myself to lift the cloth right away. Instead, I started looking through the other items scattered about. The blowtorch looked newly purchased. There were a set of tongs as well, and a clay crucible. I picked up the crucible. There was something inside. A thin, curved piece of ivory.

I'd seen it once before. In that roadside diner where I'd captured the hobgoblin. Where Mills killed me. Except back then, the ivory had formed the handle of a silver baby rattle.

I lifted a pair of heavy leather gloves. Beneath them lay two halves of a clay mold. A mold for forming the blade of a small dagger.

I cast a look at the tray of knives sitting further along the bar. But none of the knives there matched the shape of the mold. And besides, they were all stainless steel. None of them had been made from the silver of a treasured family heirloom.

I filed that knowledge away with the rest and turned at last to the cloth-covered pile. I waved my hand at the flies swarming around it, but they just parted and went right back to their buzzing as soon as my hand was clear. Taking a deep breath, I pinched the cloth by the corner and pulled it away.

"Oh, Christ," I said, planting my palms flat against the bar.

"What?" Lilian said from behind me, where she was still examining Mills.

I rubbed my face and sighed. "I found my hobgoblin. Some of her."

Brandon Mills' corpse wasn't a pretty sight, but he was still intact, for the most part. The same couldn't be said of the hobgoblin.

In some ways, that actually made it easier. It was just like looking at a slightly rotten cut of meat. By the look of it, most of her bones and internal organs had been stripped out of her. Her skin was nowhere to be seen.

The only part of her that was intact was the head. It had

been severed neatly. Her eyes were closed, thank God.

I had plenty to feel guilty for, but for some reason, this right here hit me the hardest.

I'd been trying to do good. Just like Early taught me. All I'd wanted to do was recover a stolen heirloom for a grieving father.

I'd never wanted the hobgoblin dead. I didn't want her carved up like a Christmas roast. No sentient creature deserved to die like this.

Lilian laid a soft hand on my shoulder. For a moment, my knees went weak. I wanted to collapse into her arms. I wanted to cry.

I didn't, though. I couldn't. Not yet. I turned to face her.

"What is all this, Ozzy?" she asked. She looked as drained as me. "Some kind of ritual? Witchcraft?"

I looked at the symbols painted on Brandon Mills' flesh. "Hag's magic. The final preparations for the curse."

"So where's the hag?" she said.

Good question. I glanced once more around the basement, and my eyes fell on the silver-wrought trunk in the corner.

"Help me with this," I said. I grabbed the open grimoire off the top of the trunk, putting it aside to look at later. Lilian and I took the trunk by either end and dragged it away from the wall a few inches.

"Jesus," she grunted. "What's in here?"

I had my suspicions, but I didn't want to voice them yet. There was a heavy padlock on the front of the trunk, with more silver detailing running over it.

"I don't think I can pick that lock," I said, chewing my lip. "Hand me that blowtorch. Maybe we can melt—"

Lilian stepped forward, aimed the shotgun down at the lock, and pulled the trigger.

I slapped my hands over my ears. It did nothing to stop the ringing.

"Goddamn it!" I snapped. "Didn't you complain about me not giving you any warning before doing something like that?"

She shrugged, racking the smoking shotgun and resting it against her shoulder. "Now we're even."

I gave her a scowl, but it was hard to maintain. The shotgun slug had torn the lock to pieces. I tugged it free and threw open the trunk.

A sharp smell of inhuman sweat reached out and slapped me in the face.

The hag was stuffed in there good. She was more Alcaraz's build than Lilian's: big, heavy, and not particularly suited to being contorted into tight spaces. Even looking at her, I couldn't quite see how she'd managed to fit.

She was in a bad way. Her skin hung loose from her bones, like she'd been starved. Her clothing was tattered. I couldn't see any obvious wounds from where I was standing, but something about her screamed suffering. How long had she been kept in that box?

Lilian breathed a curse. "We have to get her out of there."

Even now, I didn't really want to get involved with a hag, but Lilian was right. I sucked it up, grabbed the hag under the arms, and hauled her out of the trunk. She felt lighter than she looked. Maybe a sign of her confinement, or maybe hags just weigh less than humans. I didn't know. I'd never tried to pick up a hag before.

Lilian swept a couch clean and I dumped the hag on the cushions, sending a thin cloud of dust into the air. The hag's eyes were closed, her face frozen as if in death.

It was only then I noticed that her left hand had been severed at the wrist. The flesh around the wound was ragged and black, as if burned. I recognized the signs. A silver blade had been used for the cut.

The curse we were dealing with was hag's magic. It could only be wielded by a hag's hand.

"She alive?" I asked.

Lilian crouched at the hag's side, examining her. The hag had the look of an old woman, short and hunched, with great sagging breasts and a spare tire around her waist. But even to the untrained eye, there was something off about her, something not quite human. Something ancient.

"I don't know," Lilian said. "I need to—"

The hag's eyes snapped open and swiveled to meet mine. She opened her mouth and let loose a long, haggard cackle that came with a particularly pungent brand of morning breath.

I tried to jerk back, but her one remaining hand snaked out and grabbed me by the arm, holding me tight.

"You're too late, cunning man," she rasped. "The witch is gone. Gone to collect the blood. But I'll have the last laugh. When it's all over, you tell her, cunning man. You tell her what she did to get her vengeance. See the moment her heart breaks in two."

The hag cackled once more, a sound that sent shivers down my spine. Then her head lolled to the side, and she was out again. Or dead. I didn't know. I was no expert in hag first aid.

Her gnarled fingers still gripped my arm. I shook her by the shoulders. "Hey! Hag! What did you mean? Gone where? Where has the witch gone?"

But there was no response. I damn near shouted her face off. Nothing.

"Let me try," Lilian said.

I pried the hag's fingers off me and stood, scrubbing at my face with my hands. Too late again. Hell. Hell!

While I fretted, Lilian closed her eyes and pressed her palm against the hag's cheek. The muscles in Lilian's jaw tensed, and the air around me felt suddenly cold.

"She's alive," Lilian said after a moment, settling back on her heels. "I think. She should recover in time."

There was relief in her voice, but I was having trouble

summoning any optimism. I mean, great, the hag wasn't dead, but I'd be long gone before she was any damn use to us. We weren't done yet.

"Ozzy," Lilian said.

I ignored her. I had to think.

The hag had said something about blood. If I could figure out what kind of blood, maybe I'd be back on the trail.

I grabbed the grimoire I'd set aside earlier and scanned the page that had been left open. But my hopes were dashed immediately. It wasn't written in English. Nothing even close to English. Tall, scratchy symbols crawled in spirals across the page. The alphabet—if it even was an alphabet—was completely foreign to me. It could've been an alien translation of *Fifty Shades of Grey* for all I knew.

With a growl, I hurled the grimoire across the room.

"Ozzy!" Lilian said.

"What?" I turned, and she was standing right in front of me.

"This witch she mentioned. Who is it?"

I glanced at the wheelchair in the corner. Maybe... But no. It couldn't be. She was too frail. Mills' mother's body was probably around here somewhere, killed by the same person who'd cut out Brandon's heart. I'd been half-expecting to find her inside that trunk along with the hag.

I shook my head. "I don't know. Hell, I don't know. I've never heard of a witch powerful enough to challenge a hag, let alone do this to her."

I waved my hand at the hag's limp form, then turned to the pool table, trying to think. There was no doubt about it: this curse went beyond simple witchcraft.

It was hag's magic. But the hag hadn't been the one working it. Not willingly. Someone—something—even more powerful had bent the hag to their purpose. Kidnapped her, brought her here, used her knowledge and skill.

So if Mills was only an accomplice, and the hag a victim, then who was the mastermind? Who was this witch who could wield so much power?

I stared down at Brandon Mills, willing him to come back to life and spill his secrets. My gaze fell on his left hand. He was wearing a wedding band that was etched with a pattern of tree branches. He hadn't been wearing that when I first met him. But I remembered seeing another ring just like that around a different finger.

Something clicked into place in my head. I stood bolt upright, the implications hitting me one after another.

The last time I'd seen Mills' mother she'd been wearing the same kind of wedding ring. Maybe it was a family heirloom, something that Mills' ex-wife had given back to him when they divorced.

Or maybe there was another explanation. Maybe Brandon and the old woman both wore the same type of wedding ring for the obvious reason. They were married.

She was Mrs. Mills, yes. But she wasn't Brandon's mother. She was his wife.

A wife who had suffered just like Brandon had when her son was ripped from her life. A wife, a mother who had let her grief turn to fury. A mother willing to sacrifice anything to get answers. To get revenge.

A mother willing to trade away her youth. Her sight. Her legs. Her husband. Willing to trade all that to anyone who could give her the power she needed. The Dealer, or another of his kind.

"Dealer," I whispered. "You knew, didn't you? This whole damn time, you knew."

I looked again at the wheelchair by the stairs. Mrs. Mills must've bought herself a hell of a lot of power for everything she'd traded away. Maybe even enough power to abduct the hag and force her to help prepare this curse.

And if what the hag said was true, she was about to complete the ritual. All she needed was blood.

But what blood? It all came back to that. Even if I was right, even if Mrs. Mills really was the one responsible, I was still no closer to finding her before she could complete the curse. And by the time I brewed up a tracking potion, it'd be too late.

I turned to Lilian. She'd moved back to the bar. Unbothered by the flies, she was examining the hobgoblin's remains. Her head, specifically. I suppressed my revulsion as Lilian picked up the hobgoblin's severed head by her hair.

"Lilian?" I said.

"Yeah?" She seemed distracted.

"What the hell are you doing?"

She ignored my question, putting the head down and turning suddenly to a set of cupboards set against the wall. She threw them open and began rummaging. With a satisfied "A-ha!" she pulled out an old lamp that had been left behind.

"Hey," I said. "Earth to Lilian."

"Do people still say that?" She yanked on the cord coming out of the back of the lamp, ripping it out. Tossing the lamp aside, she turned back to me, holding the frayed end of the cord. "I need nails."

"Nails?"

She nodded. "Metal nails. For hammering into things, you know."

Frowning, I reached into my bag and pulled out a handful of the iron nails I'd scattered in Alice's basement a lifetime ago.

"Will these do?"

Lilian's eyes lit up. It was a crazy kind of light, like fairground lights viewed through broken glass.

I kind of liked it.

"I think," she said, "I know how we can get some answers."

34

I was having second thoughts.

The hobgoblin's severed head was sitting upright in a thin dish of water. Lilian had driven three nails through the poor dead creature's skull. She didn't even flinch, she just did it.

And now she was winding the bared ends of the frayed lamp cord around two of the nail heads, like some kind of mad scientist.

I started off voicing my concerns gently. "You're fucking crazy if you think this is going to work."

Lilian just smiled. "There's a lot you don't know about me, Osric Turner."

"Yeah," I said. "I noticed. But hell, Lilian. This…this isn't right."

"You're starting to sound like Early."

She thought she could wound me with that, and she wasn't half wrong. But I shrugged it off. "Even if you can do this—and I'm not convinced you can—I don't know if you should. The poor hobgoblin's suffered enough, thanks to me. She's dead. That should be the end of her suffering."

"I'm just sparking a dead brain," she said. "Not bringing her back to life."

"What's the difference?"

Lilian sighed, stopping her work for a moment to turn to me. "Do you want answers?"

The witch—Brandon Mills' wife—was out there somewhere. Seeking blood to complete her curse. A curse of genocidal vengeance. And I didn't have a goddamn idea where she was.

"Of course," I said.

She met my eyes. "Do you trust me?"

I hesitated. As she'd just said, there was a lot I didn't know about her. She'd been stabbed through with a redcap's spear and survived without even a scar. She'd done...*something*...to me at Early's place after the conclave, touching me like the black hand of death.

And now here she was, trying to reanimate the dead, Dr. Frankenstein style. That was seriously off-limits magic. Way beyond the darkest stuff I'd ever done. She wasn't exactly the good and wholesome girl next door.

Hell, that'd never been my type, anyway.

"Yes," I said. "I trust you."

"Good," she said.

Then she grabbed hold of the hobgoblin's skull and jammed the cord into the wall outlet.

There was a spark and a hum, like fluorescent lights coming to life. Lilian went straight-backed and rigid, her eyes rolling back in her head. Her mouth snapped open in a silent scream.

"Lilian!" I reached for her.

"The blood!" she shrieked. Except it wasn't just her voice coming from her throat. Overlaid with her voice was another, sharp and high pitched.

I froze, looking down at the hobgoblin's head. Its eyes were open too, open and staring. The creature opened its mouth, but when it spoke, it spoke through Lilian.

"No, no, no. Don't! Don't kill me! Not the curse!"

I swallowed. A cold chill was running up my spine.

I'd been right to be dubious. This was *wrong*. In every sense of the word. The dead shouldn't speak. The dead shouldn't feel terror.

"Hobgoblin," I said. "Listen to me."

"Not the curse," Lilian sobbed. "Please."

"Listen! I'm trying to stop the curse."

The creature mewled. "Going to cut off my head. Going to scoop out my insides. Don't want it. The blood!"

"What blood?" I said. "Whose blood?"

Lilian cocked her head to the side, as if becoming aware of me for the first time. Her sobs faded. "The blood. The blood that powers the flesh." She howled. "It hurts!"

"I know. I know it hurts. Where did the witch go? Where is she getting the blood from?"

The hobgoblin's chin waggled as Lilian spoke in its voice. "Hag told 'em. Told 'em where the hunter would take the changed. House on the hill. Blood, blood of the changed. Blood of pain." She wailed. "I heard 'em talkin'. Tried to stop it. Took the shiny, tried to run. But the hunter caught me! Now they gonna bring the mountain down!"

The hunter? Was that me? She was talking so fast I could barely understand her.

"The mountain?" I said. "The goblins, you mean?"

Smoke was beginning to trickle up between Lilian's fingers. The hobgoblin's skin was growing black around the nails.

"Hobgoblin!" I said.

"Down on their heads." Her voice was fading. "Hurt 'em all, for what one did."

"What did you mean, blood of the changed? What is that?"

The hobgoblin's jaw bobbed open and closed, but nothing came out of Lilian's mouth. The smoke was really billowing now. Lilian's face was pulled tight. I could see her veins bulging through her skin.

"Shit!" I yanked the power cord from the wall. It came away with an arc of blue lightning.

Lilian let out a small noise of surprise. Suddenly limp, she toppled backward.

I caught her before she hit the ground. She slumped in my arms, as light as a baby. Her eyes were closed.

"Lilian," I said. "Lilian, are you okay?"

Her eyes fluttered open. She gave me a weak smile as she focused on me.

"Harder than it used to be," she muttered. "Should've figured that."

I took a shaky breath. "What *are* you?"

"Uh-uh. You still have to guess." She reached up and tugged gently on my beard. "Tell you the truth, part of me wants you to win the bet. I like the beard."

"That'll be the fatigue talking," I said. "Can you get up?"

She shook her head, looking at me through half-lidded eyes. "I don't think I'm going anywhere for a while. She was more challenging than I thought." My concern must've shown on my face, because she patted me weakly on the chest. "I'll be fine. Just need to rest for a while. Did you get anything?"

I thought it over, my mouth growing dry. "Yeah. Yeah, I think so."

"Then go. Take my car. I'm not going to be much use to you. I'll stay here with the hag."

I hesitated. If the witch came back, Lilian wouldn't be able to defend herself.

But the witch wasn't coming back. She just had one last thing to do.

Lilian pulled herself up and brushed my cheek with a kiss. "Go," she said.

"Okay. Okay."

"And Ozzy?"

"Yeah?"

She slid the shotgun over to me. "You might need this."

35

"This is Early," came the old man's voice through the phone.

"Early," I said, turning the key in the ignition of Lilian's car. "Listen—"

"I can't come to the phone right now," Early continued. "Leave a message after the beep."

"Son of a bitch!" I threw the car into drive, pulled a U-turn, and raced off down the street. With one eye on the road I hung up and redialed Early's cell. It started to ring again.

"Pick up the phone, Early. Pick it up."

"This is Early. I can't come to the phone right now…"

"Shit!" I nearly hung up again, but at the last second I brought the phone back to my ear. His voicemail beeped.

"I swear to God, you better not be ignoring my calls, old man," I said. "Listen. I'm on my way to Alcaraz's now. You need to get the hell out of there. You and Alcaraz and Rodetk. You need to leave right now."

Another car pulled out in front of me at an intersection and I had to slam on the brakes to avoid T-boning him. I leaned on the horn and shouted a litany of swear words out the window. I got a few back in return.

I took a deep breath. "Brandon Mills wasn't the witch," I said to Early's voicemail. "His wife was. And she's packing some real power, Early. She didn't just trade away one little thing, like you and I did. She traded it all. Her limbs, her youth, her senses.

Some Dealer stripped her to the bone. And in exchange, she got enough power to subdue a hag and work this curse.

"The two of them forced the hag to reveal her secrets. Forced her to tell them how to create the Blackheart. They already had sentimental silver, but they also needed a hobgoblin. So they set a trap. But somewhere along the way they screwed up. The hobgoblin found out about the curse. She slipped the trap, took the rattle, and made a run for it, trying to prevent the Blackheart from being created. That was why they hired me. They needed the hobgoblin, and they also needed to get the rattle back. And that was exactly what I gave them."

I gripped the steering wheel tight. I'd been such an idiot.

"Brandon Mills is dead," I continued. "He let himself be sacrificed. Let his heart be cut out of his chest. My guess, it's going to be part of the Blackheart, along with the roggenwolf's eyes and whatever's left of the hobgoblin. It's nearly finished, Early. All the witch needs is the blood to power it. And she's on her way to Alcaraz's to find it."

Saying the words made my heart rate spike. Until now it'd all been a swirl of ideas in my head; now it was becoming real.

I put my foot down and the red needle on the dash inched higher. I raced through the streets of Lost Falls even faster than Lilian had.

"Mills' wife is going after the goblins," I said. "The whole damn mountain. You said this curse was genocidal in scale. Well, the goblins are the target. She's going to destroy them all for what was done to her boy.

"Brandon Mills wasn't lying. Their boy, Michael, was taken. Replaced, just like Teddy was. They think it was goblins. Hell, maybe it was. This curse, it's the Mills' revenge."

And in the darkest depths of my heart, I sympathized with them. When I found out Teddy had been taken, it had felt like hot coals being pressed into my chest. All my guilt, all my grief, it had mixed together and transformed into rage.

I'd gone into the Mines to try to get Teddy back. But when I'd found out I was too late, I turned to other means to sate the monster inside me.

I'd avenged Teddy. I'd wiped out the mob that'd snatched him. Who was I to stop the Mills family avenging their son?

Except this wasn't about me, or them, or their grief. Too many people had been hurt. Early was in danger.

And not even I thought that every goblin under the mountain deserved to pay for one goblin's crimes.

"Get out of there, Early. The witch is too powerful to challenge directly. Get somewhere safe. We need to call in the troops. I know how you love to do that. We get the ghouls, and the vampires, and the goblins, and whoever else we can dig up. Then maybe we stand a chance." I hesitated. "She's after Lawrence. The creature you and I caught in Alice's basement. He's linked to the goblins somehow. Brandon Mills must've seen him in the back of my van when I first met him. The hag told them I'd take the creature to Alcaraz. The witch is on her way, Early. She's going to use Lawrence's blood to power her curse. Take him with you, if you can. But if it gets too dangerous, let her have him. She'll kill you, Early, and she won't even bat an eyelid. I've seen her handiwork close-up. She's too far gone to turn back now."

I didn't say the obvious thing. If Early did that, if he let her have Lawrence, there'd be nothing stopping her from completing the ritual. Nothing to stop her getting her revenge on every goblin under that mountain, and maybe a few more besides.

Which Early would never allow. Even if it cost him his life.

"Don't do anything stupid, old man," I said.

I hung up and drove like Death himself was chasing me.

I slammed on the brakes, skidding to a halt outside Alcaraz's estate. I killed the engine and stared out the windshield. My fingers tightened on the wheel.

"Oh, hell," I muttered.

I stared up at the iron gate that usually guarded the estate. It wasn't doing such a good job anymore. The iron bars were twisted up and inward, like some great hand had reached up from the earth and punched through the gate.

I didn't want to think about the kind of power it took to bend iron like that. It wasn't good for my blood pressure.

There was another vehicle parked haphazardly outside the gate. A white minivan, with *Crown Mobility Services* printed on the side. The minivan's headlights shone toward the gate. The back door was open, the wheelchair ramp lowered.

As I climbed out of Lilian's car, I noticed the mobility taxi's driver-side door was open as well. A shadowed figure in the driver's seat was slumped nearly out of sight.

Clutching Early's shotgun, I rushed over, one eye fixed on Alcaraz's manor. Nothing moved, nothing made a sound.

That wasn't reassuring.

I came around the side of the mobility taxi, shotgun at the ready. When I saw what was waiting for me, I swallowed and lowered the gun.

The taxi driver was a middle-aged woman with curls like a 1940s film star. She was slumped half out the open door, tangled in her seat belt.

Her head had been twisted 180 degrees. I was behind her, but she was staring right at me, an expression of shock frozen on her face.

I took a couple of steps back, swallowing a sudden bout of nausea.

A vision came into my head. Early, his head twisted around, his dead eyes wide in surprise. The witch would kill him as easily as she'd killed the taxi driver.

I could see his car parked further up the driveway, beyond the gate. He was still inside. Dead already, maybe. But I couldn't leave here until I knew.

I stepped through the twisted opening in the gate and sprinted for the manor.

The door was hanging off the hinges. No sound came from inside. Heart hammering, I pressed myself against the wall next to the doorway and peered into the dark of the entrance hall. Moonlight streamed through the open door, but darkness swallowed most of the hall. The only window not blacked out was the one I'd smashed with Alcaraz's priceless troll bone. Guess she hadn't had time to cover it up yet.

I swallowed. The shotgun was slippery in my palms. Once I found the witch, I'd have to be quick. My coat was lined with protective charms, and the pockets rattled with talismans and witch bottles designed to ward off witchcraft. But I didn't rate any of it worth a damn against Mrs. Mills' power. If she caught me, I was dead.

So I couldn't let her catch me. I checked the shotgun. A silver slug was chambered. There were another two in the tube, along with three lead slugs. I had my revolver in my pocket—no silver bullets left there—but I doubted I'd get the chance to use it if I missed with the shotgun.

Nothing else I carried would be more than a distraction. I hadn't had time to brew up more witch's fire. Someone had stripped the Mills' house of anything I could use in a fetish. No hairs, no blood, and sure as hell no urine. Nothing that would give me an edge.

Hell. It was only an hour until midnight. Wasn't like I wasn't planning to live much longer anyway.

I slipped through the open door.

It took a few seconds for my eyes to adjust. I kept the shotgun braced against my shoulder as I peered into the dark corners where the moonlight didn't reach. Slowly, shapes began to resolve. And I realized the entrance hall wasn't entirely empty.

A handful of broken, twisted bodies were scattered about the hall like empty coats. Not human bodies. Strangers.

A few yards off to my right, a creature that looked like a cross between a bear and a ram had been nearly snapped in two, its tail drooping across its horns to cover its dead face. A pack of spriggans had met a similar fate over by the staircase, their wood-like flesh splintered where they'd been torn apart.

Obviously, some of Alcaraz's creatures were loose, and they'd run afoul of Mrs. Mills. I wondered if they'd broken free or been released. My guess: Alcaraz had deliberately freed some of her most dangerous specimens and set them on the intruder.

It hadn't achieved much.

A scratching sound came from behind me. I spun around, shotgun pointed toward the front door. Nothing moved.

I held my breath a few seconds, then exhaled softly. Maybe some of Alcaraz's creatures had survived. The smarter ones would've known better than to tussle with a witch of Mrs. Mills' power.

Which made my task even more fun than it already was. Not only did I have to sneak up on a witch and put her down before she could turn me into a pretzel, I had to do it without getting some monster's claws in my back.

"Thanks, Alcaraz," I muttered. "Real helpful."

I made my way toward the staircase, heart hammering in my chest. Part of me wanted to sprint straight upstairs, shouting for Early. He could be up there right now, in the witch's grasp. But I forced myself to move slowly, silently. I'd be no good to anyone dead.

I paused at the bottom of the main staircase, crouching down by the body of the Stranger lying there. She didn't look as bestial as the other creatures strewn about the room. In fact, she looked downright pitiful.

Her flesh was as pale as the moon. She was lying naked against the bottom step, one arm thrown across her stomach. Her head had been twisted around and around, tearing the flesh and snapping the bones until she'd been effectively decapitated.

It was the baiter vamp who'd tried to eviscerate me the last time I came here. I was thankful her hair was covering her face. Sure, she'd tried to kill me, but it was in her nature.

The witch, though, she'd made a choice. She knew what she was doing.

As I rose, I heard another scrabbling sound behind me. I spun back toward the door.

Nothing there. But out of the corner of my eye, I caught something slipping through the broken window above. My breath caught in my throat. I raised the shotgun.

The chandelier creaked above me. I looked up.

And found five pairs of big yellow eyes staring down at me.

I let out a strangled cry and swung the gun toward the ceiling. Too slow.

The redcaps leapt from their perches, dropping from the chandelier to surround me. The other two who'd been creeping in through the broken window dropped down in front of the door, teeth bared.

The tip of a spear touched my throat while the cold metal of a pistol barrel was pressed against the back of my head. I froze. Only my eyes moved as I took in the goblins surrounding me.

"You've got to be kidding me," I muttered.

One of the redcaps stepped forward, his iron boots clanking. I don't want to say all goblins look the same—although they kind of do. This one, though, I seemed to remember from among those that'd captured us in Likho's chamber.

On his face, patches of his skin were red and puckered, like he'd been splashed with hot oil. He'd caught some stray drops of witch's fire. And he looked like the kind of goblin who held a grudge.

With a hiss, the redcap lowered his spear and touched it to my cheek, just below my right eye. I couldn't do anything as he reached out and took my shotgun from me.

"You escaped the Mines, witch," the redcap hissed. "But you

cannot escape the sorcerer's justice."

I shook my head. "Christ, you have bad timing. You have no idea what kind of shit you've just walked into."

"You were a fool to bring the traitor here with you, witch. The sirin's call led us right here."

Shit. I hadn't considered that. The curse Likho had cast on Rodetk was powered by a sirin's magic. Magic that was designed to draw people to it.

If the redcaps had been able to follow the sirin's call, that probably meant Rodetk was still alive. Which was good news, I guess.

Unfortunately, these idiot redcaps were going to get us all killed.

"You see these corpses?" I said. "You see that door hanging off its hinges? Who do you think did that, and what do you think they're going to do to you when—"

"Enough," the redcap snapped. A couple of the other redcaps had looked around as I spoke, foreheads creasing in concern, but none of them challenged old burn-face. "Our master wants the traitor, and he wants his property back. Lead us to them, and"—the goblin made a face of disgust—"you will be allowed to live."

"What property?"

"The little one! The little one you sent your familiar to abduct."

"Hell," I said. I would've shaken my head in frustration if there weren't so many spear points digging into me. "You idiots still think it was me who did that?"

The redcap jerked forward, his eyes wide and his pupils dilated. His nostrils flared. "I know the little one is here, witch. I can smell it. I know the scent of the creature whose blood made me. Take us to it, or we will kill you and find it oursel—"

The muscles of his neck bulged. There was a loud crack, like a branch being snapped in two, and suddenly I was staring at the back of the goblin's head.

He crumpled. His head had spun 180 degrees on his shoulders in an instant.

The other redcaps began to contort. Arms bent backward, snapping like twigs. Spines cracked. The only sound, aside from the breaking of bones, was the hiss of air escaping from lungs.

I stood frozen in place, watching in horror as the redcaps collapsed dead around me. The two goblins who'd been guarding the door folded back like Christmas cards, their heads touching the backs of their knees.

"Filthy creatures," came a voice from the landing at the top of the stairs.

Sudden fire burned through the back of my calf. In his deathly contortions, one of the redcaps had sliced into my leg with his spear. I toppled, my leg suddenly unable to hold my weight.

But the pain brought me to life. As I hit the floor, I snatched Early's shotgun out of the hand of the dead redcap and I swung it around, aiming at the landing.

Mrs. Mills sat in her wheelchair at the top of the stairs, looking down at me. She manipulated something in her hand as the redcaps twisted themselves to death.

I closed one eye and pulled the trigger. The shotgun kicked against my shoulder. I sent a slug of silver flying toward the wife of Brandon Mills.

It gouged a chunk out of the banister a foot to the left of her. I racked the shotgun, adjusted my aim.

And then my body was no longer my own. My treacherous arm snapped to the side, flinging the shotgun away. My muscles tensed of their own accord. I felt like a puppet as I was hauled to my feet, my body heedless of the pain flaring in my calf.

Mrs. Mills stared down at me with cold eyes. I stood to attention, my arms pressed to my sides. Every muscle in my body quivered, ready to tear me apart. And there wasn't a damn thing I could do about it.

"Mr. Turner," she said. "I was hoping to see you. Come with me."

As if I had a fucking choice.

36

I jerked my way up the stairs like a marionette being controlled by a drunken puppeteer.

I couldn't even look down to see where I was putting my feet—or where Mrs. Mills was putting my feet. My head was locked in position, staring up at the witch waiting at the top of the stairs. I wondered how she'd got up there in the first place, with the wheelchair and all.

I decided I'd rather not know.

My leg throbbed in agony with each step. I could feel blood sticking my jeans to my calf where the redcap's spear had cut me. I wanted to grab the banister to take some of the weight off, but I couldn't even do that.

Sweat was pouring down my face by the time I reached the top of the stairs. I loomed over Mrs. Mills in her electric wheelchair. Even if she'd still had legs, I would've been a foot taller than her. I could've picked her up and thrown her down the stairs without a problem.

But my arms remained fixed to my sides, no matter how hard I strained. I tried to open my mouth, to say something. But I couldn't even move my jaw.

She looked up at me through her one cataract-clouded eye, studying me with cold, clinical precision. I couldn't read her face. If she had any emotion left, she'd buried it deep.

There was something in her hand. A complex fetish made

of sticks and string. As she ran her fingers across it, touching different parts in turn, I could feel muscles tensing and relaxing across my body.

Without a word, she touched the controls of her wheelchair, turning around in place. She started off down the hallway, and a moment later my legs began their jerky walk once more, carrying me after her.

"The hag told us about you," she said. Her voice was quiet, with a dry rasp to it. "After you attacked Brandon. She cackled like mad when she heard that we'd hired you to find the hobgoblin. She likes her little jokes."

We headed down a long, dark corridor lined with taxidermied Strangers. Glass eyes stared down at me as we went deeper into the manor.

"If Brandon had known," the witch said, "he wouldn't have done what he did to you. He told me that, before the end. He wanted to apologize. And to say he's sorry about your brother." She paused. "So am I."

She didn't sound it. She didn't sound like she knew what sorry was anymore.

"But it's good you're here now," she continued in the same soft rasp. "You, of all people, understand why Brandon and I have to do this. You understand the pain." She stopped before a door, turned her wheelchair to face me. "My name is Holly, by the way. I don't think my husband ever told you that."

Suddenly, I found I could open my mouth. From the neck down, my body was still out of my control, but now I could speak.

"Don't do this," I said.

She turned her head to the side with an achingly slow movement. I'd spoken quietly; either her deafness had been feigned or she'd read my lips.

"The hag told us what you did when those monsters took your brother," she said. "You took your revenge. Now we're taking ours." She turned her clouded eye away from me, like she was looking out beyond the walls of the manor. "They live out there, underground, creeping about in the dark. Taking our children. Our babies, Mr. Turner. They took my son. They have to be stopped."

"This isn't the way. All the people you've hurt—"

"What about the people they've hurt? The things they took from us. Brandon and I tried for years before we had Michael. We'd nearly given up hope of ever having a child of our own. And when he came, I loved him more than I thought possible." She looked at me. "And he was taken. Taken by monsters. Creatures out of old fairy tales. This isn't their world. It's ours. And we're going to make it a better one."

"You cracked open your husband's chest," I said slowly, "and carved out his heart. You lost a son, and doubled down on the tragedy by killing your husband as well."

"The spell required a broken heart," she said dismissively. "I thought you understood sacrifice. My husband did. He was brave. He was willing to die for his son."

"Yeah? And how did that help Michael?"

For an instant, a flicker of emotion broke through the stillness of her face. Pain and anger flashed behind her eye.

"How can you defend those monsters, after what they did to your family? After what they've done to countless other families?"

I licked my lips. "Because I'm done dealing death and suffering. I'm not a witch anymore. I'm a cunning man."

Holly Mills' face hardened once more. She moved a finger across her fetish, and my jaw slammed shut of its own accord. My mouth was back under her control.

"You'll change your mind, *cunning man*." She twitched a finger, and the door in front of her flew open. "Come."

She rolled through the doorway, and my legs carried me staggering after her. The door slammed shut behind me.

We were in some kind of large sitting room. The light of the full moon trickled through the dirty windows—obviously Alcaraz had never meant to house vampires here.

The creature that had been caged here was now lying in the corner, a broken mess. Feathers littered the floor around it. Still, even dead, there was something about the sirin that drew the eye, swallowed the mind. If I'd been in control of my own body, I might've wandered over to the creature, drawn in by the magic it exuded.

But my feet were fixed so firmly to the floor they might've been nailed there. After a few moments, I fought free of the dead sirin's magic, and I was able to look around the rest of the room.

The whole gang was here. Early and Alcaraz were staring bug-eyed at me from the far wall. One of Alcaraz's huge cages—the one that'd held the sirin, I guessed—had been ripped apart, and now the iron bars were twisted around Early and Alcaraz like ropes, binding them to the wall.

The bars weren't the only things holding them in place. Each wore a fetish around their necks. By the design of the fetishes, I figured they were keeping the two frozen almost as effectively as Holly Mills was holding me.

Relief swept over me as I met Early's eyes. His head was still pointing the right way. His limbs were intact. The old man was alive.

For now, at least.

Rodetk was lying on a couch, his head propped up on a pillow. More of the bent iron bars were holding him in place, but there was no fetish around his neck. Bottles and vials were scattered about the floor beside him, including a bottle of sirin urine that sparkled like liquid gold in a stray shaft of moonlight. The goblin's boils had shrunk, and it looked like the bewitchment had been broken. His eyes slid open as the witch and I came into the room.

"Oh, good," he muttered. "The cavalry's arrived."

Holly Mills twisted her head toward Rodetk. The goblin's muscles tensed and he squeezed his eyes tight, grunting in sudden pain.

"Keep your filthy mouth shut, monster," the witch said, her voice calm and even.

One of the fingers on Rodetk's left hand suddenly jerked backward with a quiet *pop*. A long, drawn-out groan forced its way out of the goblin's throat.

Instinctively, I tried to take a step forward. My feet stayed rooted to the spot, of course. But as I strained against my own body, I felt the fingertips of my left hand twitch.

The witch turned away from Rodetk, releasing him from her power, and suddenly my fingers froze again.

The warding charms sewn into the lining of my coat were having some effect, I realized. Or maybe it was the witch bottle in my pocket that'd done it. When she was directing all her power in my direction, she could easily overwhelm my minor protections. But when she was distracted, her power divided, the charms gave me back a fraction of control over my own body.

Great. Maybe if she spent half an hour torturing Rodetk, I'd regain enough control to be able to scratch my nose. It'd been itching for the last five minutes.

"There," the witch said as Rodetk's face screwed up in pain. "That's better. Remember that next time you have something you want to say, goblin." She turned away.

Panting, Rodetk glared at the back of the witch's head. It was all he could do, and it wasn't even a particularly impressive glare. Early had obviously managed to break the curse Likho had cast on Rodetk, but the goblin was still badly weakened. He shot me a look, demanding I do something to stop all this.

As if I could do anything. I was caught, plain and simple.

Pressing on her wheelchair's controls, Holly Mills rolled over to a small table next to the empty fireplace. The table had been positioned in a shaft of moonlight pouring in through the window. It was the kind of thing that people might serve tea and scones on. Today, a different delight was being served up.

The Blackheart lay in the center of the table, surrounded by a trio of unlit candles. As centerpieces go, it was...well, let's just call it *interesting*.

Brandon Mills' heart formed the main body of the thing. Strangely, it didn't look bloody at all. It was dry, almost desiccated, though she'd only cut it out of him a few hours ago.

One of the roggenwolf's eyes had been embedded into the muscle on the front of the thing, a blank white orb staring out from the center of the heart. The other eye hung from a string connected to the base of the heart, along with other trinkets: the fang of some animal, and a long, white feather I didn't recognize. The flesh of the Blackheart had been painted with more arcane symbols, the same kind that'd been drawn on Brandon Mills' skin.

Where the main blood vessels leading out of the heart had been severed, artificial vessels had been stitched in place. It took me a moment to realize—to my growing disgust—that the new vessels had been stitched together from the skin of the hobgoblin.

The hobgoblin-skin tubes looped around and connected back up with the heart, making a self-contained system. No, now that I looked closer, I saw there was one vessel standing open near the top of the heart, held open with some kind of ring. A screw cap hung from a chain next to it.

I swallowed. That opening was where the blood would be added. And once that was done, it was all over.

There was one final piece to the Frankensteinian organ. A gnarled hand—almost human, but not quite—was clutching the heart. Sharpened yellow fingernails dug into the heartflesh, holding it tight.

Guess I'd found the hag's missing hand.

As the witch moved toward the Blackheart, a hiss of fear rose up out of the darkened corner of the room. There was a small cage sitting on the floor. As the witch approached, the creature in the cage moved for the first time, shuffling back toward the far wall. Its claws clacked against the floor of the cage. A pair of eyes peered out of the darkness.

Hell. She'd found Lawrence. Which meant she had everything she needed to complete the curse.

And I'd arrived just in time to enjoy the show.

The witch touched her fetish, and my legs lurched back to life. I was carried across the room toward her and dropped into a dusty armchair sitting near the fireplace. At least that stopped my leg throbbing.

"Let me tell you a story." She reached out, and the wick of one of the candles sprang to life. The flame danced in the moonlight, though there was no breeze in the room. "My husband was a big city police officer. That was how we met, actually. I was at a party he'd been sent to break up. We were both young, and I was drunk, and I thought he was cute, so I flirted with him while he was throwing me out. When I sobered up, I found a piece of paper in my purse. It was his phone number. He'd slipped it to me when I wasn't looking."

The witch moved her withered hand, and the second candle caught fire. Maybe it was a trick of the light, but I thought I saw the Blackheart twitch.

"We dated," she said. "Moved in together. Broke up, got back together. We tried for a baby, but the doctors said I was infertile. It got too much for us. We broke up again. A few days later, when he was on patrol, he got stabbed. And on the same day I found out I was pregnant.

"We made up, had a courthouse wedding two months later. I wanted us to leave the city. I didn't want to raise a child there. I didn't want Brandon to get killed on the job, and my son to grow up without a father. I thought if we moved somewhere small, somewhere peaceful, we'd be safe."

The third candle flickered to life. A cold breeze cut through the room, coming from nowhere and everywhere at once. It bit right to the bone.

The Blackheart contracted. No doubt about it this time.

The witch was facing away from me, but I could sense her excitement as she bent toward the table, her arms raised above the Blackheart. The cold grew sharper, and it brought with it a smell like death. The heart relaxed, contracted again. Slowly at first, and then faster, it began to beat with a hollow thump.

Behind me, Rodetk let out a low groan. He knew what was coming.

"I told you to be quiet," Holly Mills said over her shoulder. "You're only alive so I can make sure the curse is working. But I can make you hurt before you die, monster. Believe me."

She moved her hands in slow circles above the table, willing her husband's heart to beat faster. It made a dry, scratching sound with every contraction. The candle flames were growing brighter.

But with her power divided, the protective charms in my coat were just enough to overcome her witchcraft. Her control over me was slipping slightly.

For what good it'd do me. The only part of me I could move was my left hand, and even that was barely twitching.

I concentrated, pushing all my energy into my thumb and forefinger. Maybe I could get to my revolver. But no, it was over in a pocket on my right side. Totally out of reach.

There had to be something. Anything!

The witch returned to her story. "My son didn't have an easy start in life. He was rushed back to hospital for emergency abdominal surgery when he was only 10 days old. It seemed like another sign. For more than a year I begged Brandon to let us move. And a couple of months ago he finally relented. We quit our jobs. He found a security position in a small, backwoods town called Lost Falls.

"So we came. We came here." For the first time, a hint of emotion crept into Holly Mills' voice. "My son was taken a week later. And they left something else in his place.

"I knew it wasn't him in that crib. I knew it. But no one believed me, not even Brandon, at first. He said it was the stress of the move, the sleep deprivation, the homesickness. But it wasn't. That wasn't my boy lying there, screaming. My boy was long gone."

I strained my muscles, trying not to focus on the sickening sight of Brandon Mills' heart beating on the table.

There were only a couple of pockets within reach of my barely moving hand. I hadn't been able to fully restock. What was left? Was there anything that could break the witch's hold over me?

Hell, if only I hadn't used the last of my silver.

"And then I found out the truth," Holly Mills said. "I found out what had happened to my son. And I was offered the chance to take my revenge against the monsters that had preyed on us. I had to make…sacrifices." She shifted in her wheelchair, and I could see her looking down at the stumps of her legs. "So did my husband. But we both knew what we had to do.

She turned her head, her eye fixing on me. "It will be humane," she said. "More humane than they deserve. I'll stop their hearts, just like they stopped mine when they took my son. They'll all die in an instant. Lost Falls will never be plagued by goblins again. No more parents will have to endure the suffering that Brandon and I went through. Tell me that doesn't sound just, Mr. Turner."

I realized she'd given me back control of my mouth again. I licked my lips. "Yeah. You're a real Mother Teresa. What about that taxi driver sitting outside, huh? She screw you on the fare? Was that *just* too?"

Her mouth tightened. "That was unfortunate. She didn't

want to drive up here. She kept saying the estate was haunted. I had to make her." She paused. "It had to be done."

"Well, I'm sure that's going to make her family feel a lot better." I laughed bitterly. "And what about us? Your husband already tried to kill me once. Going to finish the job?"

"No. I want you to understand."

"Why? Why the hell do you want my approval?"

"Because you know. You know the pain they've caused. You know they deserve this."

I glanced at Rodetk. "Not all of them."

She shook her head. "The hag was right. You've grown soft. But you'll see. When this is over, you'll see the good we've done." She turned back to the Blackheart. "It's time."

She held up her hand and spread her fingers. The heart began to groan, like reality itself was creaking under the force of her will.

A fire burst into existence in the empty fireplace, burning with brilliant red light. There was a sound on the edge of hearing, like distant screaming.

I gritted my teeth and struggled against her power, but she was still too strong. My fingers scratched at my pocket, but I couldn't get inside. My own muscles were fighting me.

"You can't do this!" I yelled. "There are thousands of them under the mountain! For fuck's sake, they have children too!"

I knew her deafness wasn't as bad as she'd feigned, but she pretended not to hear me.

She picked up the beating heart, laid it in her lap, and turned toward the corner of the room. Lawrence screeched in his cage as she rolled toward him.

I looked madly around the room. Early was staring at me, frozen in place. Alcaraz was even less help. We were trapped, all of us.

Holly Mills was too far gone to be reasoned with. Her grief had burned away everything else. She thought she was hunting monsters.

So had I, once upon a time. But something had shifted in my head. Whatever lingering anger I'd felt after Teddy's death, it had all boiled away. The goblins who'd killed him had paid for what they'd done. I'd seen to it. That was justice.

This…this was senseless. This was murder.

I looked at Rodetk. He was straining against his iron bonds, his lips peeled back. He caught my eye.

"Don't let her do this, Turner!" he shouted.

I twitched my fingers again, stretching for my pocket. Still too far. Rodetk's gaze flicked to my hand, then back to my face.

Lawrence squealed in fear as the witch stopped in front of him. He'd backed away as far as he could. He couldn't take its eyes off her. She reached out.

"We ate your boy!" Rodetk shouted at her. "Did the hag ever tell you that?"

Mills froze. Her face twitched.

"That's right," the goblin said. He threw his head back and laughed. "I was there. We stuck him on a spit and roasted him over a fire. Like a fucking pig. Mmm, I can still smell it now."

The witch slapped the joystick on her wheelchair and spun around to face him. "Shut your mouth, monster."

Rodetk licked his lips. "The young ones always taste the best. They're so soft. So succulent. They melt in your mouth. And do you know what we did afterward, when we'd stripped all the meat off him?"

"Shut up!"

"We ground his bones to make our bread. Just like that old human story, the one about that thieving little bastard and his beanstalk. We used every little bit of your son, ate him and shat him out, and I wouldn't take it back for—"

The witch let loose a scream of rage. Rodetk let out a choking noise, his eyes growing wide. I could see his windpipe flexing beneath the force of her magic.

With a groan of tortured metal, the iron bars around him snaked tighter. His left forearm got caught between two bars, and his eyes widened in pain. Bone snapped with a sickening *crack*.

But he was giving me the chance I needed. While the witch's power was divided even further, I reached into my pocket and grasped the spirit bottle the Dealer had given me.

Within the translucent blue bottle, something twitched in anticipation. The Dealer had advised me against opening it unless I had no other choice.

Well, I had no other choice.

It was time for the Hail Mary.

37

I flipped open the cap and tossed the spirit bottle to the floor beside the witch.

With a screech like a kettle boiling, something began to flow out of the bottle. It moved like liquid, then like smoke, then something in between. It was fuzzy at the edges, but in the center it began to take shape.

The thing poured upward from the bottle's opening, growing ever larger. It didn't have a face, or limbs, or anything that marked it as a creature.

But it was alive. There was no doubt about that.

And it was pissed.

Holly Mills stared up, slack-jawed, as the entity loomed over her. It billowed like steam, spreading along the ceiling, taking in its surrounding.

I felt a strange intelligence probing at me with some alien sense. It felt warm and wet against my mind.

I trembled. That was the first sign the witch had lost her grasp on my body. I could tremble.

My body was mine again. Mills was using her power elsewhere.

With a snarl, the witch reached into her collar and pulled free a collection of talismans strung about her neck. I felt something shift in the air, and a star-shaped talisman began to spin wildly.

The entity splashed back from the witch as if struck. Holly Mills had landed the first blow.

But it was like punching water. The thing swirled, reformed. Its tone changed, the screech turning into a low *thrum*. And it turned its attention on the witch.

A flash of light hit the room like a thunderclap. Mills went flying from her wheelchair, hitting the floor with a thud. But before she'd stopped rolling, she held up her talisman again, and the entity reeled, groaning. There was another flash of light, and the battle recommenced.

I couldn't follow what was happening. I was just a lowly cunning man. I could track down a hobgoblin, and brew a mean vial of witch's fire, but this...this was the big leagues.

So it was a good thing I wasn't competing. My job was simple: use the distraction to get everyone the hell out of there.

I jumped out of the chair and hobbled across the room. Hell, it felt good to have my body under my control again, even if my leg was still burning.

I could feel the entity taking notice of me, but apparently it decided I wasn't a threat. As it turned its attention back to the witch, I ran to the wall where Early and Alcaraz were pinned.

Though the witch's power was now almost entirely bound up in her battle with the entity, Early and Alcaraz still stared at me silently, unmoving within their iron bar prisons. A muscle in Early's cheek twitched, and his eyes flicked down toward his chest.

I grabbed the fetish hanging around his neck and ripped it off. As soon as it was gone, the old man slumped and caught himself on shaking muscles. His fingers wrapped around the bars holding him tight. He strained, trying to force his way free. The bars wouldn't budge.

"What is that thing?" he demanded, staring at the entity.

"Hell if I know. A gift from the Dealer." I grabbed one of the bars and tugged, adding my strength to his. I couldn't move it an inch. The iron was driven deep into the wall, and it was twisted around Early so closely there was no way for him to slip out.

"Forget it," he shouted over a roaring sound that suddenly filled the room. "You have to stop her from completing the curse."

"I'm not leaving you behind, old man!"

Color flashed behind me. A storm raged inside the room, god fighting god. The walls groaned in agony. I gripped the bars holding Early as a gust of otherworldly wind whipped through the room, threatening to carry me away.

"Listen to me, Ozzy." Early's voice was infuriatingly calm. "A cunning man protects his community. His entire community. You know what you need to do."

I stared at him. In his gray eyes, I could see the reflection of the battle going on behind me. But I stood frozen in place, another battle going on inside my head.

"My boy," Early said softly.

With a snarl, I spun away from the man who'd made me who I was. Away from Alcaraz and Rodetk. I turned to face the storm.

"Goblins," I muttered. "I can't believe I'm doing this for a bunch of stinking goblins."

I pulled my revolver from my pocket and charged into the fray.

The entity swirled overhead like a silk cloak caught in a cyclone. And below, the witch lay on the floor muttering, her hands never stopping their movement. The talismans she wore about her neck floated up around her, suspended in the air. More glittered around her wrists.

It hurt to look at them. They weren't witch's talismans; she'd swiped them from the hag's collection. And they were turning the battle in her direction.

Holly Mills' shadow stretched out behind her. It grew

bigger as I watched, creeping up the wall and along the ceiling. It twitched unnaturally, no longer mimicking the witch's movements.

Silently, the shadow began to bulge outward. The amorphous blackness took form, and a great black claw raked the swirling entity, sending it screeching back.

I charged right through the middle of it all. The winds of magic battered my coat, testing the limits of my protective charms. If the witch and the entity had been directing their energies at me, rather than each other, I would've instantly been turned into cream cheese.

I prayed I remained unnoticed.

I staggered over to the corner of the room, nearly tripping over something. I squinted down as the entity's smoky form whipped past me.

The Blackheart lay at my feet, still pumping away. It had taken on a life of its own now, free of the witch's power.

Grimacing, I stooped and snatched up the thing. It was warm in my hand, pulsating and alive. I could feel it quivering as the battle raged around it.

I swallowed my disgust. Without slowing, I headed for the small cage in the corner of the room.

The entity's tone had changed again. Its scream had become high-pitched once more. An almost fearful sound. I glanced overhead. The thing seemed more corporeal now. It twitched and thrashed, lashing out. But it was shrinking.

The witch had risen from the floor. And when I say she'd risen, I mean it.

She hovered a couple of feet off the ground, the stumps of her legs dangling beneath her. Her disembodied shadow hung overhead, bearing down on the entity.

The spirit bottle lay in front of her. Her talismans twisted and bobbed with increasing speed. The entity was being sucked back toward the spirit bottle, like the reverse of wine spilling from a glass.

There wasn't much time. I slid to a halt in front of the cage in the corner. Inside, Lawrence hissed and wailed like the end times had come. Little bastard wasn't far wrong.

I grabbed at the cage door, tried to wrench it open. It was padlocked shut. With a glance back toward the witch and the entity, I thumbed back the hammer of my revolver, aimed it at the lock on the cage, and pulled the trigger.

The crack of the gunshot cut through the screech of the fading entity. As I swung the cage door open and grabbed the panicking creature under my arm, I heard the witch scream.

"No!"

I spun back. Her face was pulled tight, like all the life had been drained from it. She was bleeding from a split lip and a half dozen other cuts and scrapes. Both hands were still moving, using every drop of her power to draw the entity back into the spirit bottle. But her eyes were fixed on me.

"Turner!" she yelled. The room boomed with the sound.

I cast one last glance back at Early. And then I turned and ran.

The squeal of the entity was now so high-pitched it was passing out of my range of hearing. The thing stuck out slivers of itself, clinging to the floor as it was sucked back into the bottle.

But it was too weak, and the witch was too strong. It bulged and twisted, desperately trying to resist.

I ran for the door. The terrified little one clawed at me, trying to squirm out from under my arm, but I held him tight. The Blackheart beat wildly in my other hand. It seemed to be sucking the strength from me with every step.

The closed sitting room door loomed ahead of me. I was so close. The floor was warped beneath my feet in places, where the magics of the witch and the entity had been deflected. I scrambled across the uneven terrain. Gasping, I reached for the door.

Suddenly, there was silence behind me. The entity's screech had ceased. I heard the soft *click* of the spirit bottle cap being snapped back into place, trapping the thing once more.

There was a split second of peace. I was suddenly aware of how warm my coat was against my skin. Most of my protective charms had probably burnt to ash inside the lining.

I felt a prickle on the back of my neck as the witch returned her attention to me.

My left leg twisted beneath me. I heard the bones break before I felt them. A *crack* that ripped through my body and echoed in the silence.

Then came the pain. And it came in force.

I hit the floor face-first, my broken leg going out from under me. Blood filled my mouth.

Lawrence squealed and wriggled free. The ugly creature darted forward, scratching at the door with his claws. He was too short to reach the handle, and too damn stupid to realize it was hopeless anyway.

Groaning, I rolled over and took a look at my leg. Bad idea. The witch's magic had twisted my lower leg at a sharp angle. The sight of it made me woozy.

"Ozzy!" Early shouted.

"Enough!" Holly Mills roared. She touched the fetish in her hand and Early's jaw slammed shut, his eyes bulging.

The witch dropped into her wheelchair with a thud. I got the feeling she wouldn't be levitating again for quite a while. She was spent. Her hair had been gray; now it was white. The muscles seemed to have withered right off her bones, leaving her a skeleton of a woman.

I started to shuffle toward the door. I was so close. If I could just open the door, Lawrence could get out. And if he escaped, Mills would be unable to complete the curse. The goblins would be safe.

Trying to block out the agony burning up my broken leg, I pushed myself as far as I could and reached for the door handle.

Invisible forces tightened around my throat. I slumped back down, gasping for air.

I clutched at my throat. My airway wasn't entirely closed off. The witch probably didn't have enough strength left to kill me while also keeping Early and Rodetk under control. But that wasn't much comfort for my burning lungs.

With watering eyes, I watched as Holly Mills nudged her wheelchair into motion. She sat slumped in her chair, wheezing as she breathed. But her one clouded eye bore all of her steely strength. She glared down at me as she rolled to a stop.

Whining, Lawrence scratched at the door, gouging out thick claw marks in the wood. Little bastard looked so damn pathetic.

I felt sorry for him. It kept me from pitying my own damn self.

"Enough," Holly Mills rasped. She touched her fetish, and the little creature froze, bug-eyed. Then the witch turned her cold eye on me. "I won't let my husband's sacrifice be for nothing. No more tricks, Mr. Turner. This ends now."

38

While I lay gasping for breath, Holly Mills bent over and picked up the Blackheart I'd dropped. It throbbed in her hand.

"No," I choked. "You can't."

My throat tightened, cutting off my air even further. She was so close I could see the blood vessels in her good eye. Close enough that I could've leaned forward and touched my nose to hers.

But I could barely move. The pain in my leg was overwhelming, and she was using what remained of her power to hold me. She couldn't control me completely, not like before, but every movement was like fighting through mud.

I looked around for my revolver. I'd been holding it just a few seconds ago. But it had fallen outside my reach, sliding away into the corner. I had no more tricks up my sleeve. Nothing left to give.

The witch reversed and moved to my other side, where Lawrence stood rigid. His eyes swiveled in his head, watching Mills approach.

"It's time," she whispered.

The little one turned clumsily in place, limbs moving with the witch's magic. His eyes were wide in fear, but he toddled toward her anyway. As the witch touched her fetish, Lawrence climbed into her lap, like a child wanting story time with his grandmother.

"The hag tried to deny me this creature once already." Holly Mills' voice was hoarse. "We'd persuaded her to use her familiar to abduct it from its cage beneath the mountain. But when it came time to hand the creature over to us, the familiar instead set the creature free. The hag laughed for an hour. From then on, we kept her in the trunk. She learnt her lesson."

The Blackheart twitched as if it could smell Lawrence's blood. The witch touched a fingernail to the eye embedded in the heart, and the orb began to swim with faint light.

"Taking the roggenwolf went much more smoothly," she said, "but the raid used the last of the hag's strength, and the familiar perished soon after. After that, we had to do things on our own. I kept the roggenwolf contained while my husband took its eyes. Brandon wanted to kill the beast when we were done, but I convinced him it could still be useful. We left it on the mountain, so the goblins would hear its howls. So they'd know their doom was coming." A flicker of a smile passed across her exhausted face. "I've waited so long for this."

She laid the Blackheart in her lap and grasped Lawrence by the skull.

I looked over at Early, at Rodetk. The goblin was staring at me, the iron bars tight around his neck and chest. He couldn't speak, but he didn't need to. He knew he was going to die, along with the rest of his kind.

I'd done my best, but it wasn't enough. I couldn't compete with Mills' power. I was just a simple cunning man.

There was a small leather bag hanging from the arm of the witch's wheelchair. Slowly, she reached in and pulled out a small knife. The blade shone silver as it caught a thin shaft of moonlight.

It was the knife that had been molded from the silver of the baby's rattle.

The Blackheart began to beat excitedly in anticipation of the blood that would soon flow. Lawrence stared wide-eyed at the knife, muscles twitching beneath his skin. But he couldn't break free of the witch's power.

The witch turned the creature in her arms, holding his head back to expose his neck. Murmuring in a language I didn't recognize, she brought the silver blade toward the creature's throat.

As I stared, helpless and choking, I caught sight of something on Lawrence's side. A long, thin scar, barely visible. Only the slightest change in the shine and texture of the creature's skin gave it away.

Through the pain and the exhaustion and the terror, I achieved a sudden moment of clarity.

Thoughts crowded my head, coming in thick and fast. A hospital wristband, found among the trash gathered by the hobgoblin in the Mills' house. Something Lilian said Alcaraz had told her, about a scar the little one bore that seemed almost like a surgical scar. The hag's sadistic laughter. And a photograph...

The photograph. I forced my hand away from my throat, down to my pocket. My muscles fought me at every step. But the witch wasn't watching me. She had eyes only for the creature now. As she touched the knife to his throat, I clumsily reached into my pocket.

I pulled out a photograph. The photo I'd found pinned to the ceiling of the Mills' basement. The photo Brandon Mills had been staring at while his heart was cut out.

A photo of Michael Mills, aged 6 weeks. The baby that'd been stolen from them. I ran my thumb along the picture of the boy.

The overexposed picture had wiped out most of the detail of the baby's pale skin. But there, along the boy's side, was the scar, still red from the surgery he'd had a few weeks before.

I looked up. The witch's murmuring had reached a crescendo. The Blackheart was practically leaping out of her lap in excitement. A single drop of blood flowed down the blade of the knife as the point pricked the creature's skin.

I tried to choke out a cry. But only a wordless grunt came out of my closed-off throat.

The witch finished her chant. The pressure in the room changed. She let out a relieved sigh.

"It's working," she whispered to herself. "It's working."

I tried again to speak. But her grip on my throat was too tight. My world was starting to black out around the edges.

For the first time, Holly Mills smiled. The muscles of her arm tightened. She readied herself to slash the creature's throat and drain its blood into the Blackheart.

I flicked the photograph toward her with two fingers. It fluttered to the floor beside her wheelchair, face-up.

For a moment, her concentration broke. She glanced away from the little one, eyes widening as she saw the photo. Her control over me faltered, just a fraction. My throat relaxed.

"Your son," I choked out. "You're about to kill your son."

39

Holly Mills stared at me in stunned silence. Her clouded eye traveled across the little one's frozen face, its body.

Then she recoiled, gasping. The silver knife clattered to the floor.

I suddenly had full control over my body once more. And so did the little one. He thrashed in her arms, scratching the witch and squirming free.

He bounded over to me, cowering beside me as I pushed myself up to a sitting position. The witch's mouth hung open.

"It can't be," she whispered. "They said he was dead."

I shook my head, looking down at the creature. The pain made it hard to think. Now that I had my breath, the full agony of my broken leg came rushing back. "Changed."

"Why?" she breathed.

I thought back to Likho's chamber, to the other little ones in their cages. Other changelings. Other children. Hell.

"So his blood could be used for dark magic." I eyed her. "Seems like everyone had the same idea."

The witch swallowed. She reached out her hand, but when the little one hissed and recoiled, she faltered. A broken look passed across her aged face.

"The...the hag. She said..."

"The hag thought this was a great joke," I said. "She was laughing about it when we let her out of the trunk. You'd have got your revenge, all right. But you'd have killed your son in the process."

"My son." She blinked, and tears began to fall, catching in the crevices of her face. "What...who did this to him?"

"A goblin," I said. "A sorcerer. You were right about that much."

She nodded slowly. She turned her head to the side, her gaze never leaving the little one. A miserable, delighted smile touched her lips, like she couldn't decide whether to grieve or jump for joy.

"This isn't magic I know," she whispered. "Can it be reversed?"

I didn't know. I looked down at the sad little creature, this thing that was once a boy.

I glanced across the room. "Early?"

The witch followed my gaze. Summoning what remained of her strength, she touched one of the hag's talismans. With a groan, the iron bars shifted enough to allow Early to drop to the ground, panting. With a wary look at the witch, he crossed the room and knelt at my side. He looked at my broken leg.

"How bad does it hurt?" he murmured.

"It's no picnic, I'll tell you that."

He put a small pouch in my hand. I opened the drawstring and got a whiff of powdered herbs.

"Rub a little into your gums," he said. "It'll take the edge off."

"Cunning man," the witch said impatiently.

He shot her a look from beneath his bushy eyebrows, like a stern school teacher reprimanding a back-talking child. Then he turned to the cowering creature, slowly holding out a hand to him. Lawrence—Michael—snapped his teeth, but he let Early touch him with the back of his hand.

"You think it's this Likho's work?" he asked me.

I nodded. "There are more of them still down there. If

they're all changelings, Early..."

He grunted. "We'll figure it out."

"Can he be changed back?" Holly Mills said. "Tell me."

Early frowned, studying the creature. "The changes are profound," he said slowly. "It will take time. I might need the hag's help." He stood, stroking his beard. "But yes. I think it can be reversed."

The witch's lip trembled. But she didn't break down entirely. She nodded.

"But," Early said, turning to her, "it will cost you."

She raised her head. "What?"

I was no stranger to the hardness in Early's face. He could be a stern, grumpy bastard when it suited him.

But as he stared at the witch, I saw something in his eyes I'd never seen there before. A touch of darkness.

"You have tormented this community," he said. "Your husband can't stand judgment for his crimes, but you can. Lost Falls tradition holds that we turn you over to your victims. The goblins would find a suitable punishment, I'm sure."

Mills swallowed. Her hands trembled. The Blackheart still lay in her lap, but its beating was growing slower, weaker.

"But the goblins were not the only victims here," Early said, turning to me. "And perhaps Ozzy has a better use for you."

I met his eyes, suddenly understanding what he was suggesting. Maybe I wasn't the only one with a little witch in him.

I nodded slowly and looked around. There was a broken table leg sitting a few feet away. "Hand me that and help me up."

He passed me the table leg and I used it as a crutch as he hauled me to my feet. The old man's herbal powder was doing its job, but I still grunted in pain as I rose, trying to keep my broken leg off the ground.

"Take Rodetk and Alcaraz downstairs," I said to Early, glancing over at the two of them. "The goblin looks like he could use some of that powder as well."

He cast the witch another look. "You'll be all right by yourself?"

"I think so," I said.

He nodded. "Free them," he said to the witch.

She hesitated.

"They won't harm you," Early said, with a special look for Rodetk. "I swear it."

The witch licked her lips, but she touched her talisman again, and the bars snaked away from Rodetk and Alcaraz. Early went over and tore off the fetish hanging from Alcaraz's neck, while Rodetk pulled himself uneasily to his feet, swearing all the while.

I hobbled aside, nudging the little one along with me, and Early led Alcaraz and Rodetk from the room. Clutching his broken arm, the goblin caught my eye as he passed. He nodded.

"That's it?" I said. "A nod? I just saved your ass, goblin. Twice."

"What do you want? A big sloppy kiss?" He opened his mouth wide, waggling his tongue and showing off his sharp teeth.

"On second thoughts, the nod's fine."

Rodetk glanced back at the witch, then grabbed me by the shoulder and hissed in my ear. "You'd better make her pay, Turner."

"Don't worry," I muttered. "I intend to."

He gave me one last long look, then nodded again. He filed out of the room along with Early and Alcaraz. Early touched my shoulder as he left, then closed the door behind him.

The little one cowered behind my leg. The witch stared at him, longing in her eyes. Flickers of emotion passed across her face: love, despair, revulsion. I didn't know whether she was more disgusted at what Likho had done to her boy or what she'd nearly done to him.

For a moment, I thought she was going to reach out, try to

take him in her arms. But in the end she just bent over the side of her wheelchair and picked up the photograph I'd dropped. Her eyes grew wet as she dragged her thumb across the image of her son as he'd once been.

She slammed her eyes closed, turning the photo face-down in her lap. When she looked at me again, her face was fixed in a look of cold anger. She glanced toward the wall, but I knew she was looking beyond it, toward the mountain.

"The one who did this to my son is still out there, isn't he?" she said.

"That's right."

"He can't be allowed to live. Not after what he did."

"No. He can't." I reached into my pocket and pulled out a strip of black cloth. I tossed it to her.

"What is this?" she said as she picked it up.

"It belongs to the sorcerer."

She stared at it. "Why are you giving it to me?"

"A show of good faith. I got my revenge. You should get yours. But it stops with the sorcerer. Understand?"

She licked her lips, running the cloth between her fingers. With shaking hands, she tied it around the Blackheart.

Bending over, she picked up the silver knife from where she'd dropped it. A thin line of the little one's blood had dried on the blade.

The witch closed her eyes and muttered a few words, and the Blackheart began to beat with a panicked rhythm. The pressure in the room changed.

Opening her eyes, the witch plunged the blade into the center of the heart. The Blackheart disintegrated, turning to ash in her hand. Only the knife remained.

The witch let out a sob. Relief mixed with disgust. She buried her face in her hands, accidentally smearing her cheeks with black dust.

Her shoulders shook. A few tears dripped from between

her fingers, splashing in her lap. Finally, she lowered her hands and wiped the dust from her face. She'd aged another ten years. "He's dead. He's dead."

I exhaled, nodding. "Good," I said. I meant it. I didn't know what Likho's death would mean for the Mines. But it needed to be done.

"I have no strength left," Holly Mills said. "Please. Change my son back."

I reached down and touched the top of the creature's head. "We'll do our best. He'll be well cared for. Once you and I make a deal."

"Anything." She closed her eyes. "Anything."

"I was hoping you'd say that."

In some distant corner of the house, a clock's chime rang out. Midnight.

There was a knock at the door to the sitting room. Before I could answer, it creaked open, and a misshapen figure entered the room.

The Dealer took off his hat and closed the door behind him. He smiled his lopsided smile at the two of us, then bent his neck to the little one clinging to my leg. It hissed and quivered.

"Thought I'd let myself in," the Dealer said. "I hope you don't mind. I've been keeping an eye on things. Very entertaining. Ah, here it is."

He stooped down and picked up the spirit bottle lying on the floor. He shook it in his hand, smiling cruelly at the shifting shadow within.

"I have to admit," he said as he tucked it into his pocket, "I still have no idea what this entity is. But I'm glad I got a chance to see it at work."

The witch stared at him. "Who...?"

"Oh, where are my manners? You can just call me Dealer." He eyed the stumps of her legs and smiled. "I believe you've dealt with one of my kind before."

With a flourish, the Dealer pulled up a chair, planted it between us, and sat down.

"Now," he said. "Your time is up, Osric. I've come to claim a body." He grinned, then turned his eye on Holly Mills. "But I believe you'd like to activate a certain transfer clause."

40

I stood before my brother's grave.

His real grave, that is. Not the one in the cemetery, with the white granite headstone and the freshly cut grass. The thing that was buried there was a doll, an impostor, nothing more.

This grave was harder to find. All that marked it was a river-smoothed stone. It sat at the bottom of the waterfall that gave Lost Falls its name, near the bank of the river. Spray from the waterfall rained down lightly, catching in my beard.

It had been a tough little trek to get here, what with a crutch and my leg in a cast and all. But it was worth it. I liked it here. I liked the way it smelled. I liked the sound of the water crashing down endlessly.

"This was a good place to bury him," Alice said as she knelt in the dirt by Teddy's grave.

"See? Occasionally I'm right about something."

"Very occasionally." She touched the stone marker with her fingertips, then stood. "Thanks for bringing me here."

"Sorry I didn't do it sooner."

She looped her arm through mine and pressed herself against me. We stood like that a few minutes, thinking about Teddy. Well, I was, at least. She could've been thinking about anything.

For some reason, it didn't hurt so bad thinking about him anymore. He was dead, and me, I was still alive. Strange to think. Sure as hell not fair.

But it was the way things were. I'd finally begun to accept that.

"Are you and Early still coming around for dinner tonight?" she asked after a while, breaking the silence.

"Depends," I said. "Are you cooking, or is your wife?"

"Are you saying I'm a bad cook?"

"I'm saying you're both bad cooks. It's just a lesser-of-two-evils situation."

That earned me a punch in the arm. It nearly knocked me right into the damn river.

"All right, all right," I said. "We'll be there. The boys can sign my cast."

There was a rustle of leaves behind us. I looked around to see Lilian emerging into the clearing from the narrow dirt trail. She stopped and looked awkward for a second, like she was intruding on a private moment.

"Oh, sorry," Lilian said. "Early said I'd find you here. I didn't know you had company."

I shook my head. "No problem. This is my sister, Alice. Alice, this is Lilian. A friend of mine."

Alice raised her eyebrow a fraction of an inch, the corner of her lip quirking upward. It was a look that said: *'Friend,' huh?*

The two women shook hands and murmured hello. Alice looked about ready to start asking Lilian what her intentions toward me were, so I cut in quickly.

"I'll catch you tonight," I said to Alice. "I'm sure Lilian can give me a ride home."

Alice's eyebrow went up a little higher. She nodded. "Bring wine."

"Will do."

She pulled me into a hug and whispered into my ear. "Your girlfriend's cute. Does she look as good from the back as she does from the front?"

"Stop objectifying my friends," I whispered back.

She pulled away, grinning, and waved goodbye to Lilian. "Nice to meet you."

"You too," Lilian said.

As Alice passed Lilian on the way to the trail, she glanced back and gave Lilian's ass an appraising look. She raised her eyebrows, nodded, and gave me a thumbs up over Lilian's shoulder.

I cleared my throat and turned away, hoping my embarrassment wasn't showing on my face. Lilian came alongside me.

"Is this where your brother's buried?" she said.

I nodded, pointing to the spot. "Here."

"I'm sorry."

"Thanks." I paused for a moment, then looked at her. "What's up?"

"I've just been to visit the hag," she said. "She's recovering well. Aside from the severed hand, of course. I think she's a little upset you spoiled her prank."

"You mean the one where a bewitched child gets sacrificed by his mother to commit mass murder against a bunch of goblins?" I shook my head. "I don't understand hag humor."

"At least she's agreed to help with the changelings. However begrudgingly. I took her new unguent to Early before I came here. He seems confident the changes can be reversed."

I nodded. "He won't talk about anything else at the moment. I'm his personal bouncing board for ideas. It's going to get even worse now that Rodetk's gone."

The goblin had left earlier this morning, disappearing upriver in a cloud of smoke from the dinghy's outboard motor. He was still injured—join the club—but he didn't want to wait any longer. Likho's wards had fallen a few days ago, and news was trickling out of the Mines. Apparently, the sorcerer had vanished. He'd gone into his chamber alone late the other night, waiting for a report from a squad of redcaps he'd sent to the surface. But when one of his attendants came looking for him in the morning, Likho was nowhere to be seen. The only thing the attendant could find was a small pile of ash sitting in the sorcerer's favorite chair.

Naturally, rumors were flying. Some thought he'd been eaten whole by the roggenwolf that was said to still be roaming the endless tunnels beneath the mountain. Others thought he'd fled the Mines in disgrace after letting the witch in the shadows slip from his grasp.

Things beneath the mountain were unstable at the moment. As soon as the Lord of the Deep had regained control of his faculties, he'd ordered his men to imprison the redcaps, who'd become weakened without Likho's magic to fuel them. But confidence in Khataz had been eroded, and rival factions were vying for power.

Which was why Rodetk was going back. He said he had an obligation to try to smooth things out, or some nonsense like that. And when things were more stable, he wanted to start building a stronger connection between the Mines and Lost Falls. The mountain had always stood apart from the rest of us. There was a lot of distrust there, on both sides. Not without cause.

But that isolation could breed fear, hatred. Rodetk wanted to make sure nothing like this could ever happen again.

It was worth a shot, anyway.

Rodetk was also going to negotiate for the release of the remaining little ones from Likho's chamber. There were other families out there whose children had become changelings. Other families who thought their kids were dead. I itched to go back there and bring the changelings home myself, but the last thing we needed was me stirring up more trouble in the Mines. Rodetk would bring the kids back, I was sure of it.

Besides, that was the easy part. Once we got them back, we had to reverse Likho's spells and figure out how the hell we were going to return these children to their families. Not to mention finding a home for Michael Mills, now that one of his parents was missing a heart and the other had become the Dealer's property.

And we had to do all of that without drawing too much attention to ourselves. Sounded like a nightmare, if you asked me. I planned to let Early do most of the work, while I sat around milking my broken leg for all it was worth.

"All right," I said to Lilian. "Spit it out."

"Spit what out?"

I gestured around us, to the falls and the river and the forest. "You didn't come out here just to tell me the hag is pissed at me. What is it?"

She hesitated, then reached into her bag and took out a small, thick book. No, not just any book. A grimoire. She held it out to me.

"It's the grimoire we found in the Mills' basement," Lilian said. "If it looks a little battered, it's because you threw it at a wall."

"I remember." I flicked open the book and was greeted again by the strange alphabet I didn't recognize. "Why are you giving it to me? It belongs to the hag."

"No," she said. "It doesn't."

I looked up. "What?"

"I tried to give it to her. She said it wasn't hers. It's not written in the hags' language."

"Then what the hell is it?"

"I don't know. But when I first showed it to the hag, she looked…"

"What?"

"Scared."

I swallowed and closed the book. "Great. That's just fantastic. So why are you giving me something that can scare a hag?"

"Well, I don't want to keep it," she said. "The thing's creepy as hell."

I considered tossing it in the river. Seemed like the smart thing to do. But something made me hang onto it. A feeling deep in my stomach.

I looked down at Teddy's grave, putting the book out of my thoughts. It was a mystery for another time.

"So," I said. "Where were you buried?"

Lilian didn't answer, but I could feel her eyes on me. A cloud shifted overhead, and the spray from the falls sparkled in a shaft of sunlight.

"The baiter vamp," I said. "Up at the estate. It couldn't sense you. Couldn't smell you. Didn't even know you were there." I poked at the ground with my crutch. "I saw that redcap skewer you. That was no trick of the light. When you went down, I felt for your pulse. Couldn't find it. You didn't bleed, either. In fact, I've never seen you bleed." I met her eyes. "Because you're dead."

She was studying me silently, trying to maintain a mask over her emotions. She wasn't doing a very good job of it. I saw nervousness there. Shame. And relief.

"My guess," I said, "is you're a revenant. Returned to take revenge on whoever killed you." I cocked my head to the side. "So? How'd I do?"

She nodded slowly. "Not bad. Not bad at all."

"It's strange, though. You're pretty rational for a vengeful spirit returned from the dead. I mean, I've never met a revenant before, but if I had to guess, I'd say most of them aren't much like you." I turned to her. "Who killed you?"

"I…I don't know." She looked down at her hand, made a fist. "I can't remember."

"What do you mean?"

"Every now and then I get images from before, when I was alive. Flickers of thought. Shadows of memories. But nothing substantial. I came to Lost Falls seeking my killer. I know that much. I was a…a monster." She licked her lips. "I got caught in one of the traps Alcaraz uses to catch wild Strangers. I nearly tore her face off. Alcaraz went to the hag, and the hag…did something to me. Gave me something. It drove the monster back inside me. Made me almost human again. For now, at least."

"That's why you need the hag so badly," I said.

She nodded. "I'm afraid to lose myself again. I can feel it. The fury. Here." She touched her chest. "Pushing me to seek. To kill the one who killed me. But to cage the monster, the hag had to dig around in my head. Wipe out the memories that were driving me. Now I'm…empty."

"And the things you can do. What you did to the hobgoblin. That's part of it?"

"I don't think so. I think I learned those things a long time ago. When I was still alive." She chewed her lip. "I don't really know what I am."

"You're a terrible driver. I know that much."

The smile I got was small and fleeting, but it was better than nothing.

"You know what this means, though, right?" I said.

"What?"

"It means I get to keep my beard. And you have to buy me dinner. I won our bet."

She eyed me warily. "I'm a vengeful corpse, Ozzy. You sure you want to have dinner with me?"

I shrugged. "That's nothing. In high school, I once dated a girl with no belly button. Now that's really freaky." I limped over and clapped her on the shoulder. "Come on. Give me a ride home, and I'll tell you all about it."

The Dealer was waiting for me when I got home.

He was sitting at my kitchen table, bent over my laptop,

wearing a shockingly white suit. The light of the screen played across his asymmetrical face. He didn't look up as I came in, but he raised a hand in greeting.

"My word, Osric," he said. "Did you always fancy yourself a writer, or did you just go a little stir crazy sitting inside all day with that broken leg?"

I hobbled across the room and slammed the laptop closed. The Dealer frowned up at me.

"I was enjoying that," he said. "I think you captured me quite well. No one has ever written a book about me before."

"You're a character in the book," I said. "That doesn't make it about you."

"Doesn't it?" He shrugged. "We'll see." He smiled, showing off teeth that were too big for his mouth. "How does it feel to still be alive, my friend? Invigorating, is it not?"

"Can't complain."

He closed his eyes and inhaled deeply. "I envy you humans. You live so close to death at all times. It must be thrilling."

"Yeah, I guess that's one word for it."

"You should feel even more alive," he said, "knowing that someone was sacrificed to keep you that way." He leaned forward. "Trading your life for the witch's wasn't a very cunning man thing to do, though, was it?"

"It was a simple trade," I said. "Holly Mills and I each had something the other wanted. She wanted her son to be human again. And I wanted to live. Neither of us were strangers to making hard deals."

He grinned. "A man after my own heart. And to think, your heart nearly *was* my heart. Oh, well. Maybe next time. I will have to be content with owning the witch's body for now."

"And the power it comes with," I said.

"That too."

"Guess I didn't need to give you a kidney after all," I said. "We thwarted the curse, and Early is just fine."

"Hmm? Oh, you're referring to the warning I gave you. What makes you think I was talking about your recent adventure?"

"What?"

"Things are in motion now, Osric. Recent events, including the hag's temporary disappearance, will not have gone unnoticed by certain outside powers. Powers who have an interest in this town." He smiled. "Big things are in store for Lost Falls. I hope you're ready, my friend."

I stared. He was just screwing with me. For sure, this time.

I chewed my lip a second, then pulled out a chair and sat down next to the Dealer. "I do have one question."

"Oh?"

"The Millses forced the hag to use her familiar to free the the changeling child from under the mountain, yeah?"

"As I understand it."

"But the hag played a little trick on them, as she likes to do. She set the little one loose instead of handing it over to Brandon Mills."

"Correct." The Dealer's smile widened.

"So how did the little one get into Alice's basement? Seems like a hell of a coincidence."

"It does, doesn't it? I suppose when you're writing your book, a coincidence like that might seem unbelievable." He tapped his fingertip on the table, then clicked his fingers. "Perhaps it was the hag. She could've bewitched the little one, sent it to your sister's house."

"There's no indication anyone but Likho laid a spell on that boy," I said. "I've checked."

"That is a conundrum, then, isn't it?"

"Unless someone else found the changeling," I said, "And led it to Alice's basement. Knowing I'd be the one to capture the creature. Perhaps it was the same someone who ensured my name and phone number were given to Brandon Mills."

"And you think this someone is?"

I just stared at him.

"Me?" He cocked his head to the side. "Why would I do anything like that?"

"Fun, maybe. Because you wanted to torment me." I licked my lips. "Or maybe because you were hoping I'd succeed in stopping the Millses from casting the curse."

The Dealer smiled and shrugged. "Well, it's certainly a possibility. But you know, I think there's nothing wrong with keeping a little mystery in your story. I think your readers will enjoy it."

He rose, making to leave. I grabbed my crutch and pushed myself to my feet as well.

"Speaking of mysteries," I said, holding up the grimoire Lilian had given me. "What can you tell me about this?"

He peered at the book, sighed, and shook his head. "Osric, you know I don't give out information for free. And I'm afraid you just can't afford what I know about that book."

"Whoever gave it to her must've had a reason," I pressed. "Is it possible another of your kind traded it to Holly Mills?"

He waggled his finger at me. "What did I just say?"

"Hey. The way I see it, you owe me. The deal we made was that I could trade my life for something of equal value. Well, you got Holly Mills' body. Now, I'll grant you, she's not as pretty as me, and she's lacking a few limbs. But the power she can wield, that's worth a hell of a lot more. From where I'm standing, you came out of this pretty damn well. I think I deserve a…a…" I waved my hand in the air, trying to think of the right word.

"A kickback?" he suggested.

"Yeah. Exactly."

Smiling, he rested his hand on my shoulder. "It's already done. I took the liberty of giving it to you while you were sedated at the clinic. I would never cheat a friend, Osric."

"What? What are you talking about?"

He pulled on his hat. "Take care, my friend. And send me a

copy of your book when you finish."

"Hey, wait. Dealer. What are you talking about?"

But he just smiled once more, then disappeared out the door. I didn't bother chasing after him this time.

"Son of a bitch," I muttered. "What the hell did you mean by...?"

I trailed off as a sudden thought came to me. I raised my hand to my head, touched the scar tissue on the left side of my scalp. It had been a little tender there the last few days. I'd thought I must've hit it when the witch broke my leg. But maybe...maybe...

I threw the mysterious grimoire onto the table. It could wait. First I had to check something.

I hurried to my piano and lifted the fallboard. Cringing in anticipation, I touched one of the keys.

The sound. It was...

It was music.

I stood in stunned silence for a moment, listening to the sound as it slowly faded. I didn't know what the note was, or whether the piano was in tune, or how to turn that one sound into a melody.

But it was there. It was real. I could hear it.

With a strangled cheer, I pulled down the box of dusty music books sitting on top of the piano. I tossed them aside one by one, littering my living room with them.

Until I found it. A thin, purple book, designed for kids. On the front cover, a cartoon rabbit played piano beneath the title: *My First Piano Book*.

I flipped it open to the first page, set it on the stand, and sat down on the stool. Trembling, I put my fingers on the keys where the book told me.

"Middle C," I read, grinning like an idiot. "Middle fucking C."

I got started. I had a lot to learn.

ABOUT THE AUTHOR

Chris Underwood spends an unhealthy amount of time in his imagination. Luckily, his wife and daughter are very tolerant. He writes the kind of urban fantasy he has always loved: stories set in a perilous, darkly beautiful worlds filled with magic, monsters, and just a touch of hope.

He has a science degree and a postgraduate diploma, both of which look very nice on the wall of his office. That's about all they are useful for.

Find out more about Chris Underwood and his books at:

www.chrisunderwoodbooks.com